# The Loop

# The Loop

NICHOLAS HOLLOWAY

JPM
Publishing co.

Published in Austin, Texas, by JPM Publishing Co. Publisher can be reached at jpmpublishingco@gmail.com or via the contact form at www.jpmpublishingco.com.

Ordering Information:
Quantity sales. Special discounts are available on quantity purchases by corporations, associations, and others. For details, contact the publisher at the address above.

Any references to historical events, real people, or real places are used fictitiously. Other names, characters, places and events are products of the author's imagination, and any resemblances to actual events or places or persons, living or dead, is entirely coincidental.

Cover by Stephanie Davenport
Map illustration by Nolan Odom

ISBN: 978-1-7332291-2-8 (Paperback)
ISBN: 978-1-7332291-1-1 (Ebook)

Library of Congress Control Number: 2019913227

Printed in the United States of America


JPM Publishing Co.
www.jpmpublishingco.com

*For Nichole,*
*who pushed me to finish the damn thing.*

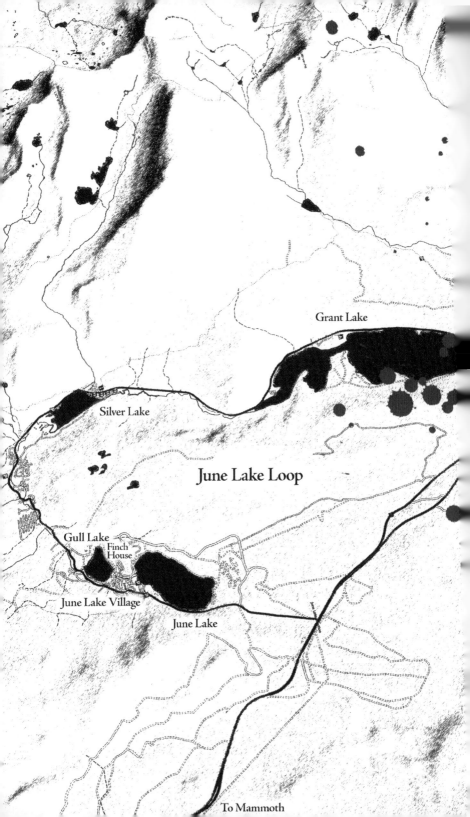

# The Loop

CHAPTER ONE

# Scarlet

∽

*T*ipp. *Tipp. Tipp...*

Droplets of scarlet pattered into a porcelain sink, fading to pink as blood intermingled with the steady trickle of water.

*Tipp. Tipp. Tipp...*

Webs of scarlet stretched across glossy eyes as bright green hues stared deep into the reflection of their possessor.

*Tipp. Tipp. Tipp...*

Curves of scarlet danced along the white pages of an open, pocket-sized notepad... story notes scribbled in lazy cursive.

Gallagher Finch swallowed back the bile burning to escape his bowels. He sighed, reached for a hand towel, and pressed it firmly to his throat. Blotches of scarlet seeped through white cotton as he pressed the towel into his flesh, applying pressure to the tiny nick in his throat. Another towel, ruined.

He had never been good at shaving.

When the bleeding subsided, Gallagher tossed the towel into the bin with the others and proceeded to finish shaving the remainder of the stubble from his neck. He would leave the stubble around his jaw and up his cheeks, of course. How else would he promote the façade of ruggedness? Certainly not through his lifestyle. But when modern women called for rugged men, he would entertain the notion that, yes, he was indeed a rugged man.

If only it were true.

He rinsed the shavings from his hands, then looked down at his palms. Large enough, stretching into long fingers devoid of any callouses save for those on his fingertips. Not from years of working in a mechanic's garage or in a steel mill, as his brothers had. These had formed from years of typing his life away behind a desk. If only the merit of manhood could be measured by the faded letters on a keyboard, he would surely be ranked an alpha among men.

If only it were true.

The most faded of all the keys was the backspace. It was now nearly illegible. His work had been a constant battle with the backspace. Much like his life.

It was time for another drink.

Gallagher rinsed the shavings from a cheap plastic razor and splashed water on his face, leaving the faucet running as he surveyed the rest of his features.

Not bad.

Not great.

Handsome, he figured. Average on days when he didn't try, days when he remained shut up in his home indulging in his favorite strain of indica. Sure, he had cut back on smoking weed. At least, that's what he told his sister.

If only it were true.

"Gal," called a soft voice from the bedroom.

"In a sec," he replied. He lifted the bottle of Evan Williams to his chapped lips, the same bottle he'd stolen from the bar. Half-full. Half-empty. He didn't care a lick either way, as long as the rest ended up in his gut.

"Make me a sandwich," the girl groaned.

"In a sec, Dani."

"It's Daphne. Prick," she admonished with a simple giggle, one he'd heard countless times during their countless romps in between countless shots of bourbon. He guessed that half of her countless cries of ecstasy were fake, yet he could count on one hand how much he actually cared.

Gallagher stared into the mirror a moment longer. He let the water run...

*The original sin of California.*

Water shortage. Drought. Call it what you like. There was plenty of snow up here in the June Lake Loop and, therefore, plenty of water. Those dried-up, money-mongering Hollywood pricks down south could screw themselves.

"I'm hungry," the young female whimpered from beyond the doorway, and it was with a sigh that he finally shut off the faucet. He staggered out of the bathroom and into the hallway. His world was a kaleidoscope of shadows. He choked back another lurch of his gut and stomached the sick aching to come up.

Perhaps he should've eaten dinner.

Perhaps he should drink more.

Gallagher reached the top of the stairs and placed his hands upon the bannister. He peered down at the entryway and the large oak front door. The same door that had left him without the tip of his left pinky when he was eight years old.

"Peanut butter and honey," came Dani's voice. *Or was it Daphne?*

He took another guzzle of whiskey and headed down the stairs. A smile crept up his cheeks as his bare foot eased onto the second-to-last step. That familiar *creeeak* in the ever-aging, mauve-carpeted wood never failed to bring back memories of his mother.

How she would chase him through the dining room, into the entryway, and up the stairs, chasing him with either a smile or a spatula.

Always chasing him.

And now, nobody chased him.

He staggered to the front door and placed his left hand upon the cold, hard oak. He curled the stub of his pinky against the coarse, tangential lines. Bloodshot eyes traced carvings in the wood, invisible to the naked eye due to countless efforts to re-stain it.

But he knew what to look for, and where.

The letter *J*, carved below the brass doorknob. A splintering *B*, chiseled sloppily beside the jamb. An *S*, larger than the others and larger even than the doorknob below it. Oh, how his sister had been spanked for that display of vanity.

And far to the right of them all, a cursive *G* the size of a quarter.

He traced his fingertips along the curves of the wooden letter. For the past eternity, or perhaps the past five hours, his brain had buzzed with too much alcohol and too much Adderall.

But for this moment, all buzzing ceased.

The G was intricately carved, not too shallow and not too deep. Subtle enough to hide from the neighbors during friendly house calls, but enough to boast to the other neighborhood children about. After all, none of their parents had allowed them to carve their initials in the family door.

He could still feel his favorite pocketknife held in his palm, the handle crafted from a stag's horn. After all these years, he kept the knife, left hidden in the bedside dresser in case some unfortunate soul decided to break in. A man could never be too cautious.

He could still feel the blade catch an unseen notch in the oak.

He could still feel the knife slip and the blade slice through his pinky nail.

He could still feel the agonizing pulse as scarlet squirted from his severed fingertip... oh, how he had cried.

So rugged a man was Gallagher Finch.

He had returned from Mammoth Hospital a day later, bloody bandages wrapped around his left hand. How he had hated changing those bandages. How they would stick to the dried blood of his festering wound. How his mother would pour a devious mixture of hydrogen peroxide and rubbing alcohol onto bare, exposed flesh. How the nerve endings of his severed pinky tip would ignite and send excruciating jolts of electricity down his spine. How he had screamed. How his brothers had laughed at his pain. How his sister had cried with him.

But the G… the G he had finished. A cursive remembrance of a loving mother, etched into a sanded down knob where the oak branch had been sawed away by his father…

*Murderer.*

The buzzing returned at full measure.

Gallagher groaned and pressed the heel of his palm above his left eye, attempting to subjugate the pulsing in his brain.

"Gal!"

"In a sec!"

A moment's pause as he admired the door once more. A quick drink. A quick yawn.

He wrenched his eyes from the front door and staggered into the kitchen, tripping over the call girl's scarlet heels in the process.

In this house, memory served in darkness. No lights needed turning on, no electricity need be wasted when every nook, every crevice, every sharp corner was etched into the inside of Gal's skull. Even with drunken feet refusing to walk in straight lines and right angles, Gal navigated around inky blotches of furniture until his feet touched the kitchen floor. He closed his eyes to further darken his sight, allowing the chilly tile to press into his heels, the balls of his feet, his toes.

Dollars and dimes abandoned on the bar top by parsimonious patrons had been scrounged and saved for three long years until finally, cold tile had taken place of hardwood. Tending the bar had been tedious, but it had been worth it.

He smiled.

*Mom would have loved new kitchen tile.*

Gal opened his eyes and walked into the pantry. A new door was set aside with a large **F** etched into the frosted glass, denoting the Finch name. And while only he resided in the family home anymore, Jimmy and Brad might appreciate the thought whenever they visited.

*If only they would visit.*

New hinges were installed into the doorjamb. Tomorrow, he would stain and mount the damn thing.

One more room, done.

Gal emerged from the pantry with a jar of Jif peanut butter, honey, and a few slightly stale slabs of bread. He pushed the three good fingers of his left hand deep into the creamy Jif and stuffed the velvety goodness into his mouth. A midnight snacking ritual he had inherited from his father. He savored the taste a moment, and then he frowned.

It tasted bitter. Acidic. Medicinal, almost.

*Does peanut butter go bad?*

He washed it down with a mouthful of Evan Williams. Yet another midnight snacking ritual he'd inherited from his father.

*Murderer.*

Retrieving a butter knife, he slathered a heap of Jif onto one slice of bread, drizzled honey on the other, and suckled the excess from the stub of his pinky.

And then, something strange occurred.

Gal's skin became hot. His eyelids grew heavy. He lost feeling in his toes, his fingers, and his face. Tunnel vision clouded his sight. The sticky knife slipped from tingling fingers and clattered on the new tile.

A sudden shift in the darkness made his blood run cold.

Gal's sluggish eyes squinted at a hulking shadow in the corner of the living room. He didn't remember owning a coat rack.

He froze.

*Who's there?!*

At least, that's what he wanted to say. Instead, he expelled a frothy gurgle. The world lurched on its side. The last thing he remembered was Dani yelling his name from up the stairs. A world beyond.

*Or was it Daphne?*

The night engulfed him.

***

Blackness. Silence.

Had the void finally claimed him from an over-excess of liquor, Adderall, and call girls? Was Heaven this bleak? Or could this be Hell?

Purgatory, most likely.

God, his head hurt.

The *creeeak* of a stair roused his senses. The gentle click of a large oak door sounded oddly familiar.

Purgatory, indeed. He must have consumed a monumental measure of whiskey for a headache this bad to carry on into the next life.

Perhaps now he could be with his mother.

Perhaps he should've had dinner.

Perhaps he should drink more.

Gallagher Finch opened bloodshot eyes.

With a loud groan, Gal pushed himself into a sitting position and rested his back against new kitchen cupboards. The stub of his pinky waded in something wet. He looked down to find the bottle of Evan Williams on its side, much of it pooled upon the tile.

No broken glass. At least he'd fallen gracefully.

He considered bending over to slurp the amber liquid from the tile. *Pluck some hair from the dog.* But for the first time in a long time, the stench of whiskey stung his nostrils and seared down his esophagus until an equally searing burn found its way back up.

Gal suddenly lamented his long-time best friend, kicking Evan Williams across the kitchen. He held his throbbing head, staggered his way up the cupboards, and placed a hand on the counter. His fingers squished into a spongey substance.

He looked down.

His left hand was smashed in the remnants of Dani's unfinished peanut butter and honey sandwich.

*Or was it Daphne?*

The smell of food provoked his bowels to regurgitate once more.

Funny how a harrowing hangover could cause a man to loathe his favorite liquor and midnight snack in the span of seconds. His sister would've recommended water, yet even the lifeblood of the earth, the one thing that Californians were crying and panicking over, made him want to be sick.

No. What he needed was Remy.

Gal slipped in his sick as he stumbled out of the kitchen and into the living room. And then something occurred to him. He looked up.

A hulking coat rack stood in the corner of the living room.

No burglars, then. A mere trick of the darkness. He sighed a breath of relief.

*I'm not crazy.*

He plopped down on the couch in nothing but a pair of time-stretched briefs sopping wet with whiskey, reached into the drawer of the coffee table, and withdrew his favorite treasure.

Finely crafted of double-walled red and black glass, blown to incorporate his favorite childhood cat's-eye marble as a grip, Remy was a work of art. She had once been clear with red swirls ribboning down her pipe and around her bowl, but years of compounded resin had given her a mature, black hue.

Gal withdrew a green plastic bottle. With a squeeze, he popped the top to emit the sweet and skunky fragrance of Rising Wind, his favorite strain of indica. He pinched off a small bud and tucked it into the bowl before sparking up the lighter and taking a drag.

Instant relief.

A buzz upon the coffee table reignited the buzzing in his head. Had he left his phone down here? The call girl could've stiffed him and stolen it like the last one had. You could take them home, but you could never trust them. The mere thought of her, however, caused his senses to awaken.

If only she were still here.

Gal picked his phone up and squinted at the screen. An event notification:

## 9:37
## Monday, January 26
### Bday plans w/ sis @ 11:00 am

Twenty-six on the twenty-sixth. His golden birthday. Where had the years gone? And why was he not a published author yet?

Gal sighed and finished off the bowl. A quick nap sounded perfect before eleven o'clock rolled around. He only wished Dani was still around to make him feel like a man, and a rugged one at that.

*Or was it Daphne?*

He had to hand it to her, she knew how to sneak out.

She had probably walked downstairs to find him passed out in the kitchen, rolled her eyes at the half-made Jif and honey sandwich on the counter, grabbed her heels, and left him with a flip of the bird.

He'd hardly even heard her leave.

*Hardly.*

Yet another reason he loved that squeaky second-to-last stair. It let him know when he was alone.

*Me, myself, and I.* Gallagher's three favorite people.

He stretched and left the living room with a yawn. He stumbled over a pair of scarlet heels, placed his foot on the bottom step of the staircase...

And stopped.

She'd forgotten her heels. *In this weather?*

Not that it mattered. She'd be back for them, and he'd bribe her with an extra hundred dollars for a quick and carnal birthday gift.

*Step. Creeeak. Step. Step. Stumble. One at a time, old boy.*

Gallagher made it to the top of the stairs and headed for the bathroom. Stubble shavings littered the sink and countertop. A notepad etched in red cursive lay beside the window. A blood-dabbed cotton hand towel hung from the bin with the others.

Everything in its place.

Gal looked in the mirror and barely recognized himself. His slightly-above-average mug looked far below par. Yellow crust was lodged in the corners of his eyes and mouth. His eyes glowed red, thanks in part to Evan Williams and, of course, to Remy.

He looked like hell.

He'd take care of it later. His bed beckoned like a missed lover. Gal left the bathroom, took the six familiar steps to his bedroom doorway...

...and stopped dead on the threshold.

White cotton sheets, normally stained brown from spilled whiskey, were now soaked in scarlet so dense it was almost black.

Blood dripped from the bed frame and onto the floor. A steady, weeping trickle ran down a soft pale arm ending in manicured French tips. The same French tips that had left marks upon his back only hours ago.

Limbs jutted out in strange directions as the blood-soaked sheets lay twisted and tangled around a nude, feminine figure.

She hadn't forgotten her heels after all.

"D—Dani—Daphne?" he whispered.

No response.

Legs wobbling, Gal stepped closer, careful not to tread on the ever-growing pool of thick, red-black lifeblood claiming the new floor molding he'd laid down just last week. He had seen enough episodes of CSI to know not to mess with a crime scene.

But, therein lay the biggest problem of all: there was a CSI-worthy crime scene in his home. In his room. In his bed. But why? By whom?

"Daphne," he repeated. No answer.

Her milky, lifeless eyes stared out the window at the falling snow, fake eyelashes looking as if they'd just been freshly glued.

Something jagged and white jutted from her throat. Something bony.

A stag's horn.

The handle of his favorite pocketknife.

He became hot and cold, flushed and clammy all at once. His stomach tied itself in a knot. He lurched forward and dry-heaved, bowels having been emptied on the kitchen floor only minutes prior.

He was still dreaming. He must be.

He opened his eyes.

Daphne's cold, dead gaze remained fixed on the snow-frosted glass. She stared at the white-gray haze, and he stared at her ensanguined face.

So beautiful, even in death.

Far off in a distant world, a melancholy tune played for her soul. It grew louder…

Gal snapped back to reality. His phone was ringing in his white-knuckled fist. He glanced down at the screen.

His sister's name stared back at him – SCARLET.

CHAPTER TWO

# White

∽

His first instinct was to run.

Leave this mess far, far behind him.

This mess of a house. This mess of a life. This mess of a once-beautiful woman, now hacked into a crimson carcass. A sad existence, likely wrought with dysphoria, withdrawal, and the outlook that one day, life could get better. And it might have, but now there was nothing for her.

Nothing but twisted limbs and a slit throat.

Gallagher's phone screeched its deafening whine. He looked down at the screen to find Scarlet Finch's name gleaming up at him. *Accusing* him. As if he had done it. As if he had plunged the stag horn pocketknife into Daphne's once pulsing carotid artery. As if he had spilled her blood and left her wrapped in expensive white sheets.

What once was white, now soaked black.

He decided to answer.

"Scar – " he began, then dry-heaved and dropped the phone to the floor. He fell to his hands and knees, retching as the pressure built behind his watery eyes.

"Happy birthday, you beautiful son of a bitch!" came his sister's muffled voice through the receiver.

His birthday. The party. The planning.

Gallagher picked up the phone with jittery fingers and placed it to his ear.

"H — hey, Scar."

"Twenty-six? God, you're old," she sniggered, a sound that never failed to ease his every worry. But not today. "I'm on my way over. Did you want something from Tiger? I was going to stop and grab some – "

"No! Don't come over," he blurted out.

*Smooth, Gal.*

"Are you kidding? Why? Do you have a girl over or something?" There was that familiar fire. That oh-so-Scarlet, ireful annoyance in her voice at his attempt to convince her to turn around. She had driven all the way from Bishop, after all. She'd make sure he was well-aware of that fact.

Truth was, there certainly *was* a girl over.

"You can't – I mean, can I meet you at the bar later? We can plan my party there," he responded, summoning some repose to his shaky tone.

*Easy, old boy.*

"Oh, my god. You *do* have a girl over! We've been planning this for weeks, Gal. You do realize I drove all the way up from Bish – "

"Yeah, I know. I'm sorry. I—I forgot to put it in my phone." He smacked his forehead against the heel of his palm. He had never once lied to his sister.

"You sound weird. Gal, have you been drinking?"

"Come on, Scar, are you serious? I haven't had a drink in months." Another lie. Oh, how he and Evan Williams had become quiet companions in habitual secrecy.

"You're high," she grumbled. She was three for three.

"Scar, no!" he lied again. It was strange how one tiny incident could compel Gallagher Finch to completely soil the fruits of truth and alliance he had cultivated with his one and only sister.

His one and only friend, really.

But *this* wasn't one tiny incident.

"I'm getting off Highway 395 right now," she growled through the receiver. Gal's eyes remained fixed on Daphne, noticing her manicured fingertips curling at the knuckles as rigor mortis began to manifest. "I'm only ten minutes away. There's a little snow on the ridge, but they're clearing it and – "

"For God's sake, Scarlet, I told you I will meet you at the bar!" he interrupted with an ire of his own. "I will make you a hot totty and I won't even charge you."

He was met with silence.

"Scar?"

"I'm still here."

"Will you please meet me at the bar?" he sighed.

"Fine."

"Thank you."

"Only because it's your birthday. I want to see the new tile, though."

"I swear I'll show you tonight. You can come over after the party. I'll pour you a couple night caps. I'll have a glass of milk or something, and it'll be cool." He glanced around the pool of blood spreading across the bedroom floor. "Just let me clean up a little bit, all right?"

"Don't make me wait long." She sounded livid. And with that, she hung up.

***

*Thump. Thump. Thump...*

God, she was heavy.

The back of Daphne's skull clunked down the stairs as Gal dragged her by the ankles. He looked down to catch a glimpse of her face, and then dropped her in surprise. She was staring up at him. Rather, her foggy, uninhabited eyes were staring up at him.

He retched once more, and then continued on.

*Step. Thump. Step. Thump. Creeeeak. Thump...*

Had time been on his side, he would have taken more care to wrap the corpse in more sheets. As it stood, he was running out of time. Scar had probably already parked in her favorite spot out front of the Sierra Inn. Was probably sitting at the bar, impatiently waiting.

Matted clumps of raven hair left syrupy streaks of blood on every stair, trailing across the entryway as he dragged Daphne's dead weight. He tripped over her high heels, cursing loudly as one stiletto stabbed into the ball of his foot.

*What am I doing?*

He knew what he *should* have been doing. He *should* have been dialing every ranger, every police station from Lone Pine to Yosemite. He *should* have been sitting alone on his front porch, waiting for the pigs to show up. He *should* have been putting together an alibi.

How would that have looked? Cops show up, nobody around to claim the blame, no leads. They might dust for prints, but what if there was nothing? They would take him in for questioning, find his prints on every door, every surface of the house, even on the handle of the pocketknife. And then, they would find his DNA on the body.

Unconditionally culpable.

He'd never been a fan of the thin blue line, but who else could he have called? Certainly not Jimmy or Brad. His older brothers would have noticed the stag horn pocketknife embedded in the call girl's neck and taken him into the station themselves. They were family, sure, but far from friendly.

His twenty-sixth birthday, gone to hell in a handbasket.

*What to do, what to do…*

He considered dragging her through the snow to the shed out back. The snowfall would cover his tracks in a matter of minutes. Maybe wrap her in plastic like they did on *CSI*. He *did* have a spare tarp in the attic, after all. Hide her behind the lawnmower until he had more time to figure out what to do…

Actually, all of it sounded genius.

He still had to clean up the blood. That could take hours.

*Scar is going to kill me.*

What better way to bide one's time than to hide the evidence? At least, for now, until he figured out what the hell happened while he had been snoozing on the new kitchen tile. Or had he been sleepwalking? It wouldn't be the first time.

He looked down at Daphne's body, a bloody visage of violence and volatility. Could he truly be capable of this? Had the combination of alcohol and Adderall become too much? Had they brought out the Hyde to his Jekyll?

*Dammit, Gal. This wasn't you. You heard the stair creak. You heard the front door.*

He froze.

He *had* heard the front door.

Gal dropped Daphne's legs, hopped over her lifeless body, and ran full speed to the oak front door. He wrenched it open on whining hinges and sprinted barefoot into the snow in nothing but his briefs. He peered through the dense curtain of falling white at the surrounding road. It looked normal, nothing but the driveway, the dead juniper, and cranky old Ruby's blue two-story across the road.

There were no footprints in the snow other than his own. No tire tracks in his driveway or in the street beneath the snowdrift. Nothing to go on. The snowfall was too heavy.

*Damn.*

Gal became suddenly aware of just how cold he was. Feet numb and packed into the snow, he shivered and ran back inside, making sure to lock the door behind him.

Gal retrieved the spare blue tarp from the attic. He bounded down the stairs, careful not to step in the large stripes of blood glistening on the stairway. Luckily, he had already planned on replacing the mauve carpeting.

He'd have to rip it up sooner rather than later.

Garbed in snowboarding pants, a pair of boots, and a flannel shirt, Gallagher wrapped Daphne's body in the tarp. He dragged her out the sliding glass door, onto the back porch, and down into a heap of fresh white powder. He glanced over his shoulder at the surrounding pine trees, and then traversed into a familiar clearing within a thicket of dilapidated conifers, unaware of the smeared trail of blood left in Daphne's wake.

And there it was.

A small aluminum shed, eaves dripping with the glistening glaze of rains passed, sharpened icicles glittering in a hazy fog of white.

Gal dug out a small trench in the snow, opened the door, and tugged the body into the aluminum interior of the small, musty shed. He took a moment to glance around at the unused yard equipment: two lawnmowers, a weed whacker, a leaf blower, three large containers of stale oil, four compost bins, and a coil of rubber hose hanging from the rafters. A thick layer of dust had accumulated on every surface.

The compost bins were packed with yard waste that had long since decayed. Dry grass, shriveled weeds, and old branches were the only remnants of a time when the full ten acres of land had actually been cared for.

He never found the time to get out and push the lawnmower around, much less the will. He hadn't touched anything in ages, not since the day the house had been left to him. The day Scar moved away. The day his brothers left. The day his mother died.

The day his father had been arrested.

*Murderer.*

Gal dragged Daphne's body into the farthest corner of the shed. He adjusted the compost bins and oil containers in front of her so that she was hidden from sight. He found himself wondering just how long he had until the body would begin to smell.

"I'm sorry, Daphne," he whispered.

And with that, he locked up the shed, kicked a heap of snow in front of the door for good measure, and then began his march back into the trees.

Gal pulled out his phone and sighed a cold breath of relief to find that Scar hadn't called him back. He may have been late, but her patience hadn't worn thin.

*Yet.*

He reached the edge of the tree line, let his gaze wander up to the back porch, and stopped dead in his tracks.

Scarlet stood on the deck with eyes wide as dinner plates, face white as the snow falling around her, and a hand clasped to her mouth.

Gal knew what she was thinking...

*What have you done?*

\*\*\*

"I didn't do this."

"You said that already."

"And you still don't believe me."

It wasn't a question. He could see it in the deep, mocha brown hues hidden behind her red hipster glasses. They sat across from each other with the coffee table between them. It might as well have been a twenty-foot high brick wall, as far as Gal was concerned. Never in his life had he felt so detached from his sister.

"Do you want me to go over it again?" he asked.

"No."

She sighed and put her face in her hands, fingertips tucked under the lenses, hair peeking out from beneath her crocheted beanie.

"No, like you don't believe me? Or no, like you don't want to hear it again?" he asked, afraid of the answer.

"Both," she spoke calmly, her neatly-plucked brows furled in confusion and frustration. "You've told me everything. I don't want to go over it again."

"And me?"

"You're my brother, Gal, and I love you. But this... *this*..."

She sounded on the verge on tears. The back of Gal's throat burned in response. He choked back the urge to bury his face in her lap and cry like a frightened child. How was she the only one who could make him feel anything other than indifference?

"And on your birthday?" she groaned.

Gal slid around the coffee table and onto his knees beside her.

"Look at me, Scar. You know me better than anyone. I don't even watch scary movies. Blood – "

" – freaks you out," she finished for him and slowly nodded her head. "I know. But who the hell would have done this, Gal? This wasn't random."

"I don't know. The last thing I remember was passing out in the kitchen. I was making her a sandwich, and then I woke up."

"So, you *were* drunk."

"Don't do that. That's not important right now."

"Your alibi isn't important to you?"

"The cops don't need to find out – "

"Listen to yourself! Gal, there's a dead girl in your shed with your knife in her neck, and goodness knows what else of yours the cops will find inside of her!"

She had a point.

"You're a mean drunk, Gal. You go off the handle. You know that. I know that. Did this girl know that?"

"I've changed."

"Are you still going to the meetings?"

He hesitated, and then sighed.

"No."

"You lied to me."

"I know."

"You don't lie to me. Right? Or is that a lie too?"

"Scar, I don't know what to do. All I can tell you is that I didn't do this. I don't know who did it. I don't know why."

He stared at her, and she stared right back. For an eternity, they stared at each other. A battle of wills. A war for truth. A staring contest, just like when they were kids.

"I don't know what to do."

Finally, she sighed and her eyes hardened.

"We need to get rid of the body."

Gal did a double take, certain beyond certainty that he was hearing things. But she had said it, loud and clear.

"I know a spot," Scar said.

\*\*\*

A blanket of gray obscured any semblance of sunlight. It had been this way for eighteen days and the weatherman had forecasted many more shady days over the June Lake Loop.

Down here near Gull Lake, the second and the smallest lake in the sixteen-mile Loop, most of the year was silent. In the spring, fishermen preferred the glasslike depths of Silver Lake. In the summer, the vast expanse of Grant Lake, ideal for speed boating. And in the fall, the sun-soaked beaches of June Lake.

The winter belonged to Gull Lake. Silent and serene. Perfect for a murder.

Scarlet drove Gallagher's jeep around the side of the house and surveyed the front of cranky old Ruby's place.

The shutters were drawn over every window except the upstairs bathroom. Judging by the old woman's weak joints and the rehabilitation bed Gal had helped install downstairs after her third knee replacement, she wasn't likely to be peeking out of the tiny round pane of stained glass.

A sharp whistle caused her head to turn. She found Gallagher peering around the side of the house, a crumpled heap of blue tarp lying in the snow at his ankles. She threw open the jeep's gate, lifted the window, and pushed up the back seat to make room. She shuddered when she noticed a manicured hand jutting from underneath the tarp, bloody fingers curled and stiff, then walked over and helped lift one side of the body.

Gal allowed her to take up the rear, eyeing her for any trace of emotion. She offered none. No angry glares. No suspicious sneer. No wrinkles of disappointment. It was this lack of anything that made Gal more hurt than any punch to the nose.

"I didn't do this, Scar," he repeated.

"Just put her in the back, Gal," she said.

They eased the body into the back of the jeep beside a pair of shovels Gal found behind the shed, lowered the back window, and locked the gate.

Getting one last look at Ruby's place, Gallagher jumped into the passenger seat. Scarlet revved the six-cylinder engine, kicked it into four-wheel drive, and slowly rolled over fresh snow down to the main road. Had it not been for the morning's misfortune, Gal might have been ecstatic for a birthday snow.

With the road to the bottom lakes shut down for the winter months, they were forced to traverse up the ridge and into June Lake Village. They passed small businesses, bars, and steep-roofed housing. A few of the taverns were lit from the inside, wintertime tomfoolery in full swing as early birds began Monday moonshining earlier than usual… a January tradition in these parts.

Gal sensed the anxiety burning off Scarlet's shoulders as she tried desperately to maintain her cool.

"I should be the one sweating," he said with a chuckle.

"Is this funny to you?"

That shut him up. Instead, he focused on the landscape.

Colossal and commanding, the sleek Sierra Nevada mountains towered beyond all points of the compass, capped in brilliant white and ribboned with frozen waterfalls. The jeep whizzed past Cathy's Candy and followed the road beyond the Tiger Bar. They passed the Sierra Inn, and Gal greeted it with a grimace. He'd had to beg for the day off, had to plead to enjoy his birthday. A single day to enjoy, now gone to hell because of a mutilated call girl stuffed in the back of his jeep.

Two miles later found them passing through Oh Ridge, a long stretch of snowplowed asphalt, a break in the mountains lending space to an expanse of snow-covered plains dominating both edges of the road. They passed a gas station at the entrance of Highway 395, one of the last pitstops before the entrance to Yosemite National Park.

With a sudden left turn onto the highway, Scarlet punched the gas.

"Where are we going?" he asked.

"Mono," she replied.

"Why?"

She fixed him with a familiar stare that said, *Don't question me.*

And so, he didn't.

Scarlet proved early in life that to second-guess her was quite possibly the dumbest move in the book. If Brad had inherited the looks and Gal had inherited the creativity, then Scar had inherited the smarts. Jimmy, well… there was still hope for him, somewhere.

They remained silent for the rest of the drive until Scar pulled off the highway and onto a hidden, icy gravel path. Working as a summer guide all through her teenage years, Scar knew this terrain and territory better than most. She killed the headlights and rolled over a hill until finally, Mono Lake dominated the landscape.

Dwarfing even Grant Lake, the largest in The Loop, Mono Lake was as massive and as beautiful as it was deadly. Mother Nature had cursed its alkaline waters with salinity five times greater than the ocean. Long term skin exposure led to lesions, a sorry fact that Gal had learned firsthand on a field trip in the third grade. An accidental gulp led to severe dehydration and, in most cases, a nasty bout of gastrointestinal infection. For the young, the sick, and the elderly, risking exposure meant risking death.

Water this deadly to humans, however, was almost mystical to the surrounding soil, providing ample nutrition to the dense weeds that spanned for miles off Mono Lake's fly-infested shores.

Gal suddenly understood why Scarlet had brought them here. The alkaline soil was sure to break down human tissue, and fast.

"Do you think I should have called the police?" Gal asked.

Scarlet scoffed.

"What would I have told them, Scar?"

Ignoring him, she pulled the jeep behind a large mound exploding in sagebrush, put it in park, and killed the engine. Without a word, she got out, wrenched open the gate, and tossed him a shovel. Gal pierced the frosted soil with a sharp downward plunge.

"Are you going to talk to me at all?" he asked.

"I don't really know what to say, honestly," she replied, launching a shovel-full of dirty snow at his chest. "My guess is that, yes, you probably should have called the police."

"She was a hooker, Scar. Do you realize how badly that would have gone down?"

"You probably would have been a right side better than you are now, Gal, do you understand that? What are you doing with call girls, anyway? Are you that lonely? Are you that goddamn pathetic?"

*That one hurt.*

Gal didn't say much after that. He bit back the discomfort in his hands and dug deeper into the earth. After an hour, they succeeded in producing a six-foot-deep hole. Once more, they lifted the stiffening corpse, careful not to let the tarp rip as they lowered Daphne into the ground.

"You should probably say something," Scar said, wiping a sheen of sweat and dirt off her forehead.

Gal thought for a moment, shrugged, and began his eulogy.

"Dani — er, Daphne, you were good at what you did," he pronounced. "One of the best."

Scarlet rolled her eyes.

"You enjoyed red high heels, Midori on the rocks, and honey with your peanut butter." He met Scarlet's gaze and shrugged.

"That's all you knew about her?"

"I mean, it's not like I paid her to tell me her favorite color."

"You're disgusting," she said. "You do realize that someone is going to come looking for her, don't you?" The thought hadn't quite crossed his mind. Newfound panic began to settle in, mainly because Scarlet was always right.

She reached forward, plucked a hair from his head, and showed it to him. The strand was as white as the snow beneath his feet.

"Only twenty-six, and you're already going white."

She turned on her heel, but Gal caught her by the arm.

"Thank you, Scar. For everything. I know I told you to wait at the bar, but I'm glad you didn't."

He smiled. She did not.

"Why *did* you end up coming over?" he asked.

"You called me Scarlet," she said.

"What?"

"On the phone earlier, you called me Scarlet. You never call me Scarlet." She pulled her arm away. "That's when I knew something was up."

And with that, her feet crunched away on the frost as she made her way back to the jeep, allowing Gal the duty of filling the grave.

# CHAPTER THREE

## Ruby

◌

She was going to murder that dog.

The little bastard had finally pushed her to her limit, and now she wanted nothing more than to catch him and wring his finely groomed little neck. She wanted to squeeze and squeeze until she collapsed his delicate windpipe, wanted to watch his slightly-askew, bulging eyes pop with the effort.

*It wouldn't be difficult.*

She remembered being young, staring out at the barren flatness of dusty, post-Depression Kansas. On a near-daily basis, she obeyed her daddy's wishes and shuffled out to the barn to strangle dozens of chickens. Had twisted until the spine emitted a wet squelch, like attempting to break a green twig. The head would sometimes dangle by little more than mere sinew until, with a gentle tug and a pop, she would discard the head and set to work plucking the feathers.

Although, her hands had been much, much stronger back then.

Ruby lifted her old, withered hands. Behind horn-rimmed glasses, she gazed upon what had once been two strong gifts from the good

Lord Himself. Father Time was a cruel man indeed, countless years warping straight and delicate fingers into lumpy masses of flesh, bone, and cartilage. Her knuckles looked as if marbles had been squeezed between the phalanges, popped into place, and left to impede any sort of dexterity she might have once possessed. Her fingers jutted in all directions, some locked at the middle knuckle while still others were forced into a claw-like state, giving the appearance that rigor mortis had set in early.

That would come soon enough, she was sure.

Her palms maintained the same curved lines she'd had as a girl, "luck lines" that a tarot reader in New Orleans had once prophesied would perform great acts of charity and heroism. Looking back on it, now, it had all been a load of crap. The most charitable thing she had ever done was offer to babysit the kids next door during the tragedy thirteen years earlier.

*Had it already been thirteen years?*

She'd always hated those damn kids, but somehow Ruby got wrangled into the occasional good deed, especially when the promise of more land was on the table.

The jingle of a dog's collar brought her back to reality.

"Copper!" she chirped in a weak, withered whimper.

Surely that couldn't be her voice. A voice that had once graced taverns, bars, and speak-easies across the beaches of the Gulf Coast with war melodies was now broken and ragged after decades of tobacco and opium smoke inhalation, not to mention screams of sensual ecstasy.

*Oh, if walls could speak…*

Not these walls, no. These walls had only watched the steady decline of both her health and her spine for the last twenty years. These walls had only seen her past her prime. Past her days of singing for men in the service and, afterward, offering her own seductive service to them.

"Copper, sweetie, mama has treats," Ruby lied a little more sweetly, shuffling her fuzzy slippers along the yolk-yellow shag carpet that Gordon had never once thought to replace. She'd begged and begged for new white carpet and always, he had given her the same response: "*Give it enough time and white carpet will end up the same color it is now.*" And that would be it.

The old bastard…

God rest his soul.

The jingle roused her again. She followed the sound of Copper's collar, stepping carefully over dozens of squeaky toys, praying to nobody in particular that she would be lucky enough to avoid another faceplant like the one she'd taken last week.

Curse her wretched feet. Curse her knobby knees. Curse the world, for all she cared.

The jingle ceased.

"Copper, sweetie?"

Nothing.

"Dammit, Copper! Come out this instant!" she bellowed. And then it occurred to her: only one thing had ever been able to rouse the one-year-old puppy. The one promise she knew she could never, ever bring herself to fulfill…

"Want to go for a *walk*?"

Loud as sleigh bells on Christmas, the jingle was back. It began upstairs and bounded down the dreaded flight of stairs she hadn't hiked up in weeks. She heard breathless little grunts and the pitter-patter of tiny paws until finally, a furry ball of white and coppery hair sped down the bottom steps and slid across the linoleum. The puppy shot past Ruby's slippers, caught his footing, and then doubled back until he sat, panting, at her feet.

Copper stared up at her as though it had been *he* who had been calling *her* name for the past hour and a half. As though it had been *he* who had found *her* fresh turd melted into the shag carpet. As though it had been *he* who had discovered *her* dragging her worm-infested little sphincter across the floor. She wouldn't have minded so much had Gordon still been alive. Perhaps, then, she could have persuaded him that, indeed, it was finally time for new carpet.

The old bastard…

God rest his soul.

"Bad boy," Ruby snapped, pointing her deformed, crooked finger in his face.

Copper cocked his head to the side, oversized tongue lolling out of his furry maw. His curly-Q tail wagged without a care. He was mocking her, the little shit. Just as Gordon might have done, had he never fallen down those damned stairs.

The old bastard…

God *damn* his soul.

"Bad boy!" she yelled louder. She reached down to smack his snub-nose.

Copper evaded the fruitless swing of her hand like a fly evading the swat of a newspaper, then darted forward and bit her knuckle.

Ruby squealed and clutched her bleeding finger. She launched an ill-positioned kick at the puppy, but remembered halfway through just how old she was.

Too late.

Her hip gave that all-too-familiar click. The joint of her femur locked in the crook of her pelvis. Everything seemed to move slowly as the horrifying realization of what was about to happen became reality.

She hoped beyond hope that her bottle of oxycodone was downstairs…

Below her left buttock, searing agony built like a shaken champagne bottle. And just as the bottle might burst if provoked, she instinctively set her foot on the ground and felt the pain explode up her left side. The world turned to pudding beneath her feet, sending her spiraling away into open air. She caught sight of the hundreds of small wooden slats of the window shutters, closing her off from the outside world.

She had always valued her privacy above all else. A habit, more than anything…

After all, the line of work that she had chosen for so many decades called for absolute secrecy. Absolute discretion. Absolute concealment.

Part of the reason she had chosen to move here in the first place was to be rid of the busy contempt of the world. Hidden within a small crook of the Sierra Mountains, a tiny woman in a tiny home perched on a tiny hillside of the June Lake Loop.

Moving here meant solitude. Moving here meant solace…

Moving here meant secrecy.

Ruby's back hit the linoleum floor, knocking the wind from her lungs. Her dentures sank into her tongue as the Poligrip fastening them to her gums became loose.

*God, I'm falling apart.*

She lie upon the floor, stiff and still as a board, bespectacled eyes staring up at the ceiling. Had that brown spot always been there? Or had the ceiling sprung a leak? It seemed as if both she *and* the house were falling apart.

Shock of the fall made her numb, but only for a moment.

Electric pain burst up her side. Unable to breathe, she wondered if here upon the linoleum would be her final resting place.

Had her entire life – the quiet Midwestern plains of her childhood, the raucous New Orleans streets of her twenties and thirties, the secret taverns and countless motel rooms of her forties and fifties, the quiet marriage and even quieter secrets of her sixties, the grief of her seventies – had it all led here, to the yellowing linoleum floor of her late husband's family home?

The old bastard…

God rest his soul.

Ruby tried to take a breath but found her lungs didn't work. She closed her eyes, intent on sending up one final prayer to the God she had never truly believed in. Better to cover all her bases just in case He truly did exist, even though He'd had one hell of a time ignoring her over the years.

*Okay, here goes.*

She took a breath…

And stopped praying before she even started. She could breathe again.

*Not dead yet.*

Biting back the pain, Ruby pushed herself into a seated position, the slight pressure on her bum feeling as though someone had bludgeoned a sledgehammer into her hip. She looked down and found that she had landed quite gracefully, both legs extended in a straight line.

No dislocation, then.

*Perhaps there is a God.*

And then, that annoying little jingle started up again.

She was going to murder that dog.

Ruby turned to find Copper crouched with his butt in the air, tail wagging mischievously as he yipped at her, bulging eyeballs askew and pointed in two separate directions. Why her niece had thought to give Ruby an ugly Shih Tzu puppy for Christmas was entirely beyond her.

"You little shit! Get over here!" she barked back, vocal cords regaining some of their usual *oomph*. She slapped the linoleum and he was gone, stealing away back up the stairs like a child who'd been caught with his hand in the cookie jar.

She grunted and reached for her cane, supporting herself as she slowly rose to her feet. Her hip threatened to give out on her again, but years of battling arthritis kept her focused on shifting all of her ninety-six pounds onto her good leg.

She needed the oxy, and fast.

Ruby limped into the kitchen, every single step sending an electric surge up her side. She wrenched open the cupboard beside the sink and rummaged through dozens of old love letters from various soldiers she'd serviced over the years. Letters she had dug up after Gordon's funeral. Letters of liaisons past, liaisons she was keen to relive, if only she had retained the strength in her hands, her lungs, her hips.

If only she had her youth back.

Deeper she rummaged. No sign of a clattering pill bottle. She sighed, and then turned to her deadliest of enemies.

*Up the damned stairs.*

"Easy does it, Rube," she whispered, preparing for the treacherous ascent. She limped across the yellowing linoleum entryway until she stood hunched at the bottom of the switchback staircase.

Copper sat at the platform dividing the lower steps from the upper, ugly eyes bulging. He stared at her for a moment and then, as if to spite all her efforts, bounded effortlessly up the stairs and out of sight.

She placed her good foot on the bottom step and hoisted herself up. Pain shot down her left side and made her to step back to the floor. Fighting that familiar frustration, she gripped the bannister and forced herself to fight the pain until finally, she stood upon the bottommost stair. She gave herself a minute to recover, then hoisted herself up.

And up.

And up.

Copper sat at the top of the stairs, head cocked like a clueless idiot. Staring at her. Daring her to continue. Slowly but surely, Ruby pushed her legs to tread ever-onward, up the mountain. Finally, she reached the summit.

*The air is thinner up here*, she considered, gasping for breath.

She was going to murder that dog.

But first, the oxy.

Ruby limped down the upstairs hallway to the master bedroom. The large bed was still messy from her last sleep in it two weeks earlier. An oak dresser, which the eldest neighbor boy had built for her a couple of winters ago, was now empty considering most of her clothes were folded neatly downstairs beside her medical bed. Large bay windows stood darkened behind closed shutters. Little slivers of gray glowing between the slats promised yet another day of snow.

Everything in its place.

An old analog television sat beside the window. The 10 a.m. news report droned on the black and white screen. She always left this TV on, day or night, rain or shine. Since Gordon's passing, the mindless dribble of current events was intoxicatingly comforting. Her electric bill had, as always, been through the roof, but it was a small price to pay for the comfort of pretending that she wasn't alone in the old house.

She limped to the bathroom, opened the medicine cabinet, and found her hidden treasure. She popped open the pill bottle, brought it to her lips, half-considered swallowing everything inside, thought better of it, and then took down a single oxycodone tablet.

After a minute, sweet relief kicked in.

Ruby's eyes glazed over as she peered out the small, round, stained glass window above the tub. Reds, greens, and blues liquified the bleak sky in a rainbow of colors. Outside, the massive, snowcapped peaks of the Sierras brimmed with glittering streams, frozen waterfalls, and vast pine forests.

It was beautiful.

*My, aren't I smiley today?*

Her attention was stolen by a shift in the snow. Careful to avoid detection, Ruby staggered to the window, adjusted her glasses, and squinted to get a better view.

Across the street, the dark-haired neighbor boy stood alone in his front yard, shivering in nothing but a pair of briefs. He glanced up and down the small cul-de-sac they shared, legs buried mid-shin in fresh white snow.

The poor boy was bound to freeze his fruits off.

He was more a man now than when they'd last exchanged words, white skin raked with pink scratches, presumably from a night alone with a woman. She had always regarded him as something of a royal pain in the ass, recalling how he and his brothers used to wrap her trees and bushes in toilet paper during warm summer nights. How they used to throw eggs at her front door on Halloween.

*The little bastards.*

She watched as he dashed back into the house.

The whole event was odd, to be sure. She kept watch, and for thirty long minutes, his home was silent, snow filling the footprints he'd left in the front yard. She was moments from relinquishing her voyeuristic fantasies into the blizzard when suddenly, a car rolled into his driveway.

A short, brown-haired female emerged from the car, adorned in a beanie and large spectacles Ruby may have considered fashionable in the '70s. Perhaps it was true, then, that old fads come full circle in time. This woman was certainly familiar. Upon closer inspection, Ruby deduced that it was the sister.

*Can it really be little Scarlet, all grown up?*

She remembered the tubby little girl, always hidden behind a textbook while her brothers threw snowballs in the winter and shot BB guns in the summer. She'd heard rumors that Scarlet had moved away after the mother was killed and the father was locked away. Scarlet had finally shed her baby fat, it seemed, now more a woman than her mother had ever been. What had brought Scarlet here now, in the middle of winter?

Ruby wondered how long it had been since she had seen all four of the siblings in one room together, even the same town.

Scarlet disappeared into the house and, again, Ruby was left standing at the stained glass window, staring out into the snow. She knew it wasn't her place to snoop, knew all too well what it felt like to be snooped upon, but something about the boy had intrigued her.

The uncertainty in his movements. The twitchy glances in his face as he scanned up and down their lonely cul-de-sac. He appeared as a rabbit might when a wolf was on the prowl. As though there was anywhere else in the world he'd like to be except where he was right then and there.

As though, quite possibly, he was hiding something.

She heard the analog television droning on about current events, every word clear yet increasingly hazy in her attempts to mentally drown out the specifics, her mind set on the house across the street and the possible goings-on inside. This was, after all, far more interesting than any of the crap television they aired nowadays.

Another thirty minutes later, her eyelids became heavy as the oxy kicked in full swing, numbing her pulsing hip and further fogging her already cloudy mind.

The sound of an engine rumbled to life and forced her eyes to snap open.

Adjusting her glasses, Ruby watched as Scarlet reversed Gallagher's jeep into the side yard. The girl got out and peered suspiciously around the cul-de-sac, just as her brother had done, and then turned her attention upon Ruby's home. A glance at the bottom floor, no doubt attempting to see past her shuttered windows, and then...

To Ruby's horror, Scarlet's gaze drifted up to the little round window. As though struck by a bolt of lightning, Ruby's old body went rigid, muscles seizing up as she tried to steal away from the window pane, certain that she had been spotted.

She gave it a few moments, and then slowly peeked out the window once more.

Scarlet was gone. The jeep sat unattended, exhaust billowing from the tailpipe.

The siblings reappeared, dragging something blue up the length of the side yard, each carrying one side. Whatever it was, it looked heavy, as though it were not a *something* at all, but rather...

Her eyes were playing tricks on her. Had to be.

In an instant, the jeep was gone. Fresh tracks in the snow led out of the cul-de-sac and toward Gull Lake, which would ultimately lead into the village.

*What on earth had those kids...*

" – escaped from Folsom State Prison sometime in the early hours of this morning. He was incarcerated in 2003 after being convicted of murdering a Mono County woman at her home in the June Lake Loop."

Ruby's heart stopped.

Her ears were playing tricks on her. Had to be.

There was no way in hell...

"Mono County Sheriff Paul Larson issued a statement today, urging residents of Mono and Inyo Counties to remain alert, as Jonathan Tanner is expected to be armed and dangerous."

The newscast played on, but her mind became even hazier. She couldn't believe what she was hearing. It couldn't be true. Could it?

Ruby knew one thing for certain…

If Jonathan Tanner had truly escaped from Folsom State Prison, then Mono County was in trouble. The Loop was in trouble.

*She* was in trouble.

Ruby had to get out of town. And fast.

CHAPTER FOUR

# Golden

～

Fresh snow fell in torrents as Gal and Scar ascended into Mammoth. The moon was obscured by rolling clouds that hadn't blown over in weeks, and Gal was beginning to yearn for a little starlight, as much as he hated looking up at the stars.

His mother had always told him stories about the stars, how the tiny specks of light in the night sky were, in fact, supermassive balls of scorching gas and flame millions of times larger than the earth. A star burned for billions of years beyond space and time and when it finally reached its moment to die, it collapsed into its own core before exploding bright enough to outshine its entire mother galaxy. In the span of a few brief weeks, the supernova would radiate as much energy as the star had emitted during its entire lifetime, all before fading into darkness. So much energy, so much golden life, so much rage, fury, brilliance, and time encapsulated in a single speck of light stuck amidst a vast sea of others just like it.

*Just like her.*

And then, in an instant, his mother had gone to join the stars. And he had become jealous of them for taking her. And now he hated them for it. Hated looking at them. But just a small glimpse of starlight would assure him that he was, in fact, still alive.

Amidst the cold.

Amidst the confusion.

Amidst having found a young woman slaughtered in his bed only hours before.

"We're here," Scar said over the soft buzz of the radio.

He looked at her from the passenger seat. They had driven her red Audi and left the jeep at home, having spent the last few hours scrubbing and bleaching and scrubbing and bleaching, over and over until Gal felt quite certain that both he and Scar would pass out from inhaling so much Clorox.

She insisted on helping him clean up the mess, but he couldn't help wondering if the mess was all his fault. Not the bloody gore left sopping upon his bedroom floor, but the mess he had created by neglecting to call the police and make a report. The more he thought on it, the more he wished he could have just played it cool.

But, Daphne had been in *his* bed. Had *his* DNA on her body. Had been murdered by *his* stag horn pocketknife. There was too much wrong with the situation already. Scar said so…

And Scar was always right.

"Thank you," he whispered. "For everything."

She looked at him and sighed. Without a word, she got out of the car and Gal followed. Snow crunched beneath their feet as they walked across the parking lot toward Ansel & Adam's, his favorite dive bar. It had been the one place he wanted to spend his birthday with just a small group of family and friends.

And now, it was the one place he wanted to be far, far away from.

"Just be cool," Scar told him as she reached up to rub his shoulder, but even over the wind, he heard the apprehension in her voice. Here they were, sharing a secret far bigger than either of them could have ever anticipated. Oh, what people would say if they knew:

He, the murderer.

She, the accomplice.

"Just be cool," he heard her whisper again. He wondered if she was repeating it to calm him or to calm herself.

The immediate and familiar warmth of Ansel & Adam's washed over Gal in a wave of aromas, from wood smoke to stale beer. The scent of rich hops, malted barley, and greasy food enticed his nostrils and, almost immediately, he felt better than he had all day.

Not quite happy. No, he hadn't been happy in months.

Neutral, he supposed.

A loud roar erupted and Gal was hefted into the air, shaken about like a rag doll. A dozen voices cheered as he was spun around, bar lights whipping into stretched, glowing neon ribbons until he thought he might throw up.

"Happy birthday, ass-wipe," Jimmy chortled, beer foam dripping down his beard. Gal's eldest brother's voice was so deep that one might have expected to find a man as large as Paul Bunyan himself. Standing at 5'4, however, Jimmy Finch was a mere six inches shy of being classified a legal dwarf. His shoulders were as broad as he was tall, and years of steroid abuse had given him the appearance of an underdeveloped gorilla. For this reason, Jimmy was afflicted with the most severe case of Little Man Syndrome that Mono County had ever known.

"I'm going to puke, Jim. Let me down."

"We ain't even started drinkin' yet! Somebody get this boy a beer," Jimmy demanded and, almost instantly, Gal felt a cold glass pressed into his palm. He looked at Scarlet, expecting her to reprimand him for even accepting the cold brew.

Instead, she wandered to a corner near the fireplace, his drinking the least of her worries.

"Happy birthday, kid," came a familiar, silken voice behind him. Gal spun and nearly dropped his IPA. Standing there was Bradley Finch, as cool and collected as ever. Where Gal was overly tall and Jimmy was amusingly short, Brad stood at a healthy average. Where Gal was lanky and Jimmy was bulbous, Brad was athletic. Where Gal's black hair hung lank and Jimmy sported an awkward curly red, Brad sported a flaxen coif and the most perfect five o'clock shadow that Gal constantly wanted to sink his fist into.

*The golden brother, in form and in fashion.*

"You made it," Gal muttered and forced a smile.

"I wouldn't have missed it," Brad said, tipping back the rest of his beer.

The brothers stared at each other for what felt like hours, but after two seconds, Brad presented his phoniest Cheshire grin.

Sensing the animosity, a pair of feminine fingertips finished in black nail polish slipped around Brad's waist as a girl's face appeared from behind him.

Gal felt as though he'd been punched in the gut.

A pair of bright, sapphire eyes popped beneath a light shade of dusky eyeshadow. She possessed an oval face, a soft chin ending in just the slightest hint of a family cleft. Tresses of golden hair fell in curtains around her face, neither messy nor kempt, as though she hardly cared about her appearance and didn't give a lick what people thought anyway.

"You must be Gallagher," she said.

"Gal," he squeaked.

Brad snorted into his beer.

Gal cleared his throat and spoke with a sudden confidence he was able to turn on at a moment's notice. A confidence that came from having to maintain a fake smile every night of the week. A confidence that came from bartending. "Call me Gal."

"Like *girl*, but with an accent," Brad added.

Gal had half a mind to crunch in Brad's perfectly-sloped nose, but decided that his words had always been stronger than his fists. He was a writer, after all.

*Or at least a semblance of one.*

"For a second, I thought you must have been Whitney," Gal spoke coolly, taking back a gulp of the rich and hoppy ale and harboring immense pride at the sudden frustration forming in the lines of his brother's stupid face. "Are you not seeing that Whitney girl anymore, Brad? God, that was fast."

"I'm Amber," she interjected, pressing her palm into his own, soft fingers wrapped around the back of his hand.

"It's a pleasure to meet you, Amber. Please, help yourself to anything."

Their eyes locked for just a moment as Gal offered a lazy grin, a laziness that she returned. His stance became more and more awkward in an effort to conceal his attraction.

She averted her eyes upon Brad and purred, "You never told me about Whitney."

Having planted the seed and deciding to let Brad's frustration water it, Gal excused himself and disappeared into the throng. John and Graham sat at one of the large oaken tables, ceremoniously locked in a fierce arm-wrestling competition. *Graham's too drunk to win.* Ellie and Michael were arguing in the corner. *Just break up already.* Pete was already drunk and half asleep, gulping straight from a pitcher. *Typical Pete.*

Everything, and everyone, in its place.

All except Scarlet.

She sat alone near the back of the room beside a roaring hearth, beanie pulled over her ears and fire reflected in her glasses. She looked scared, alone, her eyes fixated on him.

Gal sighed, brushed past Jimmy scarfing down an entire pizza, and sat beside her.

"You really should be mingling with people," Scar said.

"So should you," he replied. He let his eyes scan the crowd, catching glimpses of Amber teasing Brad about Whitney.

*God, she was beautiful.*

"I'm not good at lying," Scarlet whispered. "You know that."

"Scar, it's only lying if somebody legitimately asks if we buried a call girl today." *Always a way around things.* He ran a hand through his hair, then chugged down the rest of his ale to calm his nerves. "We aren't lying. Just keeping a secret."

"You're right."

"That means a lot coming from you, smarty-pants." He met her eyes and smiled, lifting her chin. "Just be cool."

She nodded and rested her forehead on his.

"Secrets don't make friends," Jimmy called over to them and, for a moment, Gal's blood ran cold. Had they been heard?

Both Gal and Scar stared at their brother with fearful eyes, but Jimmy furrowed his eyebrows and turned back to the beer he was pouring.

"I was kiddin'. Weirdos."

***

Even for a Monday night, the place was packed. Not only did their party of ten dominate the tiny interior of Ansel & Adam's, but four other parties had stumbled in midway through the night. Eventually, all parties merged into a hopeless mass of beer-drinking, co-mingling inebriates.

Having been the center of attention at his party all night, Gal received tender, lustful glances from an array of different people throughout the establishment. A blonde co-ed offered to buy him a beer, yet he'd respectfully declined due to her lazy eye. An Amazonian cougar with frizzy hair backed him into a corner and attempted to clean the beer foam off the tip of his nose with her tongue, but he'd all too eagerly slipped out from beneath her buxom bosom. Even a set of twins had given him a sultry glance that would've made any man swell with pride. Instead, he gave them a simple nod and averted their gaze.

What was wrong with him?

He should've been in a hotel room right now celebrating his birthday properly. But as much as he didn't want to admit it, he knew all too well what was wrong with him.

Long, messy golden hair...

Sapphire eyes...

Black nail polish…

The girl of his dreams stood five steps away.

Like a vulture laying claim to a carcass, his older brother remained wedged between them. Brad stood with his prize to the wall, one arm held lazily over Amber's shoulder. Their faces remained only inches apart as they whispered sweet-nothings over the rabble of laughter and misconduct flowing freely amongst the crowd.

Gal's palms sweated, his face burned, the hairs on the back of his neck prickled. He felt like he was going to be sick. He shoved through the crowd and made his way past the bar, between the long lines of party-goers waiting for the restrooms, through the back hallway, and out into the blistering cold of the night. The door clicked behind him, silencing the raucous and leaving him alone with his favorite people.

*Me, myself, and I.*

The snow had finally let up, but the night sky was still absent of moon and starlight.

It all felt so claustrophobic. The weight of the clouds above him. The weight of the book he'd been attempting to write. The weight of the house and its endless renovations. The weight of imagining Amber pinned beneath his brother. The weight of a dead girl pressing against the front of his skull.

And now, the weight of seven IPAs pressing against his bladder.

God, he had to pee.

Gal looked around the parking lot with half a mind to drop his fly and disembark right then and there, but the sudden glance of a police car nestled just beside the bar made his blood run cold.

*Had they found out about Daphne already?*

He had to run. He had to get the hell out of Dodge…

No. He had to play it cool.

As if daring him to whip it out, the two officers inside the vehicle watched him with matching grins, their quota not yet fulfilled for the evening. The last thing he needed was a ticket for public indecency.

As if daring them to cite him for being drunk in public, Gal placed his hand on the rail of the back courtyard and lifted his beer before taking a good, long draught. He was, after all, still on bar property. He had half a mind to pull Remy out of his pocket, pack a fresh bowl, and take a long drag just to test their patience. It was California, after all, and it was 2015. Weed was no big deal if you had a card.

Problem was, his card had been expired for months.

His bladder would have to wait. And so would Remy. That narrowed his options.

*A cigarette, then.*

Gal withdrew a pack of Marlboro Reds, pulled one between his teeth and sparked the lighter, letting the acrid smoke flood his lungs. He held it in and zeroed it out, then took another deep, long drag as a slight head change began to settle in.

*In and out.*

*In and out.*

*In – cough! – and out.*

The back door opened and Jimmy stumbled into the cold, laughing with half a beer spilled down the front of his flannel. Gal's tiny big brother wrapped hairy python arms around his waist.

"I freakin' love you for bringing cigs. Left mine at home," Jimmy lied. He had never offered to pay for his own cigarettes, let alone anything else. "Mind if I – "

"Knock yourself out," Gal muttered. He tossed the pack of Marlboros onto the ground, simply for the fun of watching his oldest brother hunker beneath his own weight and stumpy legs to pick them up. Jimmy had cuffed Gal on the ears far too often when they were growing up for him not to have a little fun now and again.

Jimmy picked up the cigarettes with a minor struggle before lighting up. He noticed the cops watching from their unit.

"Pigs. Just waitin' for people to stumble out."

He spat on the asphalt, not three feet from where the police unit was parked.

"Easy. Be cool," Gal said.

"You're the chill stoner. Not me."

"If it wasn't my birthday, I'd say go for it. But we don't need Scar bailing you out of jail. Not tonight, at least."

"What's up with her anyway?" Jimmy growled. "She's been actin' all weird. 'Specially around you."

Gal felt the weight in his skull grow heavier.

"You two fight or somethin'?"

"She's been quiet all day," Gal replied with the cigarette between his chattering teeth. Chattering not from the cold... at least, not anymore.

"We were talkin' about the house, and she was sayin' that it's comin' along pretty damn well. New kitchen tile and all that. I might have to move back in." Jimmy chuckled and punched Gal on the shoulder, but Gal knew that Jimmy's rouse was far from a joke.

Gal remained silent, and that was the catalyst that Jimmy was waiting for.

"I'm kidding, obviously. What kind of older brother would I be if I just barged back in?"

"Yeah," was all Gal could manage before stifling the awkward silence with a fake cough and another inhale.

God, he had to pee.

Jimmy looked at him, then at the ground, then at the police unit, shuffled his feet, and then set his dark eyes back on Gal.

"I mean, if the circumstances were to go south, like with my house — "

"Your apartment?" Gal corrected him.

"Whatever. I mean, you'd let me — I wouldn't be a — it would be different this time around, you know?" Jimmy stuttered.

"You're talking like things have already gone south."

"No! Things are great, kid. One hundred percent solid gumbo," Jimmy retorted, louder than he needed to.

So, things truly were going south.

"Then what are we talking about?" Gal asked.

"Never mind. I just want to come and see the house is all."

"Drop by any time," Gal replied with a shrug. He finished off his final cigarette and flicked it at the police car.

And with that, he walked back inside, leaving Jimmy alone in the cold.

God, he had to pee.

Gal rushed through the back hallway and to the restrooms. He stood at the back of the monstrous line leading into the head. The girls had an even rougher time, their line stretching nearly three times as long and moving twice as slow.

A sudden flash of golden hair caught his eye. Amber stood hardly an arm's length away.

*And no Brad in sight.*

The men's line lurched forward, and Gal seized his chance. Feigning being more inebriated than he actually was, he bumped shoulders with Amber and pretended not to notice.

"Well, well. The birthday boy himself," he heard her say.

"Apologies. I had one too many."

"That makes two of us," she said.

"Lose my brother already?" he asked, looking ahead rather than directly at her. *Make her feel like you don't care about the conversation.*

God, it was hard not to look at her.

"He's somewhere around here. Probably grabbing another round," Amber replied. "You two don't get along very well, do you?"

"Blunt, aren't you?"

"Guilty."

He smiled. "I like blunt."

"So does your brother."

Gal thought long and hard about what to say next, then decided on remaining silent and giving her naught but a slight nod of the head. She watched him a moment, as if trying to decide whether he was friend or foe. Three stumbling men emerged from the restroom, and the line shuffled forward. He stepped ahead of her, proud of maintaining his cool composure, but also disappointed they hadn't said more to each other.

Gal suddenly felt a slight tug on his jacket and turned to find her sapphire eyes focused on the small handwritten label on the bottom hem of the jacket:

*FINCH*

"Cute," Amber said with a brightness in her eyes that could outshine the stars. "Brad labels his clothes too."

"More of a habit than anything. Mom used to label everything. Whenever we went camping, one of us would end up losing something, but we always got it back."

He smiled and reminisced about the bright red fishing pole he had begged for on his tenth birthday, only to leave it unattended at Grant Lake. He'd returned to find it gone, and had cried and cried on his mother's shoulder. Two days later, a man from a neighboring campsite had returned the labeled pole good as new, as well as the large fish that had pulled it into the lake. Gal recalled just how sweet that trout had tasted.

"Mom labeled *everything*."

"He doesn't talk about her," Amber said. "Can I ask you how she died?"

Blunt, yet again. Gal thought about his mother often, but always shied away when strangers asked him about her.

Her life. Her love of The Loop. Her infectious smile. Her husband. Her murder.

Perhaps he did, in fact, have something in common with his older brother. Gal realized then that he, like Brad, did not like talking about his mother.

"No," he answered.

He was suddenly eager to be anywhere else.

Gal turned to glance at Amber once more, but her gaze had shifted to the wall, as though she was used to being ignored. He wanted so badly to talk to her, to apologize for being rude, but the line of men behind him beckoned him forward.

He disappeared into the restroom to find the first open urinal.

*Ah, sweet bliss.*

***

By midnight, Ubers had come, tabs had been settled, and only Graham had been forced to clean vomit off the bathroom floor from one too many shots. A clean and composed night, then, to be sure. The bartenders wiped down the bar top while the servers settled out their tips, the latter and the former both grateful for the business yet annoyed from the night's drunken antics.

"You did a great job setting this up," Gal murmured to Scar, his head buzzing from countless beers. "Couldn't have asked for a better birthday."

"You sure about that?" Scar asked, obviously still dwelling on Dani.

*Or was it Daphne?*

Gal sighed and rested his head on her shoulder.

"I guess you're right. Like always."

He yawned and tipped back the dregs of his final beer, wanting nothing more than to drive back to The Loop and collapse into his bed.

Then again, maybe he would sleep in the guest room for a few nights, at least until the smell of bleach faded. With all of the lights on, of course, and with a baseball bat next to him in case whoever slaughtered Daphne decided to come back for round two...

*What if he is still in the house?*

As though reading his thoughts, Scar ruffled his hair and asked, "You want to stay at my place for a while? If it were me, I wouldn't set foot back in that house for months."

"That might look odd, me up and leaving after a girl goes missing. Wouldn't it?"

"No one is going to find her, Gal."

"What are you two whisperin' about?" Jimmy called from the restroom door. "Seriously, Scar, you've been weird all night. And you barely drank. What's up? You pregnant?"

Scarlet tossed her head back and laughed. It was the first time Gal heard her laugh all day, and the sound of it warmed his belly.

"If I were, it would be an immaculate conception," she said with a shake of her head. "Are you ready to go, Gal?"

"Yes," he replied and stood up on staggering legs.

He glanced out the window to find Brad with his arms wrapped tightly around Amber, their hoods up and their lips locked in a slow, passionate embrace as fresh flakes of snow cascaded down upon them. It was a scene straight from a romance novel, and the thought of what they would be doing when they got back to Brad's place made Gal sick to his stomach.

And here he was, with no one to hold. No one to kiss him on his birthday.

"I ain't kiddin', brother," Jimmy said as he pulled Gal into a bear hug. "You're going to be seein' a lot more of me. I promise." Whether that was a good thing, Gal wasn't entirely sure.

He looked outside to find Amber walking alone to Brad's truck. *But where was...*

"Happy birthday, little man," came Brad's voice in Gal's ear. "It was good seeing you."

"Same," Gal lied. The only good thing about Brad coming tonight was Gal's brief talk with Amber in the restroom lines. And even that had gone sour.

Brad ruffled his hair, gave Jimmy a high-five, hugged Scarlet, and left. Gal watched him go, eyes narrowed as Brad traversed the snowy parking lot, hopped in his truck, and tore out onto the street with Amber inside.

Through a sudden break in the clouds, silvery moonlight glittered into the passenger window.

Amber stared straight at Gal. She smiled at him, tucking a strand of golden hair behind her ear. Their eyes remained locked for what felt like hours. Then, with a roar of the engine, she was gone.

And for the very first time in years, Gallagher Finch was hopeful.

FIVE

# Blue

∽

Straight to voicemail.

*Not even so much as a dial tone...*

Could she have changed her number? Or had she been so busy behind the bar for the past three weeks not to have the decency to return her calls? Her aunt. Her *only* aunt.

Her only relative.

Sandy groaned, hung up the phone, and redialed for the seventh time, just to be on the safe side.

Straight to voicemail.

*I am going to kill her.*

"It's me again. Aunt Sandy. I miss you. Just— just call me back, please. I'm getting worried. Call me back as soon as you get this. I love you, Daph."

Sandy hung up and launched the phone into the passenger seat. She sucked on her gums and fiddled lazily with her gun belt.

Her head hurt. Either she had tied her bun too tight this morning, or the stress of the force was finally getting to her. The country was on the brink of an all-out war, and the thin blue line was right in the thick of it. The trepidation of wearing a badge pinned to her chest was becoming a strain. She longed for the old days, when all she had to do was wake up in the morning, throw on a t-shirt, and bag groceries. Days when average citizens didn't detest and undervalue her role in society.

*What happened to those days?*

Well, she had grown up. Learned who she truly was. Learned what the world truly was. Had chosen not to live a lie anymore. Had evolved from Little Pecan Sandy to Deputy Sandra Castro. Chose to follow a dream, one that promised money, power, safety, and a nine-millimeter strapped to her hip.

And then, she learned the hard way that dreams don't mean anything.

The LAPD was a joke, and she was the punchline. The money wasn't great, not when you had to pay twice as much rent in the city and egregious gas prices continued to inflate.

The power wasn't what she had been expecting, having spent nine long years being passed around the city jails, acting as a glorified babysitter and nothing more. A year ago, she'd finally been put on patrol – at a local middle school. Her career had shifted from chaperoning rapists and murderers to patrolling pretentious, pimply preteens.

At least in the jails, she got to watch Netflix.

Sandy sat alone in a parked patrol car, mirrored shades pulled over her eyes. The Southern California sun had become overbearing, and it was only March. She glanced at the computer propped on the dash, listening to the occasional hiss of a nearby call. Nothing but whirring static all day. She would have given her left arm to have just one real call. A shooting. A robbery.

*Anywhere but here.*

She needed a vacation. Somewhere cool. Somewhere with snow-capped mountaintops. Somewhere she could cast out hook, line, and sinker, then soak in the landscape while she waited for the bobber to dip below the surface. Natural beauty, no concrete.

*Lake Arrowhead?*

Too close.

*The Adirondacks?*

Much too far.

*Montana?*

A good place to retire, maybe, but that was twenty years away. Sandy was only thirty-eight, after all, and Montana was intolerably country-bumpkin. She wanted a place she could kiss her girlfriend in public and never meet the distasteful glance of a bigot.

The world was changing, but some places never did.

No, she and Kim would remain in California, regardless of the traffic, regardless of the earthquakes, regardless of the drought. It was the only place in this country gone to hell that she and Kim could live together in peace.

Her mind drifted back to her niece. To Daphne. To the Sierras. To Mammoth. To the calming canvas of towering peaks capped in snowfall, the undulating rhythm of water lapping a lake's edge, the fresh air offered by the altitude. She closed her eyes, imagined herself there, Kim at her left and Daphne at her right.

She smiled. Her first in days.

*Thwack!*

A wad of pink bubblegum slapped the windshield, tugging Sandy out of her daydream. Adjusting her shades, Sandy put on her hardest face and glowered at a group of giggling twelve-year-old girls.

"God, she is so ugly," Sandy heard one of them say, the one with streaks of blue in her hair. The one whose crooked posture and mini skirt looked more akin to a twenty-something call girl than a preteen Selena Gomez wannabe. The one that would end up either a drunk, a meth head, a prostitute, or all three.

*Kids just aren't kids anymore*, she considered. Nothing like Daphne. These little girls could learn a thing or two from her niece.

Sandy got out of the car.

The girls stopped giggling, eyes wide as colossal Deputy Castro rested her hand on the butt of her gun. She pointed a finger at the blue-haired offender.

"You. This your gum?"

The girl glanced around at her posse. They had already fled. Her legs began to tremble as Sandy's shoulders blocked out the sun, casting a hulking shadow over the tremulous tart. The deputy pulled the melted, stringy gum off the windshield, rubbed the smudge out of the glass, and then dropped the pink wad on the baking asphalt beside her.

"Pick it up, Miss Priss."

*Not a request. A demand.*

"Now."

Miss Priss gulped, kept her eyes locked on Sandy's gun, lowered to her haunches, and reached down with manicured French tips.

"Did I tell you to pick it up with your fingers?" Sandy growled.

The tween furled her eyebrows. "How — "

"Teeth," Sandy demanded. "Better hurry before it gets too hot, otherwise you're going to be down there a while."

"I don't have to listen to you," Miss Priss stammered.

"Shall I tell Principal Arana that I caught you and your brood of babbling bimbos ditching school?"

"We weren't ditching! We were still inside the gate!"

"And who do you think Principal Arana is going to believe? A deputy of the law, or some little girl with a crappy root job?"

The tween touched the roots of her hair.

"Gum. Teeth. Now!"

The tween mewled as she got down on her knees. Tears welling in her eyes, she lowered her face, bared her teeth, and set to work. She cried as her braces scraped the asphalt, doing her damnedest to pull the stringy gum off the hot ground. The sun had done its job, causing the melted gum to stretch and leaving behind a sticky mess.

"All of it," Sandy said.

She watched the girl chew the remaining gum off the asphalt. She sobbed, opened her mouth, and obediently showed Sandy the gravelly pink wad.

"Swallow it."

Sandy almost felt sorry for her.

*Almost.*

"No one is watching," Sandy assured her. She'd made it her duty to know where all of the school cameras were positioned and at which angles they were directed. The windows of the front office peered out into the front parking lot, though Sandy always preferred to park her police unit in the shady side entrance.

At that moment, the perverse display of power unfolding at her boots was altogether invisible.

"Swallow it," she repeated. "Then you can go."

Miss Priss stared with defiant contempt in her eyes. She closed her lips and with a gut-wrenching gulp, took the gravelly gum down her gullet.

"Good girl. Be sure to pick the rocks out of your teeth. Now, get back to class."

Absolute power. *But only over teenagers...*

An agent of the thin blue line. *A glorified babysitter...*

Devoted to the law. *Devoted to nobody but Kim...*

Deputy Sandra Castro watched the tween mope back to class, head down and shoulders hunched. Broken. Defeated. Perhaps this was why people hated cops.

In a split second, Sandy felt that familiar kick of guilt in her stomach.

*What if somebody were to treat Daphne this way?*

For the first time in her career, she felt ashamed to be a member of the force. After all, was it really meant to be a *force*? Do sheepdogs *force* lambs into their pen? Or do they *guide*? She got back in the police car, grabbed the cell phone, and tried her niece one more time.

Straight to voicemail.

***

She felt blue.

And so, Sandy threw back the rest of her Johnnie Walker.

Johnnie was an old friend, one who definitely had a way of pulling her back onto her feet when she was feeling down. She paid her tab and shook off the natural tendencies of her body, walking in a straight beeline when her feet wanted nothing more than to stumble.

A beeline she had perfected after nine long years of drinking.

Nine long years in the jails, listening to prisoners rattle the bars of their cells. Nine long years of sitting behind a computer when she wanted to be out on the streets. Nine long years of pretending that the system was finally equal, that female deputies were no longer regarded by their gender.

*Nine long years of crap.*

Having traded her uniform for a flannel Duluth and a pair of jeans, she contemplated making the trade permanent. Was she willing to trade an old dream for a new one? Did she even have any dreams left?

Sandy sighed, climbed into her blue Chevy Silverado, revved the engine, and tore off down the highway. She knew her blood alcohol content was over the legal limit, yet that same pride of the badge trickled down her spine and guided her in driving all the safer. If all else failed, if she got pulled over, a flash of the badge was a quick reassurance.

*Am I willing to give up all the perks?*

Three rights and a U-turn later, she parked on the street below the apartment she shared with Kim. Having picked up an extra shift at the jail, Sandy let her love know she would be home later than usual.

What a surprise, then, to have been relieved early. Kim would be ecstatic to spend an evening in after two weeks of non-stop work.

Sandy walked up the steps of the apartment complex, red roses in hand. A smile spread across her freckled cheeks, the thought of holding Kim's delicate frame bringing butterflies to her stomach. She unlocked the door, turned the knob...

...and the roses fell to the floor.

She was greeted by the stark naked, tattooed backside of a male, thrusting away into the back of her couch. Upon closer inspection, she saw a pair of familiar legs between those of the man.

*Kim, naked as the day she was born.*

Time stopped.

Was this real? Sandy figured she must still be at the bar, drunk and anesthetized.

*I have to stop doing that.*

Kim was a free spirit, but how free was too free? Free enough to switch between love and lust? Free enough to switch between women and men? Free enough to cheat?

Sandy's instincts kicked in. She launched herself across the living room and clapped her hands onto the man's shoulders. She wrenched him off of Kim and smashed him effortlessly into the nearest wall. The impact rattled the windows, knocking picture frames to the floor with a resounding shatter.

Kim screamed, collapsed onto the couch, and covered herself with a throw blanket.

Sandy stared at her beautiful girlfriend, but the beauty began to fade as the weight of current events began to sink in.

*Kim would never cheat...*

Kim cheated.

A dense silence settled between them, save for Kim's sobs. Not knowing what to say, or if there was anything to say at all, Sandy looked at the male crumpled on the floor.

A stream of blood trickled below a receding hairline. He was an older man, likely in his fifties, judging by the laughter lines on his bloody forehead. His entire torso was covered in faded tattoos. The skin of his arms, however, was left untouched, where no one would notice his ink had he been wearing casual clothing.

*As though he would need to hide it for his career...*

"Captain Pike?" The name slipped from Sandy's mouth, as though from a dream.

*A nightmare.*

Her boss remained silent, unmoving. What had she done? What had Pike done? What had Kim done?

"Baby," Kim sobbed from the couch. "Baby, it's nothing. He's nothing. I just – you know, I just like to – I just wanted to – "

"Shut up."

Sandy unfastened her gun belt and let it fall to the floor. Then and there, Sandy decided to leave it all. The glass on the floor. Captain Pike bleeding on the carpet. Kim sobbing on the couch.

And with it all, the force.

"I'm done," Sandy said. She went into the bedroom to pack her things.

Kim's silent sobs became woeful wails. Whatever would she do without Deputy Sandra Castro to keep her safe at night?

*Former* Deputy Sandra Castro.

***

On a "clear" day in L.A., the sun beat down upon a brown-gray sky laden with vermilion clouds. Southern Californians attributed the unnatural tint to smog. To climate change. To the oil derricks scattered within the coastal waters, slurping up the lifeblood of the earth to fuel mankind's constant race to its own demise.

Sandy attributed the tint to greed. To selfishness. To loathsome attitudes. To oversized veneers in fake smiles on plastic faces.

*To cheating girlfriends.*

Getting out of the city seemed the right thing to do.

Up here, the sky was a deep blue. A natural blue. The blue that God intended. The Mojave Desert crept north and traded sand for foliage, then crept higher still to offer the majesty of the Sierras, sentinels capped in fresh snow and a halo of looming storm clouds.

As the hours slipped by, the blue Silverado maneuvered up Highway 395. From Pearsonville to Lone Pine. From Lone Pine to Independence. From Independence to Big Pine. And finally, after five long hours, Sandy arrived in Bishop.

Sandy had visited Bishop only once before, back when Daphne decided that she no longer needed the charity she'd been offered since being orphaned at seven. Daphne decided to make a living on her own.

She had, however, accepted one final act of charity by allowing good ol' Aunt Sandy to do all of the heavy lifting, as well as assembling the IKEA furniture they had found for next to nothing on Craigslist.

Sandy hadn't minded, though.

Daphne was a tiny thing and used her looks to get the things she wanted. It was half the reason she considered a service industry job in the first place, to utilize her beautiful bone structure, pale skin, lush raven hair, and pouty red lips in exchange for mountains of tips.

Daphne was probably running the restaurant now.

She drove the Silverado at a snail's pace down Main Street, nodding curtly at simple country folk who seemed happy about nothing in particular. As if to simply be alive in this beautiful small town was reason enough to wear a smile.

By memory alone, Sandy took the first left and followed the road until it ended in a small mobile home park.

*Third from the end. Third from the end. Here we go.*

Daphne's Camry sat in the driveway. Sandy parked behind it, got out, and walked to the front door. She took a deep breath, held it, and knocked.

No answer.

She knocked again.

Nothing.

"Daph, it's Aunt Sandy!"

No response.

Sandy peered through the front window. A half-eaten pizza sat on the coffee table, fuzzy with green mold.

*Odd.*

She looked around at Daphne's front lawn. Other lawns in the neighborhood had already taken to seed with the impending arrival of spring. Daphne's yard was a brown stain on an otherwise emerald street.

*I raised her better than this.*

She called Daphne's cell phone, and again, was met with her voicemail.

*Something's not right.*

Sandy got back in the truck, started it up, and flew across town to Big's Saloon & Barbecue. Upon arrival, she stalked straight to the bar and helped herself to one of the larger barstools. She lifted her mirrored shades and began searching the crowd for that familiar tuft of raven hair.

"Welcome to Big's."

Sandy turned to catch the stare of a fat, bald, greasy man with half his teeth missing from his head. His nametag read: BIG.

"Is Daphne working today?" she asked.

"Daphne? Nah, she ain't in today." Big narrowed his eyes. "Ain't seen you in here before. You know her?"

"She's my niece."

"That right?" Big regarded Sandy with one lazy eye, the other peering down at the dirt underneath his fingernails. "Ain't seen Daphne for three weeks now. Missed every one of her shifts this month. I tried callin', but I can only leave so many messages, y'know?"

Sandy *did* know.

"Been itchin' to get rid of her, but she ain't been in for me to give her the pink slip. Nothin' personal. She is — *was* a great waitress. Lot o' people loved her. Would ask for her personally. Still do."

Big shrugged and chewed off one of his dirty fingernails.

"This ain't no charity, though. I need my waitresses to get their shifts covered before they ditch town."

Sandy's blood began to boil.

*Where in the world are you, Daph?*

"Is there anyone else I might be able to talk to? Someone who might know where she is?" she asked.

Big's eyes narrowed further still. He stared across the bar top at Sandy for a few moments, and then sighed. "Hang on." He disappeared into the kitchen, then reappeared with a pretty blonde.

"Go on," Big beckoned her towards the bar, and then disappeared into his office.

*Odd.*

"What can I pour for you today?" asked the blonde. Her voice was shaky, her eyes shifty. As though she would rather be anywhere but here. Her nametag read: WHITNEY.

"I'm looking for Daphne Cas--"

"I haven't seen her," Whitney blurted out.

Sandy sighed.

"Look, I'm not playing games here. I'm Daphne's aunt. The only family she's got, actually, and I've never once had a problem reaching her. Yet, here I am with three weeks' worth of voicemails and not a call back. Mr. Big back there's acting like he knows something he'd rather not say. So now, I'm asking you. Where is Daphne?"

"I honestly have not seen her," Whitney replied. "We worked a Sunday night shift together last month."

"You're lying," Sandy growled. She turned on her barstool and pointed to the sign out front. "You are closed on Sundays."

Whitney chewed on her top lip. Sandy began to wonder if she might bite clean through.

"Not here," Whitney said.

"She has another serving job?"

"You could say that."

"Another bar in town?"

"Not exactly."

Sandy cleared her throat and leaned in close.

"Listen to me. You are going to be straight with me, because if you aren't, I will rip off those fake eyelashes and shove them right up that pretty little button nose."

"Miss, can I get another beer over here?" called a geezer at the end of the bar.

"One second," Whitney told him, then shifted her gaze back to Sandy. "You really don't know what Daphne has been up to, do you?"

"No, I don't. But *you* are going to tell me."

Whitney sighed and ran a hand through her blonde locks.

"You're going to need a drink for this. Anything you want. This one's on me."

It was Sandy's turn to feel nervous. She wrenched her eyes from Whitney's, looked at the top shelf, and made her pick.

"Johnnie Walker," she said.

"Black label?" Whitney asked and reached for the bottle.

"Blue."

SIX

Red

⌣

The names were all there, pure as sin.

*M. Hopper*

*J. Smith*

*T. Anderson--*

Sandy flipped another page. Dozens upon dozens of names were scribbled upon the pages of a small red notebook. A date was written beside each name, as well as a price point. The higher the price, Sandy guessed, the longer the liaison.

*J. Fortezzi*

*B. Finch*

*R. Walker*

A few of the names had been written in red ink. Whitney confessed that these particular entries belonged to women. Women who, as Whitney described, were mainly conservative female bureaucrats looking to escape the watchful gaze of their husbands and take a dip in the devil's hot tub. Women who had been married right out of high school, who'd never had the chance to experiment in college.

Sandy felt as though she had stumbled onto the set of a tawdry Hollywood movie. Was waiting for someone to tell her that it was all a big parody. That Daphne was fine, tucked away in her bed with nothing more than a cold and the Holy Bible by her bedside.

"It helps to not think about it," Whitney sighed, leaning up against a large pine tree as she lit up her second cigarette. She took the red notebook out of Sandy's hands and tucked it back into her purse.

"How can you *not* think about it?" Sandy inquired, scrunching her nose as the wind carried aloft the smell of tobacco and tar.

"You tell yourself that it's just sex. A body is a body is a body." The blonde shrugged, keeping her gaze fixed on the alpine panorama. "Unless it's more than one body, and then it's a party." Whitney cracked a tiny smile.

Sandy did not.

"And that notebook is what? A list of conquests?"

"A ledger," Whitney said. "Each of us keeps our own records. We never disclose to each other. Never tell stories. Never share experiences."

"There must be a hundred names in there," Sandy guessed.

"At *least* a hundred. Some of the names belong to recurring clients, but a lot of the time, they come in under pseudonyms."

Sandy stood silent for a moment, lost in the repugnance of her niece's reality.

"The longer you're in the game," Whitney continued, "the harder it is to keep track. Hence the notebooks. They help us remember faces and fetishes. The happier the client, the higher the tip."

"Sounds a lot like bartending," Sandy said.

"Probably the main reason I got into it. Bartending always came natural to me, so it wasn't a shock to find that this also came natural." Whitney stamped out the cigarette, rummaged through her purse, and withdrew a stick of gum. She bit off half and offered the rest to Sandy.

Sandy declined. "Not a gum fan."

"You don't know where my mouth has been," Whitney sighed.

"That too."

"I don't blame you."

Sandy sighed and looked down at her giant boots. "So, you haven't seen her."

"Like I said, not since our last Sunday shift. Which was – "

"Three weeks ago. Right," Sandy muttered as she rubbed her now aching head. "Tell me the details of that night."

For the first time, Sandy saw Whitney blush.

"I'd rather not."

"That wasn't a request," Sandy snarled.

"All right. It was some sort of house party. A bunch of rich guys. There were maybe thirty of us hired for the night."

"Where?"

"I'm not sure. Our Lodge Directors told us to meet – "

"Lodge Directors? You mean pimps – "

"Madams, actually. All female," Whitney explained. "There are Lodges up and down the Sierras. Each region has its own Director."

"And who do the Directors answer to?"

"I've only ever heard of her. Someone they call The Old Lady."

"Where are the Lodges?"

"We're made not to know. That's how the Lodge System has lasted so long." Whitney shrugged. "That's all I know. I just do my job."

That would have to do. *For now.*

"Okay. So, your Lodge Directors told you to meet – " Sandy waved her hand for Whitney to continue.

" – just off Highway 395 near the Devil's Postpile turnoff. They blindfolded us. Had us cram into a couple of limos, and we were off. I don't like being blindfolded, so I counted the minutes. Counted the turns. We didn't drive long, so I'm guessing we ended up somewhere in Mammoth. Big house. There weren't many other houses around it, so we must've been west of the ski runs."

"Smart girl. Then what?"

"The usual. We drank, we mingled, and then people started to bid on us. Around ten, it started to get weird. They began *trading* us, like we were nothing but baseball cards. Made it difficult to keep our ledgers in check."

Whitney scoffed and fiddled the toe of her shoe into the grass, hugging her arms a little tighter.

"I've never been traded before. It was barbaric."

"Did you see who bid on Daphne?"

"No. She disappeared pretty early that night. I assume she ran into one of her regulars. Someone she was comfortable with. Someone she was willing to go home with rather than someone she didn't know. A few of the smarter girls did that. I wasn't that smart."

Whitney's eyes began to water, as though the reminiscence of the night in question scared her to death.

"That's all I remember."

"All right," Sandy said. "Is there anything else you can tell me that might help?"

Whitney pulled the red notebook out of her purse and held it up.

"I didn't show you this to brag about how many men I've been with. In the wrong hands, this notebook could destroy me. Destroy me, my Lodge, my Lodge Director."

The wheels in Sandy's head began to turn.

"Everything you need to know about your niece – about Daphne," Whitney continued. "About the girl you never knew Daphne was – it's all in her notebook."

She offered Sandy a sad smile.

"Find it, and you might find her."

\*\*\*

The moldy pizza remained unmoved upon the coffee table. All the lights were off, leaving the entire property in darkness save for the slivers of moonlight begging to break through the clouds.

Sandy knocked on the door for good measure, but was met with silence. She bent down and lifted the doormat in the hope of finding a spare key.

Nothing.

Up and down the small side street, all was quiet except for the soft crunch of Sandy's boots upon the gravel. She walked along the side yard and lifted herself effortlessly over the tall wooden fence, her bulky weight landing softly upon hard-packed dirt. She may have possessed the physique of a gorilla, but she retained the agility of a cat.

Sandy checked everywhere for the key. Under every rock. Inside the bird house. Within the rain gutter. She used the LED light of her cell phone to search through every single rose bush, springtime thorns slicing her fingertips.

She could have gone to the police. Could have taken Whitney's story, played the part of the concerned aunt, and let the police take over looking for Daphne. But with no leads and no destination of where to begin their search, the cops would prove just as useless as not doing anything at all.

*Not that they weren't useless already.*

Besides, Daphne's name was at stake. Her reputation – or as much of one as she had established beyond her alleged prostitution. Even if the police did end up finding her, she and her new group of friends would surely be taken in for questioning, possibly even sentenced to jail time. Roots would be ripped up. Vengeance would come snooping. Daphne would be further from Sandy's reach than she was now.

*No cops.*

For now, Sandy was determined to find her niece by herself. For now, Sandy would utilize her own skills, skills she'd possessed for nine long years, but never had an outlet for. She was determined to find Daphne as quickly and as quietly as she had arrived, and then the two of them would leave town. Move farther north, maybe up into Portland or Seattle.

*Scratch that. No more cities.*

The outskirts, then. Somewhere near the western seaboard. Somewhere warm in the summer and cold in the winter, as it should be. No more stifling, year-round heat.

Not California. Never again.

After an hour, she collapsed with her head in her hands. No spare key. Not a trace of one anywhere. She would have to get creative.

Sandy unbuttoned the right wrist of her flannel jacket, dipped her hand inside, and wrapped it in the fabric. She approached the window beside the back door and, with a swift strike, shattered the pane.

No alarm. *Thank Jesus.*

Reaching inside, she unlocked the back door, opened it, and was met with the musty odor of moldy pizza, stale beer, and dewy decay. Evidently, Daphne had had a few guests over before she disappeared. That, or she had one hell of a time by herself.

*I taught her better than this.*

The kitchen was filthy. A mile-high mound of dirty dishes teetered within a lime-crusted sink. The living room was small and unkempt, dirty blankets strewn over the couch and flattened pillows upon the floor.

*I have to find her.*

Sandy went to work. She wrenched open every cabinet, rummaged through every drawer. Pens. Old Christmas cards. Highlighters. Silverware. Car keys. Two bags of Skittles.

And in the back of a kitchen drawer, she found an open box of Durex.

*Whitney wasn't lying, then.*

She turned the kitchen upside down before heading into the living room. She upended couch cushions, searched for loose slats in the floorboards, felt around for bulges beneath the carpet. She stomped into the bathroom and delved through boxes of makeup and hair care products. She kicked the side of the tub and buried her face in her hands.

Nothing.

All that was left was the bedroom. What horrors awaited her in there? Did she really care to discover any sultry paraphernalia? Did she really want to learn more about the real Daphne? The Daphne she'd never known existed?

*What happened to the shy little girl with crooked teeth?*

Sandy kicked open the bedroom door. She ripped the sheets off the mattress and flipped the bed onto its side. She searched a bedside closet littered with skimpy lace, rifled through dresser drawers packed with nylons, baby doll lingerie, and Ziploc bags full of marijuana.

Not a trace of a red notebook anywhere.

It must have been true, then, what Sandy had been fearing all along.

*Daphne has the notebook with her.*

But where would she go? Why would she leave behind all her clothes? All her makeup? Her toothbrush? Her car keys?

Sandy's racing mind slowed to a stop. She looked up and out the window...

Daphne's Camry sat parked and dusty in the driveway.

*How could I have been so stupid?*

Sandy retrieved the car keys from the kitchen. Outside, she unlocked the driver's side door and opened the glove compartment.

No notebook.

*Damn.*

Something did catch her eye, however. A small business card was wedged between Daphne's car insurance renewal and an unopened granola bar. She grabbed the business card and let impatient eyes scan the font:

### Sierra Inn Restaurant
*June Lake Village, CA*
*Since 1973!*

And on the back, in red ink, was a phone number. Judging by the lazy, subtle intricacies of the handwritten numbers, she assumed a man had written it.

*The Sierra Inn.*

Sandy felt a familiar rush.

A clue.

***

Whitney Burges stood in front of the bathroom mirror, staring at her disheveled reflection while a silent black tear rolled down her cheek. She wiped away the liquefied mascara.

It was natural to be nervous.

Whitney had taken quite the risk showing off her red ledger and its contents to a complete stranger. It had been justified, however, considering the woman looked as if she could break even Big's back with minimal effort.

Whitney illuminated the fractured screen of her cell phone and checked the time.

### 8:47 p.m.

God, she needed a new phone. Her ex had promised to buy her one for Christmas. Instead, the pompous ass had blocked her number and cut off all communication before she could get the goods out of him.

Although, the goods she *had* gotten out of him were beginning to blossom within her womb. She touched her belly, caressed the small, firm bump, then sent up a silent prayer.

*Please, God, let this be my way out.*

She had a long night ahead of her. Her newest client had instructed her to practice complete and absolute discretion. Total privacy. No names. No numbers.

He had given her instructions, and she would comply.

Wearing a red lace corset, Whitney applied a brush of dusky eyeshadow above each set of false lashes, using a finger to smudge the powder into a smoky tinge. Lined her lips in fire-engine red. Curled her long blonde tresses and pulled them into a loose ponytail. Pinched her cheeks for some natural rosy hints. Stepped into matching high heels and a long overcoat, tying it at the waist.

She was ready.

Two sharp honks blasted from outside. As always, Whitney tucked her red notebook into her purse, locked the front door of her dingy apartment, and hopped into the back seat of the deeply-tinted black Camaro.

"Right on time, Big," she said.

"Ain't I always?" the bar manager chuckled from the driver's seat. He adjusted the rearview mirror and tore out of the driveway onto the icy road.

"Cold tonight," she spoke more to herself than him. "I hope this guy has a working heater. The last two haven't."

"That woman today. What did she want?" Big grumbled.

She decided to play dumb.

"Which woman?"

"You know who I'm talkin' about, Whit," he growled, weaving the Camaro around slower traffic as he pulled onto Highway 395. "The big one. The dike."

The word made Whitney cringe. She may have been a lot of things, but a bigot wasn't one of them. She'd shown compassion to a relatively kind woman searching for her missing niece. That was all.

"You know everything I know, Big. She's looking for Daphne." Whitney cracked the window and lit up a cigarette. "At least *somebody* is looking for her."

"Nature of the business," Big grunted while chewing his already nubby fingernails. "Girl goes missing, it ain't our job to look. Or to care."

"I *don't* care. Daphne knows the rules. It's just a little sad is all. I mean, it could have just as easily been me that went missing."

"The Old Lady isn't going to be happy about some big broad snoopin' around the cornfield," Big warned. "And you flappin' your trap. Get it?"

"Don't worry about The Old Lady, Big. You're just a driver. And besides, that's even *if* she finds out. Could be Daphne shows up before anything gets out."

"You're treadin' on egg shells, girl," Big muttered. "But what do I know?"

"Nothing," Whitney said. "You know nothing. Like it should be. Just drive."

They pulled off Highway 395 and onto a dirt road that Whitney had never been down before. Big remained silent as the Camaro trudged along sand and gravel, the road all but disappearing into sparse vegetation and the remnants of small, filthy snow drifts.

"Where are we, Big?"

"We're here."

Whitney peered out of the tinted glass. The Camaro sat in the middle of nowhere, under a moonless night. Just up the path stood a log cabin. Light spilled out of two bay windows. A single oil lantern swung in the breeze from a front porch awning.

"Stay close by, just in case."

"You want to leave?" Big asked.

"The funds have already been transferred. I'll be fine," she whispered unconvincingly. She stepped out of the car into the brisk night air and sauntered up the dusty drive.

Big killed the lights and reversed the car behind an outcropping of trees, disappearing from sight. She took a deep breath and rapped gently on the door.

Loud footsteps echoed from within and grew louder with each footfall. She held her breath. The door opened, barely a crack.

"You her?" came a deep, gravelly voice.

*Like rocks in a blender.*

"Call me Sapphire. I don't recall your name," Whitney purred gently, fingertips stroking the wood of the front door.

"I never gave it."

"I need a surname, at least. Records purposes," she said, the modest anxiety in her tone becoming evident.

"No names," the man growled. "At least, not yet. The pay is well worth the discretion."

"Fine." She tucked the notebook back into her purse. "No names."

The door opened fully, and Whitney's eyes widened.

Towering over seven feet tall, shoulders broad as the door itself, the man stepped into the light. At first glance, he was terrifying. Deep lines split like trenches across his face. A ragged gray beard hung to midchest. Corded, python forearms that could have snapped her like a twig ended in hands large as dinner plates. Her gaze traversed along a jagged scar that stretched out of his beard, up his cheek, and over the bridge of his nose …

As though someone had tried to carve his face in half.

*But his eyes.*

His eyes were a piercing green, tender in nature as he surveyed her every bump and curve. Crow's feet stretched from the edges, looking as though they had formed not from fury and hatred, but from laughter.

"Gorgeous, ain't I?" he grumbled.

"I've seen worse," she said.

He stepped aside and allowed her to pass the threshold. He sealed the door, cutting her out of Big's sightline from beyond the blackened trees.

Her high heels clicked on the wooden floorboards as she untied her overcoat and let it fall, cashmere pooling at her ankles. A colossal, calloused hand slid up the side of her arm, gentle as velvet, causing goosebumps to erupt upon her flesh.

"Are you hungry?" he asked. "We have a lot to discuss."

"I'm confused," she said.

"About?"

"It's just – I mean, you paid *a lot* for my services. And here I am. And you want to talk?"

"That a problem?"

She stared at him, and he stared right back. As though he were peering under the surface of her skin. As though he were glancing into her soul. Reading her.

"Put your coat back on," he grumbled.

She did as he said.

"Are you hungry?" he repeated, turning to a large wood-burning stove. He ladled the soupy contents of a Dutch oven into two bowls.

"I could eat."

She watched as No-name approached and slipped a warm bowl of stew into her hands. She sniffed it, ate a spoonful, and was met with a rich, surprisingly delicious blend of meat, potatoes, and gravy. They sat down at the table and ate in silence, simply watching one another. When the silence became unbearably awkward, she spoke.

"You're quite the chef."

"Not my recipe."

"Your mother's?" she asked.

"No," he said. "It belongs to The Old Lady."

She choked on her stew and dropped the spoon with a heavy clatter.

"How do you – "

"We go way back," he said, slurping the broth. "I haven't seen her in thirteen years. I'd like to thank her for giving me the recipe."

He wiped his beard with a napkin and folded it neatly upon the table.

"I need you to help me find her," he said.

"Look, I don't feel comfortable talking about – "

No-name tossed a wad of bills onto the kitchen table, and Whitney fell silent. She stared at the thousands of dollars sitting in front of her, touched the small bump of her belly, and made her decision.

*Please, God, let this be my way out.*

"When do we start?"

SEVEN

# Amber

∽

For the fourth consecutive hour, the screen was blank.

Moreover, his mind was blank. Writer's block had begun as a small stone lodged in a trickling stream. Now, it pressed against the front of his skull like a dam holding the edges of the very ocean in its grip. All his story notes, scrawled in lazy red cursive in his trusty black notepad, stared back at him as though they were written in Martian.

Having begun writing on the first day of the New Year, Gallagher planned to have the first draft of his new novel completed by the first of April. How deliciously ironic, then, that his date of completion was now one big joke.

*April Fools, dummy. This is going to take you years to finish.*

How was he supposed to envision a rugged, Indiana Jones-type protagonist exploring the riches of the Amazon rainforest when he, the author of the damn thing, was the poorest excuse of rugged this side of the Mississippi? That, and the only information he had on the Amazon was what he'd pulled up on Wikipedia.

He popped an eight-hour Adderall just before sitting down to write.

Without any fresh ideas, he focused his drug-induced blank stare on an equally blank computer screen.

The first of April was only two weeks away, and all Gal had to show for it was an admittedly poor prologue.

*Quite the author, sir. Quite the author.*

Gal groaned and shoved his laptop aside. He stood up and stretched his aching limbs. Bent over the keyboard for half the morning, he found that working the blood back into his fingers felt like fighting the onset of rigor mortis.

*Rigor mortis… Daphne.*

Surely, she should be decomposing by now.

Had the worms chewed through the blue tarp, only to feast on the flesh beneath? Had the snowmelt compacted the dirt around her into a sort of cement? Was she forever entombed, destined to become the forgotten ghost of Mono Lake?

And where was her killer now?

For the first two weeks after discovering Daphne's body in his bed, Gal hardly slept a wink. During the night, he left every single light on, slapping himself each time he started to doze off in case the murdering bastard came back for seconds. Electricity bills had skyrocketed, but safety meant more than money. During the day, he searched every nook and every cranny of his home, and for every moment he was alone, he kept the stag horn pocketknife held firmly within his grip.

Yes, he had kept the pocketknife. He could never tell Scar…

Just before burying Daphne, Gal had wrenched the blade out of her throat and tucked it away into his jacket. If Daphne's body ever ended up being discovered, he wouldn't allow his belongings to be found at the grave. How many of his friends had he boasted to about that pocketknife? Surely too many. Someone somewhere in this quiet little Loop could point out the owner of such a treasure.

He didn't kill Daphne, but his pocketknife sure had.

It felt as if all he'd been doing was waiting. Waiting and watching. Waiting for someone to turn up and profess their guilt. Watching every news channel in the hope that another call girl had been found dead somewhere, and that a perpetrator had been caught. Perhaps, then, he could come clean.

In truth, a few years in prison for burying a corpse seemed altogether brighter than a life sentence for a crime he didn't commit.

All he could do was hope that Daphne remained hidden, lost to the world until a shred of evidence presented itself. He had searched for clues around the house, had prayed to a God he wasn't even sure existed for something, anything that might lead him to some sort of trailhead. If he had a lead, he would go to the police. He and Scarlet promised each other that much. She, too, promised to keep her eyes and ears peeled.

Gal walked into the kitchen and began digging through the pantry. Rice cakes. *Blah.* Cheez-Its. *Blah.* Trail mix. *Shoot me in the head.* And then he saw it.

*Bingo.*

The half-empty jar of Jif sat near the deepest reaches of the bottom shelf. Surely, he hadn't stuffed it back that far. Scar probably stole a spoonful or two the last time she was here and hid it away in case he decided to devour the rest. His sister had been over a lot lately, cooking for him, cleaning up when he was at work, doing her best to keep him calm in his otherwise chaotic situation. And yes, he was beyond grateful.

*But the Jif… the Jif is mine.*

Without a second thought, he took a large spoonful and gulped it down. His tongue smacked noisily against the roof of his mouth as he struggled to get it down, stomach anxious for a gulp of milk.

The jar was half-empty, but it tasted fresh, as though he had just purchased it. Had he? He recalled the night of Daphne's murder, of the bitterness of the Jif. Now, however, it was sweet.

*Odd.*

Perhaps Scarlet finished off the last jar and replaced it.

Gal stared out the kitchen window and noticed cranky old Ruby in her front yard, hunched over and scolding her unsightly rat-dog. He considered how easy she had it. Sure, the weight of death lingered heavily on her shoulders, but judging by the pain and discomfort she exhibited whenever she moved around, perhaps death would be something of a welcome guest at her age. All Ruby had to worry about was enjoying the last years she had on this earth.

Gal, meanwhile, found himself unable to sleep, unable to think, unable to write because of the constant, clammy breath of fear and guilt trickling down his neck.

There in the kitchen, his heart began to race. His breath came out in sharp gasps. Sweat beaded on his forehead.

Another panic attack.

He imagined Scar there with him, imagined what she would say to calm him down...

*Sit. Breathe. Hold it. Exhale slowly. And again.*

And he decided to do just that.

Gal held his heaving chest as he clambered for the coffee table, withdrew Remy from the drawer, quickly packed her bowl full of fresh herb, sparked the lighter and took Scar's advice. He sat. He breathed in deeply. He held the skunky fumes in his lungs. He exhaled slowly.

*And again.*

He took another rip, and another, allowing his head to grow lofty.

Gal glanced outside. He watched Ruby collect her prized lawn gnomes off the grass and tuck them away into a box. He noticed cardboard boxes piled high in her garage.

Was she going somewhere?

Gal shifted his glossy red hues back to the screen of his laptop. He watched the tiny vertical cursor blinking at him, impatiently waiting for him to vomit out some literature.

What the hell was he doing writing about adventures in the Amazon? He had been jotting notes for months, but what did it all mean? Who was it for? Why this stupid story?

*Hell, I should just write about my own life.*

It was wrought with imperfection, sadness, secrets, and a broken family.

*And now, a dead call girl.*

None of it felt real, but there it was. It was his life. It was interesting. Wrought with emotion. Tainted with liquor and pain and longing and a drive to get the hell out of this tiny Loop. Why not vomit out all of his insecurities, all of his inner torture, all of his regret? Isn't that what the best writers do?

*Yes, it certainly is what the best writers do.*

A sudden rush of inspiration washed over Gallagher like a dip in the lake on a blistering summer afternoon. His chest tightened up again, but this time from excitement. He gathered his black notebook full of red cursive notes and tossed it into the fireplace.

He had no use for it anymore.

Gal set his fingertips to the keyboard and let them fly. Letter after letter. Word after word. Sentence after sentence. Paragraph after paragraph...

Page after page.

***

The room was humid. The air thick with chlorine.

Whitney stared down at the glassy water of the indoor pool.

She knew what she should have been doing, what she should be searching for. But she would have all the time in the world to accomplish the task that No-name had set for her. Sheriff Paul Larson was already asleep upstairs. Having gone for a solid hour without a break, she wanted nothing more than to cool off with a quick dip.

Whitney removed the towel from around her chest and let it fall around her ankles. She rubbed the kinks out of her shoulders and peeled the dry candle wax off of her hips before diving gracefully into the lap pool. She couldn't remember the last time she had swam in a pool.

*Too cold during too many months of the year.*

From what Sheriff Larson said, however, he had money pouring out his ears. Why not splurge a little? He splurged on this luxurious, heated indoor pool much like he splurged on this four million-dollar home. Moreover, he had splurged on Whitney's services for the night. The large wad of bills stashed away in her purse proved more than enough for one measly hour.

She swam a few hard laps, retreated beneath the surface for a final dip, and then came up for air.

"Enjoying yourself?" Sheriff Larson's voice echoed off the wet tile walls.

"The water is fantastic," she replied, catching him staring at her from the doorway.

"I meant in general?" he asked in a nervous tone. That same nervous tone a man shows if he isn't sure how he performed between the sheets. Strange how a man who carried a gun for a living was so nervous in the presence of a beautiful woman. Or was the good and righteous Sheriff simply scared of getting caught with a call girl?

"You were... good," she shrugged.

*Ouch.*

He frowned, not entirely satisfied with her all-too-honest answer.

Whitney wiped the water out of her eyes and pushed back her long blonde hair.

"I'm sorry. Is this room off-limits?"

"Not at all," the Sheriff replied as he stepped into the steamy room in pajama bottoms. Larson had paid her a lot for tonight's liaison.

No-name, however, had paid her triple the amount to obtain a single piece of information from the good Sheriff. It was No-name who discovered where Paul Larson would be dining this evening. It was No-name who purchased her elegant white dress. And it was No-name who pulled a few strings to get her into the VIP section of the illustrious Italian bar, right smack dab in view of the gluttonous Sheriff.

*Enough small talk.*

"Would you like to join me?" she asked.

"I'm okay. I took a shower." Larson pulled a lounge chair to the edge of the pool and let her play with his toes. "You had a question for me?"

*Play stupid.*

"I did? When?"

"Earlier at dinner, right as I was paying the bill," he answered, scratching the scruff under one of his three chins. "You said, *may I ask you a question?,* and I told you – "

" – 'after I'm satisfied, you may ask any question you like,'" she completed the sentence for him, tenderly stroking his fat ankles.

"Precisely."

*Act naive.*

"And are you satisfied?"

He inclined his head proudly and nodded hard enough to set his belly a-jiggle.

*Divert your true intention.*

She could hear No-name's voice in her head. And like a good pupil, she obeyed.

"You never called after our first little romp. Why?" It was a stupid question, one she didn't truly care about, yet it would set in motion a thread of conversation which would eventually lead to the information she was being paid to unveil.

Larson sighed.

"I apologize for that, baby doll. Truth is, I found another call girl. One who was closer, one whose schedule wasn't so tied up."

*Make him feel important.*

"You're a busy man," she said. "An important man. Any of us girls would be lucky to have you even for a single night."

The fat idiot's grin widened to match the breadth of his stomach.

"Truth be told, though, you're much better," he confessed, a rosy flush rising in his plump, unshaven cheeks.

*Become the victim.*

"Can I be completely honest with you?" she asked.

"Please," he said.

"I want out."

"Out? But you're so good."

"I just want out. You're high on the totem pole, Paul. I'm nobody." She raised her eyes to him. "Help me."

"What can I do?"

*Go in for the kill...*

"Help me find her," she said. "I need to find her. To beg her to let me out of all this."

"Who?" he asked and avoided her stare.

"Don't play dumb. You know who I'm talking about, Sheriff," she cooed and kissed his vile feet. He smiled.

*Of course he knew.*

"Where can I find The Old Lady?" she asked plainly.

"Why do you think I know where to find her?"

"The fact that you haven't told me otherwise is proof enough," she said, rubbing a hand on his thigh for a little extra encouragement.

"You're smart."

"You're not the first person to tell me that."

"What will you do for me?" he asked.

"Anything you want."

She watched as Sheriff Larson slipped a hand into his pocket, dark eyes glazing over in lust and hunger.

"The Old Lady doesn't like to be found. Last I heard, she was living in Mono County. One of my guys got wind of her up near June Mountain, back before the runs went bankrupt."

"The Loop?" she asked.

"The Loop," he confirmed. "You repeat that to *no one.*"

*Technically, No-name is no one.*

"Of course. Thank you, Paul. Now, what can I do for you?"

Larson slowly withdrew his hand from his pocket and brandished a taser.

"Just a little something my other call girl used to do for me."

He helped Whitney out of the pool, wrapped a towel around her, and slipped the taser into her hand. She gave the device a few good sparks, crackling the air.

"What happened to her?" she asked. "Your other call girl?"

"She stopped answering. Just sort of – disappeared."

Whitney's heart sank.

"What was her name?" she asked, though was certain she already knew the answer.

"Started with a D, I think," he said.

Whitney chewed the inside of her cheek, her focus suddenly shifting from No-name's assignment to her own general worry for her beautiful, raven-haired cohort.

"Sheriff, there's something you need to know about Daphne."

***

God, his fingers hurt.

*Better than writer's block*, Gal considered.

He counted to four, measuring two ounces of Midori into a rocks glass. He topped the neon green candy liquor with sweet & sour and a freshly cut lime wedge.

"Midori Sour for the lady. And for you, sir?"

"Just a Coors Light," squeaked the pug-faced kid.

Gal stared at him for a moment, knowing for a fact that this delinquent was nowhere near twenty-one years old. Gal glanced at the prettier-than-average redhead beside him and gave her a smile, one she returned with excited fervor.

"Got your ID on you, sir?" Gal asked. The pug-faced kid tried to maintain a straight and hardened look, but the tremble of his upper lip was enough to give him away. He took out his wallet and passed Gal the California driver's license.

Going with a California ID had been the kid's first mistake. Bartenders were far too lazy to memorize every detail about every state's identification card requirements other than their own. He'd have been better off with New York, Iowa, or even an Arizona license. The second mistake had been in the lamination. Gal bent the top right corner down to touch the bottom left corner, and the plastic lining buckled into a sharp crease. The third and most crucial mistake was the signature. Gal ran his thumb along the messy cursive and found that the ink wasn't raised.

The boy began to sweat.

Gal looked at the redhead. "First date?" he asked her.

"How did you know?" she giggled.

Gal smiled and then handed back the fake ID.

"Coors Light it is. Open or closed?"

Pug-Face looked as though somebody had smacked him across the face. He was either shocked by the fact that Gal hadn't kicked him out, or had no idea what Gal was asking him.

"Did you want to open a tab or close it out, bud?" Gal repeated slowly, chuckling as he glanced at the redhead. "Don't mind his nerves. He's in here all the time with different girls, but you are by far the prettiest."

The redhead blushed. She leaned in to plant a sweet kiss on Pug-Face's rosy cheek. The kid looked on the verge of fainting and handed over a credit card, most likely one he'd stolen out of his dad's wallet.

"Open tab, then," Gal deduced. He rang in the two drinks, left the young couple to their awkward conversation, disappeared behind the bar, and massaged his aching knuckles.

*Thirty pages in three hours.*

God, his fingers hurt.

"That was really sweet," came a familiar voice.

Gal poked his head around the expanse of liquor bottles and felt as though his heart might just explode out of his chest.

Long golden hair cascaded over slender shoulders. Plump and pouty lips were pulled up into the most flawless smile on the planet. Those sapphire eyes were the same, staring at him as though they could see right through him.

Amber looked as beautiful as ever. And this time, she was alone.

"There's no way in hell that kid is legal," she told him with a smile. "You really upped his confidence just now, you know that?"

Gal looked back to find Pug-Face flirting ostentatiously with the redhead.

"As long as he doesn't use that shady I.D. anywhere else, he should do just fine. How long have you been sitting there?"

"About three hours," she replied. "And still no drink in front of me."

"My apologies. Too bad we only opened twenty minutes ago."

"You caught me," Amber giggled. "I can be a pathological liar sometimes."

"Me too."

"You're lying."

"If I am lying, doesn't that make me a pathological liar?"

"Touche." Amber kept her eyes locked on Gal, as though daring him to look anywhere else. "But, I still don't have a drink in front of me."

"Pick your poison."

"Vodka and soda. House vodka is fine," she said and pulled her golden locks back into a ponytail. "I don't make enough for Grey Goose."

Gal smirked, wiped down the bar, and poured her drink.

"Brad doesn't pay for your drinks?"

"Bradley isn't here," Amber said. Whether or not that was an invitation to continue flirting, Gal couldn't tell.

"He's still working?" Gal asked.

"Isn't he always?" she sighed. "Don't get me wrong. He has a great job. Pays well. But it's way more restricting than what you and I do."

"You bartend?"

"Only recently."

"Anywhere I know?"

"I would hope so," she muttered and sucked down her drink before he mindlessly poured and passed her another, this time with Grey Goose.

"Why is that?"

"Because it's right next door." Amber smiled and sat back in her barstool, putting her black, loose fitting shirt on display. A cartoon tiger leered at Gallagher.

"So, you're the newest cougar prowling the Tiger Bar?"

"I'm hardly old enough to be considered a cougar, but yeah. Started a few weeks ago. You don't go in there much?"

"Not really my cup o' joe."

"Why is that?"

"You're a nosy one, aren't you?"

"Guilty."

"Let's just say that my reputation at Tiger isn't the greatest," he said with a shrug, quickly pouring another Midori Sour for the redhead fawning over Pug-Face.

"Let me guess. You worked the bar and you got involved with one of the waitresses."

"A couple of the waitresses."

"And what? They had boyfriends?"

"Guilty."

"I'll have to be careful then, won't I?" Amber said with a smile.

Gal shook his head and began tending to the bottles in the well, wiping off the muck that accumulated on each of the pour spouts.

"I wouldn't be too concerned. I'm nowhere near as perfect as my brother."

*A little blunt, but resounding nonetheless.*

"Perfect is boring," she said. "See you around, Gal."

And with that, Amber sucked down the rest of her Grey Goose, slipped a twenty across the bar top, and walked out the door. Gallagher watched her hips swing from side to side until she disappeared into the hazy evening.

What was her game? Was she even playing a game? Or was his brain the one playing tricks? Imagining something that wasn't even there…

He was wrenched from his daydream by the cell phone buzzing in his pocket. Not the singular buzz associated with a text. Not the three long buzzes associated with a call.

Long, drawn out. Beckoning.

He dried his hands and pulled out his phone.

The screen read:

**AMBER Alert**
**Daphne Castro**

Inyo/Mono Counties, CA
Missing Adult Female
19 y.o., Hr: Blk, Ht: 5'4, Wt: 120 lbs
Last seen 01-25-15

Gallagher's heart, swollen from Amber's coy remarks, suddenly deflated.

# EIGHT

# Silver

Of the four lakes that hugged the ring of the June Lake Loop, Silver Lake had always been Gallagher's favorite.

Silver Lake reminded Gal of Scarlet. It was the third lake in The Loop, and Scar was the third child. It was the quietest, yet the one that harbored the most beauty. It was the only lake that made Gal feel safe, the only lake that eased the tension in his brain. While summer tourists flocked to June Lake and Grant Lake for paddle boarding, boat races, and rambunctious barbecues, the more artistic visitors settled into the small campsites along Silver's shores for fishing, quiet peace, and creative inspiration. Nestled in a small basin surrounded by towering peaks, Silver was also the least temperamental of the four lakes.

*So very much like Scar.*

A light breeze caught Gal's hair and sent a chill down his spine. He stared at the glasslike surface of the water as the small fishing boat rocked gently beneath him. The handle of his fishing rod sat unmoving in his sweaty palms, yet his mind was elsewhere.

*Who raised the alarm?*

As always, Scar had been right. She said early on that someone was bound to come asking questions. Now, only two weeks after the AMBER alert had been broadcast to every cell phone in the Sierras, Inyo & Mono County policemen were searching high and low for the missing raven-haired girl.

*Why is Scar always right?*

"You all right, G?" Jimmy slurred from the bow, swaying more from his consumption of six beers than the rocking of the boat. "You look sick as a dog."

"I'm fine," Gal lied. He reeled in his line to find the wad of rainbow fishing bait untouched.

"Bastards ain't bitin' today," said Jimmy. He unzipped his fly and released a steady stream into the otherwise pristine lake. "I don't get it. Beginning of April is trout season."

"Haven't you been watching the news?" Gal asked. Jimmy snorted and hacked a loogy into the ripples. "I'll take that as a no."

"Ain't got a TV, Gal. You know that."

"I haven't seen your new place, so no, I wouldn't know," Gal replied lazily before drawing back his pole and casting a fresh line. "People on the news are saying it's because of the drought. Less snow melt means warmer water. Fish are swimming deeper to stay cool. Swimming deeper, biting less."

"Let's go to deeper water then," Jimmy suggested.

The brothers reeled in their lines, Gal yanked the motor's pull cord, and they were off. It was still too early in the year and too early in the morning for tourists to enjoy the fruits of Silver Lake's placid depths, granting Jimmy and Gallagher the entire south end of the lake. Here, the water reached 170 feet.

*I wonder if dumping her in the lake would have been smarter…*

Jimmy cleared his throat.

"Speakin' of the news, I's at the grocery store yesterday…"

"So you were at a bar," Gal corrected him over the dull rumble of the motor. Judging by the sudden flush around Jimmy's ears, Gal's guess had been correct.

"Anyway, you heard 'bout that girl that went missin'?"

"No," Gal spluttered over the rim of his freshly cracked Pabst.

*Smooth, Gal. Very freaking smooth.*

"What happened?" he asked. Jimmy eyed him for a moment.

"You livin' under a rock, G? I ain't even got a TV and – "

"What happened?" Gal repeated, turning away to kill the motor and drop the anchor. "You ain't even got a TV, but you know something I don't. Enlighten *me* for once."

"Pretty little number, by the mugshot they got. Hot little body."

Gal's heart began to beat against his ribs. Could Jimmy hear it? Surely all of Silver Lake could hear it, even the fish 170 feet down.

"About your age. What was her name?"

Gal froze.

*Does he know? Scar said something. I'll kill her.*

He turned to find Jimmy's eyes upon the sky, scratching his bushy, untamed beard.

"Donna—Diane—Denise—Dede—" Jimmy mumbled to himself, racking his brains. "Started with a D. Anyway, you should look into it. Might be someone you know, if she's from around here. I asked Scar, but – "

"What did she say?" Gal blurted out.

"Said she saw everything on the news. That she didn't recognize her." Jimmy stared at him, cocking a bushy eyebrow. "You sure you're okay?"

"I'm fine," he lied. "Just not used to drinking this early."

Jimmy threw his head back and laughed. "That's a good one, Gal. This comin' from the guy who used to pass out in the Tiger Bar, wake up, and start pounding a bottle of Jack before his shift. Looks like AA did you a hell of a lot of good." Jimmy tossed Gal another Pabst.

"Thanks for the reminder," Gal growled and tossed it back. "I've had enough."

*Enough of the Pabst and enough of you, Jim.*

"More for me," Jimmy chided.

For the next hour, they remained silent in the hope that less sound meant more luck. At a quarter past eight, Gal felt a gentle tug on his line. He carefully took hold of the reel, gave it a tug, hooked his unseen catch, let the line zip out a few yards, and then began to wind it in.

"'Atta boy, G!" Jimmy called happily, nearly stumbling over the side of the boat as he stood to grab the net. "Reel 'er in, nice and slow. Not too fast now! Gal, you're going too – "

"Jimmy, shut up! I'm fine!" Gal yelled, tugging harder and tightening the slack.

"Y'ain't fine! You're going to lose it! Loosen the slack!" Jimmy stumbled drunkenly forward and grabbed the quivering pole.

Without a second thought, Gal swung a fist into Jimmy's nose.

A loud crack resounded off the surface of the lake, reverberating along the high peaks that surrounded Silver Lake like a mountainous bowl. Jimmy's bloodshot eyes widened as the impact sent him reeling over the edge of the boat and splashing into the freezing water. Gal turned back to his reel and tightened the slack even more, winding and winding as the fish fought to break free. Twenty feet away and struggling. Ten feet. Five feet…

He could see the monstrous, silvery trout just below the surface.

*You're mine.*

The tension in the line was so great that Gal was doubled backward in an effort to land the giant fish.

He gave one final tug, and *snap!*

The line broke, sending Gal off balance as his foot caught the edge of the boat. He tumbled backwards, reached for anything to hold onto, but felt only the cool morning air between his fingers.

The breath was wrenched from his lungs as he plunged into the freezing water. He kicked, but found his leg caught in the anchor's chain. He tried to swim upward, and suddenly felt something hard and sharp slice the top of his head.

Light pulsed behind his eyelids. The crown of his head erupted in a surge of pain. He opened his eyes to find the water above him flooding red. He was bleeding, and badly.

But how? And why?

*Where's Jimmy?*

His vision began to fade. His arms refused to swim to the surface. Tunnel vision set in as the swinging anchor dragged him deeper, the murky depths pulling him into the abyss.

*Where's Jimmy?*

And then a final thought presented itself…

*Jimmy wants the house.*

Jimmy was the one who had knocked him on the head. An oar, probably. The old bastard never liked Gal. Sure, he acted like he did. But when a chance to better his own life presented itself, Jimmy always seized it. Gal was going to drown at the hands of his eldest brother. He was going to join Daphne in the afterlife, nothing more than the forgotten ghost of Silver Lake.

He sank into darkness. And then, the world was gone.

*** 

Former deputy Sandra Castro guzzled down a cup of steaming black coffee, biting back the burn that threatened to singe every one of her taste buds.

"Do you have an appointment?" asked the silver-haired receptionist.

"I don't need one," Sandy grunted.

"Sheriff Larson is very busy this afternoon. I must insist that you set up an appointment. I can pencil you in for Wednesday the twenty-ninth if you – "

"I'll see him right now," Sandy replied calmly, picking the dirt from beneath her fingernail and flicking it on the receptionist's desk.

"Ma'am, you really need to – "

"Paul Larson!" Sandy bellowed from the bottom of her gut. "I need a word with you, Sheriff!"

The entire waiting area went silent as the geriatric receptionist silently fumed from behind the protective glass.

"Larson, you pile of dog crap! Get out here!"

From the hallway beyond, a door burst open. A round, obese man stomped out, face red as an overripe tomato.

"What in the holiest hell?!" Larson screamed, tightening his much-too-small trousers and causing his colossal belly to fold over, nearly busting the bottom buttons of his uniform. "Mary Ann, I thought I said no appointments!"

"I'm sorry, Sheriff. She – "

"I let myself in," Sandy growled, sizing up the short and stout Sheriff behind the glass. She stood a foot taller and twice as broad. "Still a little gremlin, aren't you? I don't remember you being this fat."

Larson's tomato-red face plunged into a plum-purple.

"And just who the hell are you, woman?"

*He hasn't changed one bit. The chauvinistic pig.*

"You don't remember my magnificent mug, Pauly? My hair was a bit shorter, but I think the years have been pretty damn good to me." Sandy chewed the nail off her middle finger, making sure to extend her digit tall and proud, just for him. "Can't say the same about you, sadly. You used to have all the female deputies in the palm of your stubby little hand. What happened?"

"Deputy Castro?"

"Former deputy," she corrected him.

"So, the southland finally chewed you up and spit you out."

"The opposite, actually."

"And you're here for what?" Larson growled as he stepped closer. As if a single pane of glass could deter her fist from making contact with his fat nose. "A job?"

"Nope. Just the fresh air."

"I doubt that."

"The southern scum can keep their smog," Sandy replied, spitting her freshly chewed fingernail at the glass and causing Larson to flinch. She inhaled deeply, held it in, and sighed with satisfaction. "But I guess no matter how far north it migrates, southern scum keeps on scummin'.

Isn't that right, Pauly?"

Larson's temple began to twitch.

"So, what? You kick down the door to my station just to rouse old tensions? To insult me in front of my people?"

"The insults are more for shits and giggles, Pauly, considering how easy it is to make your fat face look like an eggplant."

Sandy leaned in close, moist breath fogging the pristine glass, much to the chagrin of Mary Ann and her trusty bottle of Windex.

"I want to know who raised the AMBER alert on the missing girl last week," Sandy said.

"The Castro girl?" Larson stared at Sandy for a moment. His angry eyes suddenly shifted to a widened, unbelieving stare. "Are you two – ?"

"She's my niece, Larson."

"Ah, hell. I'm sorry to hear that, Sandy," Paul muttered. The tension slackened and warped into an uncomfortable silence. He turned to Mary Ann and nodded his head. The secretary, bewildered as she was, turned up her nose and pressed a buzzer on the desk. The glass door clicked, and Larson pushed it open.

"Come into the back."

Jokes put on hold, Sandy shoved past Mary Ann. She followed the squat Sheriff down a long hallway and into his office. The unimpressive room was decorated with file folders, a large pinned map, and a wall covered in pictures of missing persons. Sandy's stomach did a backflip when she noticed a photograph of Daphne, clipped from a newspaper article. It was an old photograph taken on the edge of the Balboa Pier, a photograph Sandy recognized from Daphne's Facebook photo album…

A photograph that Sandy herself had taken.

"Forgive me, Sandy. I didn't even think to put two and two together. There are a lot of Castros, you know. If I had any inkling that you – "

"Don't worry about it," she sighed. "Who told you about Daphne?"

He cocked a bushy eyebrow and plopped down into his overly faded leather chair. "You know I can't tell you that. I've tried getting a link on the parents."

"She has no parents. Only me," Sandy said. "My deadbeat brother is currently serving fifty to life in Theo Lacy Jail. Four counts of manslaughter after his meth lab blew sky high." She averted his stare and looked out the window. "Daphne's mom – my sister-in-law, Eileen – was one of the four."

"I'm sorry to hear that."

"Don't be. Eileen was a bitch." Sandy snorted and put on a face as hard as stone. "Daphne's a good girl. She just got into some bad stuff. Stuff that I'd rather not let the media find out about."

Paul Larson's lips squeezed into an uncomfortable straight line. "Like what?"

"Have you heard of the Sierra Red Lodges?" she asked.

She watched Larson's beady eyes shift nervously from his desk to the door.

*What are you hiding?*

Finally, he cleared his throat and nodded. "Of course, I have. There ain't a deputy up here who hasn't heard of them."

"And, what, you condone them? You just let illegal call girls sip tea in their Lodges while they wait for the next batch of horny old men to show up? What the hell kind of ship are you running?"

It was Larson's turn to return the smug look of educated interest.

"How much do you know about the Lodges?" he asked. "Besides the fact that your niece– "

"Daphne," she corrected him.

" – is a working call girl for at least one of them," he finished without skipping a beat. Sandy's heart pounded against her ribs. She fought back the urge to leap over the table and choke him silly for associating her sweet, lovely niece with the money-crazed harlots roaming the Sierra Mountains.

Instead, she shrugged her massive shoulders.

"Obviously not very much," Larson said. "Let me enlighten you. A Sierra Red Lodge isn't a lodge at all. It isn't concrete. It doesn't have a mailing address. It can't be found on Google Maps. It doesn't have a front yard or a backyard. It doesn't have a garage or a staircase. It doesn't have a roof or a chimney. A Sierra Red Lodge isn't a place, Sandy. It's a network."

He stood up and walked over to the pinned map of Inyo & Mono Counties, strings of silver yarn stretching in all directions like a spider's web.

"It's a web of people who are very good at covering their tracks and their business practices."

"You're well informed," she said accusingly.

"It's my job to be," he retorted.

Sandy stared at the sweat stains under his pits, on his brow, and along the fat folds of his back. Funny thing was, the air conditioner was on full blast.

*What are you hiding?*

"Sheriff Larson," Sandy whispered in her most respectful tone. Intrigued at the newfound acknowledgment of his title, Larson looked at her. "All bullshit and bickering aside, I would really appreciate it if we kept Daphne's case under wraps. At least until we find her."

"*We?*" he asked with a laugh. "What makes you think you are involved in any of this?"

"Because she is *my* niece, and *my* responsibility," Sandy snarled. "And you are going to help me find her whether you like it or not."

"*I* am going to help *you*? Forgive me for saying so, Castro, but you aren't even in the force anymore. Hell, I shouldn't even be discussing this case with you. In fact, why don't we just adjourn this little meeting and you can let me get back to work?"

He turned his attention back to the silver-webbed map, let up a wet belch, and thumped a fist on his chest to clear the indigestion.

"Staring at some stupid map isn't going to help find my niece," Sandy said. "So, get your ass out that door, get into a unit, and go look for her."

"I have my best men on it, Sandy, trust me."

"That's the main problem, Pauly. I don't trust you. I haven't trusted you since our first day in the academy together. Nothing personal, but you are a slime ball. I wouldn't trust you enough to pour me a scotch, let alone to find the only person on this earth that means any sort of shit to me."

"Then why are you here? What are you asking me to do, Sandy?"

"No more alerts. No more media coverage. No more news interviews. Daphne is a smart girl, she has a bright future, and I will not have it all screwed over because you let slip that she's involved in some shady network of two-bit call girls looking to make some extra cash."

She rose out of her chair and towered behind Larson.

"I have my best men on it," he repeated, then strolled to the door and pulled it open. "I'll be in touch. Leave your information with Mary Ann."

"Who told you Daphne went missing, Paul?"

"Goodbye, Castro."

And in case she didn't quite understand that this meeting was indeed over, the Sheriff of Inyo County placed one hand on the butt end of his gun, daring her to press him further than she already had.

Sandy stared at the round little man, reached over his shoulder, and ripped the silver yarn from the map before balling it up and tossing it into the trash.

"Damn cops," she growled. Sandy spit on the floor at Larson's feet and left the office. She walked a few paces down the hallway, and then turned to find Larson staring at the photograph of Daphne upon his wall.

The photograph that Sandy herself had taken.

*What are you hiding?*

***

From what Gal had always imagined, death meant the end of all pain. In his mind, when someone died, all physical and emotional anguish were lost to the cosmos. Lost among billions of trillions of stars, to the expanse of black inky space where his mother had resided for the past thirteen years. Why, then, did his head feel as though someone were dragging a knife back and forth along his scalp?

*Am I dead?*

After all, everything was black. Did he now float among the darkest reaches of the cosmos? Had he followed his pain all the way here? Or had his pain followed him? Was he about to be reunited with his beautiful mother? The woman who had left him all alone in the world with nigh but a deadbeat father, two brothers who internally despised him, and a sister who felt sorry for him? Would it hurt to see his mother again?

*Am I dead?*

He vaguely remembered the rush of ice-cold water, remembered how his lungs had seized up, remembered how his leg had wrapped around the chain of the anchor, remembered struggling for the surface. And then the pain had taken over, rushed from the crown of his head and numbed his entire body.

Jimmy had won, then. They had both seen their mother's will, after all. She had left the house to Gal, her favorite child, though if anything were ever to happen to him, Jimmy was the next in line to receive the property.

But now that he was dead, did Gal even care about the stupid old house?

To be honest, he *did* care. He had slaved over that house for the past three years, had saved up to transform it from a two-story dump into the renovated kingdom he had become fond of calling his home.

*All that work, for nothing.*

In this state of pure inky darkness, Gal could hear the sounds of rippling matter sloshing gently through his own abyss. The cosmos sounded strangely familiar... like gentle waves lapping the side of a boat. So strangely familiar.

Small, odd shapes of dim light appeared in front of him, fading and reforming. The darkness became a dull pink, as though sunlight were pressing upon his eyelids. He still had eyelids? Did that mean he still had a body?

*Am I dead?*

*Only one way to find out.*

Gal opened his eyes.

A pale blue sky stretched like an endless ocean above him. Silver-lined thunderheads blocked direct sunlight, yet the mid-April afternoon was still bright as could be. He lie on his back in the bottom of a boat, listening to the water lapping against the hollow underbelly.

*Not dead, then.*

Gal tried to sit up, felt himself go dizzy, and collapsed onto his back.

"Easy there, kid," came a deep and familiar voice. Gal adjusted his gaze from the sky to find Jimmy seated beside the rumbling motor, holding the rudder and easing it slowly from side to side. "Don't try to sit up. Relax, G."

"What happened?" Gal croaked.

"What happened is your damn fish got away," Jimmy muttered with a chuckle. "I told you the slack was too tight."

Gal noticed a brown streak just below Jimmy's nose. Dried blood.

"I'm sorry," Gal whispered. "I shouldn't have – "

"Shut it. It's all right. I was bein' a drunk asshole. I deserved it." Jimmy pushed the rudder to the left and Gal felt the boat sway to the right. Birch branches hung over the boat on either side as tall reeds drifted by, swaying gently in the breeze.

"Where are we?"

"Still at Silver, don't worry. Just back in the channels."

"Why? I need a doctor. Call Scar or – "

"You don't need a doctor," Jimmy growled. "I'm going to take real good care of you."

What the hell was going on? His brother had saved him from a watery grave, sure, but did he have bigger plans in mind for Gallagher? Did he plan on killing him and leaving him to rot in the back channels of Silver Lake? Or would he bury him, as Gal had buried Daphne?

"Jimmy, please, I – "

"Seriously, Gal, just shut up and relax."

"My head – "

"I took care of it."

"You what?" Gal groaned and reached up, scared out of his wits to feel the gaping gash in his head. He was relieved to feel a small slit, skin flaps pulled cleanly together by tight stitching.

"You hit your head on the propeller. Cut it clean to the bone. I pulled you up, tossed you back in the boat, and stitched you up with that extra-thin fishin' line you got me last Christmas."

Jimmy smiled warmly, and for a moment Gal imagined it to be genuine. Or was it truly genuine? It'd be the first genuine smile Jimmy had given him in years.

"How do you know how to – "

"Hell, Scar has stitched me up so many times. Used to hate watchin' her do it, but after enough times, I got the rhythm down. Don't even need her help anymore, can you believe that?"

Jimmy chuckled, and Gal was suddenly surprised to hear himself chuckling along with his older brother. The boat gave a lurch as the bow hit soft sand. Jimmy jumped out to pull the vessel ashore.

"We're here."

Gathering up the remaining strength he had, Gal sat up, allowed the world to right itself, and then drank in his surroundings. They were alone on a small embankment shrouded in tall birch trees, the likes of which stretched high enough and thick enough to leave them in complete isolation.

"Where is *here*?" Gal asked. Jimmy tied off the boat to one of the thicker birch trees and turned to Gal with a tiny shrug.

"Home, I guess you can call it."

"I don't get it."

"Follow me."

Jimmy grabbed a stringer holding two silver trout from the side of the boat and disappeared into the trees. Gal clambered out of the boat and followed. After a two-minute hike up a steep pile of shale and boulders, they reached a rocky glade where a small tent was erected.

Gal's jaw fell open in disbelief.

"This is where you've been living?" he asked. His nose turned upward at the stench of a small hole dug into the earth just beside the tent, a roll of toilet paper set neatly beside it. "Jesus, Jim."

"It ain't much, but it does the job," Jimmy replied with a shrug of his stocky shoulders.

"What happened to your place in Bishop? You said you had a huge apartment."

"I never had an apartment in Bishop, Gal. I was livin' with Scar. She let me have the back room. I felt bad, though. Started to feel like a burden, so I told her I got an apartment and I booked it over here and set up shop."

"How long have you been here?"

"Since October," Jimmy confessed. He had outlasted an entire winter, countless feet of snow and ice, on this rocky glade back in the channels of Silver Lake.

Gal suddenly understood why Jimmy had grown his beard so long. "Are you still working?"

"If you call fishin' for dinner every day workin', then yes."

"Jesus, Jim," Gal repeated. He rubbed his head and instantly regretted it, sharp pain exploding across his scalp. "You can't live like this."

"Ain't much else I can do, G. Nobody wants to hire me, and no girl wants to date a homeless guy." He chuckled, but the sound was pitiful.

Gal's conscience began to nudge at him. As horrible as it felt, he tried hard to ignore it.

"It's fine though. I'm makin' due."

Gal's conscience nagged him harder with each moment he was forced to inhale the stench of an old tent and a hole filled with Jimmy's waste. At last, he found he could fight it no longer.

"Pack it up, Jim. You're coming home."

"I can't do that to you, Gal. You made it very clear at your birthday party that I'm not welcome. I don't blame you one bit, I promise."

"Shut up and fill in that hole. We're going home."

Gal clambered back down the shale and rocks. He silently prayed that he wouldn't end up regretting his decision.

# NINE

# Oak

∾

Gallagher's fingertips flew across the keyboard of his laptop in a flurry of sharp clicks. The document upon the screen showed far more black than white, words upon words filling each page until he found himself struggling to find the next loop in his story.

*Tom DeLevine, a crass and degenerate novelist struggling with writer's block, wakes to find a dead call girl in his bed.*

The hook was pure gold.

The opening of the story was set. The less-than-classy introduction of Tom DeLevine. The reveal of a bloody corpse. Tom's inner struggle to maintain his cool. A stunned sister walking in at just the wrong moment. An improper burial deep in the woods…

But something was definitely missing. A very important something.

*With no recollection of her grisly passing, Tom must…*

*Tom must what?*

And then it hit him.

"Who is the antagonist?" Gal asked no one in particular. He popped another Adderall and swallowed it down with a glass of oak-aged bourbon. He sat for a moment, staring at the cursor blinking eagerly up at him.

*Who makes DeLevine's life so difficult that he must eventually face them in a final, head-to-head confrontation?*

An enraged pimp declaring retribution for dismembered property?

The call girl's love interest, come back to claim revenge?

A sad and emotionally unstable family member looking for answers?

The possibilities were endless.

Gal leaned back in his chair, balancing on the back legs. His mind raced from one possible antagonist to the next. Each had its perks, yet each would determine how the rest of the story would play out. It wasn't necessarily writer's block – rather, what he was struggling to navigate through was a blinding blizzard of ideas.

*Creeeak.*

He stopped.

His eyes widened.

His spine tingled.

The unmistakably familiar noise roused him out of his own head and tugged him back into the unholy reality that was his life. Gallagher pulled the plugs out of his ears to find the silence in his home even more pressing.

Jimmy had left the house hours ago…

As quiet as possible, Gal closed his laptop and reached into his desk. He pulled out the stag horn pocketknife, unhinged the devilish blade, and stepped cautiously out of his bedroom, into the lightless upstairs hallway.

After all these silent weeks, the killer had finally returned to finish the job…

But Gal wouldn't go down without a fight.

A rustle from the kitchen made his heart skip a beat. His white-knuckled fingers wrapped tightly around the handle of his pocketknife. Back pressed to the bannister, Gal slowly inched his way down the stairs. He took heed to step silently over the creaky second-to-last step until he placed his foot on cold new tile.

Pupils dilated in the darkness, Gal held his breath when he saw it…

A shadow hunkered over the kitchen sink.

The sinister figure was tall and slender, a black hole against the dim starlight filtering through the kitchen window. Gal slowly approached, bare feet silent against the new tile…

The shadow raised its head. It sniffed the air.

Gal stopped. He turned on his heel and pressed his back into the wall separating kitchen from entryway. He clenched his jaw, squeezed his lips shut, and held his breath.

Silence.

Knife clenched in his right hand, Gal's left hand slid along the wall and found the kitchen light. He switched it on. Light flooded his vision as he whipped around the wall and into the kitchen, intent on facing his would-be killer.

The kitchen was empty.

A bone-numbing breeze wafted over his cheek. The back door was ajar. For a moment, Gal's feet were rooted to the tile, unsure of whether he should give chase.

*I need answers.*

Gal grabbed a flashlight, pulled on his boots and stepped out onto the back porch. He shined the light onto fresh boot prints etched perfectly in the midnight frost. They looked oddly familiar. He pressed the sole of his boot into one of the prints…

A perfect fit.

Shaken, Gal let the flashlight follow the boot prints leading into the darkness of his property, deep into the trees. He knew exactly where they would lead.

*It really is time to buy a gun*, he considered. The pocketknife felt more like a toothpick than a weapon. The pocketknife had, however, proven its deadliness once before.

He followed the boot prints down the porch steps, followed them through the yard, into the trees, and pressed deeper until he saw it.

The boot prints ended at the old aluminum shed. The door was ajar...

An invitation.

Panic flooded Gal's veins like ice water. He hadn't pursued anyone. He had been led to a dark, isolated place. A trap.

"Come out!" he yelled.

Silence.

"I've got a gun!" he lied.

Nothing.

The cold picked up, causing his teeth to chatter as he approached the shed with the knife held high. He kicked the door open and let the flashlight illuminate the interior.

Everything was in its place: two ill-used lawnmowers, waste bins filled with dried leaves, cans of expired oil dripping in excess.

And in the middle of it all, a large, lumpy blue tarp.

*No fucking way.*

Gal squatted beside the tarp, tracing his fingertips along a small inscription written in permanent marker:

*FINCH*

God, how his mother had labeled everything. *Who the hell would steal a tarp?*

The tarp began to move. It rose an inch and fell an inch. Over and over. Perfect rhythm. Perfect breath.

Gal ripped back the tarp.

Scarlet writhed on the floor of the shed. She stared at him, white-faced and wide-eyed. She clutched at a deep neck laceration stretching from ear to ear. Blood squirted and splashed against the oak floorboards. She clawed at her throat, gulping and gasping for the oxygen now escaping her body.

"Scar! Scarlet! No! Hold on!" Gal screamed. He dropped the knife and pressed both hands against the deep wound. He felt Scar's blood squirting against his palms, dripping between his fingers, running down his forearms.

Scar wheezed, choked, gasped. Her bulging eyes became soft. Her breathing slowed to a stop. Her look of panic eased into an expression of release.

Gallagher Finch watched his sister's pupils dilate for the last time.

"Sc – Scarlet? Scar – " Gal heard himself whisper.

She was dead.

His throat closed up tight. His eyes welled with tears. He looked at his blood-soaked hands. He looked at the pocketknife beside him.

Fresh blood glistened along the edge of the blade.

*My blade.*

"No," he groaned.

"Yes," came a soft, wheezing voice behind him. He turned...

She was naked, her pale skin like wax, eyes white as the moon, skin rotting away. Flesh and sinew dangled from her face, arms, and legs. Her joints popped as she stepped closer, the stench of her decomposing corpse flooding Gal's nostrils.

"Yes," Daphne wheezed.

Horrified, Gal stumbled backward into the pool of Scarlet's blood.

Eyes as dead as Daphne's, Scarlet slowly sat up. She picked up the stag horn pocketknife, gazed lifelessly into his eyes, and pressed the bloody knife into his hand.

"Yes," Daphne repeated in that awful, post-mortem hiss, placing a kiss on the back of Gal's neck.

Without a care in the world, Gal pierced the blade into his beloved sister's windpipe, silencing her once and for all. And then...

Gallagher Finch awoke in his bed, soaked in sweat.

***

*It should've been so easy.*

If there was one thing that Jimmy Finch's mother had always wanted when she was alive, it was a widow's watch.

Sure, their family home was hundreds of miles from the California coast. Sure, it was densely curtained in the midst of large pine trees. Sure, the fog in winter would never allow her to see five feet in front of her face. But, the mere idea of having her own deck to await her husband's return had always seemed romantic... even if she had only ever waited and watched for him to return from the bar.

After the snowfall of the past few months, the monstrosity that Gal had attempted to build on his own now sloped at a dangerous angle. The eastward lean of the widow's watch was immense.

Jimmy and Gal sat harnessed to the oak beams supporting the unsteady structure.

"Remind me why you didn't call a professional," Jimmy grumbled, arms pushing up on the sloping planks as Gal hammered a support beam into place.

"Don't need one," Gal said between hammer strokes.

"Apparently you do, kid," Jimmy chuckled. "Or was this slope on purpose?"

"You wanted to help, Jim. Lift it higher."

"I'm tellin' you, this is as high as it goes. And why the hell did you use oak? Pine would've been so much more – "

"Do you want to rebuild this whole thing, Jimmy? Because I swear to God – "

"Let's call my buddy, Stan. He builds these kinds of things all the time."

Jimmy looked over at Gal. His younger brother was staring daggers, nostrils flared, knuckles white around the hammer.

"What the hell is your problem?" Gal snapped.

"S'cuse me?"

"You've been here for three weeks now, eating my food, clogging my toilet, dragging your knuckles around my house – "

"*Your* house? We all grew up here, you little prick. Since when is it *your* house?"

"Since mom left the deed to me!"

And there it was.

The only thing that Jimmy had ever wanted, cast like a stone at his face by his ungrateful little brother. Why their mother had always favored Gal remained a mystery these past twenty-six years.

Before Gal, life was better. That much Jimmy remembered of his childhood.

"Is that supposed to hurt me?" Jimmy growled. "I don't need your charity. I'll go back to Silver Lake. Back to my tent. You'll never have to worry about me, Gal."

He looked at the rope of Gal's harness, how it was wearing against the oak beam. All it would have taken was a small flick of Jimmy's wrist to unfasten it, and Gal would have fallen thirty feet onto the driveway below.

Splat.

*It would've been so easy.*

A sharp whistle blasted through the chilly April breeze, followed by a familiar, cocky laugh.

"Look at you two! An ape and a weasel, up in the trees." Brad guffawed at his own joke as he crunched his boots over the frost below. "Is it supposed to slope like that?"

"Ask Gal," Jimmy said, dark eyes never leaving his youngest brother or the unsteady rope of his harness.

"It was fine a couple of weeks ago. The weight of the snowdrift buckled a couple of the support beams," Gal grumbled, hammering away to hide his displeasure at the arrival of their golden brother.

"Should've called a professional," Brad suggested and sparked up a cigarette. "And why oak? Why not pine?"

Jimmy couldn't help but grin.

"Is there something you want?" Gal asked impatiently.

"What? I can't come by and check out your, uh, handiwork?"

"In that case, grab a rope and a hammer."

"Maybe next time."

"Is there something you want, then?" Gal repeated louder, hammer missing the nail completely.

"Damn, Gal, which bug crawled its way up your ass?" Brad yelled up at him. "Both of you take a break and come down. I wanted to come and share the news."

"What news?" Jimmy asked. He abandoned his chore and scaled down the rope.

Without the extra manpower, the widow's watch sloped lower and splintered the new support beam Gal had been hammering in. The curse words that spilled from Gal's mouth made Jimmy smirk.

"Would you come down here and chill out for a sec?" Brad yelled over Gal's cursing.

"I'm fine up here," Gal barked. "Go on then, what's your news?"

Brad reached into his jacket and withdrew a small oak box. He opened it, and inside sat a band of silver topped with a black diamond.

"Yes, Brad," Jimmy said. "Yes, I'll marry you!"

Brad slugged him on the shoulder. Jimmy smiled and wrapped a gorilla arm around Brad's shoulders.

"Congrats, brother! I knew you'd quit whorin' around one day."

"Amber's a good girl. I want her forever."

Brad glanced up at Gal, who made no effort of congratulations. Instead, he began dislodging the splintered beam.

"Don't worry about him. He's been a shit all day," Jimmy muttered, clapping Brad once more on the shoulder. "Let's grab a beer later. First round's on you."

"Just like old times," Brad smiled. He closed the small oak box and tucked it back into his jacket. "Call me later, Jim."

Brad looked up to leave Gal with one final disapproving glance, chuckled at the failed attempt at a widow's watch, and then strolled back to his Mercedes.

As Brad sped away, Jimmy looked up as an angry Gal struggled with the oak beam. Was Brad unaware of how jealous Gallagher was? Had he never noticed the way Gal looked at Amber? The way their eyes met?

Say anything for Jimmy Finch, say he was perceptive.

He stared at Gal, and then at the loosened knot of Gal's harness.

*It could've been so easy.*

\*\*\*

Gal had never felt so sick in his entire life.

His stomach gave a sharp lurch as he vomited his lunch into the toilet bowl of the Sierra Inn's guest bathroom. Thanks to the rain, hardly anyone had shown up for Happy Hour. Nobody at the bar would miss him.

Brad's news that afternoon had set Gal's eyes ablaze, had caused his senses to go fuzzy, had twisted his stomach into knots.

It was a reaction he hadn't foreseen, one he wasn't entirely sure what to do about. Nobody had ever made him feel outside of himself. No girl had ever hooked him so fiercely, so quickly. No woman had ever left him dreaming about the future. It wasn't him. He wasn't supposed to think this way.

Or perhaps he was absolutely supposed to think this way.

His stomach lurched once more, but there was nothing left in his guts to expel. He dry-heaved until he had no more strength, then rested his face on the toilet bowl before flushing down the remains of his lunch.

*Maybe Jimmy just undercooked the beef in the chili.*

Yes, that had to be it.

And yet, the idea of Amber wearing that black diamond on her left hand caused his eyes to burn once again.

He sent his fist into the stall's partition, caving it in and feeling at least three of his knuckles crack under the pressure. He bit back the pain, stood up, washed the vomit off his face, and stepped back into the bar.

Gallagher stopped dead in his tracks.

A sweet smile etched onto her beautifully perfect mug, Amber sat patiently at the bar top, tapping manicured black nails on the oak. She had already helped herself to a cocktail napkin and looked up as Gal trudged behind the bar. Rain pounded against the windowpane while a flash of lightning illuminated her lustrous golden locks.

"I was starting to wonder if you still worked here," she spoke in that terribly gorgeous and confident tone. "How have you been?"

"What can I pour for you today?" he grumbled, green eyes downcast and laden with darkened circles.

"Oh my god. Gal, you look awful. Are you okay?"

Unable to meet her gaze, Gal glanced at her left hand. It was bare. Brad hadn't yet popped the question. His stomach relaxed a bit, but his heart was still heavy as lead.

"What happened to your hand?" she asked, reaching out to touch his swollen and bloody knuckles. He allowed the sensation of her fingertips to ease his mind a moment, and then tugged his hand away.

"It's nothing. What are you drinking?"

He found the courage to look up, noticing her eyes fixed on him with a look of perplexity and pity.

"So, what? You're just not going to talk to me?"

"There's nothing to talk about," he lied.

"Are you sure?" she pressed with a comforting smile, reaching out to touch his knuckles again. "Because if you want to talk, I'm more than happy to – "

"Don't touch me," he interrupted. "What are you drinking, Amber?"

Her smile faded. They stared into each other's eyes before she finally shook her head.

"You know what, I'm not thirsty."

And with that, she stood up, grabbed her purse, stalked out of the bar, and into the pouring deluge.

*You're such an idiot.*

Without realizing the propulsion of his feet, Gal followed her out into the rain. Head on a swivel, he searched for her through the deluge, a brief flash of lightning illuminating her golden streaks.

"Amber!"

She turned. He approached, both of them soaked to the bone.

"I'm sorry."

"What's wrong with you?" she yelled over an ear-shattering clap of thunder.

"A lot of things."

"You think you're the only one with shit going on? I was just trying to – "

But before she could finish, Gal closed the distance between them. He grabbed hold of her face and crashed his lips firmly against her own. Her eyes widened a moment before falling slack, lashes fluttering closed while her arms wrapped around his neck. She stood up on her tiptoes to deepen the kiss. Gal lifted her off her feet as her fingers tangled into his sopping wet black hair until finally, she pulled away and rested her forehead on his chin.

"Oh my god," she whispered.

"Yeah," he replied. Gal set her back down and for a moment, they simply watched the lightning in each other's eyes.

"I have to go," she told him with a smile.

"Yeah," he repeated, giving in to his first smile of the week. She touched her lips and walked off. He watched her until she disappeared into the fog.

Enraptured by the moment, Gal never noticed the blue Silverado across the street.

He never noticed the pair of eyes watching him from within.

                                    ***

The rain pattered loudly against the roof of the Silverado.

Former deputy Sandy Castro watched as the dark-haired young man stared off after the golden-haired young woman. She glanced down at the business card she'd found in Daphne's Camry, and then at the matching name of the restaurant – The Sierra Inn.

*It's go-time.*

Sandy hurried through the rain and hunched her massive shoulders as she eased her way into the tiny tavern. The place was empty, save for an elderly couple bickering in the back corner. Making her way to the bar, she took a seat and caused one of the old stools to creak loudly under her bulk.

The dark-haired young man appeared from behind the bar, choking back what she assumed was a shot of some sort, bright green eyes mildly bloodshot, heavy bags beneath. His skin was pale, face unshaven, yet there was a brightness to his eyes that only comes from the touch of a woman's lips.

"Evening," the young man spoke confidently. She caught a glimpse of his left hand, a cringe sliding down her spine when she noticed the severed tip of his pinky.

"Shit, that must've hurt," Sandy said.

"From what I can remember. I was really young. Passed out when enough blood squirted out." He chuckled, giving her time to glance at his nametag.

"Gal. That's a funny name," she said.

"Can I pour you anything? You don't look like you prefer martinis. How about a beer?"

"Scotch."

"Dry or oaky?"

"The oakier, the better," she replied, and the bartender known as Gal disappeared behind the bar. She heard the clinking of bottles until he emerged with an elaborately carved bottle, the cork topped with brass elk's antlers.

"Don't ask what it is. Just taste it," he said, pouring her a sample.

She lifted the glass and inhaled a lungful of peat and phenol indicative of a very rare scotch, interlaced with the smooth and extremely subtle breath of oak. She sipped, and then groaned as the most incredible spirit she'd ever tasted slid down her throat.

"Jesus, Mary, and Joseph."

He chuckled and poured her a couple fingers.

"*Fuil na Talhainn*," he said.

"Never heard of it." She looked at the bottle a little more closely, then withdrew her phone and took a picture of the label.

"It means *blood of the earth*." He stared at the bottle like a long-lost lover, stared at it like he'd stared after the blonde.

*Enough flirting, Sandy.*

"Have you worked here for a while?" she asked.

"Longer than I care to admit," he replied, wiping down the bottle like a baby in swaddling.

"That your girlfriend that just left?"

He stopped. "Excuse me?"

"I don't mean to pry. It's just, she's gorgeous. You're lucky to have a girl like that to go home to every night."

"No. She's not my girlfriend."

She watched as he did his best to hide the grin on his face.

"I could sure use one myself," she said, sipping the scotch.

"A girlfriend?"

"Hell no. Come on, we both know what we're talking about here," she pressed, giving him a smirk. "A lady of the night. Someone to make me forget my ex."

"No, she's not like that."

"Well, maybe you know somebody who can help me out. A little lady in need of a little extra cash?"

She watched his eyes for a moment. He opened his mouth, the confirmation on the tip of his tongue.

And then, he shook his head.

"I should probably start cleaning up. We close in five."

And with that, Gal walked across the restaurant to hand the elderly couple their bill. He approached Sandy and gave her a clap on the shoulder.

"That one's on me. Come back any time."

"I didn't get your full name. I want to put a good review on Yelp for you," she muttered.

"It's Gallagher. Gallagher Finch."

"Well, it was great meeting you, Gallagher Finch."

Sandy gulped down the rest of her *Fuil na Talhainn*, left a ten spot on the bar, and walked back out into the rain. She climbed into the Silverado, pulled out her phone, and dialed the phone number on the back of the Sierra Inn business card.

It started to ring.

Through the window of the Sierra Inn, she watched as Gallagher

Finch pulled out his phone, furled his eyebrows at the unknown number, and then answered.

"Hello?" she heard through the receiver.

Former deputy Sandy Castro hung up and then started the engine.

*Got you.*

TEN

# Steel

〜

The sky opened up. A bolt of lightning ignited the steel gray clouds hiding the face of the moon.

Amber stared straight ahead through the windshield, her eyes unfocused as she sped over the ridge along Highway 395. Her knuckles whitened as she clutched the steering wheel.

*What the hell just happened?*

The country croons of Shania Twain brayed from the speakers, interspersed with radio static. And while she normally would have belted "I Feel Like A Woman" with fervor, tonight Amber could not find her voice.

She watched the windshield wipers whip to and fro as rain spat loudly upon the glass. Her mind raced faster than the balding tires of her '95 Volkswagen beetle. Wakes of rainwater sprayed upward from either side of the car, blurring her vision.

Amber hated driving in the rain. She willed herself to think of Bradley, alone at the apartment, waiting for her to walk in. She'd be soaked to the bone and freezing. He would pick her up, carry her to the shower, and together, they would peel the clothes from her body. He would lead her under the steaming torrent.

She would press herself against his lean frame.

Push her fingers into his dark, lank hair...

She closed her eyes and shook her head.

*Brad has light hair,* she had to remind herself. *And he isn't lean... not like Gal.*

The thought of Brad's younger brother seared the nerve endings in her lips, like a bolt of lightning that flashed from above. She touched her lips, just as she had for the last half hour.

*He kissed me. It was stupid. It was nothing. It meant nothing...*

Lies.

The ear-splitting blare of a truck horn suddenly roused her from her thoughts. White light blinded her through the rain-soaked windshield. She punched the brake and wrenched the steering wheel to the right. The world faded into a dizzying blur of white and red as the Volkswagen spun like a top upon its balding tires. The blare of the semi's horn passed on the heels of a roaring wind and finally, she opened her eyes.

*What the hell just happened?*

Deafening rain bleated against the windshield. Amber watched the flaming taillights of the semi grow distant before disappearing over the ridge she'd crossed only a minute earlier. The car had spun on its axis, much like her life had spun with one little kiss. The remaining ten miles found Amber driving slower than she had in years, hands shaking with adrenaline. The Volkswagen trudged along the northern bank of Mono Lake and up a muddy access road, through a set of towering steel gates, and into the parking lot of a massive steel mill.

She parked, took a deep breath, and glanced up at the immense structure. Even in the darkness, behind sheets of cold rain, she despised the bulky mill and shadowy warehouse set against the hills. It was sheer industry, a blemish of corporate greed on the insurmountable beauty of the Sierras.

The steel mill was the legacy of Brad's father, Charlie Finch. And now, it had become Brad's legacy. His burden.

Eager for the warmth of a shower and a lover, Amber shut off the car. She covered her head and ran through the deluge, across the parking lot, and up three flights of stairs to the apartment atop the mill. She wrung the rain out of her golden hair and walked inside. She found Brad on the couch, munching a Hungry Man, eyes glued to the TV.

"I'm home," she announced with a dash of dalliance.

"Where've you been?" Brad grunted through a mouthful of mashed potatoes.

"They kept me late."

She waited for a response, but all she received was a nod.

"Who are we playing?" she asked, feigning interest as she shivered and waited for him to whisk her off her feet.

"Damn Dodgers."

"Oh. Do we not like them?" This earned her a moment's silence. Brad turned to her with a cocked brow.

"No. We hate them."

"Oh."

"Amber, what the hell? You're soaked."

"I was thinking about taking a shower," she purred with a suggestive smirk.

"Well, for the love of Christ, lay some towels down," Brad grunted. He stood up, sucked down the rest of his beer, then walked to the kitchen to throw away the scraps. She watched and waited for him to give in to her advances, a small puddle glistening under her boots.

"Amber, towels!"

"Do you want to take a shower with me or not?" she asked impatiently.

"I already took one."

"Oh."

Amber watched him for a moment as he tucked his fork into the dishwasher and grabbed another beer from the fridge. She sighed, then walked down the hall and into the bathroom, soaking wet shoes squelching sadly beneath her. She peeled the clothes from her body, turned on the shower, and set her gaze upon the mirror. She stared into her sullen sapphire eyes, wiping away the mascara dripping with rain and tears.

Her lips continued to tingle. She touched them, closed her eyes, and shook her head.

*It meant nothing.*

A deep cough roused her from her thoughts. She opened her eyes to find Brad in the mirror's reflection, eyes hungry and scanning her naked backside.

"I got something for you," Brad said. He approached her from behind, towering over her and allowing his crotch to press firmly against her bum.

"Perv," she giggled.

"Not that. *This.*"

He reached into the pocket of his pajama bottoms, pulled out a small wooden box, and set it on the sink beside her.

"Open it."

She did as he instructed. Her stomach twisted at the sight of a small silver ring set with a large black diamond.

"Wh—what's this?"

"What does it look like?" Brad responded with a confident smirk.

"It looks like a ring." She met his gaze in the reflection, and for a moment, they stared at each other.

"Do you?" he asked.

"Do I what?"

"Do you want to – you know – *wear* it?"

"Right now?"

"No, dammit," Brad huffed. He took the ring and slid it onto her left ring finger. "Do you want get married?"

And there it was. Her heart sank.

"Is that your proposal?" she asked.

"I've always told you that you'd be Amber Finch one day," he grunted into her flesh. "We both knew this was coming."

She stared at him through the mirror, but said nothing.

"Are you surprised?" he pressed.

"I'm just – it's not what I was expecting."

She chewed the inside of her lip as he looked up and met her gaze. The steam began to fog up the glass as the shower continued its tumultuous gurgle.

Brad's smile vanished.

"Is that a no?" His eyes hardened like the steel his mill so effortlessly produced.

"What do you want me to say, Brad? That was — it wasn't really a proposal. You didn't even get down on your knee. I mean —"

In an instant, his demeanor shifted from lukewarm to boiling. Amber wondered whether the steam flooding the bathroom was emanating not from the shower, but from Brad's shoulders. For the first time, he scared her.

"Do you know how much that ring cost?"

"It's a beautiful ring, Brad, but I want you to mean it when you ask me."

She suddenly felt very vulnerable, naked and sopping wet with him fuming behind her, strong fingers digging into her flesh.

"You're hurting me. Let go," she demanded.

"Fuck it," Brad whispered. He turned on his heel, stormed to the door, and turned to her with fire in his eyes.

"I would *kill* for you," he said.

And with that, he slammed the door. The walls shook. The mirror cracked. Amber stared at the jaggedness of her face within the broken shards before the steam obscured her reflection once and for all.

She touched her lips.

*What the hell just happened?*

***

"Can I get you anything else?"

Sandy gulped down the rest of her beer, ignoring the overly

enthusiastic waiter hovering like a vulture over her half-eaten steak. The interior of the Sierra Inn Restaurant was surprisingly packed, a change of pace from the previous evening. It was a welcome change, to be sure, a chance to watch her prey from the comfort of a warm booth amid a sea of prattling patrons.

Unfortunately, her prey had not shown up for work.

Sandy watched an older gentleman tending the bar, presumably the manager. A young woman shadowed him, as gorgeous as she was young. Dark, lustrous hair. Mocha skin. A soft, sultry frame that Sandy wouldn't mind getting her hands on. But judging by the way she flirted with the men at the bar, the young woman obviously had different tastes.

"Ma'am?" the waiter pressed.

"What?" Sandy burped.

"Can I get you anything else? Another beer? The bill?"

"You trying to steal my table?"

The waiter shook his head vehemently.

"No, no, not at all. It's just, we're very busy tonight and, well, you haven't touched your steak in forty-five minutes. I just wanted to make sure you were all right. I'm sorry. I didn't mean to…"

"I'm screwing with you, kid. Give me the bill."

Intimidated by Sandy's mass, the waiter sighed a breath of relief and set the bill on the table. Sandy paid in cash, watched the waiter frown at the minimal tip, and then stood up to tower over him. "Don't spend it all in one place."

"It'd be hard not to," the waiter scoffed, then left to tend to another table.

Sandy approached the bar top. She sat at the empty stool perched opposite the manager. His nametag read: **FLETCH.**

"What can I get you?" Fletch asked, eyes never leaving the bottle he was polishing.

"Not thirsty," Sandy said. The old bartender looked up, eyes widening at the size of the woman in front of him.

"Goodness," he muttered, then caught himself and smiled. "Well now, what can I help you with?"

"Are you the owner of this fine establishment, Fletch?"

"Why, posilutely, absotively," the old man chuckled. "Been behind this ol' bar for nigh on thirteen years now. Cheapest prices in town, can't do no better!"

"I believe it," Sandy replied. "I was actually in here last night. The gentleman behind the bar really knew his scotch. Tall guy. Dark hair. Missing the tip of his pinky."

"Gal," the old man smiled sadly. "Good ol' boy. Poor kid. Everything that happened, and he still ain't missed a beat."

"What happened?"

"Oh, hell. Dumbass I am, can't keep my mouth shut. Just a bunch o' family stuff when he were younger. People in town don't like to talk about it. Dark time in The Loop. Don't pay me no attention. He's a good boy. Rough around the edges, don't get me wrong, but a good boy. His daddy and I were pals before – well, never mind."

Judging by the redness around Fletch's furry ears and his sudden interest in a chip on the wooden bar top, Sandy knew he was finished gossiping.

"Well," Sandy said. "I'm new to the area. Gal was so cordial and so helpful. Thing is, he hurt his hand and I wanted to send him a little Get Well Soon card. I have it all written up in the truck. You don't happen to have his address, do you?"

*Come on, Fletch. Give me the goods.*

"Well, that's right nice of you, ma'am. I'm sure he'd like that. Thing is, it's against company policy to give away our employees' personal info."

"Ah, come on, Fletch, he really hurt it bad. It's the least I could do," Sandy pressed.

"Nah, I can't. I'd be breakin' my own rule. I'm sorry, ma'am," Fletch shrugged, placing his weathered and wrinkled palms on the bar top. "Now, if you'd like, you can leave it here with me and I'll be sure to pass it along."

"Will he be in tonight?"

"He took the rest of the week off. It's a sad time for the family, this time o' year," Fletch said. He then shook his head and slapped himself on the forehead. "Dumbass, quit gossipin'! My 'pologies. But again, just leave it with me and I'll pass it along." Fletch swung a wet bar rag over his shoulder and disappeared into the kitchen.

*Shit.*

Sandy sighed, stood up, and was about to leave when fortune reared its lovely head in the form of the beautiful mocha bartender.

"Hey," she said.

"Hi," Sandy replied and scanned her nametag. "Yvette."

Yvette looked back toward the kitchen, then back at Sandy. "You looking for Gal's place?"

"Just his address," Sandy lied. "He hurt his hand, and – "

"Yeah, I heard you. Bastard probably deserved it."

"I take it you two aren't friendly?"

"Oh, we used to be friendly. We used to be *very* friendly. About as friendly as two people can get. He got me the job here," she spat. "As if that was payment for making me get an abortion."

Sandy sat back down. It was clear now that where Fletch had been overly fond of Gal, Yvette possessed the fury of a woman scorned.

"I'm sorry to hear that."

"Yeah. Well, fuck him, and fuck his privacy. You want his address? Here you go."

Yvette withdrew a pen from behind her ear and scribbled something on the back of a receipt, folded it, and slid it over to Sandy.

"Do me a favor, though. Next time you see him, tell him thanks from me. Tell that asshole that I can't have kids now."

It was more information than Sandy cared for, but if Gal was involved in Daphne's disappearance in any way, Yvette was revealing a side to him that only supported her theory. She watched tears glisten in Yvette's cappuccino hues and suddenly, Sandy began to harbor a bitter antipathy towards Gallagher.

"Scumbag," Yvette whispered, dabbing at her moistened eyes. "All the Finches are scumbags."

"Tell me, Yvette, what did Fletch mean when he mentioned a *dark time in The Loop*?" Sandy asked.

Yvette leaned against the bar on her slender forearms.

"Well," she said. "It all began with the mom, the dad, and a steel pipe."

***

"Why did we have to bury her here?" Gallagher croaked.

"Where else would we have buried her?" Scarlet replied.

"It's an ugly cemetery."

"You say that every year."

The grounds of Mt. Eugene Cemetery were never green. During the winter months, the ground was covered in snow so high that it completely buried Annie Finch's tombstone. When the snow melted in spring, even the occasional California rain couldn't encourage grass and flowers to push through the rocky soil. The cemetery was situated just south of Mammoth-Yosemite Airport, and funeral-goers were forced to mourn their loved ones over the dissonant roar of expensive private jets flying overhead.

Gal and Scarlet's feet shuffled on the brown, arid dirt as they stood awkwardly over their mother's marble slab.

"Well, the mountains are pretty," Scarlet offered, ever the ray of hope in an otherwise gloomy world. "The rain's made *them* green, at least. It looks like the drought is finally letting up."

"Why'd she have to die in May? It's so hot in May," Gal grumbled, squashing a stinkbug when it scuttled too close to Annie's burial plot.

"It's not like she had a choice, Gal."

Scarlet pulled him close, wrapped her arms around his neck, and buried her face into his chest. He failed to return the sentiment.

"I should've been there," he muttered into her shoulder. Gal's throat tightened as melancholy memories flooded his thoughts. His vision became wet and blurry until he closed his eyes and let a tear roll down his cheek.

"Gal, don't. Not again."

"I shouldn't have left you two alone with him."

"It's not your fault."

"It could've been you, Scar," he cried into her shoulder. His bandaged hand found the back of her head, holding her close. His only sister. His only friend. He listened to her quiet sobs before she pulled away and lifted her hipster glasses to wipe the tears from her eyes.

"You don't know how often I've thought of that," she said, resurrecting that all-too-familiar strength she could pull out of a hat. "But thankfully it wasn't me, Gal, and we *can't* think like that. Do you want to talk about it?"

"Not really," he said. He hated himself for crying.

"Are you sure? It might help."

"I just — I don't know. I was so pissed off. Pissed off at both of them. Him for the things he'd say. Her for not standing up to him. If I would've just stayed – "

"Stop it. You can't do that to yourself."

"Jimmy and Brad were gone, Scar. I was the only one who could've done something."

She shook her head. "No. You couldn't have. You were young, Gal, and dad — dad was a big guy back then. He put Uncle Rich in the hospital with one punch, remember? He could've killed you if you tried to get in the way. And I'm so, so glad you didn't, Gal, because life would just really suck without you."

Gal finally offered a sad smile.

"Shut up," he chuckled.

"You shut up," she giggled and slugged his shoulder. "Come on."

Scarlet took Gal's arm and led him away from their mother's grave. An hour vigil had proven long enough.

"What do you remember?" he asked.

She sighed and remained silent.

"Scar. Please. You never talk about it."

"I was sleeping, Gal. I don't remember a lot. Michael Branson broke up with me over a text, so I went to bed early and cried myself to sleep. I remember a lot of shouting. I thought I was dreaming. I heard mom scream, and then I woke up. And then it was quiet."

"That's all you remember?"

"I was scared, obviously, so I didn't leave my room for a while. When I finally did, I just poked my head out, and – "

She stopped and stared at the mountains. The jagged, ice-capped spine of the Sierras basked beneath a cerulean sky.

"Mom was just lying at the bottom of the stairs," Scarlet continued. "She was on her stomach. The front door was open. Dad was on his knees next to her. His hands were bloody, and he was crying. And then I called the police, and that was it."

Scarlet kept her watery eyes fixated on the peaks. Gal watched her for a moment, silently pondering how petrified she must have been the night their father killed their mother. He pulled her in for one more hug, kissed the top of her head, took her hand, and led her out of the ugly cemetery through the rusted steel gates.

"I love you, Scar," he whispered.

"I love you more."

***

According to Yvette, the late spring and summer months found most of the snow melting away as bohemians and mountaineers began their ascent into Mammoth and Yosemite. On the way, many tourists drove along the breathtaking sixteen-mile bend of The Loop, drinking in the spectacular visage of the four famously glassy lakes. Southern celebrities ventured north to pamper themselves, spending thousands of dollars in a matter of hours at the world-famous Triple Hawk Resort & Spa.

Sandy hadn't driven this far to pamper herself. She had work to do.

Having accepted the folded receipt from the beautiful, jaded bartender the night before, Sandy wasted no time in plugging the address into her phone and saving it to Google Maps. Without a tent and without an RV, she half-considered renting a room somewhere, but hell, the prices around here were highway robbery. She managed to find an inexpensive campsite on the shores of Grant Lake, the final and most massive body of water in The Loop. Considering the wind chill could fall below freezing at night, even in the spring, she kept the heater on high until she felt comfortable enough to fall asleep, then woke up halfway through the night to shut off the engine.

She awoke in the cab of the Silverado as a dewy dawn cracked over the ridge, rubbing her aching neck where she had slept on it wrong. She paid her camp fare through the rest of the week, filled up at the nearest gas station, chugged three cups of coffee, and opened the map on her phone.

There was one thing, however, that she enjoyed about her current situation, and that was the winding drive along The Loop's only road. As she weaved the Silverado around each bend, she surveyed the dramatic landscape.

Stretching over three miles long, Grant Lake reminded Sandy of herself. It was massive and docile until a sudden wind rustled its waters. Then, Grant became choppy and unforgiving. She followed the rocky western shore as rolling hills suddenly gave way to jagged peaks, emerald green with foliage.

Here was Silver Lake, a shy, watery haven hidden by pine and maple and nestled in a bowl of mountains. Sandy raced the early morning sunlight until its rays exploded over Reversed Peak, bathing old aluminum fishing boats in golden hues.

Deeper into The Loop she drove until she almost passed tiny and glittering Gull Lake, on whose northern shore her quarry lived. She found the access road and followed it into a cul-de-sac containing two houses: one for sale and one in the throes of renovation.

She spent all morning watching both houses.

A black jeep sat in the driveway of the renovation. Jeeps were popular with young men, Sandy considered. She assumed it belonged to Gallagher Finch. She parked the Silverado three hundred yards from the renovation, at the entrance to the cul-de-sac. She donned her sunglasses, pulled down the vanity shades, and then, she waited.

And waited.

And waited.

At half past eleven, she noticed a dark-haired young man emerge from the renovation, adorned in black clothes and sporting a gloomy grimace.

*There you are.*

Sandy rolled up the tinted windows of the Silverado and forced her bulk lower into the front seat, albeit with some difficulty. She watched Gal climb into the jeep and pull out of the driveway. She hunkered lower, listening as the jeep slowed down beside the Silverado. She held her breath, knowing that if she looked up, he would see her.

After what seemed like an eternity, the jeep rolled past and continued on down the road.

Sandy counted to thirty, and then sat up. She reached into the glove compartment and withdrew her nine-millimeter Glock. She gripped the cold black steel, opened the door, stepped onto the pavement, and stared at the old house.

*Please be here, Daphne.*

# ELEVEN

# Mauve

～

An army of Jeffrey pines stood sentinel around the disheveled driveway.

More than once, Sandy peered into their emerald canopies, feeling as though she were being watched. Cracks in the concrete stretched like veins along the length of the driveway. Oil splotches and stamped-out cigarette burns tarnished the ground like liver spots.

She let her hardened gaze drift to the old house.

A set of stone steps, one of which had shaken loose of its concrete cradle after decades of weathering the elements, led up to a small wooden porch. The front door was massive and built of heavy oak, the exterior possessing the gnarled bark and growth rings of its host tree. A large brass knob sat in the center of the door and was shaped like an eye, as though the house itself was staring right back at her.

The exterior walls built around the bottom floor and garage were a stonemason's pride and joy, a mosaic of old boulders shaded with moss and red lichen. The top floor, however, was constructed of stacked logs, giving the indication of being added on long after the initial rocky foundation had been hoveled. Thick, silvery cocoons of spiderweb swayed between cracks in the logs, giving the appearance of an old man's unkempt whiskers.

The structure was decrepit indeed.

Stretching along the crown of the house was a poorly constructed widow's watch, which sagged in favor of the east. A couple of rope harnesses hung over the wooden railing and for a moment, Sandy cursed to herself. Had the harnesses been lowered ten more feet, she would've had easy access to a door on the top floor.

*I'll have to get creative.*

Sandy eyeballed the property for home security cameras and was relieved to find none. She checked the wooden side gate and found it locked. Stepping back a few paces, she got a running start and jumped, pulling herself up and over the beams before landing quiet as a cat in the side yard.

Six trash barrels were filled with rolled-up mauve carpeting that, upon closer inspection, was stained and moldy with age. She found a door she assumed led into the garage and jiggled the handle. It was locked, but the door thumped loosely against the jamb.

*No deadbolt.*

Sandy kicked the door open. Her eyes adjusted to the darkness within and found nothing but a few oil stains, a workbench, and empty rafters.

"Daphne," she whispered.

Silence.

She abandoned the garage and made her way into the backyard, eyes widening at the expanse of property that suddenly exploded in all directions. Dry, knee-high brown grass and towering Jeffrey pines spread nearly ten acres. As she scanned the vast expanse of the property, her mind settled upon a horrific truth.

*She could be buried anywhere.*

Intent on keeping hope alive, Sandy shook her head and abandoned the thought. She told herself that Daphne was still alive and that, if her investigative instinct once again proved correct, Daphne was here.

*She has to be.*

Squinting her eyes, her gaze wandered beyond the yard and down a sloping knoll until finally, she saw it. Had it not been for a sudden glint of sunlight against its metal frame, she might've missed it entirely.

Tucked invisibly amongst the trees stood a small aluminum shed.

Without thinking, Sandy sprinted across the yard, down the dry grassy knoll, and darted through the trees. She hadn't seen or heard from her niece in six months and now, finally, here she was. A rusty padlock was fastened to the door of the shed. Her nine-millimeter could've easily blasted a hole clean through the lock, but she thought better of firing off any shots. Instead, she slammed the butt of her gun against the lock. After the eighth attempt, the corroded shackle broke. She held her breath and wrenched open the shed door.

"Daphne!"

Her heart sank.

All she found were an assortment of cracked barrels half-filled with old sod, two lawnmowers, a weed whacker, a leaf blower, and a coil of rubber hose hanging from the rafters.

Sandy rubbed her eyes, sighed, and then punched a softball-sized dent into the aluminum paneling. She took a few moments and forced her breathing to slow. She opened new eyes, eyes belonging to a former field deputy and not to a worrisome aunt.

She noticed cobwebs hanging throughout the shed. A layer of dust an inch thick coated the machines and carpeted the floor. She noticed that the dust was much thinner in the farthest corner of the shed, behind the lawnmowers, as though something had disrupted the even dusting. Her gaze followed a thin path etched across the dusty floor, as though…

*As though something had been dragged out.*

Sandy snapped a few pictures on her phone and then abandoned the shed. Instincts led her back through the trees, up the yard, and onto the back porch. Fortune seemed to be in her favor, as the kitchen window had been carelessly left ajar. She carefully removed the screen and pushed the window wide, forcing it back on its hinges as she squeezed her bulk through the frame and onto new marble countertops.

A fresh, glossy lacquer gleamed on a newly-stained bar top, and Sandy's nostrils stung with the sharp aroma of nitrocellulose fumes. An attractive pantry door inlaid with frosted glass depicted a large, intricate **F**, one she could only assume signified the Finch name. Brand new black appliances gleamed in their respective corners. She climbed off the countertop and set her feet on tortuously laid mosaic tile.

She had to hand it to Gal…

*The kid has great taste.*

A quick exploration of the first floor led Sandy through a small but cozy living room. An old-fashioned fireplace built entirely of river stone, possessing a hearth larger than any she'd ever seen, dominated the room. She inspected the hearth for bone fragments among the ashes, but found nothing.

Her big feet tripped clumsily over a coat rack as she peeked behind the couches for clues. A handcrafted coffee table played host to a crumpled and greasy takeout bag, several beer cans, and a red and black glass pipe that reeked of pot.

Downstairs were two bedrooms connected by a Jack-and-Jill bathroom, one of which was entirely empty. The other contained nothing but a blow-up mattress and messy sheets.

*Does Gal have a visitor?*

Wooden slats of the floorboards were exposed and rotting in areas, while more bundles of the old mauve carpeting lay heaped in the entryway. The oak front door appeared even more grand from the inside. As Sandy looked closely, she made out four letters carved into the wood: **J**, **B**, **S**, and **G**.

She stared at the **G**. The memory of Yvette crying at her inability to conceive had been etched into the front of Sandy's skull and now, it begged for revenge. She retrieved a steak knife from the kitchen and, with a scowl, carved an **X** over the **G**.

Sandy opened the hall closet at the bottom of the stairs. She shoved aside coats and jackets and was about to close the door when she saw them…

Stuffed into the back corner of the closet were a pair of scarlet high heels. They were clean and appeared brand new, small enough for Daphne to fit into. Judging by the immense height of the spiked stilettos, Sandy could only imagine the type of woman brave, stupid, or slutty enough to wear them. And while the loving aunt in her struggled to cope with the idea of her niece's covert erotic persuasions, the ex-deputy in her deduced that they must have indeed belonged to a prostitute.

She sighed and snapped a picture.

Sandy glanced up the flight of mauve stairs. Apparently, Gal had only just finished ripping up the downstairs carpeting. She walked up. The second-to-last step gave an almighty creak, a noise that put her on edge. She'd already been searching for forty-five minutes. How much longer did she have?

The top of the stairs met a perpendicular hallway that stretched to a bedroom on either side. She decided on the left room first.

It was small, possessed a door that led out onto the widow's watch, and was devoid of any furniture. What she did find, however, intrigued her enough to merit further investigation.

Two portraits were mounted to adjoining walls.

The first portrait showed six people in matching flannel. The father was a broad-shouldered and stern looking man, his smile void and vacant. Beside him stood a gentle-looking woman with raven hair and sad yet brilliant green eyes, features matching those of the scrawny raven-haired toddler she held tightly in her arms.

*Gallagher,* Sandy assumed.

Two older boys, one with reddish-brown curls and the other with flaxen hair and a piercing gaze, sat cross-legged at their father's ankles. The young daughter with coke-bottle glasses clutched her father's forearm, eyes wide as she attempted to shy away from the camera. An unhappy family, to be certain.

*But a family nonetheless.*

Sandy turned her attention to the larger portrait, hung below a singular round window that cast radiant sunlight across its surface. Bright green eyes burning with life, the mother beamed with the most exquisite smile Sandy had ever seen. Cake frosting was smeared across her right cheek and nose, a messy mixing bowl propped under one arm while the other sat draped over Gallagher's slender shoulders. Nine or ten years old, the young Gal had his lips pressed to his mother's cheek, black hair streaked with white flour. As filthy as they were, never had Sandy seen such a display of love between a mother and son.

For the most fleeting of moments, Sandy imagined Gallagher's unrelenting love for his mother, imagined his unending devotion to being the source of her smile. And then she imagined the heart-shattering pain and infinite anger he must've felt after her death.

Her *murder*, Yvette had mentioned.

Sandy left the room.

She peeked her head into the small bathroom at the other end of the hall and found nothing suspicious, just a damp towel hung over the shower and beard trimmings in the sink. She considered perusing the magazine rack next to the toilet, but brown and yellow stains in and around the toilet bowl discouraged any further scrutiny.

The master bedroom belonged to Gallagher, evident by the messy king-sized bed and dirty laundry strewn across the floor. Sandy tore back the sheets, checked the closet, rifled through the dresser drawers, and found nothing save for a few bags of weed stashed away in a shoebox under his bed.

She groaned.

Wherever Daphne was, it was suddenly very clear that she was nowhere in this house. As Sandy tucked the shoebox back under the bed, something suddenly caught her eye…

A long strand of black hair lay tucked in the corner under his bed. She picked it up and stretched it out. It was far too long to belong to Gal. The thickness of the strand reminded Sandy of Daphne's lush raven hair and as she pictured her niece, she couldn't help considering how similar Daphne looked in comparison to Gal's mother.

Sandy tucked the strand into her pocket and emerged from under the bed, content that her search was over. She was about to leave when she noticed Gallagher's laptop tucked carefully under his pillow.

*Men keep photos of female conquests on their laptops,* she considered. *Why not Gal?*

She opened it up and was met with a screen requesting a password. Of the little she knew of Gal, Sandy typed anything and everything she could think of:

F-I-N-C-H- Enter. *Invalid Password.*

S-I-E-R-R-A- Enter. *Invalid Password.*

J-U-N-E-L-A-K-E- Enter. *Invalid Password.*

W-H-I-S-K-E-Y- Enter. *Invalid Password.*

S-C-O-T-C-H- Enter. *Invalid Password.*

And then, suddenly, a revelation. She quickly swiped through the pictures on her phone until finally, she found what she was looking for: a bottle of aged scotch with brass antlers as a cork topper. And on the label:

F-U-I-L-N-A-T-A-L-H-A-I-N-N- Enter.

The screen lit up.

A Word document had been left open. Dozens of pages containing tens of thousands of words of prose. The name of the document read:

## MURDER MYSTERY NOVEL, TITLE TBD.docx

Intrigued, she began to read:

*Tom DeLevine bolted up in bed, soaked in ice cold sweat. Never in his life had a nightmare roused him from the catalepsy of his slumber. His chest rose and fell in agony as he buried his face into his palms.*

*He screamed, knowing nobody could hear him. It was the beauty of living this deep in the hills. It was the complacency of knowing that nobody else knew his secret. But now, it was the silent torment of a dead soul pressing on the backs of his eyeballs, scratching at his eardrums through the deafening quiet.*

*She was dead, and he was partly to blame...*

The slam of a car door made Sandy's heart stop.

She looked up and out the window, horrified to find a Cadillac de Ville parked in the driveway. A stout man with curly, reddish-brown hair climbed out the passenger side and knocked on the hood.

"Wait here," she heard him yell.

*Time's up.*

As quickly as she could, Sandy launched Chrome and opened her email account. She dropped the Word file into a new email draft and waited for it to upload, noticing the battery life was only at 7%.

"Come on, come on," she muttered.

Downstairs, she heard the front door whine on its hinges.

"Hello?" came a gravelly voice.

She watched the small bar slowly filling in as the document uploaded.

"Gal, you home?" Footsteps on carpet-free wooden floorboards echoed like dynamite in her ears. "Gal!"

The bar continued to fill, barely passing the halfway mark as...

*Creeeak!*

He was coming upstairs.

Keeping the laptop propped open, Sandy tiptoed across the bedroom and stuffed her massive frame into the tiny closet. She silently pulled the sliding door closed just as the bedroom door squeaked on its axis.

"Gal?"

Through a small crack in the closet door, Sandy watched as a short, apelike man thumped into the bedroom. She held her breath, watching as he looked around. She recognized his pudgy face as one of Gal's brothers from the family portrait, albeit twenty years older. Realizing Gal's absence, the older brother smirked, got down on his knees, and pulled the shoebox out from under the bed. He took his time sniffing through each bag of weed and stole a nugget from each before tucking the shoebox under the bed.

And then, to Sandy's horror, he spun around and looked at the closet door.

"Gal?" he muttered.

Sandy gripped her nine-millimeter. She lifted the barrel and aimed through the tiny crack in the door as the older brother slowly approached.

His hand reached for the sliding door.

Her fingertip grazed the trigger, and…

Two loud honks blared from outside.

"I'm comin', you impatient fuck!"

The brother's hand dropped, he turned, and then he left. Sandy waited until his footsteps disappeared before breathing out. She eased out of the closet and moved to the window, watching the older brother sell off Gal's weed to the driver.

Sandy checked the laptop and was livid to find that the battery had died.

With everything she'd learned, she bolted across the hallway to the portrait room, onto the widow's watch, and carefully scaled the rope harness onto the dead grass below.

*** 

The market was absolute shit.

In all her life, Ruby never had to sell a home on her own. Part of the reason was due to her constant shifts in scenery, from Kansas to the Gulf, nightclubs in Vegas and Reno, and finally to the last forty years in the Sierras. Her only real home had ever been this one. It was the home that Gordon, God rest his soul, had built in this tiny little cul-de-sac. It was the home that had first rescued Ruby from her duty as matron of the Sierra Red Lodges. And when she'd missed her old life so much, it was the home that had served as her new base from which to gather funds left on her doorstep by a devoted business partner.

*Where did I go wrong with him?*

Nearly five months after she placed the house on the market, only two offers had been placed, one by a Hollywood actress that Ruby had never heard of, and another from a San Diego County fireman looking for a winter getaway. Both offers, however, bowed out when the winter cold had become too much for the selfish southerners. Becky Hall, the best real estate agent in Mono County (or so her flyers suggested), had proven far too incompetent and now, Ruby had no choice but to meet with prospective buyers herself.

"It really is a beautiful home," the young woman professed, long blonde hair fluttering in the mid-June breeze. She gazed up at the house, hands caressing her grapefruit-sized belly. She was beautiful, but the longer Ruby squinted behind her sunglasses, the more familiar the young woman appeared.

"When are you due?" Ruby asked, hip nearly giving out as Copper yipped and tugged against his leash. "Knock it off, you little rat!"

"That's the question, isn't it?" the dolled-up young woman responded. "I'm not really one for doctors, so I've kind of been doing this on my own. Mid- to late-September, I imagine."

Suspicion nagged at Ruby's senses.

"Pardon me for being forward," Ruby muttered, lazily picking a fresh scab off the back of her spotted, gnarled hand. "I noticed you aren't wearing a ring. Is the father still around?"

"Oh, he's around. Around me? No. But around."

"I'm sorry to hear that."

"Don't be. I'm in the company of a very generous man," the pregnant blonde confessed with a smile, her heavily-shadowed eyes glancing up at the old house before settling firmly on Ruby.

The sudden stare made her nervous.

"And where is this gentleman caller now?" Ruby asked. She reached casually into her coat pocket to grip the small can of pepper spray hidden within. "Surely he should be here with you. If buying a home is as stressful as selling a home, a woman in your condition shouldn't be doing it on her own."

"I imagine you'll meet him soon enough," the young woman prophesied. She took a step forward, and Ruby took a step back.

"You look so familiar," Ruby said, tugging Copper's leash and causing his ugly little eyes to bulge. "What did you say your name was? Becky forgot to mention it to me."

The pregnant young woman smiled.

"My name is Whitney Burges. Ring a bell?"

"Not entirely," Ruby said.

"I go by a few names, actually," the blonde said with a coy grin. "Evelyn to some, Mary Beth to others… most people call me Sapphire."

Ruby pulled the pepper spray out of her coat and pointed it at Whitney.

"How did you find me?" she demanded.

"It wasn't hard. I was able to loosen Sheriff Larson's tongue," Whitney crooned. "Would you really mace a pregnant girl? Especially one of your own?"

"Don't test me, bitch. I've done things far worse to much prettier girls."

"He wants to know how you've been collecting. Who took over for him when you sold him out?"

"Is he paying you? Because I'll double it!" Ruby yelled.

Whitney smirked.

"Like I said, he's a very generous man. He buys me whatever I want. But more than that, he *protects* me. He wants to protect all of us."

"I want you to leave. Now!"

"Old Lady, you haven't protected us in years," Whitney said, her eyes burning. "One of your girls is missing, did you know? She has been for five months. Have you been watching the news? Daphne Castro. She's yours and you never came forward. Never once contacted any of the Lodge Directors. She's my friend, and you – "

"Get off my property!" Ruby yelled.

Whitney nodded and then turned towards her small car.

"He's watching you."

And with that, the girl known as Sapphire sped off.

***

Gallagher Finch breathed in slow and deep.

Fierce, flowery fumes flooded his lungs, and then he cleared the pungent smoke out of Remy. All the hard work of the past eight months had left newfound callouses on his palms and fingertips. As he gazed down at them, he couldn't help but smile.

Between the house and the book, he had never worked so hard in his life, and, well...

*It feels good.*

His mind began to buzz with the effects of a new strain of indica he'd purchased, a strain he made sure to never smoke around Jimmy, knowing his eldest brother would steal it the moment Gal turned a blind eye.

His shoulders were sore. A sharp pain eased down the left side of his neck. His thighs felt weak after months of carrying wood, stone, and heavy rolls of carpet up and down the stairs. The discomfort in his muscles was the fruit of his labor.

*It feels good.*

He finally felt it, if only just a ping of it: the ruggedness he'd so longed for. He finally felt like a man, and...

*It feels good.*

Gal opened his eyes and set to work ripping up the remaining mauve carpeting on the second floor. He rolled it up and tossed it over the bannister before turning his attention to the stairs. It was the last little bit before he could finally put in new wood flooring. He cut a seam into the carpet, dug his fingertips underneath, and ripped it up. Stair by stair, he made his way down, exposing the wooden steps underneath until finally, he heard that familiar sound...

*Creeeak.*

After all that had happened in his life, after all the people he'd loved and lost, after the unfair and bloody situation he'd been forced to deal with five months earlier, the creaky stair had always been there. It taunted him and teased his memories.

He was determined to never again hear that creaky stair.

Gal ripped up the mauve carpeting and found the source of the creak. Where the rest of the steps were constructed of solid birch, the second-to-last step was a cheap and moldy slab of fiberboard.

"What the hell?"

He grabbed a hammer and wedged the claw beneath the fiberboard. With a push, he managed to lift off the top, and then tossed it aside.

Inside of the step sat a manila folder. Curious, Gal removed the folder and opened it. A single sheet of eggshell cardstock was emblazoned with a golden notary seal. He read the curvy, bold lettering and suddenly, his heart stopped.

## CERTIFICATE OF ADOPTION

This is to Certify that
GALLAGHER NATHAN FINCH
has been formally adopted into the Family
and is Entitled to all the Rights and Privileges herein
ON THIS 11ᵗʰ DAY OF NOVEMBER, 1990

Underneath were three scrawled signatures: his father's, his mother's, and one he assumed belonged to the head of the adoption agency.

Stunned, Gallagher read and re-read the certificate, again and again until he had memorized it word for word.

His brain was numb.

His fingers trembled around the edges of the certificate.

He heard the rush of pulsing blood behind his eardrums.

He pressed his back to the wall and sank onto the bottom mauve step, eyes drifting to the large oak front door. And there, freshly tainting the wood, was a large **X** carved over his cursive **G**.

# TWELVE

# Mud

~

"Maddy, what happened to your face?"

"Tucker James, that is *enough*!" his mother scolded from the front seat.

"I was just – "

"She didn't look like that yesterday, mom."

"And I don't want to hear *anything* out of you, Timothy! You're in trouble as it is."

"She looks like a piece of road kill," Tucker muttered under his breath. Timothy snorted apple juice from his nose in an attempt to stifle his laughter.

"Or a mushy tomato," Timothy whispered to his brother. The twins broke out into unanimous laughter.

Madison sobbed from the back seat.

"Darren, do you mind?"

"Listen to your mother, boys," Darren Fullerton yawned. One hand gripped the steering wheel while the other balanced a steaming cup of coffee.

"That's it? That's all you have to say?" Tara turned the scolding on her husband. "Your daughter is crying."

"What do you want me to say? They're eight-year-old boys. Besides, Maddy, it doesn't even look that bad," Darren said assuredly, eyes scanning the rear view to give his daughter a wink. As she looked up, he couldn't help but wince at the sight of her, spilling a bit of coffee onto his leg. "Ouch. Dammit..."

"Why didn't you grab a lid?"

"We've been over this, Tara. There's no point. You put the lid on, and it keeps the coffee scalding hot for too damn long. I hate waiting for it to cool down."

"You hate waiting for a lot of things," Tara griped, peering out of the rain-streaked window. A flash of lightning lit up the dull gray sky. Mud splattered the back window as the car sped over a pothole.

"Do you even know where you're going?" she asked.

"Don't start," he growled. "I've been to Yosemite a thousand times. A little rain never hurt anybody."

"You're sharing a bed with her," Tucker muttered to Timothy.

"Gross, no! One of 'em might pop on me!" Timothy whined. "You sleep with her!"

"Shut up!" Madison screamed from the back seat. "Both of you just *shut up!*"

"KNOCK IT OFF, OR I'LL BEAT ALL YOUR ASSES!" Darren roared.

In an instant, all three children went silent, eyes wide as they stared, perplexed, at their father. None of them had ever heard him curse. They'd never even heard him yell.

Tara stared at her husband, brows furled and mouth agape.

"What was that?"

"They're quiet, aren't they?"

"That is *not* how we parent our – "

"Tara, not another word," he warned, turning to her as another flash of lightning lit up his electric blue eyes. They were the first things she'd ever noticed about him twelve years ago. She'd found them stunning.

But now, they scared her.

Madison Fullerton's eyes matched her father's, piercing silvery-blue orbs that were puffy and bloodshot after her unexpected morning.

Womanhood had hit her like a freight train.

Three days prior had been the last day of seventh grade before summer break. Madison and her two friends ate lunch at the losers' table, forced into submission by the popular girls who contentiously mocked their below-par hairstyles and thrifty clothes. So, it came as a complete and utter shock when Jake Fallon, the cutest guy in school (and an eighth grader, no less), shot her a smile from across the cafeteria. At first, she was sure she must have been mistaken.

*Why would Jake Fallon smile at me?*

But then, she watched in astonishment as he walked over. "Maddy, right?" he'd asked. All she could do was nod. "I like your eyes. They're big. Come on. Come sit with me." She looked around nervously at her friends, who appeared just as surprised, but who nodded in encouragement. Maddy grabbed her sack lunch with a smile, stood up, and then she stopped.

Her inner thighs felt warm and wet.

"Oh my god, she's bleeding!" Cassie Murchison squealed. The girls at the popular table pointed and laughed as the entire lunch hall exploded into cacophonous jeers of disgust. Madison looked down at her red-stained shorts and then at Jake, who slowly backed away in revulsion.

"Never mind," he said. *Never mind.* No two words had ever hurt so much. She didn't remember much after that, only that she burst into tears and spent the rest of the afternoon locked in the bathroom.

Her mother picked her up earlier than usual with ice cream and the old worn-out homily: *You're a woman now!* But if being a woman meant blood in weird places, stomachaches, body odor, and showing her face in school, she wanted no part of it.

This morning had proven even worse.

Madison fell asleep to a clear and starlit Santa Barbara sky, the ocean's steady ebb and flow lulling her to sleep. She dreamt of pine trees and warm lakes. She dreamt of colossal Half Dome, and how her father promised that this year, finally, he would take her to climb it. She dreamt she was flying over Yosemite Valley, toes grazing the clouds and fingertips brushing the coarse granite face of mighty El Capitan.

Anticipation of the first day of summer break buzzed in her head when she awoke. She dressed quickly and pulled on her brand new hiking boots, eager to scuff them on dusty Sierra hiking trails. She went to the bathroom, squeezed a little Colgate on her toothbrush, looked in the mirror…

…and screamed.

Overnight, her face had flared up with white-capped red bumps that spread across her forehead, greasy cysts throbbing painfully on her chin and cheeks. She locked herself in the bathroom once again, and only after hearing the soothing words of her mother did she emerge, teenage dreams of summer suddenly shattered.

Wiping her eyes, Madison stared out the muddy back window of the SUV.

"Psst…" Tucker whispered over the middle seat. "Maddy…" She ignored him. "Maddy…"

"What?" she hissed.

"Who's Jake?"

"What did you say?"

Tucker nodded at Timothy, who chuckled and lifted a small brown journal.

Madison's eyes widened in horror. She lunged and swiped for her journal. "Give me that, you little monsters!"

"What is going on back there?!" Tara yelled.

"They stole my journal!"

"Boys!"

"Mom, it's juicy!" Tucker laughed, pushing Timothy out of the way of Madison's swinging arms.

"Careful, don't touch her face!" Timothy laughed.

"Give it back!" Madison screamed.

"ENOUGH!" Darren yelled.

Out of the fog, a deer bounded onto the highway.

"Darren!" Tara screamed. "Look out!"

The deafening impact of shattered glass and twisted steel rang in Madison's eardrums. The SUV slammed head-on into the deer's ribcage. Blood and hair splattered the windshield as the airbags deployed in unison. The twins hit their faces against the backs of the front seats. Stars twinkled behind Maddy's eyelids, ears ringing, nose burning with the smell of oil and panic.

And then, silence.

"Is — is everyone okay?" she heard her father grunt.

"Boys? Maddy?" Tara whimpered. "My babies — "

"I'm okay," Timothy grumbled. "Tuck, your nose is bleeding."

"Cool," Tucker chuckled.

"Maddy?" Darren called back at her. "Madison!"

For a moment, Maddy considered not answering at all. They didn't care about her. How could they? Perhaps it would've been better if she remained unresponsive. But after a couple of seconds, she muttered through shaky vocal cords, "I'm okay."

"Oh, thank God," her mother groaned. "Darren, where are you going?"

"I have to get that thing off the road. Come on. Everyone out."

"But Dad – "

"No buts, boys."

"Come on, kids," Tara beckoned. She climbed out of the SUV and opened the door to help the twins out, wiping the blood off Tucker's nose and upper lip. "It's not broken, Tuck. Just pinch it there to stop the bleeding. Out, Maddy. The rain's stopped."

Madison rubbed her head and climbed out of the smoking vehicle. She slipped in the mud as the family moved to watch Darren heaving a dead, bloodied deer carcass to the side of the road. He pushed it over

Highway 395's sloping shoulder and together, they watched it roll into the mud.

"Oh my god. Poor thing," Tara whispered.

The front of the SUV was caved in. Smoke spiraled skyward from under the hood. Darren tried starting the car, but they were met with the telltale *click-click-click* of a dead engine.

"Shit," he groaned.

"Darren, language."

Darren pulled out his cell phone, punched in a few numbers, and held it to his ear.

"Yes, hello? Hi, my name is Darren Fullerton. My family and I just hit a deer and we need a tow – yes, of course – yes, uh huh – yeah, we are members. My card's in the car somewhere. We're on northbound Highway 395, uh – " He looked around and noticed the fog clinging to a massive, circular lake. " — just south of Mono Lake."

Madison walked to the edge of the shoulder. She peered down at the mangled and lifeless stag. Tears welled up in her eyes as, for the first time in her life, she realized just how fragile and unfair life could be. Then, she heard two pairs of feet approach behind her.

"Way to go, Maddy," Tucker groused under his breath.

"Yeah," Timothy chimed in.

"What? How is this my fault?" she retorted, turning fierce eyes on her young brothers.

"You pissed off dad."

"You made him hit that deer."

"You little assholes stole my journal!" she screamed.

"Madison Lee Fullerton!" her mother yelled from the front of the car. "What did you just say? You do *not* use that word, young lady, do you understand me?"

"Mom, they stole it! They read it!"

"It's not all about you, Madison! It's just a stupid diary!" her father shouted.

And that was it. Fire and anger blistered in Madison's veins. Her eyes burned with tears. Her head ached with loathing for her brothers, her mother, and her father. Without restraint, she bolted down the muddy slope past the bleeding deer, sprinting with all she had through the weeds and the shrubbery, new boots squelching ankle-deep in the mud.

"Madison, get back here!" she heard her mother scream.

Maddy sobbed as she ran, not knowing where she was running to, only that she wanted out. She wanted nothing more to do with her family, with her school, with her womanhood...

*...with Jake Fallon.*

Madison looked back, seeing her father and brothers running after her while her mother hollered from the highway.

She looked forward and suddenly, her feet felt nothing but air.

Madison tumbled over the side of a ravine. She hit the mud and rolled down the embankment of a large wash. A tumult of opaque rainwater roared through the ravine. Just as she was about to be washed away, she hit something and stopped.

Pulling her face out of the mud, Madison wiped her eyes and opened them. She lay atop a muddy blue tarp. She scrambled to her knees, her boot catching one end of the tarp and lifting it. Madison's blood ran cold.

A pair of lifeless white eyes stared back at her. A young woman's naked body lay tangled in the tarp, limbs twisted, throat sliced from ear to ear.

She screamed in horror.

Never again would Maddy Fullerton be happy to see the first day of summer.

*** 

The large oak front door swung open.

Rain dripping from his reddish-brown ringlets, Jimmy stumbled into the house, stamping his muddy feet before kicking off his rain boots. His head swam with an overindulgence of gin and marijuana, extremities still tingling from the talents of the call girl he'd purchased for the afternoon.

Sure, the motel had been dingy and the cost a little high, but Violet had made him feel like more of a man than he'd felt in years.

*Violent Violet*, he mused.

He thought of her tattooed legs, the strength of her thighs wrapped tightly around his beer belly, so strong in fact that she would have no trouble cutting off his oxygen. He asked how she'd gotten so strong. "Kick boxing," had been her answer. "In my business, girls have to be pretty, but we also need to be able to hold our own, sugar."

Jimmy shrugged off the soaking wet jacket he'd blindly borrowed from the downstairs closet. He considered drying it out on the back patio, but his drunken brain offered another, more vengeful solution.

*It's Gal's jacket, and he's been a jerk lately. Let it get moldy.*

Jimmy pulled open the downstairs closet door, balled up the soaking wet flannel, and pushed aside the multitude of coats and jackets.

*Hide it in the corner. Let it stink up the place.*

He stuffed the soggy jacket beside a pair of scarlet high heels tucked into the back corner. He considered the sanguine stilettos and scratched his stubbly chin.

*Now whose are these?*

Surely not Scarlet's. His younger sister was a plain Jane. Maybe they had belonged to their mother. Gal definitely had a weird obsession with her, Jimmy considered with a scowl.

*He was always her favorite.*

But these shoes looked far too new, and she'd been dead for years.

*Maybe Gal is a closet tranny.* Jimmy burst out laughing as he imagined Gal in women's wear and a wig, swinging a purse and clicking around in stilettos.

*No. His feet are too big.*

And then Jimmy considered the call girls that he, Brad, and Gal had passed around over the years.

*Some girl probably left them so she'd have a reason to come back.*

Jimmy swung the closet closed and then staggered to the kitchen.

He grabbed a beer from the fridge, cracked it open, and guzzled down half, letting out an almighty burp before checking his wallet.

*Damn.*

Violent Violet had taken all of his cash. Jimmy pulled out his phone and sent off a quick text to Aiden:

*Need money.*

In the minute it took to guzzle down the rest of his beer, Aiden responded:

*Got more green?*

Jimmy's brain ventured to the shoebox under Gal's bed. He typed back:

*Always. Swing by tomorrow.*

Raiding the back of the fridge, Jimmy stole Gal's final beer and headed upstairs. He cursed out loud as he twisted his ankle in the crook of the second-to-last step. Gal had yet to replace the wood, but the moody turd hadn't been home in two days.

Something was up with Gal, that much was evident.

Not that Jimmy minded the privacy, however. It finally felt as if he had his own place again and, more often than not, Jimmy considered what life might be like if Gal just gave him the house. *I'm the oldest*, he often told himself, *so it should be mine.* And yet, as it always had been when she was alive, their mother had played favorites one final time. This time, in her will. Jimmy still despised her for leaving him nothing.

Jimmy hobbled up to Gal's room, found him absent once more, then got down on his knees and tugged the shoebox out from under the unmade bed. He pulled off the top.

*What the hell?*

The shoebox was completely empty, save for a small, folded piece of paper. Jimmy unfurled it and found Gal's handwriting:

### *Quit stealing my shit.*

Red in the ears, Jimmy slammed the lid onto the box and slung it at the wall. He stood up, shovel-width hands clenched into white-knuckled fists. His shoulders became tense, adrenaline and habitual anger wearing off the carnal bliss that Violent Violet had inspired. He launched his foot straight into a baseboard, kicking it hard and causing the walls to rattle. His ankle twisted, searing in agony at the impact and sending him to the floor. He cursed and clutched his leg, lying still and fuming until something rather curious caught his eye...

The baseboard had come loose. Jimmy noticed a coppery-brown, flaky substance, as though something had seeped underneath, dried, and now molded with decay. He ripped the baseboard from the wall and found the brownish substance becoming thicker as it neared Gal's bedframe.

In all the fights he'd been in over the years, of all the bones he'd broken, and of all the noses he'd caved in, Jimmy knew the substance well...

*That is a hell of a lot of blood.*

\*\*\*

"Well, well, well. You finally decided to visit *me* at work. Hey – hey! Wake up!"

A sudden smack to the back of Gallagher's head caused his eyelids to flutter. His brain throbbed, vision spinning as he opened his eyes.

*This can't be happening.*

"Gal," came a familiar voice.

His mouth was bone-dry, tongue like sandpaper against the roof of his mouth. He raised his head, squinting through bloodshot eyes. Amber stood behind a long, polished bar top.

"How many drinks have you had?" she asked.

Dazed and drowsy, Gal looked around. All he saw were tigers. A vicious watercolor painting of the Bengal beast devouring an antelope. Black and orange statues with sharp claws and gaping maws. Tigers everywhere, lining the interior of a small restaurant.

"What?" he grumbled, rubbing his aching head. "Where – "

"Gal, you're at the Tiger Bar. Here, drink this."

He felt her push a cold glass into his palm. *Another whiskey coke*, he thought he heard her say. All too willing to continue drinking himself to death, Gal put the glass to his parched lips and guzzled down whatever was in it.

Instantly, he regretted it.

"What the hell is that?" he slurred, spitting it out on the bar top.

"It's water," Amber answered angrily. She grabbed a rag, wiped it up, and refilled his glass. "Drink it."

"Give me another whiskey coke."

"You've had enough, Gal."

"Is there a problem, Amber?" the manager asked from the other end of the bar.

"Nothing I can't handle, Joe. Thanks," she replied. She whipped her beautiful sapphire eyes back onto Gal and forced the water glass into his trembling hands. "You're making people stare, Gal," she whispered under her breath.

Gal looked around at the mid-afternoon lunch rush crammed within the small restaurant. Dozens of deplorably disapproving gazes were set upon him.

"Screw them," he yelled.

Amber slapped the wet rag onto the bar top. She emerged from behind the bar, grabbed Gal's arm, and tugged him roughly off his bar stool with a strength he never knew she possessed.

"Come on," she snarled into his ear. Gal knocked over two more stools as she led him away from the bar and to a back corner of the restaurant, out of sight of the public.

"What the hell's the matter with you?" she reprimanded. "I'm so close to kicking your ass out into the mud."

The warmth of her breath on his face was like a sweet summer breeze after a ravaging storm. He tried to focus his eyes.

"I'm sorry," he sighed. "I've had a very shitty couple of days."

"What's wrong? What happened?"

"Just… I don't know. Family stuff, I guess." God, his head hurt.

"Maybe I can help," she suggested.

"You can't. I'm sorry, but there's really nothing you can do," he said.

"Oh." She looked away and a painful silence settled between them. When it became too much, Gal leaned in to kiss her.

She pulled away.

"Whoa, whoa. What are you doing? You can't – we can't – "

"We can't what?" he asked. "I thought we – "

"We did," she interrupted him. "But we can't. Not anymore."

"Why not?"

"Because – well, just because, Gal, okay? I'm with Brad. I – that is, I love him and – "

"You don't love him," Gal said. He peeled his eyes off her and focused instead on a tiger sporting a top hat and monocle painted on the door of the men's restroom.

"And how would you know?" Amber retorted.

"Did he propose to you yet?"

"Yes, in fact, he did."

"Well, you're not wearing the ring."

Amber slapped him hard enough to send his face swinging to the side. He rubbed his jaw, stubble thick with drunken neglect.

"Get out," she whispered.

"Amber, I'm sorry. I just – " He touched her waist, but she shoved him.

"Get out," she spoke sternly, glaring at him in disgust. "Now."

*This can't be happening.*

The final dregs of his pride suddenly drained, Gal brushed past Amber and walked back to the bar. He found the check waiting for him, and as he began to rifle through the bills in his wallet, he noticed that the packed interior of the Tiger Bar was eerily silent. He looked around and watched the patrons staring at the bar's only television.

Confused, Gal followed suit. His blood ran cold.

The four o'clock news displayed a high school photograph of a raven-haired young woman. Gal knew her well. For one night, she had haunted his bed sheets. And for five long months, she had haunted his dreams.

"...have confirmed that the body of Daphne Castro has been unearthed by floodwaters near Mono Lake basin. The body was discovered after Madison Fullerton of Santa Barbara County nearly fell into the wash after the family car hit a deer on northbound 395..."

The photograph was replaced by an image of a mother, father, and two twin boys holding a teenage girl close, her eyes wide in horror.

The newscast droned on.

"...the body was found tangled in what appears to be a large blue tarp. The Mono County Sheriff's Department has stated that no leads have yet been made official, but that a singular clue may lead to the search and arrest of the person responsible for Castro's murder..."

The image was replaced with a photograph of the tarp.

And there, in his mother's handwriting, the tarp was labeled:

### FINCH

Gal looked around the restaurant.

The locals were staring at him. A few whispered to each other. A couple of them pointed.

Neglecting to pay his bill, Gal sprinted out into the rain, ankles deep in mud.

*This can't be happening.*

## THIRTEEN

# Green

～

A dull pain thudded within his skull.

Gal opened bloodshot green eyes, and the world began to spin. Bright sunlight blinded him through broken glass. His cheek rested against the firm support of an airbag. The burn of stomach acid seared his esophagus on the way up. He closed his eyes, opened the driver side door, and vomited. Wiping his mouth, he squinted through the brightness.

The front of the jeep was smashed against the trunk of a large Jeffrey pine.

He groaned, sidled out of the driver seat, and nearly slipped in his own sick. The engine was smoking. Judging by the irregular inward tilt of his front tires, he could only assume that the front axle was irreparably bent.

Forcing himself to focus, Gal looked around to gauge his surroundings.

His boots scuffed against an unpaved dirt road. Tall Jeffrey pines surrounded him, sunlight filtering through bright green canopies.

Swaying on jelly legs, he choked back a dry-heave and wobbled up the road to higher ground.

He found the summit of a small hillock and breathed in a fresh blast of cool mountain air. The snow-capped peaks of The Loop towered all around him.

To his right rose a broad cliff face, red rock covered in lichen. It reminded Gal of copper peppered in green oxidation. He knew the cliff face well, having climbed it in his youth alongside his older brothers – the backside of Reversed Peak.

To his left, a dirt road swung down about a quarter mile until the pine trees met soft yellow sand. The wind shifted. He could just make out the faint rumble of a boat engine and the giggling of children splashing in the water.

The beach at June Lake.

In that moment, Gal knew exactly where he was, but couldn't remember why he was there. He bit back the throbbing hangover constricting his brain. He closed his eyes and took in another lungful of sweet, crisp summer air.

The last thing he remembered was a mouthful of mud. He had been running and he had slipped. He had been running... *from what?* He remembered the taste of whiskey and coke, remembered the taste of ice water, remembered the taste of Amber's lips.

*The Tiger Bar.*

He remembered Amber's voice, not sweet and soft, but firm and cruel. *Get out*, he remembered her yelling. He remembered the swing of her hand. Gal touched his cheek and felt the slight sting of a raised welt.

*She hit me.*

He remembered the feel of her body as he brushed past. He remembered a very large bar tab, remembered rifling through his wallet. And then he remembered...

*The eyes.*

All the eyes staring at him. Reprimanding him. Accusing him. He remembered the television. He remembered the four o'clock news. He remembered seeing her face, remembered that a family from out of town had found her, remembered seeing the tarp. Remembered that it was labeled with his last name.

Gal's eyes snapped open.

A fresh wave of nausea rippled through his core like a violent tide constrained by an unstable levy. The levy suddenly cracked, broke, and a tidal wave of panic flooded his entire world.

He remembered the desire to get home as quickly as possible. He remembered slipping, falling, and spitting out mud. He remembered stumbling to the jeep, remembered the fallen pine branches that had blocked the road to Gull Lake, remembered deciding to navigate the dirt roads behind June Lake instead.

And then, he remembered seeing Daphne. He remembered her cold, dead eyes. He remembered the tarp wrapped around her naked, mangled body. He remembered her stepping out in front of the jeep, remembered her raising her hand to stop him. He remembered swerving out of the way, remembered a loud crunch…

And then he remembered darkness.

Gal leaned over and felt his stomach lurch. His insides burned, but he had nothing left to expel. He dry-heaved, and then he forced himself to stand. He had to get home, and fast.

Gal abandoned the smoking jeep and began to run.

Half an hour later, his legs were on fire.

The large oak front door swung open, and Gal stumbled inside. He staggered into the kitchen and guzzled water from the tap. He dipped his head under the faucet and allowed the cold torrent to soak his shaggy hair and the back of his neck. He breathed slow and deep, lungs burning from sprinting along three miles of unpaved hills and dirt roads.

Gal dried his head with a dish towel, left the kitchen, and walked up the uncarpeted stairs. He narrowly avoided the second-to-last step he'd neglected since discovering the unknown truth of his heritage. He felt the urge to puke again but choked it back, knowing his body needed the water he'd just gulped down.

"Jimmy!" he called out hoarsely, receiving no response. "Jim!"

The discovery of Daphne's body, of the tarp she'd been buried in had latched onto Gal's brain like a spidery tumor. All he could think about were the last five months. Five months that he could've used to come up with a plan, an alibi should Daphne's body ever be found. Five months he could've used to contact the police and attempt to explain what had happened on his birthday, what he had woken up to on that ill-fated January morning.

*Five months of could'ves, should'ves, and would'ves.*

Instead, he had fed the ravenous maw of his creativity. He had cast aside any notion of attempting to clear his name in favor of a half-finished novel that had no ending. A half-finished novel that, now that he thought about it, would only incriminate him further.

*Tom DeLevine may not have murdered the girl in the woods, but he* had *found her. He* had *panicked. And then, he* had *buried her. And now, the cops were most certainly on their way.*

*Tom DeLevine needed a plan.*

Gallagher Finch needed a plan.

He gathered up an old backpack and stuffed it with a week's worth of clothes, his laptop, Remy, the final bag of weed he'd hidden from Jimmy, and the stag horn pocketknife.

*The murder weapon.*

He pulled on fresh clothes, rinsed his mouth with Listerine, and scurried back down into the kitchen. He pulled out his phone and dialed Scarlet's number.

"C'mon... pick up!" he yelled at the dial tone. He cursed when he heard the voicemail's telltale beep.

"Scar, they found her. They found Daphne. It's all over the news. I'm so sorry. I should've never tangled you up in all this. You were right. You've always been right. Please, call me as soon as you get this. I love you."

He hung up.

"Turn around."

Gal's blood ran cold. He turned to find Jimmy in the doorway, pointing his phone camera at him. *Filming* him.

"I didn't want to believe it," Jimmy said. "I saw the news, Gal. I swear I didn't want to believe it."

"You don't understand."

Jimmy continued filming.

"I understand that girl was wrapped up in the old tarp. The same tarp that's been in the attic for years, Gal. The same tarp that has our last name on it. All of us. Me, Brad, Scarlet, and you. I found her high heels in the closet. I found her blood under the baseboard in your room."

"Jimmy – "

"The police need to know it was you, and not me, or Brad. And you got Scarlet mixed up in all this? What the hell, man?"

"You have to let me explain, Jim," Gal said, raising his hands.

"I called the sheriff, Gal. The cops are on their way. You can explain it to them."

"Please, just – "

Jimmy stopped filming and lowered his phone.

"Go," he said.

"What?"

"Leave, now."

Police sirens blared from the end of the cul-de-sac. Jimmy turned to see red and blue lights flashing in the driveway, bathing the living room in a flood of color. He turned back to find the back door wide open...

Green Jeffrey pines swayed in the backyard.

Gal was gone.

***

The silence between them was deafening.

Amber stared into the deep green of her steamed broccoli, using her fork to push it around the plate. She felt light-headed, knowing food would help but unable to bring herself to eat anything. She looked up.

Brad held his head in his hands, hunched over a cold steak.

"You have to eat something," she finally said, her voice piercing the stillness.

Amber let her gaze sweep to the eight glass beer bottles beside Brad's plate. The stagnant light from above the kitchen table refracted through the empty green bottles and stained the wood with splashes of emerald.

"Another beer?" she asked with a sigh.

Brad nodded. Without realizing it, she stood up and walked to the fridge, pulling out the final IPA and setting it beside him. She lifted her hand and let it hover over his back, and then she pulled it away. "I'm sorry."

Brad fixed her with a hard, gray stare. He grabbed the fresh beer and roughly twisted off the cap. For a moment, she wondered if he was imagining it to be Gal's neck.

"Are you?" he growled.

"I should've told you sooner."

"Yes, you should've."

"I'm sorry."

"You said that."

Amber pulled her gaze away from Brad's cold, gray eyes and focused instead on the green refractions on the table.

*The same color as Gal's eyes.*

She hated her mind for wandering, but considering the unfolding of the day's events, she found it difficult to think of anyone else.

*I hope he's okay.*

"Have you heard anything?" she asked.

"No."

"Is Jimmy certain what he heard?"

"Why are you so interested?" he snapped.

"Why are you *not?*" she barked back. "He's your little brother."

"And a potential murderer!" He stood and swept his arm across the table, sending bottles and plates smashing against the wall, silverware clattering to the floor.

Amber stepped away. "Brad, you don't honestly think that Gal – "

"I don't know what to think anymore! You saw the news. You heard what Jimmy and the police said. Everything points to him! And then you come home, and you tell me you kissed him?"

"He kissed me," she corrected him.

"You *let* him kiss you! Twice!"

Amber puffed her shoulders and stared him straight in the eye.

"I told you I was sorry. It was a mistake the first time. I pushed him away the second. I told him no, Brad, because I'm with you. I'm with you now, and I want to be with you."

"Oh, right," he scoffed. "Is that why you turned down the ring?"

"It was a shit proposal!" she yelled.

The silence that followed pressed on her ear drums as if the kitchen were submerged beneath the deepest ocean. She stared at him, and he stared at her. And then, she softly pressed her hands to his chest, feeling it rise and fall, searching for a heartbeat she couldn't find.

"I'm sorry," Amber whispered. "Truly and without fail. I am sorry."

Brad's eyes softened.

"I love you. I want to marry you," he said.

"And I haven't said no, Brad."

"I know."

For the first time in a week, he pressed his lips against hers.

The seconds ticked by. After what felt like an eternity, she opened her eyes and glanced around. Brad continued his assault on her mouth. She looked at the wall, admiring the emerald green refractions left by the broken bottles on the floor.

Slowly, Amber realized something…

She didn't feel a thing.

Her feet were lifted from the floor as Brad hoisted her up onto his waist. He grunted into her mouth and chewed on her tongue.

"Ouch," she whimpered as his teeth sunk deep into her bottom lip, suddenly tasting the coppery tang of her own blood. He carried her through the apartment, banging her into walls and windows, digging his crotch against her inner thighs.

"Brad, hang on… wait…" she whimpered in between his brutal

bites and hungry lips.

He ignored her, holding her up with one hand as he reached down to unbutton and unzip his jeans.

"Brad! Stop!"

"What?" he yelled.

"Who is that?" she whispered, peering over his shoulder. He turned.

A massive shadow watched them through the streaked glass panes of the front door. Three loud knocks followed suit.

Brad set Amber down. He grabbed the copper pipe he left beside the front door, unlocked it, and cracked open the door.

"I hope I'm not intruding," came a woman's voice.

"Yes, in fact, you are," Brad snarled.

"I wanted to talk to you about Gallagher," said the woman.

The copper pipe fell from Brad's fingertips and clattered loudly on the tile. He opened the door, and Amber set widened eyes upon the most intimidating woman she had ever seen.

"My name is Sandy."

***

For the first time in a long time, the night sky was clear.

Stars ignited the inky blackness and shimmered like specks of shattered glass. Only when the Milky Way met the sleepy sentinels of the Sierra Mountains did the stars disappear behind the rugged outlines of giants.

He still did not trust the stars, but for the first time since his mother went to join them, Gal admired their iridescent beauty. He picked out the brightest in the sky, a star glinting a soft green beside Orion's right shoulder, and imagined it to be her.

*Help me out, ma.*

Gal breathed in the cool night air and listened as the last generator rumbled through the RV campground, and then shut off. He knew from countless nights camping on the western shore of Silver Lake that RVs were required to shut off their generators at 10 pm.

Gal's shoes crunched on the gravel leading down to Silver Lake's boat dock. The moon cut a bright white streak along the glassy surface of the lake, lighting his way.

He found a small break in the trees that led into the campground nearest the lakeshore. Following the promenade path, he listened to the gentle lapping of the water against the rocky shore, the full view of the lake obscured by tall thickets and nettles. Every ten paces, a break in the foliage exposed small fishing alcoves. Many of the alcoves were empty. A few housed fishing boats chained to trees.

One contained a gem hidden amongst the tall grasses...

A small green kayak.

*Thanks, ma.*

A gentle wake cut through the moonlit surface as Gal slowly and silently dipped the paddle-heads through the water. He guided the stolen kayak across Silver Lake's northern inlet to Rush Creek, disappeared into the shadowy cover of trees along the east bank, and paddled hard. Log cabins along the eastern bank cast light from triangular windows onto the water's mirrored face, which rippled as Gal weaved the kayak through the shadows.

With each stroke of the paddles, Gal allowed the events of the day to drift behind him, into a swirling wake of forgotten panic that slowly smoothed over Silver Lake's mirror face and descended into its murky depths.

He looked up at Carson Peak, hard-packed snow glowing in cracks along the summit. He could just make out the ribbon of Horsetail Falls cascading down from higher lakes nestled among the peaks. The distant roar of the falls soothed him.

For a few precious moments, he imagined that he didn't have a name, that he didn't have a face, that he didn't exist. He was no longer Gallagher Finch.

*I am the Ghost of Silver Lake.*

After a mile's paddling, he found the entrance to the channels. He followed the twists and turns of the snakelike gulley, dipped his head to avoid low-hung branches, and listened to the occasional splash of trout leaping for midnight mosquitos. A doe and her fawn watched with black marble eyes as he glided past and, more than once, he thought he heard the grunts of a black bear rustling through the brambles.

Deeper into the channels he paddled until the moon drifted over the mountainside. He rounded a final bend and found his path blocked by the trunk of a large fallen birch.

*Finally.*

Having found his marker, Gal guided the kayak to a small embankment shrouded in birch trees. He climbed out, dragged the hull onto the bank, and unsheathed the stag horn pocketknife. Eyes and ears on alert, he pressed into the trees of the embankment. He hiked up a steep grade of shale, climbed over a boulder, and found what he had been looking for.

The tent was water logged. It was battered. It was torn.

*But it's still standing.*

Say one thing for Jimmy, say he knew a good hiding place.

*** 

"Beer?"

"Scotch, if you've got it."

"I have beer."

"Beer it is, then."

Brad nodded and walked back inside.

Sandy watched him through the sliding glass door, noticing a pink cell phone on the kitchen table. She nestled into the wooden chair that was far too small for her. She heard the legs creak under her bulk, but she paid no mind. She watched Brad re-emerge onto the deck and accepted the cold frosty he offered her.

"Fresh out of IPA," he grumbled.

She observed him a moment, guessing he was already a few sheets to the wind, a cool breeze wafting through his flaxen hair.

"You look nothing like him," she stated.

"Lucky for me," he replied, cracking open his beer and sucking down the foamy head. "You look nothing like *her*."

Sandy paused mid-sip, and then lowered her beer.

"Did you know Daphne?"

"No," he blurted out. "I meant from her picture on the news."

"Right," Sandy whispered. She wrenched her gaze from the older Finch boy and stared out at the endless expanse of stars stretching beyond the shadowy peaks. "No, thankfully for her, she looked nothing like me. She was my brother's kid. Got her looks from her mom."

"I'm sorry," he whispered, then sucked down another guzzle.

"For?" she growled.

"For... your loss. For my brother."

"Where is he?"

"I told you, I have no idea. I haven't seen him in, let's see, about three weeks now." He gulped down the rest of his beer, burped, and chucked the empty can over the edge of the deck, where it clattered onto the roof of the steel mill below. "Truth is, we're not close. For some reason, he hates my guts and... well..."

"She kissed him," Sandy said. She watched him, watched as he gripped the deck's railing until his knuckles turned white, watched his eyes stare blankly into the night, watched the clench of his jaw as his teeth grinded together.

"He kissed her," he said under his breath.

Brad reached into the pocket of his sweater and pulled out a small silver ring set with an opulent black diamond. Sandy watched, intrigued, wondering if he was considering tossing it over the rail and into the woods below.

"I saw them," Sandy confessed.

He turned and set his gray eyes on her. "What?"

"Sometimes, the old ways die hard. I don't need Sheriff Larson to conduct an investigation I'm fully qualified to conduct myself." She smirked. "I saw them, outside of the Sierra Inn. I watched them. It was cute. I don't swing that way, but it was cute. He ran out into the rain. He kissed her. He pulled away. She flung herself at him and kissed him right back."

"Stop."

Sandy smiled, watching his gray eyes burn green with envy.

"Look, I don't want anything from you. I don't want to stir up any trouble because, frankly, your family's had enough trouble over the years, haven't they?"

He didn't respond.

"I'm sorry about your mother," she continued. "And your father."

"Fuck him."

She stood up and placed a large hand on his shoulder.

"You feel that? That hate? That anger? That's what I started feeling the moment Larson called me and told me that my niece was dead. My little Daphne, torn to shreds and left to rot in a godforsaken hole." Her voice began to shake, but she continued. "All the signs point to your brother. It doesn't help that he ran off. But, I met him. I talked to him. I laughed with him. I don't want to believe that he did this, but I need to find him to make absolutely sure. The police won't listen to him. They'll lock him up so fast."

Sandy lifted Brad's chin and forced him to stare into her eyes.

"I need you to promise me that if he calls – "

"He won't call. He never does. You'd be better off asking my sister."

"Well, they've already taken her in for questioning, so that doesn't do me any good."

"Then I can't help you!" he yelled.

"Please. We've both lost someone we love because of this whole thing," Sandy said, calming her shaky voice. "I'm not asking you to do anything. Just – "

"All right. If he calls, I'll let you know."

"Thank you," she whispered. She set aside her unfinished beer and walked inside. He followed and closed the deck door behind them. "Before I go, I'd like to apologize to Amber. I think I may have frightened her when I barged in. She's a beauty, she really is."

Brad smiled proudly, as though Sandy had just complimented his new shoes.

"One second," he said, and walked off down the hall.

Quick as a flash, Sandy grabbed the pink cell phone from the kitchen table and unlocked it, thanking her lucky stars that no passcode was required.

"Amber!" she heard Brad call down the hall.

Sandy opened Amber's contact list, found Gallagher's name, and sent him a text:

*I'll keep you safe. I miss you.*

When Brad led Amber into the kitchen, Sandy was gone.

FOURTEEN

# Copper

∽

*B*reathe, she told herself. *Just breathe.*

As the summer sun set behind the Sierras, Whitney closed the blinds. The final light of Sunday evening passed through the wooden slats and cast a copper glow on the interior of the small office. One hand ran softly along the wood of the disheveled desk. She looked down at the unorganized pile of paper tumbling over the ancient computer's keyboard...

Electrical bills from last winter.

Past due notices from alcohol vendors.

A notice to seize property.

Tax evasion letters from the IRS.

*He's in over his head.*

Whitney sat down in the old rolling chair behind the desk. The leather padding was eaten away. Loose springs dug into her buttocks. Her hands moved over the bulbous curve of her belly, cradling the only thing that mattered – her ticket to a new life.

*He is not going to like this. Not one bit.*

The baby gently kicked her lower abdomen, and she smiled.

*Just breathe.*

Whitney gathered up all the forms, bills, and letters. She organized them by severity, by price, and by date, and then placed them in a neat stack to one side. She collected all the torn envelopes and disposed of them in the trash.

She picked up a shiny copper letter opener on the desk, used the hem of her skirt to polish the fine metal, and placed it on top of the stack.

A toilet flushed from the employee bathroom upstairs. She listened for the sound of running water, for an indication of the man washing his hands, but it never came. Loud clunking footsteps echoed overhead as he descended the staircase. Moments later, the office door opened.

Big walked inside, scratching his rear. He stopped in the doorway when he noticed Whitney at his desk.

"What are you doin' here? We're closed tonight, you know that," he said.

"I know."

His eyes scanned the desk, cocking an eyebrow at its newfound orderliness.

"You been snoopin'?"

"I had a look around. You really need to pay some of these," she said, nodding towards the neat stack of bills. He sneered and stepped closer to her.

"It's kind of hard to pay bills with no money comin' in."

She shrugged her delicate shoulders. "Maybe you should start opening the bar on Sundays."

"The bar ain't the problem, Whit."

"So, what is the problem?" she asked, wanting to hear him say it.

"*That* is the problem," he growled, pointing a grubby finger at her pregnant belly.

"I'm keeping it."

"I don't see why," Big spat. He scuttled across the darkened office to hover over her. "Baby-daddy ain't comin' back for you, Whit. To him, you're just a whore."

The words cut her, but the sting was short-lived.

"Even so," she replied.

"So, what? You're going to make me drive *and* babysit when you need to bump a client? I'll have to start chargin' you double."

Whitney rolled her eyes, stood up, and brushed past him. Big took a seat in the weathered old chair.

"Just hurry up and push that thing out. I need cash."

"I'm done," she proclaimed from the doorway.

"I'm sorry?"

"I'm done."

"Says who?"

"You know who."

"That piece o' shit orangutan?" Big laughed. "He still makin' you call him *No-name*? You know who he is, don't you?"

"Of course, I do," she whispered.

"Then you know he's dangerous. Do yourself a favor and quit talkin' to him. He's trash, Whit. Prison trash that got lucky. He'll get what he wants out of you, and then he'll flush you down the toilet, just like the bastard that knocked you up. You're a whore. That's all you'll ever be." Big leaned back in his seat with a smug grin. "That there's the truth."

"Is it?" came a deep, gravelly voice from among the shadows.

Big's eyes widened. The blood drained from his face, leaving him with a waxy pallor that gave him the appearance of a pudgy, pockmarked corpse.

Jonathan Tanner emerged from behind the door. His once-ragged gray beard was twisted into a wide fishtail braid, exposing the sharp angles of his scarred face. The top of his head nearly brushed the ceiling, long white hair pulled back and falling in torrents down his shoulders. He wore a pressed white suit and a sinister sneer. But what frightened Big most of all were Tanner's eyes.

Toxic green. Unblinking. Deadly.

All was silent, save for the deafening *clack-tap* of Tanner's ostrich skin boots along the dusty wooden floor. He walked to the desk and stared down at Big. The bar owner's jowls trembled as he watched Tanner remove colossal, tattooed hands from the pockets of his suit.

"We're all friends here," Tanner spoke. He held up his gnarled hands, palms out in a gesture of good faith. "No need to be alarmed."

"Wh- wh- what do I owe the pleasure?" Big stammered, choking back the dread in his throat.

"I'm simply here to ensure that this lovely young woman makes herself abundantly clear," Tanner replied, the low and slow gravel in his voice crackling the humid air. "For reasons involving her impending maternal responsibilities, she's found it necessary to resign her post as head waitress of this establishment. In addition, she no longer has need of your, shall we say, services of accountability. Is that understood?"

Big stared at Jonathan Tanner for what felt like hours.

Finally, the bar owner produced a greasy grin.

"Well, well, well. Who could'a guessed that scary ol' Jonathan Tanner had such a fine fuckin' vocabulary?" He shot Whitney a poisonous glance, then turned his attention back to the monstrous convict. "Y'know, I don't have much. I don't need much. I don't ask for much. I *have* this bar. I *need* some business..." His eyes darkened and his grin disappeared. "But one thing I do *ask* is for promises made to be kept."

"Respectable," Tanner said.

"Something I'm sure you can agree with," Big added. "Now, this young lady has done a bang-up job at this restaurant. I won't deny her that. Hell, I've even agreed to give her a couple o' days for maternity leave."

"Generous," Tanner countered.

"I aim to please," Big declared. "As far as this bar is concerned, she's got no strings. She can quit whenever she wants. No hair off my balls."

Big placed his fat, grubby hands on the desk, one stacked on the other. He leaned forward and leered at Tanner.

"As far as my, as you say, *services of accountability*, she and I have a contract, signed by The Old Lady herself."

"The Old Lady won't be around much longer."

"Even so, part of her nightly earnings are indebted to me. The money she makes helps this fine establishment run smoothly."

Big waved at the stack of bills and IRS reports.

"But as you can see, her fraternization with you these past few months, sir, has rendered her unwilling to garner any new clients." He smirked. "See, I know some pretty words too."

Tanner looked at Whitney, and then at Big. Uncomfortable silence pervaded the static air of the decrepit office.

Without warning, Jonathan Tanner burst into laughter.

Startled by the sudden uproar, Big watched Tanner cautiously. After a few moments of watching him howl with glee, Big joined in. The two men hooted and hollered until both were crying, and then...

Tanner picked up the letter opener and swung it downward. The copper blade pierced cleanly through Big's hands, penetrating into the wood with a loud *plunk*.

A moment of silent confusion led Big to peer down at his bleeding hands. He was pinned to the desk.

Pain and panic overtook him, and he screamed.

Whitney watched in horror as Jonathan Tanner forced a massive hand into Big's mouth, burrowing large fingers down his throat. His fingertips dug into Big's gullet and effortlessly ripped through his esophagus. He pressed his thumb downward and collapsed Big's windpipe.

A quick jolt of the wrist snapped the fat man's jaw.

Tanner removed his hand. He wiped blood and esophageal matter onto the bar owner's shirt, then turned and strolled out of the office.

Whitney held a hand to her mouth. She followed Tanner out of the office, not bothering to spare a final glance at her old accomplice.

Big's eyes rolled back into his head. He choked on his tongue. Blood gurgled down his dislocated throat and jaw.

After five long minutes, his head hit the desk, and he was still.

The neat stack of bills tumbled into a mess once more.

***

Three days passed since Daphne's body had been found.

Three days that Gal used to brood over his predicament in the silent solitude of his new outdoor home. Three days of fresh air, which did wonders for the short bursts of panic that gnawed at his insides. Three days of traversing the coiling inner channels of Silver Lake, utilizing all he knew of the outdoors to stay alive.

The first day, he'd found an old fishing line tangled up in the lower branches of a water-logged birch tree. After spending two hours unraveling the damn thing, he was elated to find a discarded, rusty hook embedded in the knot. A child's snack box had been abandoned in the kayak and, after devouring an apple and a bag of almonds, he tore off bits of string cheese to use as fishing bait.

The first night, he didn't sleep. His mind raced with images of policemen searching for him all over The Loop. Of Jimmy divulging the conversation he'd filmed. Of Amber slapping him in the face. He decided to take his mind off it all, at least for a little while. Under cover of darkness, Gal paddled out of the channels and across the lake to the western shore. He silently invaded the nearest campsite and stole an entire case of water bottles.

He spent the following mornings paddling deeper into the channels, trailing the fishing line behind him and, every so often, hand-reeling in a juicy brown trout. He returned to the birch embankment at mid-afternoon, pulled the kayak ashore, filled the cockpit with water, and allowed his catch to swim in their own little prison.

Each night after sundown, Gal gathered dried brush and wood, lit a fire with the lighter he kept in his pack, and allowed the flames to build while he indulged in a pinch of indica from Remy's bowl. Gal cleaned the fish with the stag horn pocketknife and cooked them over the flames. He devoured every fish he caught and disposed of the entrails in the channels, letting the stream carry the carcasses upstream to avoid attracting black bears in search of a midnight snack.

Each night, alone inside Jimmy's ragged old tent, he held his breath and turned on his phone. The cell service back in the channels was nearly non-existent, but when he held the phone at just the right angle, he obtained a single bar. He knew full well that cell phones were traceable, that the Mono County Sheriff's Department would have had a ping notice on his cell phone number as soon as they realized he'd fled. He also knew that cell phones were only traceable when turned on. In the end, Gal decided to keep the phone with him. He only turned it on in short bursts, praying Scarlet might leave him a voicemail or a text. The first two nights, he'd received nothing.

But on the third night, he received a text. Not from Scarlet, but from Amber:

*I'll keep you safe. I miss you.*

Eager to taste Amber's lips again, he devised a plan...

On the fourth day, Gal slept in. He caught a large rainbow trout, cooked it on the coals left over from the night before, and devoured it. Reeking of sweat and filth, he took a dip in the stream, drip-drying in the summer breeze. He made sure his phone was turned off and then packed up his belongings. He bade farewell to the makeshift campsite and silently thanked Jimmy for discovering such an inconspicuous hiding spot. He paddled away from the birch embankment one last time and followed the channels back out onto Silver Lake.

The lake was bustling with out-of-towners. Small fishing boats were anchored everywhere, manned by retired old-timers and their sleepy wives. A younger crowd favored more lively summer activities, coasting along the water on paddleboards, kayaks, and canoes. The owners of the kayak he had stolen would have a tough time distinguishing it from the dozen other bright green kayaks out on the lake. And even if they did manage to catch him in the act, they would have a difficult time swimming half a mile to steal it back.

Gal paddled the length of Silver Lake to the northern inlet of Rush Creek. He avoided eye contact with fishermen on the shore and maneuvered the kayak along the various twists and bends of the narrow creek. For hours, he suffered irritating mosquito bites among the reeds and low hanging shrubbery.

When the sun reached its apex in the noontime sky, the creek opened up in all directions. And there, dominating the horizon, was gargantuan Grant Lake. The entire afternoon and much of the evening were spent paddling the span of its enormity. The rumble of speedboats matched the tumultuous rumble in his stomach, but he knew he had to keep going. And when the sun finally dipped behind the mountains, he landed on the northern shore of Grant Lake.

Gal abandoned the kayak just south of Highway 395, crossed the turnpike on foot, and hiked five miles along familiar dirt paths and backroads.

He saw his destination at midnight under a muggy moon, tucked among the hills near Mono Lake...

The steel mill.

***

She was going to murder that dog.

Copper yipped loudly from the backseat, ugly little eyes bulging with the effort.

"Shut up, you little rat!" Ruby yelled, reaching behind her seat to smack the Shih Tzu on the nose. He yelped and fell silent. She drove on, livid that her monthly dues hadn't been delivered to the hotel where she had been staying.

Yesterday, Ruby received an email from Violet, her Collector.

Violet claimed her motorcycle was in the shop, that it would be easier to make this month's particular exchange in person. It was to be a one-time exchange until Violet's bike was fixed, and then collections could resume as usual. After a chain of bickering emails, they decided to arrange a midnight rendezvous at Ruby's cul-de-sac home on Gull Lake. The old house had yet to find a buyer, but that didn't mean Ruby couldn't use it for business.

The pregnant blonde had made her nervous. She didn't want to stay longer than she needed to.

Ruby parked in the driveway and shut off the car. She grabbed Copper by the collar, lifted the little dog onto her lap, and fastened his leash. Copper growled and bit her finger, and then Ruby smacked him.

"One of these days…" she warned him.

As they walked to the front door, Ruby noticed the lights on upstairs. She unlocked the door, yanked Copper inside, and heard hurried footfalls coming from upstairs.

"Let's make this quick," she called out.

Copper's leash slipped through Ruby's fingers as he bolted off in pursuit of the noise.

"Get back here, you little shit!" Ruby screamed after him, fixing her eyes on the mountainous staircase. "Violet, grab the dog when you come down."

No response.

"Violet – " Ruby repeated.

Again, she was met with silence.

Ruby hobbled over to the staircase, focused on the task at hand, and began to climb. Up and up she went, her hip clicking in protest until, after twenty painful steps, she reached the top. The upper hallway was bathed in yellow light, save for the dark bedroom at the end of the hall.

"Hello?" she called out. "Violet?"

Copper emerged from the shadows of the bedroom and cocked his head.

"Get over here," she shouted.

Copper disappeared back into the shadows, trailing the leash behind him. Ruby heard the unmistakable creak of the floorboards inside the shadowy bedroom.

"Violet, get your ass out here and give me my money," she yelled, hobbling angrily across the hall. She reached in through the door and switched on the light.

Her heart stopped.

Jonathan Tanner sat comfortably on the rocking chair beside the window. Copper sat on Tanner's lap, the giant's fingertips stroking the puppy's furry head.

"Hi, Rube."

Ruby's eyes swung to the telephone beside the bed. If only she could reach it.

Tanner placed Copper on the floor and stood up, brushing the Shih Tzu's hair off his immaculate white suit.

"You look… disheveled, Rube. Everything all right?"

"Where's Violet?" Ruby whispered, her old and withered heart racing.

"Your new Collector? I imagine she's out enjoying the new motorcycle I purchased for her." Tanner stroked his long, braided beard, taking a few steps towards her. "Her old one was irreparable, according to the mechanic."

"What do you want?" Ruby stammered. She backed away towards the stairs.

"Thirteen years," he spoke slow and calm, matching her steps. "Thirteen years, and all because of you."

"Johnny, I – "

"You sold me out, Rube. When the shit hit the fan, you sold me out. I made this business what it is, Old Lady. And now, I'm going to take it back."

"Back off!" Ruby screamed. She pulled a small handgun from her jacket pocket and pointed it at Tanner, an arthritic finger hugging the trigger.

Tanner smiled and stepped closer.

"I will fucking kill you," she growled.

Tanner held up his large hands in surrender. And then…

Ruby stepped on Copper's tail. The dog yelped and bolted through Ruby's feet, the leash wrapping around her ankles. She lost her footing, stumbled backward, reached for the bannister, and missed. She tumbled down the stairs and landed on her neck with a guttural twist. Her spinal cord snapped on impact.

Jonathan Tanner looked down at Ruby's lifeless body. He picked up Copper and stroked the Shih Tzu's head.

***

He watched her from the shadows.

Amber stood in the kitchen window, washing a small bowl while her eyes stared unblinking at the wall ahead, as though she was trying to think about anything other than the bowl in her soapy hands.

Gal hadn't visited his father's old steel mill in years. He looked around and noticed that Brad's Mercedes was nowhere to be found. As he stood and watched her, he couldn't help wondering if Brad had put her up to sending the text in the first place. To set him up, and then sell him out.

*Only one way to find out.*

He watched Amber rinse and set aside the final glass in the sink. She yawned and ran her fingers through her golden hair. At this point, he could only assume that Brad was either asleep or he wasn't home. In any case, Gal knew that his window of opportunity was closing, and fast.

His feet took on a mind of their own and raced up the steep driveway of the mill. He stayed in the shadows until the light from the kitchen illuminated his path. He slowed to a casual walk, watched her, and then softly knocked on the window.

Amber saw him and froze. They stared at each other through the glass, and then she walked away. Moments later, the front door of the apartment opened, and she stepped into the moonlight.

"Oh my god, Gal. Are you – are you okay?"

"I'm fine," he whispered, unable to take his eyes off of her. "I'm so sorry. I never should have – I haven't stopped thinking about – Hi."

"Hi," she whispered, offering a sad smile.

Gal walked slowly towards her and noticed the sudden shift of her feet.

"Amber, I swear to you. I didn't do it. I didn't kill that girl. Please – " he stammered, holding his hands out to her, begging her to understand. "Please believe me."

"What are you doing here?" she asked.

"I got your text," he said and held up his phone.

"My what?"

"Don't come any fucking closer," growled a deep and threatening voice from the doorway. Brad emerged from the apartment, one hand sliding possessively over Amber's shoulders. Gripped in his other hand was a large copper pipe.

"Brad – "

"What did you do?"

"I didn't – "

"Why are you here?"

Gal took a deep breath and spread his shoulders. "Because she told me to come."

"What?" Amber stammered. "No, I didn't."

Brad stared at Amber, and then looked at the phone that Gal held in his hand. He breathed heavily, brandished the copper pipe, stepped off the front porch, and advanced on his younger brother.

"She doesn't want you!" Brad screamed.

Gal ducked as Brad swung the pipe. He buried his feet into the concrete and launched himself at his older brother, tackling him at the stomach.

The pipe swung out of Brad's hand and clattered to the concrete.

The brothers hit the ground hard. Brad swung his arm, fist connecting with Gal's jaw with a resounding crack. Gal fell to the ground and Brad crawled on top, sending his fist into his jaw once, twice, three times.

Stars flashed behind Gal's eyelids. He pushed Brad off of him and staggered to his feet.

*Clunk.*

The back of Gal's head erupted in white, painful light. His vision faded. He fell.

The last thing he remembered was Amber standing over him, copper pipe in hand. And then, he slipped into darkness.

# FIFTEEN

# Violet

∽

The sullen summer sun dipped behind snow-capped peaks. The first stars twinkled in the sky as splashes of blue and orange waned into a soft violet evening.

It was his favorite time of day.

He listened to the hollow clunk of stacking firewood.

His favorite sound.

He relished in the pulsing of his temples as he lifted another heavy log and tossed it onto the pile with the others. He wiped the sweat from his brow and filled his lungs with cool mountain air laced with pine.

His favorite smell.

He looked up at the violet sky, green eyes searching until finally, he saw it. A single star glittered a soft emerald just to the left of Orion.

His favorite star. Even now, after all these years, it still reminded him of her.

"Need some help?"

Jolted from his trance, Jonathan Tanner chucked another thick slab of dried pine onto the pile. He cracked his neck.

"All done," he said.

"Kind of big, ain't it?" the woman asked, remaining at his heels like a loyal pup.

"It'll burn quickly."

"Let's hope so. Here."

Violet stepped forward and placed a bottle of lighter fluid into his hands. He noticed that she kept her eyes locked on the large pile of wood, avoiding his gaze.

"You don't have to be afraid of me," Tanner said.

"I'm not afraid," she spoke in a smoky, confident tone. Violet looked at him and smirked, swinging shoulder-length purple hair to the side. "I'm intrigued."

He let out a gravelly chuckle and shifted his gaze lower, admiring the peculiar tattoos swathed like spiderwebs around her thighs.

"What are they?" he asked.

"Rorschach," she answered, turning slowly to give him a better look. The inkblots seemed to ooze down her calves and disappeared inside of her shoes. "Believe it or not, I used to want to be a psychologist."

"There's always time," he replied.

"I like this business better." Violet reached down to rub some warmth into her thighs, tenderly caressing her beloved tattoos. "Besides, I still get to play psychologist. Men love it."

"Do they?"

"Oh yes. They see my ink, they ask me what it means, and then they ask if I'll give them a personal psych test. I giggle and tell them I'm not free. I tell them that, like all psychologists, I charge by the hour... and then I touch them."

"Who could resist?"

"No one has," Violet answered. She pulled a cigarette from behind her ear, lit it, savoring the menthol smoke, and continued. "They pay for the room, I tie them to a chair, and then I slowly start to peel off my clothes. I have them look at each of my tattoos, they tell me what they see, and I tell them what it means. Most of the time, it's something to get them going, something like, 'In my professional opinion, you're repressing something. Something dark. Something you've always wanted to do to a woman, but never had the chance to.'"

"Stoking the flames," Tanner replied.

"By this point, they're usually trying to untie themselves. Trying to get at me. I just smile, peel off the rest of my clothes, and then I ask if they want to release that dark repression. They're panting now, nodding like crazy men. I start to untie them, and then I stop and say, 'Your hour's not up yet.'"

"Tease," Tanner chuckled.

"I move to the bed, I lay back, and then I ask if I should show them the mother of all inkblots. I ask if they think they're crazy enough for that test."

"And are they?"

"Only if they fork up another hundred."

Violet took another slow drag of the cigarette. A sudden breeze whisked between them, and she shivered.

"Cold?" he asked.

"Well, I was under the impression we were going to have a bonfire," she retorted sarcastically.

Tanner smiled.

*You'll go far in this business, girl.*

He popped open the bottle of lighter fluid and squirted the clear, pungent liquid all over the large stack of logs, vapors rising like ripples in the night. He circled the stack, making sure to douse every corner, then took Violet's hand and together, they stepped back.

"Care to do the honors?" he asked.

Violet took a final drag of the cigarette and flicked it.

The logs burst into a tornado of flame. The sudden heat of the inferno drew the breath straight from Tanner's lungs. He turned to find Violet's hardened gaze fixed to the blaze, her lips curled into a malevolent sneer. Her eyes burned with hunger, with revenge, with fury. He knew, then and there, that he had chosen the right girl.

"Do we need to go over it again?" Tanner asked.

"No. But, can I ask you something?" Violet purred over the roar of the flames.

"Always."

"Does this have anything to do with the dead girl? The one they found in – "

"Daphne," he corrected her. The wind shifted, driving a spiral of black, acrid smoke between them.

The smell of burning flesh singed his nostrils.

"The cops are looking for the guy who killed her, right? The Finch guy?"

Tanner sighed. "Whitney has reason to believe that it wasn't him. At least, not entirely. She thinks it was someone else, someone close to the guy they're chasing, and – "

"And you want to get him — or her — first."

She watched the infamous Jonathan Tanner wipe wetness from his eyes. She knew the tears hadn't come from the smoke.

"I'll kill every last one of them if I have to," he growled.

"You must have really adored her," Violet cooed, reaching out to touch his shoulder.

"That's a story for another time."

"Why not send Whitney?"

"Whitney is weak. She's doing her part, but this is something I need you to do. You're tough, you're not pregnant, and you have the balls to bring me what I require."

The fire popped and sizzled, and the air stank of decay and seared flesh.

"Can I count on you?"

"Consider it done," Violet purred and then sparked up another cigarette.

They turned back to the fire and together, they watched The Old Lady burn.

\*\*\*

Gal opened his eyes.

He felt strangely warm and, oddly enough, he was naked. His limbs were tangled in soft violet sheets. The mattress under him made him feel weightless, as though he had been sleeping on a cloud. The sheets to his left had been pulled aside and, as he reached over, he noticed they were still warm. He leaned over and smelled them, a heavenly sweetness causing his body to awaken.

They smelled like her.

"Amber?" he called out, but he was met with silence.

Gal slid out of the large, unfamiliar bed, and pulled on the boxers he had discarded on the lampshade. He padded barefoot out of the bedroom and into the hall.

Quite suddenly, he knew where he was.

He was at the steel mill, in Brad and Amber's apartment. He couldn't remember why he was there, or how he had ended up naked in Brad's bed, the sweet scent of Amber on his flesh. The floor felt strangely warm under his feet. He reached the large round window in the hallway and was surprised to find snow falling outside.

*But it's summer.*

The sound of running water and clinking dishes caused his ears to perk.

"Amber?" he called out again.

"I'm in the kitchen," her sweet voice called back.

He followed the noises down the hall and into the living room, stopping in his tracks when he saw her at the kitchen sink, washing dishes. Her hair was messy, she wore no makeup, and she sported nothing but a tank top rising just above her knees. Gallagher Finch had never seen anything more beautiful.

Amber turned to him and gave him that playful little smile he loved so much.

"Good morning," she said.

"Morning," he replied.

She dried off her hands and walked over to him. "Sleep good?" she whispered, leaning up on her tiptoes to place a gentle kiss on his lips, one he certainly did not deny.

"Yeah, I think so." He looked around at the interior of the apartment. "Did we – you know – do the deed?"

She blushed and gently kissed his chest. "We did."

"How was it?" he asked.

"It was perfect. Like always."

"What do you mean, 'like always'?"

Amber looked up at him and cocked an eyebrow. "Are you feeling okay?" she asked, reaching up to push back his flaxen hair, feeling his forehead.

"Where's Brad?"

"What do you mean? You're right here, with me."

Gal turned to the mirror above the fireplace, but it was Bradley Finch's steely gray eyes that stared back.

"Brad," he heard someone whisper.

He turned to look at Amber and froze in horror. Her eyes were like frost, skin like putrid wax. Blood glistened down the front of her shirt, squirting from a deep gash in her throat.

His fist was clenched around the stag horn pocketknife, fresh blood dripping from its razor edge.

"How could you?" Daphne wheezed, reaching out to grip his throat.

Gal bolted awake. He saw nothing through the darkness.

The back of his head throbbed. Panic flooded his senses. He sat in a hard, wooden chair, wrists and elbows bound behind him with thick rope. He struggled against his bonds, chair legs scraping across a concrete floor. The chair gave way to one side and he fell hard.

"Easy there," came an oddly familiar voice. "Calm down." He felt cold water being splashed in his face.

"Who are you?" he gasped, choking back the water that trickled down his throat.

A single light switched on, the bulb dangling from the ceiling. He was confined in a small room with brick walls and a sliding hatch door.

It looked like…

*A storage unit.*

Gal felt a pair of massive hands grip his shoulders, lifting him off the floor and righting the chair he was bound to.

"Who are you?" he repeated louder. His captor stepped out from behind him and into the light. He recognized her instantly.

"Remember me?" she asked, lowering to her haunches and staring him in the face.

*Who could forget a woman that big?*

"S — Sadie — Sandy?"

"Great memory."

"What — where am I?"

"We have a lot to discuss," she said. "I need you to be completely honest with me, understand? Because I'll know if you're lying."

"What – where – " he stammered, hazy with confusion as he watched Sandy reach into her jacket. She pulled out a small picture and held it in front of his face. His eyes slowly adjusted to the light, and he felt his blood run cold.

It was a photo of Daphne Castro. She looked to be about eleven or twelve in the photo, but there was no denying that raven hair, those pouty lips, and her olive skin.

"Did you know this girl?" Sandy asked him.

He stared at the beautiful visage, suddenly hating himself for having defiled her that night so many months ago. Seeing her at a younger age made him realize that she hadn't just been a call girl. She had been a child. Somebody's daughter.

*And now, she's a bloated corpse.*

He stared at the young girl in the photo, and he thought of Scarlet at that age. The innocence. The joy. The careless love of a little girl.

Without warning, Gal puked. Sandy wiped his mouth on his shirt.

"Did you know this girl?" she repeated.

"Yes," he said.

"Did you sleep with this girl?"

He gulped, choked back a sob, and nodded.

"Did you murder this girl?"

"No," he said. Gal looked up into Sandy's eyes. They stared at one another for an eternity, and then, she tucked the picture back into her jacket.

"Did you wrap her in that tarp?" Sandy asked. Gal noticed a sudden crack in her voice.

"Yes," he said. "But I didn't murder her. I swear." Sandy continued to stare into his eyes, and he knew that she was reading him. "I *swear*."

"She was my niece," Sandy told him. "She was all I had. My entire world. And now, she's dead. My entire world, gone. You know what that's like, don't you?"

He felt as though he'd been punched in the gut. He knew exactly what it was like. Had known since he was thirteen years old.

"I'm so sorry," he whispered. And truly, he was.

"My instincts tell me not to believe you," she growled at him. "My instincts tell me to break your arms, your legs, and your skull. My instincts tell me to fucking kill you, because my instincts tell me that you killed my Daphne."

She stood up and reached back into her jacket.

Gal closed his eyes, knowing he was moments from being beaten to death by this giant of a woman. He accepted it. He deserved it. He was moments from seeing his mother again.

He heard nothing but silence, and then opened his eyes.

Sandy stood over him, still staring, but her eyes had softened. She held a stack of paper between her hands, and then dropped it into his lap.

"My instincts aren't always right," she said.

Gal looked down at the stack of papers and at the familiar title page:

## MURDER MYSTERY NOVEL: TITLE TBD

"Where did you get this?" he asked, shocked to find the first half of his unfinished novel in the possession of a stranger.

"'*Her raven hair flowed like spilt ink across the newly fallen snow,*'" Sandy spoke the familiar words that Gal had written only a month ago. "'*Her cheeks were still warm, but her eyes deceived her. Soft almond eyes, fixed forevermore upon the snowy canopy. He knew he was too late to save her. And so, in grief and in panic, he buried her.*'"

Silence settled between them and, for a moment, it was deafening.

"You have a gift," Sandy told him.

"Thank you," he said.

"It doesn't matter how this came into my possession," she muttered. "But you should be thankful that it did."

"Why?"

"Because, Gal, there is a horrible, beautiful truth in the words you've written." It all became too much and, without warning, Gal broke down and started to sob. "Tom DeLevine was dealt a shitty hand, wasn't he?" Sandy asked, and Gal sobbed even harder. "Tom DeLevine panicked, and he did the only thing that made sense, in a moment that made no sense at all."

"I'm so sorry," he whispered once more. "I didn't know what to do."

"How does Tom DeLevine's story end?" Sandy asked, her large, calloused fingertips lifting Gal's chin.

"What?"

"The last thing you've written is that he's plagued by awful nightmares. What happens next?"

"I don't know."

"You don't know?"

"I don't have an ending," he confessed.

"Well, then, let's figure one out."

\*\*\*

Amber's head ached. She'd never been more ready to clock-out.

She didn't want to go back to the mill, not after she had whacked Gal over the head with the copper pipe. But, she didn't want to be at the Tiger Bar either. For days, the mere act of coming to work had made her sad, had made her angry, had made her question everything she thought was logical.

In a way, she felt responsible for what happened to Gal.

She didn't know what transpired between him and the dead girl, but she knew that he wasn't responsible for her death. He wasn't a murderer. He couldn't be. He was crass, sure. He was an alcoholic, absolutely. He drove her absolutely crazy… in more ways than one.

But she could never admit any of it.

*Never.*

"Look, I don't give a shit what your manager says. I'm not paying for this," the plastic redhead shouted.

"I'm sorry, ma'am. You drank the martini, so I have to charge you for it."

"Are you kidding me? Do you know who I am?"

"Somebody important, I expect," Amber sighed with an unimpressed shrug.

"This is going on Yelp, I hope you know," the woman threatened.

"Would you like to speak to my manager again?" Amber asked, almost automatically. She was done with this elitist, LA-born-and-bred, Southern California trash.

"No, I don't."

"Then what would you like me to do or say, that already hasn't been done or said by the person who runs this establishment?"

Amber fixed her quarry with a firm and indignant stare and, after a few seconds, the woman let out a forced and dramatic screech. Amber watched her storm back to her table, casting furious glances in Amber's direction and filling her cohorts' ears with complaints of the hick-town bar they'd chosen for the evening's outing.

Amber rolled her eyes and went back to wiping down the bottles in the well. Never did she believe that at twenty-five, and with a master's degree in sociology from UC Davis, she would still be serving martinis to narcissistic SoCal women in the heat of The Loop's touristic summers.

"What a self-absorbed bitch," came a smoky voice.

Amber looked up and smiled at the purple-haired woman who had been sitting at the end of the bar all evening, all alone. The woman gave Amber a wink and turned in her barstool to address the fuming C-list actress.

"Hey, honey, nobody here cares about which Hollywood director you sucked off, so take your fake friends and get the hell out."

The bar went silent.

Amber's jaw dropped, but she couldn't help suppressing a smile. She watched as the plastic redhead turned with fire in her eyes. She approached the bar and suddenly stopped as the purple-haired woman stood up, flaring broad shoulders and powerful, tattooed thighs.

If a fight did break out, it was clear to Amber who would win.

"Test me, bitch," the violet avenger growled. "I'll rip off that plastic nose so fast, you won't even be able to smell my knuckles."

She stared down the redhead until, finally, the fuming actress and her plastic posse left the Tiger Bar amid a restaurant-wide cheer.

"Thank you," Amber said.

"Violet," the woman replied.

"Violet. Makes sense." Amber nodded to the woman's purplish locks. "Maybe you should take my job. I'm Amber."

"I know who you are," Violet said, then guzzled the final dregs of her beer.

"You do?"

"You're dating the rich steel guy."

"How did you — "

"Please, honey. Every girl up here knows that pretty boy."

"They do?" Amber cocked an eyebrow and went back to polishing her glass. "He is kind of pretty, isn't he?"

"His little brother's pretty too."

Amber froze. Her hands trembled.

"What?"

"Do you think he killed that girl?"

In the short amount of time it took to enjoy Violet's company, it took even less to want to get out of it.

"I have to get back to work."

Two hours later, Amber closed out the rest of her tabs, wiped down the bar, and locked up the darkened restaurant. The main stretch of June Lake Village was eerily quiet. A streetlight flickered, and the sound of swaying pines whispered to her through the darkness.

It was summer, sure, but midnight still got nippy. Amber tugged her jacket tighter around her and walked down the side street where her car was parked a few dozen steps away, footsteps echoing along the pavement. As she fumbled for her keys, she felt someone watching her. Amber looked up.

Violet walked out from a side alley and offered a smile.

"I'm sorry if I caused any offense earlier," she said.

Amber relaxed her shoulders and shook her head. "It's fine. Look, I should be the one apologizing. It's just – it's a sensitive subject right now."

"I get it," Violet replied with a saddened expression. "Well, again, I'm sorry. Let me buy you a drink sometime to clear the air."

"I'd like that."

"Cool."

"Well, have a good night," Amber muttered.

"You too." Violet smiled and held out her arms for a hug.

Amber relinquished a smile and gave in to the woman's advances, closing the distance between them and offering the obviously drunk woman a hug. She felt the warmth of Violet's body heat, and then…

A sharp pain pierced the side of her neck.

She heard Violet's voice lulling her to sleep. The last thing she remembered was the strange, purple-haired woman standing over her, a syringe in hand.

And then, she faded.

# SIXTEEN

# Tan

∽

Jonathan Tanner sat alone in his cell, listening to the incessant whimpering of the inmate in the cell next door. He tried not to lift his eyes to the carnal scene unfolding within. Instead, he kept his gaze upon the cement wall of his cell, bricks painted tan and blemished in areas where inmates before him had attempted to scratch, dig, and chip their way out.

*Nobody escapes Folsom…*

He'd heard the guards say it when he'd arrived almost twelve and a half years earlier, and he'd heard it from the other inmates whenever any of them attempted to escape.

They spent months coordinating, many with the intent of scaling the southwest perimeter where the barbed wire had apparently dulled enough not to rip the skin. Others, with counts less severe than Tanner's, would remain on their best behavior until they were granted access to the Minimum Support Facility, wait until dark, and then make a dash for the American River. Still others went with a more physical approach and simply started riots, carved shanks, and attempted to steal guns from the guards. Most of these incidents ended in bloodshed on one or both sides.

Nearly all escape attempts failed. Of those who succeeded, escape meant death at the hands of the elements or apprehension by other state police.

*Nobody escapes Folsom...*

*Nobody except Glen Stewart Godwin.*

Glen Stewart Godwin was convicted of abducting and brutally stabbing a Palm Springs cocaine dealer with a serrated butcher knife. Not once, but twenty-six times. Godwin and his roommate, Soto, loaded the body into a pickup truck strapped with explosives, drove out to the desert, and blew the thing to kingdom come. The explosion was meant to incinerate the evidence, but some residents of a ghost town nearby, unknown by Godwin or Soto, discovered the remains of both the pickup and a human body. A charred license plate was found half a mile south of the wreckage, and Godwin and Soto were both charged with the murder. Soto testified against Godwin, claiming he was merely an accomplice meant to hold the man down while Godwin, he claimed, hacked the man to pieces.

In 1983, Soto was sentenced to 25 years. Godwin was sentenced to life.

Glen Stewart Godwin's first attempted escape from Deuel Vocational Institute had failed. In response, the state moved him to the maximum-security Folsom State Prison. Little did the state realize that Godwin had made a valuable new friend during his time at Deuel, a man by the name of Lorenz Karlic. Karlic had been released from Deuel on parole two months after Godwin was relocated to Folsom.

For a year, Karlic managed to smuggle various tools into Folsom through Mexican gardeners he'd paid off in advance, gardeners who buried the tools and passed along the plan to Godwin. The tools were hidden in various areas around the yard and finally, on a warm summer night in 1987, Godwin went on a scavenger hunt. Among other things, he unearthed a hacksaw buried beside the northeastern guard tower.

Secluded in the shadows, Godwin cut a hole through the fence wire and escaped into a storm drain that emptied into the American River. Karlic had left a raft tied to a tree beside the river, and Godwin used it to float downstream to freedom, following arrows that Karlic himself painted on the rocks.

Godwin was then indebted to his friend Karlic, and vowed to repay him for his loyalty.

Two weeks after Godwin's escape, Karlic was apprehended by police in Hesperia. It seemed to Godwin that his time had come for repayment, but he never got the chance...

Karlic managed to escape on his own. He left the policeman's body at the scene, throat torn, jaw dislodged, and neck snapped.

The man known as Jonathan Tanner smiled at the memory.

"Let's go," the guard barked. "You got a visitor."

"I never have visitors."

The guard chuckled as he unlocked Tanner's cell. "Oh, you're going to want to have this visitor, old boy. Sexy young thing. Dark hair. Trust me."

The guard stepped back as Tanner stood up, long white hair matted and his beard disheveled, shoulders broad as an ox and two sizes too large for his tan jumpsuit. Tanner allowed the guard to restrain him before being led down two hallways and up a winding staircase. He was led into the visiting area and seated at a booth with a thick pane of glass between himself and...

His heart skipped a beat.

Raven hair. Plump red lips. Supple white skin. Soft, sad eyes...

*But it can't be her.*

Annie Finch's eyes were green. She had died twelve years ago. And this girl was far younger than he'd ever known Annie to be.

Tanner let his vision adjust to the fluorescent lights around the glass pane. He picked up the phone as the young woman did the same.

"Who are you?" he growled.

"A friend," she replied.

Tanner drank in the young woman's revealing, low-cut top and noticed the small red notebook on the desk beside her.

"Did The Old Lady send you for a conjugal visit?" he asked. The mere mention of Ruby caused his blood to boil with hatred.

"Nothing like that, no," the young woman replied, tucking the notebook back into her purse. "She can burn in hell for all I care."

"Careful now," Tanner mused. "Too much talk like that and she might hear you. I used to be her ears, y'know. Her ears, her eyes, her fists."

"She's a tyrant without a face. All she does is collect. She takes more and more every month. Most of us can't even afford our rent anymore. We've all been working double shifts. We're exhausted. She's even soaked up the contraception funds. Some of the girls are getting pregnant, and she won't do anything about it."

"And what would you like me to do?" Tanner asked.

"Escape," she said. "Apparently, you're good at it."

"How would you know what I'm good at?"

"Some of the older women talk about you. They talk about how smooth everything ran when you were around. They talk about how much better you treated them. They talk about how The Old Lady framed you, how she testified that you helped that Gull Lake man murder his wife." The raven-haired young woman leaned in closer, pressing her hand to the glass. "If everything they say about you is true, then we need you back."

"You're a brave girl to come and talk to me. Haven't they told you how dangerous I am?"

"I'm not afraid of you."

Tanner fixed the young woman with dangerous eyes, willing her confident demeanor to break, until she finally fixed him with an even more toxic stare.

He grinned.

"What's your name, girl?"

"Daphne," she purred. "Daphne Castro. It's a pleasure to meet you,

Mr. Karlic."

Tanner's stomach twisted. "How did you—"

"I grew up in Hesperia. Everyone knows the story." She smirked. "I just did the math."

"You're a smart girl."

"You've been in here, what, almost thirteen years now?" she asked. "Glen Stewart Godwin isn't coming back to repay you. Not on his own. But, I can help you find him."

*God, she looked like Annie.*

"I can help you," Daphne continued. "Just tell me what I need to do."

This girl was good.

"First, never again call me Karlic," he told her. "Second, you'll need to obtain a raft."

***

Gallagher Finch felt like a rat trapped in a box.

*At least she untied me.*

He relaxed on the concrete floor of the storage unit, feet elevated and propped upon the edge of the chair Sandy had untied him from. For two days now, he and the giantess shared and slept in the cramped unit, discussing the events that had led them both here.

Gal explained, over and over, everything he could remember about the night he shared with Daphne and the following morning he found her murdered in his bed.

He explained that while he and Brad never got along, Brad had surprised him with an early birthday present, an event he called a "meet-and-mingle" at a mansion in Mammoth, owned by one of Brad's colleagues in the steel industry. Upon arrival, Gal realized that the women he was meeting and mingling with were call girls from up and down the Sierras. Multiple men, and even a few women, were buying and trading the call girls, and then disappearing upstairs to indulge in more carnal activities.

He was immediately drawn to one in particular: a young woman whose raven hair seemed strangely familiar. Looking back on it, he realized just how much Daphne had resembled his mother. Perhaps that was why he'd been so drawn to her. They talked for a while and found a fiery connection that far surpassed mere friendly conversation. He recalled that Daphne said she knew Brad through a friend, and that she found him to be a narcissistic asshole.

This solidified Gal's eagerness to take her home.

He described in detail, much to Sandy's chagrin, the countless romps he shared with Daphne amid countless bottles of liquor. He told her how Daphne complained about his stubble, and how she begged him to go and shave. He remembered that he had nicked himself with the razor, and then heard her begging for a peanut butter and honey sandwich. He went downstairs, drank a little more, ate a dollop of Jif peanut butter, and began to make the sandwich. He recalled seeing a strange, shadowy figure next to the coat rack.

And then, everything went black.

Sandy deduced that Gal had been drugged, that the killer had tainted either the bottle of Evan Williams or the jar of peanut butter. Gal recalled drinking the whiskey the next morning, and that it tasted normal.

He also recalled that the peanut butter had indeed tasted bitter.

*The killer poisoned my Jif.*

One thing, however, proved incredibly useful during his sessions with Sandy. Repeating the events over and over led Gal to believe that he truly did have a winning story on his hands. He began devising new plot twists and shady characters encircling Tom DeLevine that embodied, at least partially, those in his own life...

Two bitter and hateful brothers.

One supportive and sensible sister.

A truly terrifying, yet tender opponent.

And to top it off, a darkened web of lies and secrets surrounding Tom DeLevine's lonely cottage in the woods.

The ideas swirled in his head like a shaken snow globe. His fingers itched to provide the conduit between mental images and written words. His laptop, however, was back at the steel mill, along with everything else he had taken in his backpack.

*Well, almost everything.*

Hidden in the waistband of his jeans was the stag horn pocketknife and his cell phone.

Gal wiped the sweat that beaded upon his brow, somewhat resentful towards Sandy for having locked him inside the storage unit while she went out to "run errands." He had the feeling that traditional errands were the least of her concern and, more than once, Gal wondered if Sandy might return with the police in tow.

*I wish Scarlet was here.*

Gal tugged out his cell phone and turned it on, thankful when he noticed that the battery still had a little juice. He quickly dialed Scarlet's number and, again, was met with her voicemail.

"Scar, you have to call me back. I'm locked in a storage unit. I don't know exactly where, but you have to find me. Please." And then, he hung up.

He guzzled down the last of the water that Sandy left for him, then munched on the final scraps of beef jerky stranded at the bottom of the bag.

Perhaps Sandy planned to let him starve to death in this tiny, windowless prison.

Perhaps it was retribution for burying Daphne's body.

*Christ, it's hot.*

Gal looked up at the small vent in the ceiling. If he angled his shoulders just right, he might just be able to pull himself up and out.

*I have to get out of here.*

He pulled the pocketknife out of his pants, climbed onto the chair, and used the flat end of the blade to slowly unscrew the four corners of the vent. The vent fell and clattered to the floor as Gal gulped in deep lungfuls of fresh mountain air. He felt a late summer breeze wafting his now shaggy salt-and-pepper hair, smelling freedom on the other side of the square opening.

He reached through the hole and gripped the roof flashings as best he could, using every ounce of strength he possessed to lift himself skyward. He shoved his head and left arm fully through the hole, and let sunlight warm his face for the first time in days. He pulled himself higher, but struggled to squeeze his right shoulder through. He squirmed and twisted, and his legs accidentally kicked over the chair.

He was stuck.

Pain crept down his neck and along his right side, pulling muscle after muscle as he tried to free himself, twisting his limbs in all the wrong directions. He considered yelling for help but knew anyone who found Gallagher Finch stuck in a vent would simply call the Sheriff and claim the reward for his capture.

Suddenly, he heard it.

The rattle of a key being stuffed into a lock sent his panic into overdrive. Sandy would find him trying to escape, and she would either tie him back to the chair or beat him to a pulp. He heard the storage unit door rising on metal casters, followed by two voices, neither of which he could make out.

*She brought the Sheriff. I'm done for.*

Gal felt two strong arms wrap around his waist and tug him downward. He fell through the hole, back into the darkness of the storage unit. He squinted and let his eyes adjust to his fate. Sandy held him in her python grip, and then set him down.

"You ain't going to want to escape once you see who I brought with me," she said.

Gal looked up.

Eyes tired and bloodshot behind her hipster glasses, she stepped into the light like an angel from a nightmare.

"Scar?" Gal whispered.

As if to stifle his worries, Scarlet walked closer with tears in her eyes, and then wrapped her arms around him.

"You never answered your phone," he mumbled into her shoulder.

He pulled her closer, as though afraid she might float away if he let go.

"The police have it, Gal. They took it," she whispered. "But I'm here now."

"Somebody was in the house with you, Gal," Scarlet deduced, pouring three fresh mugs of coffee. Moonlight cascaded in through the hole in the ceiling while Sandy lifted the storage unit door just enough to let in the fresh mountain breeze.

"You said you checked for forced entry and you didn't find anything," Scar continued. "That means whoever killed Daphne must have had a key."

Sandy sat down on an old crate and took out a pen and a pad of paper. "Let's make a list then, shall we?"

"I have a key. Brad has a key. Does Jimmy have a key?" Scarlet asked.

"He didn't at the time," Gal said. "But he did know where the spare key was hidden."

"What spare key?"

"The spare key I keep under the loose rock in the foundation under the porch."

"But why would Jimmy or Brad sneak into the house, drug you, and then kill your call girl?" Scarlet asked. "I know you don't like them, Gal, but for God's sake, they are still your brothers."

"We discussed that a bit," Sandy cut in. "Jimmy has obviously wanted the house for a long time. The way I see it, he feels like he was duped out of an inheritance when your mother was killed and your father was arrested. He feels the house should've gone to him, because he's the oldest. Framing Gal for murder would get him out of the house for good."

"And Brad?" Scarlet asked, unconvinced.

"That's a bit trickier," Gal told her. "He knew Daphne somehow. She told me so herself. She thought he was scum, which is part of the reason I'm guessing Brad didn't go to the mansion with me that night.

Maybe she knew something about him that he didn't want getting out."

"He could've been rushed for time," Sandy added. "There's no immediate reason why he would've wanted to frame Gal. Maybe he was just lazy and didn't clean up."

Scarlet sighed.

"I don't want to believe that any of my brothers are capable of this," she said. She sipped her coffee and then buried her face in her hands.

"Did anybody else know about the spare key?" Sandy asked.

Gal stared at Sandy, eyes unfocused as he racked his brains. He recalled their first meeting, how they shared an oaky taste of Fuil na Talhainn at the Sierra Inn.

*The Sierra Inn.*

And suddenly, as if he'd been slapped right in the face, it came to him.

"Yvette," he whispered.

"Who?" Scarlet inquired.

"The bartender?" Sandy asked.

"She always begged me for her own key," Gal told them. "I never gave her one, but she knew where the spare key was hidden."

"But why would she – " Scarlet began.

"For revenge," Sandy answered. Gal and Scarlet both looked at her. "She was very quick to condemn you when I spoke with her. She told me exactly where you lived. She said you made her get an abortion."

"That's a lie," he shouted.

"Jesus, Gal," Scarlet groaned, rubbing her eyes.

*** 

Jonathan Tanner sat inside his cabin, listening to the steady drum of summer night rain pattering on the tin roof, trying not to let his memories get the better of his resolve. He kept his gaze upon the log walls lining the spacious kitchen, admiring the tan curves and knots that each slab of wood provided, as though each were its own work of art.

"I had no idea, Tan," crooned a soft, smoky voice behind him.

"Nobody did," he answered. "Nobody but her."

"You must have really taken to her."

"She reminded me of an old friend."

Violet took another long drag of her cigar, blowing rings as she lounged heavier upon the large leather couch.

"Why would you trust her? She could've just been helping you escape to get more cash out of the system."

"No," Tanner spoke calmly. "Daphne came to me in desperation. For the sake of the Lodges. For the good of her own kind." He turned to face Violet, fixing her with a grim stare. "The Old Lady is dead, and things are going to get better. You owe that to Daphne. I'm back *because* of Daphne."

"And what about the Finches?"

"What about them?"

"Why kill all of them?"

"What do you mean?"

"Well, with you and Godwin, everything seems like it was so well-thought-out. Very planned. Methodical. Not that I'm complaining, but why the blood bath?"

"I'm an old man, Violet," Tanner sighed. "After thirteen years, method goes out the window. I don't know which one of them killed Daphne, but I am going to bring a reckoning. If I have to murder the entire fucking family, then so be it."

Loud whimpers echoed beneath the floor boards. The rattling of chains around hollow metal pipes rang upward from an open door that led into the cellar.

Violet groaned. "God, doesn't she ever shut up?"

"Will of the living, my dear," Tanner replied.

"But why are we keeping her here, Tan? I can barely sleep. Can't I dose her again?"

"An eye for an eye, Vi. Besides, she wouldn't survive another dose."

"Can I at least give her the muzzle?"

"Fine," he conceded.

Violet stood up, stretched, and disappeared through the cellar door. After a few silent seconds, Tanner heard the unmistakable muffle of Violet shouting harshly while the lovely prisoner with golden hair screamed under her muzzle.

He adjusted the newspaper he'd stolen in town earlier that day, perusing the same headline he'd been reading for the past two hours. The same headline that had him reminiscing about his past:

### GLEN STEWART GODWIN SPOTTED IN FRESNO AFTER NEARLY TWO DECADES AT LARGE

Tanner read the headline one more time, folded the paper, and tossed it neatly into the garbage. The last he'd heard of Glen Stewart Godwin, the man had been locked up in Puerto Vallarta on drugs and weapons charges. Before he could be extradited back to the United States, however, he killed a fellow inmate and escaped into the Mexican countryside in 1991. For 25 long years, he'd remained silent.

If what the headline read was true, then Daphne had succeeded in finding Godwin. She had succeeded in letting him know that his old friend, Karlic, was ready for repayment. If what the headline read was true, then Godwin was heading north.

Even in death, Daphne had fulfilled her promise.

The girl was good.

***

Say one thing for Gallagher Finch, say he could be a tad forgetful.

He, Scarlet, and Sandy had made more progress in three hours than he'd made on his own in six months. What was more, he might finally have discovered an ending to his book...

*Tom DeLevine's co-worker, a woman he'd shared his bed with a few times, had fallen headfirst into her slow-building obsession with him. She tried to win him back with a fake pregnancy and, when that didn't work, she threatened him with a fake abortion. When he continued to ignore her, she killed an innocent woman and left her on Tom's porch, effectively framing him for the murder.*

It all fit too well.

Curled under a sleeping bag in the darkness, he listened to Sandy's low snores and Scarlet's soft, fluid breathing beside him. He teetered on the edge of sleep and was already beginning to dream when he was suddenly jolted awake by an eerily familiar buzzing sound.

In all the unfolding excitement of the past few hours, Gal had forgotten to turn off his phone. He squinted as he read the name on the screen – **SCARLET**.

It all happened so fast.

The storage unit door swung upward. Men shouted. Scarlet screamed. Beams of light flooded the interior. Sandy roared in defiance.

Gal was dragged out of the storage unit and into the pouring rain. He tried to fight his captors, but was flipped onto his stomach while his arms were yanked painfully behind his back, wrists cuffed.

"Larson, you can't do this," he heard Sandy yell over a sudden crack of thunder. "He's not who you think—"

"Shut your damn mouth," Sheriff Larson screamed back, his arm wrapped tight around Gal's neck. "I told you not to get involved." Larson lifted Gal to his feet and led him to one of the several police cars surrounding the storage unit.

"Gallagher Finch, you're under arrest for the murder of Daphne Castro."

## SEVENTEEN

# Orange

〜

"Are you eating?" Scarlet asked. Her hand trembled as she held the receiver to her ear. She had never seen Gallagher so pale, so sickly, his hair falling in messy curls about his ears and neck, black curtains streaked with ashen white.

"Not very much," he muttered, staring back through the glass with bloodshot eyes. Thick dark circles and a malnourished pallor gave him the guise of a corpse who refused to die. "Gorgeous, aren't I?" He gave her a weak smile.

"Orange never was your color," she replied.

Gal scoffed, glancing down at the orange jumpsuit that hung from his emaciated frame.

"I never thanked you," she said. "You didn't have to take the rap for the entire thing."

"I buried her."

"But I drove you."

"Yeah, well, there's no point in both of us being locked up in here."

"Look, Gal, you're doing everything right," she tried to reassure him. "You told the judge everything. You just have to stick it out here for a little while longer."

"It's already been three months," he said.

"I know, but we're looking, Gal. Sandy knows people down south. Private investigators. Lawyers. If Yvette is responsible for all of this, Sandy will find the right person to convict her."

"Have you talked to Yvette?"

Scarlet sighed and looked down at her feet.

"Scar," he grumbled. "What happened?"

"Nobody's seen her."

"What?"

"After you were arrested, Sandy and I went to the Sierra Inn to talk to her, but she wasn't there. We asked Fletch where she was, and he said she hadn't shown up for any of her shifts. He wouldn't give us her address, said it would be going against his own policy, but – "

"But what?"

"We told him that it might help you." Scarlet smiled. "You know how Fletch adores you. He always has, ever since we were little. So, finally, he gave us the address."

"And?"

"Nothing," Scarlet said. "There was nothing. Her car was gone. We looked in the windows. No furniture. Nothing."

Gal looked up. "Well, isn't that a good thing?"

"How do you mean?"

"Think about it. I get arrested, she packs up all of her stuff, and then she books it. That looks terrible. If we were to bring the case against her, it would look like she saw her chance to leave and she took it."

"I don't know, Gal. We don't really have anything other than Sandy's testimony that Yvette knew where you lived, your testimony that she knew where the spare key was, and a possibility that she might have had it in for you because you made her get an abortion."

"I told you, that's a lie."

"Then tell me what happened, Gal."

He hung his head.

"Yeah, I got her pregnant. I told her I didn't want it, but the more I considered it, the more I realized that I was actually excited to be a dad. I thought it would inspire me. I thought it would help my writing. I wanted that baby."

"What happened?"

"I never told her I wanted it. We fought. She got drunk. And then, she miscarried. She had to abort it, and she's blamed me ever since."

"Oh, Gal. I'm sorry."

"Whatever. It's done." Gal scratched his thickening stubble. "Can't we use that against her?"

"I don't know if it's going to be enough."

"Then you have to search the house."

"The police *have* searched the house, Gal. They seized it for evidence."

"I bet Jimmy loved that," he chuckled, and suddenly felt very smug. "The big bastard finally got what he always wanted, and they took it away."

"Don't blame Jimmy. He was just protecting the rest of us."

"Oh, please. He's had it in for me ever since mom left me the house. Hell, I still have half a mind to think he killed Daphne just to get the deed out of me."

"Jimmy isn't smart enough to pull off something like that."

"I know," he sighed. "So, they searched the house. Did they find anything?"

"They didn't find anything except for a couple strands of Yvette's hair behind your bed."

"Isn't that something?"

"No, Gal, it's not," Scarlet snapped and shot him a look of reproach. "Do you know why? Because they also found DNA from eleven other girls behind your bed. Your reputation as a man-whore doesn't help your case."

Gal smirked and shrugged his shoulders.

"Wipe that stupid grin off your face," Scar shouted. She lowered her voice as a guard glanced in their direction, swinging his baton. "This is serious."

"I know. I'm sorry. I was an idiot." He met her gaze, and for a moment, he looked like her little brother again. "I've changed."

"I know you have, Gal."

"I've been thinking," he said. "The judge offered me bail."

"Where the hell are we going to get three-hundred grand?"

Gal stared at her for a moment. His eyes fell with a sudden sadness Scar had never seen in them before.

"The house," he said.

"No."

"Scar – "

"No, Gal," she repeated. "Bail is only good until your trial. What happens if – "

"What happens if I'm convicted?"

"It'll all have been for nothing. All that hard work," she said. "No. Not an option."

"It's not up to you, Scar," he said. "The house is mine."

"The deed might be yours, but the memories belong to all of us," she shot back. "Our family, Gal. Our entire family."

"*Your* entire family," he grumbled and looked away. "Not mine."

"What the hell is that supposed to mean?"

Gal hung his head.

"The creaky stair. I ripped up the carpet, and I found it."

"Found what?"

"I'm adopted, Scar." He didn't know what to expect. He wondered whether she would cry, whether she would refuse to accept it.

But all she did was stare.

"You knew," he muttered.

"Yeah."

"You knew, and you never told me?"

"I never told you because it never mattered. I love you, Gallagher

Finch, regardless of where you came from."

"How long have you known, Scar?"

"Since before mom died," she answered calmly.

"What?" he choked. "Why didn't you tell me?"

"It wasn't my duty to tell you."

"You're my best friend," he started to yell. "If it was anyone's duty, it was yours!"

"Have you talked to dad yet?" she asked.

"What? Hell no. Screw him!"

"Maybe it's time you did."

"What's that supposed to mean?"

Scarlet sighed, touched the glass, and fixed him with a tender gaze. "Dad didn't kill mom," she said.

"What are you talking about? Of course, he did."

"No, he didn't. You deserve to know everything, Gal." Scarlet gave him a weak smile. "He's in the hospital ward. You don't have much time. Talk to him."

Gal couldn't believe what he was hearing. He couldn't find the words, didn't know whether to be livid, sad, or curious.

"I have to go," she said.

"No. Please, don't leave me," he begged.

"I'll be back soon. I swear. It's only a four-hour drive." Scarlet tugged her purse onto her shoulder, and then stared at him as though aching to tell him something she didn't have the heart to say.

"What?" he asked.

"I don't know how else to tell you, so I'm just going to say it." She took a deep breath. "Amber's missing."

His heart stopped in his chest.

"What?"

"Brad hasn't seen her since before you were arrested. The police are searching for her, but – " She shrugged, indicating that nobody knew where she was.

Gal couldn't see straight. He couldn't speak. He couldn't breathe.

"He thinks *you* did something to her."

And with that, Scarlet left Gallagher all alone in his orange jumpsuit.

***

Fall was in the air.

The October evening burned a rusty crimson. In all directions, fiery elm trees swayed in the breeze. Orange, serrated leaves danced upon the stark autumn chill. Just east of Mono Lake, a large and imposing steel mill sat atop a dry, grassy knoll.

Far below, an orange Volkswagen Beetle sat parked on the shoulder of Highway 395. In the front seat, a purple-haired woman watched the mill from behind a pair of binoculars. Violet stalked the two police units stationed at the entrance of the mill. She took a long puff of the Cuban cigar she'd stolen from Jonathan Tanner's cabin, smoke pouring from her nostrils and engulfing the cab in pungent fumes.

"It's a no-go," she spoke in her sultry, smoky tone. "Unless you're looking for a fire-fight." Her phone sat upon the dash. A low growl emitted from the speaker.

"How many are there?" she heard Tanner's gravelly voice.

"Two units. Four pigs."

"Ah, hell."

She took another puff and spit out the window.

"He must know we're after him. You'd think he'd be desperate to find his pretty little peach."

"Some of the richest men on this earth can't afford an ounce of courage," Tanner responded.

"What if we give him a little clue?" Violet suggested. "Leave some breadcrumbs."

"No. He'd bring the pigs with him. That's the last thing I need."

Violet peered through the binoculars again. She watched as the target in question emerged from the small apartment above the mill and offered the policemen a large canteen of steaming coffee.

"He's cute. I wouldn't mind giving him a little psych evaluation."

"Don't get too attached," Tanner growled through the phone. "He won't be around much longer."

"Shame," she said lazily, chewing the cigar and picking the dirt from beneath her fingernails. "What would you like me to do?"

"Focus on the oldest brother for now. We'll come back to this one."

"And the kid? Kind of hard to get at him while he's in Folsom."

"The wheels are turning. I'm just missing the axle."

"Do you think he killed her?"

"I told you, I am going to bring a reckoning on *all* of them. I don't know which one killed her, but each of those boys is going to answer for Daphne's murder."

"And the sister?" she asked.

"I have something special in mind for her."

***

The normally bleak, eggshell walls of the hospital ward were lined with colorful cartoon cutouts of Frankenstein and his bride, ghosts, goblins, and bloodthirsty vampires.

Each door of the ward displayed a bright orange jack-o-lantern cut from construction paper, though they were without their usual ghoulish grins. Instead, the prison deputies had chosen to remind the inmates of their incarceration. The paper pumpkins depicted shapes of brass scales, handcuffs, police badges, and handguns.

Wrists and ankles bound in rattling chains, Gal was escorted by two guards down the decorated corridor. He found it ironic that only two years earlier, he had attended a Halloween party dressed as an escaped convict. And now here he was, with the realization that his costume had been spot on.

At the end of the narrow hall, the guards ushered him into Ward 137. The room was small, bathed in orange twilight swimming through barred windows. Three empty beds stood in three barren corners, while the fourth contained a decorative skeleton.

Gal's breath caught in his throat.

It was no skeleton.

Gal's father was nothing like he'd remembered. Broad, powerful shoulders were now bony and stretched like a bent coat hanger. His face was long and gaunt, and while Gal's own pallor was nowhere near rosy, his father had the complexion of melted candle wax. The old man was garbed in striped scrubs that were stained in food, urine, and god knows what else. He was attached to wires, hoses, computer monitors, and a colostomy bag.

Gal took a startled step backward, but felt the guards grip his shoulders to keep him from going any further. His chains rattled, and his father raised ghostly eyes.

"I was wondering when you'd come, boy," the old man spoke little higher than a whisper. "Come closer."

Gal hesitated, and the guards pushed him forward until he stood at his father's bedside. He was no longer the massive, brutal monster that Gal had envisaged for thirteen years. He was a shell. A husk. A weed not long for the earth. Charlie Finch was only sixty-three but could have passed for a hundred. He raised a withered, gnarled hand and waved off the guards.

"It's fine. He's my son."

"I'm not your son," Gal stated, having convinced himself of the notion for thirteen long years. And now, thanks to the manila folder under the stair, he knew it to be true. He wanted to be furious with the man he'd always thought to be his father. He wanted to yell at the top of his lungs. He wanted to feel the desire to murder the old man for killing his beautiful, perfect mother.

But all he could do was stare at the decrepit man before him.

Charlie groaned and raised the back of his bed into a more comfortable position. He swept a skeletal arm across the bedside table and gathered a small jar of candy corn, offering it to Gal.

"Your sister brought me this."

Gal hated candy corn, but took a couple anyway. "I didn't think anyone actually ate this stuff," he said.

"Tastes like dogshit," Charlie agreed. "How are you, son?"

"I'm not your son," Gal repeated.

"I see. So, you found the secret under the stair."

"Why didn't you ever tell me?"

"Because your mother wanted to be the one to tell you – before she died."

He wanted to strangle the old man for simply mentioning his mother. Had it not been for the guards, he would have been sorely tempted to end the old man's life right then and there. He would have relished the sound of the incessant beep of his monitor striking a sharp, final flatline.

"How dare you talk about her?" Gal yelled.

"I can't change what you think about me, Gallagher. All I want you to do is listen. I don't blame you or your brothers for never coming to see me. I understand what you must think of me – what others have probably told you about me."

The old man gripped his chest and heaved as he let up a series of phlegm-ridden hacks, sunken eyes bulging as he settled back down.

"I'm dyin', boy. Just listen to me one last time. Hear me out, regardless of what you think. I won't try to change your mind. Just hear me out."

"Fine," Gal said, then settled into a chair beside the bed. "I'm listening."

"I loved your mother with all of my heart, body, and soul," Charlie said. "I wanted to save her, right from the get-go. Your mother, God rest her beautiful soul, and I met under very unique circumstances."

"You met at a Christmas party," Gal recalled. "Not very unique."

"Well, that was only a half-truth. We met at a very unique Christmas party," Charlie continued. "The type of unique party, your sister tells me, where you met Daphne Castro."

Gal's stomach dropped like a brick.

"Your mother was involved with the Sierra Red Lodges. She was a call girl."

Gal didn't believe it. He couldn't.

"You're lying."

"I wish I was," Charlie whispered with a shrug of his skeletal shoulders. He popped another candy corn, chewed it with difficulty, hacked up another lung, and continued. "I paid for her services, but we never even touched. She sang to me instead. You remember her voice? Voice of an angel."

"But – "

"Let me finish," Charlie begged. "I met with her every Sunday after that. She would sing to me, and then I would teach her to read. It went on like that for months, but I never touched her. Her profession aside, she was the most innocent woman I'd ever met. I loved her. I wanted her. I wanted to *save* her. I already had three young children from my first wife. Two little boys and a beautiful little girl."

He stopped and closed his eyes. His smiling lips trembled, and for a moment, Gal wondered if he could continue. The old man wiped tears from his papery eyelids and went on.

"The Lodges, at the time, were run by a woman from the Gulf. We called her The Old Lady. She saw how close Annie and I were becoming and, one day, she pulled me aside and told me not to get involved. Said that another man had claim to her. Not just any man, but The Old Lady's right-hand man. Her Collector."

Charlie stared into Gal's piercing green eyes for a moment, as though seeing someone else within, and sighed.

"She didn't love him, but he took her every night. He forced her. He bruised her. Hurt her. And then, one day, she told him no. So, he broke her arm."

Gal watched the memories fog Charlie's already foggy eyes. He noticed the old man's withered fists clench with a fraction of the strength they once possessed.

"She'd had enough. So, your brothers, your sister, Annie and I ran away to The Loop. Her Uncle Gordon owned two houses in a cul-de-sac behind Gull Lake. He lived alone in the big one, and he gave us the cottage. A couple months went by, and we were happy. But, one night, Annie disappeared. She was gone for three days and three nights, and I knew she'd gone back to the Collector. When she came home, she was covered in bruises. She cried. She apologized. But, we carried on."

Charlie took a deep breath and licked his dry, withered lips.

"A month later, she told me she was pregnant. But in all that time at the cottage, she was still innocent Annie. I never, ever touched her. The baby belonged to him."

"Me," Gal whispered.

"You," Charlie sighed. "The more you grew in her belly, the more depressed she became. She hated him for what he'd done to her. She wanted to get rid of you, but I wouldn't let her. At Christmas time, I gave her a ring and I swore to her that you would be mine. I would raise you right alongside Jim, Brad, and Scarlet. That made her happy, and at the end of January, you came into the world."

The old man's smile disappeared. He reached over to place a hand on Gal's shoulder.

"As you got older, she would look in your eyes, she would see him, and she would cry. On your third birthday, Scarlet, who was barely five, woke me up. She was cryin', she was screamin', she grabbed my hand, she pulled me out of bed. *'The lake, the lake!'* she kept sayin'. I held her in my arms and we ran to Gull, and there was your mother, knee deep in the water and holdin' you under. I jumped in and had to wrestle you out of her arms. You weren't breathin', so I cleared your airway as best I could. I prayed that God would bring you back. I kept pumpin' your little belly until finally, you started breathin' again."

Gal couldn't believe what he was hearing.

"Your mother took it as a sign that you were supposed to live. We had a relatively regular marriage after that. We had a family. But after thirteen years, things got ugly. Your mother's Uncle Gordon met a beautiful old woman who finally decided it was time for a husband. She moved in to the big house and, after a while, innocent Annie and The Old Lady realized they were neighbors. Annie became paranoid that she was in danger, that you were in danger. She begged Ruby never to reveal where she was. Ruby swore not to say anything – but she lied."

Charlie let out a loud sob. He convulsed under the weight of his own grief, and Gal held his hand to calm the old man down.

"I came home from work and he was there, crouched over her. She was bleedin' from her head, all over the entryway. She was dead. I tried to kill him, and he tried to kill me. When the cops showed up, we were both covered in her blood. Ruby was screamin' that we both did it. Screamin' that we killed her together."

Charlie raised his eyes to Gal's and looked weaker than ever before.

"I swear I didn't kill her. I swear to you. I loved her so much."

Gallagher Finch wiped the tears from his father's eyes.

"You're my son," the old man said. "No matter what."

EIGHTEEN

# Sapphire

⌒

The house was enormous.

Perched upon the eastern peak that overlooked the glittering town of Mammoth Lakes, the old mansion had recently been renovated by a Swiss entrepreneur who made millions in drone technology, a man who decided to abandon the Italian Alps for the Sierras half a world away. European women were lovely, he'd said, but nothing beat the undeniable candy coating of American women, specifically those of the Sierra Red Lodges.

The log mansion stood sentinel in the darkness, set alight by dozens of three-story-high windows that glowed from within. The bass of loud music vibrated the glass, dozens of voices ringing with song, laughter, and catcalls. It was the closest thing to a castle that Whitney had ever set foot in. But tonight, she wasn't Whitney…

Tonight, she was Sapphire.

Or at least, she was supposed to be.

Whitney walked out of the mansion for a bit of fresh air. She wore her favorite cocktail dress, brown satin hugging her hourglass frame as though she'd been dipped in chocolate. It was far, far too cold up here. She'd much rather be wrapped in some flannel jacket and a pair of baggy sweatpants, but very few men, if any, would ever pay for that. She needed to make money, but as it stood, money was the last thing on her mind.

The cold night air pressed in on her, and suddenly, she felt very alone.

"You okay?" a familiar voice asked behind her.

"Just needed a smoke," she replied.

"You have any?"

"No." She turned and smiled at a familiar head of lush, raven hair and piercing eyes. "Has anyone made a bid on you yet?" Whitney asked.

"A couple," Daphne sighed. She reached into her bra and pulled out a pack of menthols. "Not really in the mood to go home with some sixty-year-old tonight, though. Here," she said, placing a cigarette between Whitney's lips and lighting it.

"Thanks." She took a long, slow drag and held it in. God, it tasted good. "I really shouldn't be smoking."

"One won't kill you," Daphne replied, lighting one up for herself.

"It's not me I'm worried about."

"What do you mean?"

"Nothing," she replied much too fast.

Daphne watched her for a moment. Those lovely sapphire hues widened and her cigarette fell to the ground.

"No fucking way," she exclaimed. "Goodness, Whit."

"You can't tell anybody. Please."

"How did this happen?" Daphne picked up her cigarette and dusted it off. "I mean, I know how it happened – but, my god, how could you let it happen?"

"Please don't preach to me."

"I'm sorry."

Silence settled between them as they puffed, silvery spirals rising into the night.

"What are you going to do?" Daphne asked.

"I don't know," Whitney said. "I mean, I know what I should do, but – "

"But what?"

Whitney bit her bottom lip to keep from trembling. She looked up at her friend and, without warning, tears began to flow down her cheeks.

"Oh, Whit. Come here," Daphne whispered. She pulled Whitney in close and held her tight. For the first time since she'd realized the bitter truth, Whitney felt warm in Daphne's arms.

"Don't cry. Your mascara is going to run. Nobody's going to pay for that," Daphne joked, lifting Whitney's chin with a smile.

Whitney emitted a half-sob, half-giggle, and then wiped her cheeks and fanned her lashes. "To be honest, I'm kind of happy," she confessed.

"Why?"

"This – this could be my way out, Daph. This guy, he's – he's different. He's fun. He's good looking. He has a *lot* of money," Whitney professed. "If I follow through with this, he could take care of me. Of both of us." She touched her stomach, which had only recently started to display the telltale firmness of the life growing within.

"Does he know?" Daphne asked.

Whitney chewed the inside of her cheek and shook her head.

"Who is he?" Daphne pressed.

"He's, well, he's a regular."

"Oh, no. Whit, you are so stupid."

"I know I am," she whimpered, and the tears began to flow again. "I was going to tell him tonight. He told me weeks ago that he'd be here. He promised. His brother showed up, but he never did."

"Did you call him?"

"I've been calling him for days," she sobbed. "He won't answer."

"Do you know where he lives?"

"No. We've only ever met up at the Triple Hawk. You know, that hoity-toity place in the June Lake Loop."

Daphne sighed. "Are you sure this is what you want? I mean, it doesn't seem like he's being very good to you, Whit."

Whitney wiped her eyes again and sniffed. "Yeah, well, that's another reason I'm thinking of keeping it. He can ignore me, but he can't ignore a baby."

Daphne stared at her friend. "You're going to trap him?"

"If I have to."

The silence settled between them again, and Whitney finished up her cigarette before stamping it out.

"I'm just worried about The Old Lady, and – "

"Screw The Old Lady," Daphne replied with defiance. "She's worthless. I have a feeling she's going to be gone very, very soon." She smirked and took another drag.

"What makes you say that?" Whitney asked. Something in Daphne's sapphire pools was sharp, almost wicked. "Daphne, what did you do?"

"It's not important." She stamped out her cigarette and stood up, smoothing out her carmine dress. "What is important is finding your mystery man."

"How?"

"Where's this brother of his?"

"Why?"

"I'll get it out of him," Daphne said. "I'll take whatever bid he offers, I'll let him take me home, I'll show him a good time, and then I'll get your man's address."

"Daphne, you don't have to – "

"Hush." Daphne turned to peer into the large window and watched dozens of men make their bids on the extensive array of Lodge girls. "Which one is he?"

Whitney peered in and saw him. "That one," she said and pointed out a tall, slender, dark-haired male with deep green eyes.

Daphne smirked.

"Piece of cake."

It was then that something truly odd happened. A rustle in the trees caught them off guard, and they became suddenly aware that their conversation was no longer private. The leaves trembled a moment before a short, obese man stumbled out onto the walkway, a bouquet of roses in one hand. Dressed in a pressed and pompous Burberry suit, greasy hair combed over his ever-widening scalp, the man scratched at his jiggling third chin and presented them with a yellowing grin.

Whitney watched him, intrigued, as he stepped toward them. She looked over at Daphne, who watched the man with vitriol and disgust.

"What the hell are you doing here?" Daphne barked at the man.

The bulbous, crow-beaked man stopped dead in his tracks.

"Ah. Well, I just thought — I mean, I figured I would ask you if — "

"No, I will not!" Daphne interrupted with fire in her eyes. "Stop following me."

"But, I just – "

"Leave before I call the men out here!"

Whitney stood, mouth agape. She had never seen Daphne so furious… or was she frightened?

"Leave. Now!"

The obese man watched her with a hardened stare, dissecting her from head to toe. And then, he melted back into the trees.

"Who was that?" Whitney whispered.

"Don't worry about it," Daphne answered, voice shaky. She then turned her attention back on the tall, green-eyed, dark-haired young man inside. "That guy, right?"

"Yes, that one."

"I'll call you in the morning," Daphne said. She kissed Whitney on the cheek and sauntered back inside, leaving Whitney freezing cold and all alone once more.

It was the last time the girl known as Sapphire ever saw Daphne Castro alive.

"Ouch, not so hard," Whitney groaned. She bounced the newborn boy as his gums gnawed at her chest.

Her eyes were glued to the television, mouth curved in a satisfied grin.

There he was, cut straight out of her memories. She hadn't seen him in ten months, but she knew that face like the back of her hand. She knew that jawline. She knew that flaxen hair. She knew those enigmatic, steel gray eyes. She also knew that steel mill. She'd driven past it on Highway 395 at least a thousand times before.

Bradley Finch was on the news.

He stood beside an older couple, the parents of the missing girl, the golden-haired bitch who had stolen him away from her. What Jonathan Tanner was doing with her, Whitney had no clue, nor did she care. She had devised the entire plan, had told Tanner that Brad would follow Amber right into his grasp.

But there was a part of the plan that Whitney never mentioned to Tanner…

She would get to Brad first.

She would steal him back with the revelation of their baby boy. They would name him. And then, they would go into hiding. She didn't care what Tanner did to the rest of the family, or with the girl.

"Time to meet your daddy," she whispered, the nameless infant sleeping softly against her bosom.

***

He had wanted to attend so very, very badly.

Brad imagined all the beautiful women dressed in their most revealing. He knew that tonight, there would have been plenty to choose from. He knew that with so many call girls in attendance, prices would be much lower tonight. He knew that the January chill would give them all the more reason to find a warm man with a warm bed and an even warmer wallet.

But he also knew that *she* would be there.

He had taken this whole thing much too far. He had given her far too much money. He had given her far too much hope. He had given her far too much of himself.

The girl known as Sapphire was becoming clingy, and he was tired of it.

Sure, it was Gal's birthday, but he had to send Gal off by himself. He couldn't risk being in the same room with her any longer. She'd been calling for days, and he'd been declining her an answer.

He was done.

"Babe, are you going to answer that?" Amber whispered softly, beautiful golden tresses resting on his chest. He turned to look at his phone, alight and vibrating on the bedside table. He rolled his eyes, knowing it had to be her. He reached over to check the screen, and was pleasantly surprised by the name he saw:

**GALLAGHER.**

"Enjoying yourself?" he answered.

"Yes, he certainly is," came a female voice on the other end. For a moment, he wondered if it was Sapphire.

"Who is this?"

"My name is Daphne," the voice cooed. "Is this Brad?"

"Yes," he responded, now a tad confused. He heard the dull thud of music in the background, could hear the familiar call of men bidding on girls. "Where's Gal?"

"In the bathroom."

"Why do you have his phone?"

"Mine's dead," she answered. "You never showed up. Sapphire was asking for you."

"I'm hanging up now," he growled.

"She's pregnant."

Brad's blood ran cold.

Amber glanced up at him with curious eyes. He gave her a false smile and stroked her head, willing her to yawn and fall back asleep.

"She's keeping it, you prick," Daphne spat through the receiver. "Call her back, or else your little girlfriend is going to hear about it."

The line went dead.

***

"How's her mom doing?" Scarlet asked.

"Scared out of her mind," Brad responded. He rubbed his tired eyes, a splitting headache making it hard to see or think straight. Together, he and Scarlet drove up the winding dirt road that led to the steel mill. He'd needed to get away from the apartment for a few hours and now, he sipped on the lukewarm Americano Scarlet bought for him at the Tiger Bar.

"And her dad?" she asked.

"A trainwreck," he said. "They flew in two weeks ago and he hasn't said one word to me. He forbids them from staying at the apartment. Says they'd rather stay in Mammoth." In truth, the old Milwaukee man scared the hell out of him, and in truth, he guessed he knew why.

"What is it?" Scarlet asked.

"I think – I think he thinks I had something to do with it," Brad confessed.

"Did you?"

"How could you even ask that?" he asked defensively.

"I believe you, Brad, I do, but your story – well, it's weak."

"It's the truth," he yelled. "I was asleep. I usually wait for her to get home, but we'd been fighting, so I went to bed early."

Scarlet took one hand off the wheel and placed it on his forearm. She turned to look him straight in the eye, that same look that never failed to make him feel guilty for questioning her.

"I told you that I believe you," she said. "That's the truth."

"I know. It's just – it's all so messed up."

"Now you know how Gal feels."

They drove in silence for a few minutes until the shadow of the gates came into view, stretching across the grounds to the east as the sun made its descent in the west. He peered out through the windshield and saw that the police units were positioned at the top of the driveway, a quarter mile up from the gates.

"Who's that?" Scarlet asked. She pointed at a small, sapphire-blue convertible parked at the gate. A blonde-haired woman stood beside the car, a small bundle held against her chest.

"Stop the car."

Scarlet punched the brakes, and Brad jumped out. His boots crunched on the gravel as he approached the buxom blonde.

"What are you doing here?"

"Really? That's how you're going to greet me after all this time?" Whitney jibed. She bounced the small bundle against her chest, soft suckling noises causing Brad's stomach to turn over. "Do you know who this is?"

"No," he lied.

"Brad, is everything okay?" Scarlet called.

"Everything's fine! Stay in the car."

"Who's that?" Whitney asked. "Your new whore?"

"She's my goddamn sister," he yelled. "What do you want?"

"Just a few minutes of your time."

"Talk."

"Not here," she replied, then turned and glanced up at the steel mill. "I need access past these gates."

"I have nothing to talk to you about," he spat, then turned and began to walk back to Scarlet's car.

"I know where she is."

He stopped dead in his tracks.

"What did you say?"

"Your girlfriend."

"You know where she is?" he asked, a shred of hope dousing the fury searing his every nerve. "Where?"

"No, no. Not yet. First, the gates," she said.

He was stuck. There was no way he was getting onto his own property without the obsessive call girl in tow. She had information that he desperately, desperately needed.

"Fine. Follow behind us. We'll talk to the cops."

"No."

"No?"

"No cops, or else I tell you nothing."

"I should kill you," he seethed.

"Is that any way to talk to the mother of your child?" she purred, patting the baby's back until Brad heard a soft, infantile burp.

Glittering stars graced the winter night like sapphires scattered in black tar, but Brad didn't seem to notice. He sat upright with a rigid back and arms folded tightly across his chest. His gray eyes were focused solely on the tiny infant, asleep on a linen towel on the living room floor. Scarlet leaned against the fireplace, her eyes glancing from Whitney, who sipped a glass of Brad's finest Grenache-Syrah, to the snoozing infant.

"Handsome, isn't he?" Whitney said. She nibbled the edge of her wine glass before savoring another swallow of the decadent blend. "Looks just like his daddy."

Brad gulped. He couldn't deny it. The baby boy had his chin, his upturned nose, wisps of his own flaxen hair.

"What do you want from me?" he asked.

"I don't want anything *from* you, silly," she replied. "I just want *you*."

"You can't have me. I'm already taken."

"Oh honey, you haven't been taken for three months."

"Where is Amber?" Scarlet asked.

Whitney rolled the bulb of her wine glass in her palm and sneered at the lackluster sister.

"I don't know that you need to be here. You should leave. Let us speak in private."

"Where the hell is she?!" Brad yelled. A dense silence settled upon the living room. The baby boy gave a gentle hiccup and rolled onto his side.

"I'll tell you what," Whitney said. "I'm leaving tomorrow. Come with me, and when we get settled, I'll tell you where he's keeping her."

"Where *who* is keeping her?" Scarlet pressed.

Whitney smirked and allowed a few more seconds of silence to linger before she whispered a name that made Brad's blood run cold.

"Jonathan Tanner."

He couldn't believe what he was hearing. The man who had helped kill his mother had escaped, and was now in possession of the love of his life.

"You work for him?" Brad asked, careful to keep the edge out of his voice.

"I did," Whitney answered. "He set me free."

"You're a lunatic."

"A lunatic with your baby."

"You can't prove that," Scarlet interjected.

"A DNA test will," Whitney sang lazily. She gulped down the rest of her wine and set the glass on the marble kitchen island. "Come with me, and I'll tell you everything."

"Tell me now," he said.

"Now, I can't do that, can I? If I did, you'd just go looking for her," Whitney retorted. "Or else, you'd run outside and tell the police. The problem is, if you send the cops, he'll kill her. If you go searching for her, he'll kill her. And then, he'll kill you."

Whitney sauntered towards him, swinging tipsy hips as she walked.

"The only way to save yourself, and to save Amber," she said, "is to disappear with me."

"Why is that?"

"Because he wants you dead."

"Why?"

"Because you killed Daphne Castro."

His heart sunk.

"I didn't kill her. My brother did."

"Brad – " Scarlet interjected.

"Tanner's not sure he believes that," Whitney said.

"Why not?"

"Because of what I've told him."

"And just what did you tell him?"

"I'm not going to say anything else until *she's* gone," Whitney crooned and nodded at Scarlet.

"I'm not going anywhere, you crazy bitch," Scarlet yelled. "This is my family too, and I deserve to – "

"Go on, Scar," Brad interrupted. "I can take care of this."

Scarlet scoffed, unable to believe what she was hearing. Brad kept his gaze firm and nodded to the front door.

"Go on. I got this."

"And remember," Whitney added. "If you say anything to the cops outside, I'll personally make sure Amber is dead by morning."

Scarlet stared incredulously at the scene, from Whitney, to Brad, to the sleeping infant. Then, she spun on her heel, bolted out the front door, and slammed it behind her.

Whitney turned to Brad.

"I know that Daphne called you the night she died. She texted me everything. I know she called you from your brother's phone. I know she told you I was pregnant. You knew exactly where she was. You wanted out, so you drove over there, and you killed her."

"That's a lie."

"Is it?"

"Gal killed her."

"You seem very certain of that," Whitney purred, leaning in to trace soft kisses along his neck. "Why would he want to kill her? He'd only just met her. And from what she texted me, he seemed to be in love with her. Or, at least, to the things she did to him."

"I don't know. He's nuts. He used to sleepwalk. He's an alcoholic. He's a druggie."

"You've put a lot of thought into it."

Brad pushed her back and glared in revulsion.

"Do you really think I killed her?"

"I don't think that you're in any position to decide who killed her. You're just as liable as your brother." Whitney smiled and closed the distance between them once more. She placed a soft kiss on his lips.

"Come with me," she said.

"Will you really tell me where she is?"

"I might," she answered. "It's all about keeping the mother of your child happy. Speaking of which, I need a place to stay tonight." She glanced around the apartment and helped herself to another glass of wine.

"Fine."

"Good. We'll sleep in, and tomorrow, the three of us will start our new life."

"Swear to me he'll let her go."

"I'm in no position to make any promises for him," she replied with a satiated grin. "But, if you keep me happy, I'll make a call, and I'll make sure he knows she's no longer a liability."

"Okay. Fine. I'm yours," he grumbled in defeat.

"Good. I'm hungry. What's for dinner?"

"I don't have anything."

"I have to eat something," she told him. "I have to feed the baby. I'm feeling Thai. There's a really good place in Mammoth. Right up near the mansion you ditched me at all those months ago. Thai. That's what I want."

Brad stood up mechanically, he the puppet and she the marionette. But as he turned to her, his gray eyes glazed over.

"You're going to pay for this," he said.

"I'll see you when you get back," she answered.

***

She drank far too much wine.

After nine months of abstaining from her favorite indulgence, an entire bottle of aged Grenache-Syrah had gone straight to her head. She snored soundly from the living room couch, and had absolutely no idea that she was being watched.

A pair of muddy boots stepped across the hardwood floor, over the sleeping baby. The mere presence of someone in the room roused the little tyke. His soft, tiny voice whimpered in his sleep.

His mother's eyes snapped open. Before she had time to utter a sound, a swift and sharpened blade sliced her throat.

The girl known as Sapphire released a final, guttural note, then slumped to the floor.

## NINETEEN

# Gray

∽

The idiot had proven harder to find than she was expecting.

She called him multiple times over the past couple of weeks, having found his cell phone number scrawled under a dog-eared page in her red notebook. She normally never called clients, previous or potential, but the number itself had proven a delicious turn of fate.

*If only the prick would answer his phone.*

Violet stood in the shade of a large Jeffrey pine, black leather pants and jacket providing protection from a bone-chilling wind. She looked up at a night sky black as pitch, an unseen moon casting a faint glow behind thick, gray clouds.

It was the coldest fall she could remember. The rain was constant, purging any remembrance of the drought that had choked California for nearly a decade. Sure, the clouds threatened another downpour, but for now, no rain today.

From her shadowy vantage point at the end of the cul-de-sac, Violet watched the old log house. A bright yellow band of police tape stretched from her tree to another, whipping and popping on the breeze. She frowned, having not considered that even after four months since the youngest brother's capture, the house was still an active crime scene. She doubted she would find the oldest brother asleep inside, but there was no harm in checking.

*If only the prick would answer his phone.*

She glanced at the only other home on the street, the residence where The Old Lady had met her fall from grace, quite literally. Tanner suggested that the yappy little dog had been responsible. Why he had decided to keep the little rat was beyond her. Company, perhaps.

*The killer of my enemy is my friend,* Tanner suggested while stroking his fingertips along the little dog's spine.

The FOR SALE sign creaked softly in the wind. Tufts of unkempt crabgrass stretched along the yellowing lawn. All the windows were blacked out, and Violet knew that she was alone. She pulled out her phone and dialed Jimmy Finch's number once more.

No answer.

*If only the prick would answer his phone.*

She ducked under the police tape, hugged the shadows, and slinked her way across the driveway. She pulled herself over the fence into the sprawling backyard, waded through knee-high grass, found herself at the back porch, and tried the sliding glass door.

Locked.

She'd expected as much. It was time to get more hands-on.

Violet shrugged off her jacket and wrapped the leather around her fist. With a swift strike, she broke the window above the kitchen sink, a sharp shatter piercing the silent stillness. She waited, half-expecting to hear panicked police footfalls or the shrill wail of a home alarm system.

A final sliver of glass rattled onto the wooden porch before a deafening silence fell once more.

She couldn't believe her luck.

A quick sweep of the entire house laid bare the terrible truth: the oldest brother wasn't there. She'd entertained the notion that, with the youngest brother in prison, he might have snuck into the log house at night to sleep in a warm bed.

Obviously, she'd been wrong.

Violet stood at the top of the stairs and rubbed her throbbing temples. She'd been unable to get past the cops stationed at the steel mill to lay her hands on the pretty brother, the oldest was nowhere to be found, and the youngest was safe behind bars in Folsom State Prison… at least, for now.

And why had Tanner been so adamant on letting the sister roam free? What unspeakable harm did he have in store for her?

It was time to go. There was nothing here.

But first, she had to pee.

Violet followed the path of her flashlight into the large bathroom beside the master bedroom. She lifted the lid on the toilet, squeezed her leather pants past her bum and to her ankles, and took a seat on the cold rim. She set the flashlight down on the floor…

And then she saw it.

The flashlight's beam struck an old magazine rack beside the toilet. Tucked amongst a plethora of *Playboy* and *Men's Fitness* magazines was an oddly familiar red notebook.

She had one just like it.

Violet tugged the small red ledger from the rack and opened it. She found the all-too-familiar list of names written in red and black ink. She flipped the pages from cover to cover until, suddenly, a faded envelope slipped out from between the pages and fell to the floor.

She picked it up, turned it over, and found two words scrawled on the front:

*For Daphne*

Violet's heart skipped a beat. She opened the envelope and unfolded the single sheet of paper hidden inside. Her eyes scanned the messy handwriting.

*My love,*
*I never got the chance to say Happy New Year. I can't stop thinking about you. I find myself dreaming of you almost every night.*

*I beg you to re-consider my proposal.*

*As to our mutual friend, I've relayed your message, and I am eager to announce that he has sent his response:*

*He does not know how you discovered his whereabouts, but he has decided to fulfill his promise to Mr. Karlic. As I write this, he is headed north.*

*I need you.*

*You know where to find me.*
*Yours in life and death,*
*Gray*

Violet read and re-read the letter, trying to make sense of it. Daphne had done it. She found Glen Stewart Godwin. She made contact with him through this person, Gray. In death, she found the missing axle that would keep Jonathan Tanner's wheels spinning.

Violet folded up the letter and tucked it back into the envelope. Her fingernail grazed something else hidden inside. She pulled out a small, white business card, elegant black ink embossed on the front.

**Godwin & Gray**
*Funeral Services, Mortuary and Crematorium*
*San Francisco, CA*

*Bingo.*

She tucked the business card into the envelope, the envelope into the notebook, and the notebook into her jacket. She flushed the toilet, bolted downstairs, and climbed out through the broken kitchen window. She snaked through the knee-high grass, leapt over the fence, and slunk back into the shadows of the Jeffrey pines.

And then, she noticed something peculiar...

Across the street, a single light was on in The Old Lady's house.

\*\*\*

"Your sister tells me you're writing a book."

"It's nothing."

"Two hundred and sixteen pages isn't nothing," Charlie replied, choking back a series of deep, phlegmy wheezes. When he'd composed himself, he asked, "What's it about?"

Gal took a few moments to channel the logline of his tale, and decided there was no way to make it sound less autobiographical.

"It's about a writer who is wrongfully accused for the murder of a beautiful call girl."

His father smiled.

"Sounds familiar."

He reached a withered hand across the void between them and, for the first time in thirteen years, touched his son's arm.

"Let me guess: the experience inspires the greatest thing he's ever written."

"That remains to be seen," Gal sighed.

"Sounds like this writer is caught in his own loop."

"More or less."

"How does it end?"

Gal shrugged. "I don't know if I'll ever get the chance to finish it." He looked up into his father's gray eyes and saw Brad in their hues.

"I don't buy that," Charlie muttered.

"What am I supposed to do? Write on a damn napkin?"

"If you have to," his father answered. "Write your story. Finish it before it finishes you."

It was the last bit of advice that Charles Gallagher Finch ever gave his youngest son.

Gal sat alone in his cell, face buried in his hands. His head hurt. His eyes were puffy. His throat grew tight as he choked back another sob.

Why had he never come to visit his father sooner? There was so much more he could've done. So much more that he could've tried to do. Tried to see. Tried to believe. He'd been selfish for so many years, and that selfishness had finally run its course. He never got the chance to ask for his father's forgiveness. Never got the chance to apologize for telling so many people that his father was a monster.

And now, he would never have that chance again.

Jimmy neglected to come and pay his respects.

Brad was nowhere to be found. Scarlet guessed that he ran off with the ex-call girl who had blackmailed him with an illegitimate child. She'd dropped by the steel mill a couple of times the past couple of weeks, but the door remained locked and his car was gone. He wouldn't answer his phone, and as much as she wanted to tell the police, she knew that Amber's life was at stake.

Gal was furious at his brothers' neglect. He was heartbroken that his time with his father had run out. He was terrified at the idea of having lost Amber forever.

There was nothing he could do.

There was nowhere he could go.

There was no one he could talk to.

Nobody but Scarlet. But even her visits were becoming few and far between.

After Charlie died in his sleep, Scarlet was made responsible for making arrangements for his body. She appealed to the court, begging that they rule to allow for the simple burial of her father at Mt. Eugene Cemetery, pleading that he be laid to rest beside Annie. The law hadn't been on her side, however, and Charlie's body was instead ushered out of Folsom, his organs harvested for medical study, his husk cremated, and his ashes packed carelessly in a cardboard box.

"We'll drive to Yosemite," Scarlet told Gal through a pane of glass. "When you get out, we'll climb Half Dome and we'll sprinkle his ashes over the edge. Together."

"I'm never getting out," Gal whispered before hanging up.

He was done.

It was over.

\*\*\*

In all his years on the run, up and down the length of California, he had never laid eyes on the Golden Gate Bridge.

He didn't know what he should have been expecting.

*It's just a damn bridge.*

A hulking expanse of twisted steel cables, two massive towers, and nearly a mile and a half of suspended asphalt supported the weight of hundreds of vehicles and thousands of individuals. Its vivid red hue had dulled over time, leaving behind a rather depressing, rusty tinge. Some people traveled halfway around the world to walk across the bridge, while still others traveled the entire world to jump to their deaths into the freezing bay below.

As he stared at the bridge from the shade of a large birch tree, his toes buried in the sand of a small seaside inlet, he couldn't help but scowl.

To Jonathan Tanner, the Golden Gate Bridge was nothing more than another pretentious beacon that arrogant Californians polished their rocks to. Why was this bridge better than any other? Nothing about it was golden.

"Beautiful, isn't it?" came a quavering voice behind him.

Tanner turned and found that he was being watched by the fat, crow-beaked sap who greeted him upon his arrival to the Godwin & Gray Mortuary and Crematorium.

The middle-aged man's belly was wider than he was tall. His quadruple chin was saturated in what Tanner imagined was either sweat or hamburger grease, the latter more probable considering the lapel of his pressed and pompous Burberry suit sported a mustard stain. He held a shining leather briefcase in one hand, knuckles white as he clenched tightly to the handle. The man's tie was wrinkled and seemed to choke him, its dull and lifeless color indicating that Tanner had found exactly who he'd been searching for.

"Gray."

"As promised," the fat man affirmed. He reached out a pudgy hand, which Tanner squeezed a little too hard. "Quite the grip you have," he chuckled nervously and pulled his hand away. Tanner watched as Mr. Gray's shifty beetle eyes suddenly became very interested in the briefcase.

"Will Godwin be meeting us?" Tanner asked.

"Ah. Well, no," Gray stammered. "Mr. Godwin passes along his humblest regards. He was, ah, met with some, shall we say, opposition in Fresno about a month back, and he's gone back into hiding."

"He was always good at blowing his cover," Tanner mused. He picked up a flat, smooth stone and skipped it across the smooth, brackish waters of the inlet. "And hiding."

"Indeed," Gray replied. "He enlightened me on the, ah, the history you share, and the debt he owes you. There shouldn't be a problem with – "

"What about you?" Tanner interrupted.

"I'm sorry?"

"How do you know him?"

Mr. Gray's eyes fogged over as he reached into the furthest depths of his memory. "Oh, I've known Glen a long, long time. Since we were boys, in fact."

Tanner followed the fat man's gaze as he peered nervously over his shoulder, as though Tanner's presence was starting to unnerve him. The man arrived alone, and suddenly seemed to regret it.

"Our fathers were in business together. Godwin & Gray. They opened the mortuary back in '62. My father, ah, handled the monetary endowments. His father, well… he was more interested in the science of it. Embalming. Waste expulsion. Reattaching severed limbs." Mr. Gray wiped his sweaty forehead. "My father passed in 1999. His father passed last year."

Tanner picked up another smooth stone and skipped it across the water.

Gray peered nervously over his shoulder again.

"Long story short, Glen and I grew up in the mortuary," Gray concluded. "Helped our fathers out with it."

"And now it belongs to you."

"To both of us," Gray corrected him. "Well, at least until the money clears. Speaking of which – " Gray tapped his grimy sausage fingers against the leather briefcase. "Per your request, Mr. Godwin has agreed to sell me his share of the company for – "

"Three hundred thousand," Tanner growled.

"Yes. Yes, of course." He took a few cautious steps forward and set the briefcase down on the sand. He unlatched the locks, opened it up, and spun it around.

Tanner reached inside, pulled out a thick wad of cash, and flipped through the bills.

"It's all there," Gray assured him.

"Relax," Tanner replied with a grin. He closed the briefcase, latched it, picked it up, walked past the sweaty fat man, and began to ascend the small gravel path that led to the road.

Gray let out a shaky sigh of relief.

Tanner stopped and turned, his towering and imposing build blocking the path.

"One more thing." He reached into his pocket and withdrew a small, faded envelope. "You never asked about Daphne."

Gray's beetle black eyes widened. He choked back a gurgle and adjusted his necktie.

"Yes. That, ah, well… I'm very sorry to hear of her passing."

Tanner chuckled.

"You make it sound as though she died peacefully in her sleep. You saw what happened to her, right? It was all over the news." He began to step back down the path towards Gray. "Stabbed to hell. Throat slit. Beautiful girl, hacked to ribbons."

Tanner waved the envelope in midair.

"I notice that there's no stamp on this letter. No address, even. That leads me to believe it was hand-delivered."

"Mr. Karlic, I – "

" *'I never got the chance to say Happy New Year,'* " Tanner recited. "You paid her a visit around the time she was killed."

"Please, I just – "

" *'I beg you to re-consider my proposal,'* " Tanner growled. He set down the briefcase and advanced on the nervous tub of lard. "So, she rejected you and, what, you got upset?"

"No! What?" Gray stumbled backward. A fierce, sudden wind

kicked up, spraying the mortuary owner's back with sullen seawater.

"*Yours in life and death,*" Tanner finished. "Whose death? Hers..."

Tanner's hands were on Gray before the fat man could make a sound.

"...or yours?"

***

Thanksgiving Day found San Francisco Bay flooded in a bank of thick, gray fog.

While the inhabitants of the Golden City celebrated everything they had to be thankful for, a single fishing trawler hoisted its catch out of the freezing water. The net was released, and nearly a ton of bluefin tuna and Pacific herring flooded the deck.

The crewmen cheered their thanks to the bay, but only for a moment.

Amid the flapping fins, shining scales, and gasping maws, the body of Lester Gray lay bloated, twisted, and purple.

A culprit was never identified.

TWENTY

# Ink

∽

It was all there, typed in black ink.

Gal scanned the newspaper article for the tenth time that morning. His fingertips were already chalky black as he traced them, line for line, down the length of the front-page piece published in the most recent issue of *The Folsom Telegraph*.

### 'FINCH' killer puts second victim on display, raises more questions than answers

Mono County Sheriff's Department deputies were baffled when the body of a twenty-two-year-old female was discovered early Tuesday morning. The body was found wrapped in a blue tarp, hung by the ankles from the rafters of a steel mill located off a Highway 395 access road east of Mono Lake.

The victim has since been identified as Bishop resident Whitney Burges.

Officials say a forensic autopsy revealed that Burges died of severe blood loss from a two-inch deep laceration along the length of her throat. Thirteen additional stab wounds were recorded on her chest, stomach and lower back.

According to the medical examiner, the thirteen additional

stab wounds appeared to have been administered to the body post-mortem and inflicted in the exact same places as were found on the body of Daphne Castro in June.

The autopsy report also revealed that Burges's uterus was inflamed, suggesting that she had recently given birth. No child has been documented by any hospitals in the area.

The word 'FINCH' was found written on the tarp wrapped around Burges's body, nearly identical to that of the tarp wrapped around Castro's.

"This appears to be the work of the same killer as Ms. Castro," Sheriff Paul Larson said at a press briefing on Friday. "Either that, or we are dealing with a copy-cat."

Bradley Finch, owner of the steel mill in question, is the older brother of Gallagher Finch, the June Lake Loop man suspected of Castro's murder.

Investigators report that Bradley Finch hasn't been seen by employees since before Burges's body was discovered. Police were able to gain entry to Finch's apartment above the steel mill and discovered a pool of Burges' blood inside.

A murder weapon has not yet been identified.

Amber Evans, a Milwaukee native and Bradley Finch's girlfriend, was reported missing in late July. Police are currently searching for both Evans and Finch, and a warrant has been made for his arrest.

Reporters pressed Sheriff Larson for more information regarding Gallagher Finch, who is now being held at Folsom State Prison. One reporter asked, "Is it possible that the older brother framed the younger?"

"You all know as much as I do," Larson countered. "The younger brother confessed to burying Ms. Castro's body, but denies having killed her. Burying a body is still a crime, folks."

**FINCH**, continued on A1

Gal looked at two black and white images underneath the title of the article.

One showed the high school photograph of Whitney Burges, a beautiful blonde with a saddened smile. He recognized her instantly. She was a call girl belonging to the Sierra Red Lodges, a call girl that Gal knew Brad had favored, even dated, once upon a time. He'd last seen her hanging around with Daphne that fateful January night at the mansion.

She had spoken to him, had asked about Brad...

Had held her stomach tenderly, her eyes desperate and obsessed.

*Brad's baby*, he guessed.

The second image was a grislier visual. Wrapped in a tarp, Whitney's body hung upside down, ankles clamped in chains and strung from the familiar rafters of his father's steel mill. *Brad's* steel mill. As he stared at the picture, Gal was reminded of a chrysalis, as though the mangled body contained within was merely transforming.

*Was it a message?*

Gal looked up from the newspaper. He rubbed his aching temples, fingertips smearing gray streaks across his forehead.

*What the hell is going on?*

He sat up on his much-too-firm excuse for a bed, the stench of his backed-up toilet doing nothing to make his headache lessen. He'd only recently been moved into his own cell, and the previous occupant had apparently attempted to pass contraband through the pipes. No one had been by to fix the issue.

He assumed that nobody really cared.

Gal reached into his pillow case. He pulled out a stack of napkins and a red Sharpie he'd nicked from one of the guards. He rifled through the wrinkled napkins, shuffling through his notes scribbled in red ink.

*Write your story. Finish it before it finishes you.*

He uncapped the Sharpie and began to jot down everything the news article had helped to reveal about his own story. *Tom DeLevine's story...*

The person who killed Daphne was still out there. He killed again. This time, Whitney's murder had been a show of arrogance. A display of vanity. A work of art.

*What the hell is going on?*

*Think, Gal, think.*

Amber had been missing since July, and it was now December. She had either run away, had been abducted, or... he didn't want to think of it... she was dead. If Brad was indeed responsible for all of this, Gal could think of no reason why he'd want to kill Amber.

He killed Daphne because she knew about Whitney's pregnancy, and didn't want to risk Amber finding out.

He killed Whitney because she'd followed through with having the baby and, presumably, she had confronted him.

He sent Amber away until he sorted it all out…

*Does Amber know that Brad is a murderer? Could she have helped?*

Brad was now missing, either because he ran off to meet up with Amber, or he panicked and ran away to escape capture.

*But why would he show off his work by hanging Whitney upside down in the steel mill?*

Could it be that someone was framing him, just like someone framed Gal? And where had Yvette run off to? Why would Yvette want Whitney dead? There was no connection there.

Daphne. Whitney. Yvette. Amber.

Two dead. Two missing.

*What the hell is going on?*

Gal jumped as his cell door clanged open. The guard stepped inside, glancing curiously at the hundreds of red-stained napkins littering the cell floor. "Let's go."

"Where are we going?" Gal asked.

"To Disneyland," the guard quipped sarcastically. "Grab your stuff."

"Where are we going?"

"Jesus, boy, if you want to stay locked up in here, be my guest." The guard grabbed the cell door. "You made bail, but if you don't want to go – "

Before he realized he had moved, Gal jumped off the bed, gathered all the napkins off the floor, stuffed them into his pants, and bolted out of the cell.

*Scarlet sold the house.*

Gal sighed, suddenly relishing in an equal measure of relief and melancholy.

"Hang on a sec." The guard grabbed Gal by the shoulder, spun him around, and plucked something from the top of his ear. "Steal my Sharpie again, and I'll kill you."

***

*Desperate times…*

It was cold, and he needed a beer.

Jimmy Finch's breath projected a thick cloud of vaporous steam in the chill midnight air. Every night this week saw at least two inches of snowfall, and it was finally cold enough in The Loop for the powder to stick.

He stamped his feet on the asphalt, kicking blood back into the numbed toes curled within his shoes. The soles had worn away from walking, melted snow seeping in through the decayed rubber and soaking his socks… not that his holey socks provided any protection anyway.

It finally happened. *Again.*

He was homeless. A vagabond. A man without a car. A man with no money to hire a cab. A man with no friends to drive him around. He'd screwed over too many acquaintances over the years. Had borrowed too much money. Had spent all that borrowed money on booze and call girls. Had neglected to find, and keep, a job. And when he'd finally sold out his little brother for the family house that was rightfully his, the police seized it for evidence.

*Pigs.*

He wanted new shoes.

He wanted cash.

He wanted warmth, but he absolutely needed a beer.

His clothes were starting to stink, but his current lodgings were zero help. No water to do laundry. No heat to dry his sodden socks. No gas to warm his hands over the stove. All the amenities had been turned off, all except the electricity, but Jimmy had a feeling it wouldn't be long before even light in the darkness of winter would be hard to obtain.

Old Ruby hadn't been seen in months. She'd most likely given up any hope of selling the place, had given up paying her utility bills, and had probably moved back to find some warmth and solace that only the Gulf could provide during her final years.

*Lucky ol' bitch.*

She left one thing behind, however.

For the first couple of days, he searched the old house for food, but all he managed to find was a moldy sack of potatoes hidden under the bottom shelf of the pantry. Underneath the potatoes, however, he found an old can of Folger's coffee. And inside the can, Ruby left behind an interesting little artifact.

The small handgun with the pearl handle was now tucked safely in the waistband of his boxers. Sure, it was a little girly, but it was loaded and it was dangerous.

*Desperate times…*

A sudden gust of wind and snow blew onto the back of his neck, causing him to pull a black beanie lower over his ears. He tugged the black jacket he'd stolen from the house tighter around his simian shoulders, pulled a black ski mask over his mouth and nose, and then brushed the snow from the soaked denim of his faded black jeans.

In the dead of night, he was nothing but a shadow. All but invisible.

The rev of an engine roused Jimmy's attention. He swung his eyes to the Shell gas station across the street and watched as a semi pulled out and sped off down the highway.

Too many people recognized him in the various general stores in town. But here, at the dilapidated southern entrance of The Loop from Highway 395, there was nothing but the gas station. He looked up and down the highway and, seeing no lights coming from either direction, he dashed across the street, pulled the small gun out of his boxers, and kicked open the front door of the convenience store.

Halfway through devouring a granola bar, the stoned hippie behind the counter glanced from Jimmy's shadowy getup, to the mania in his eyes, and finally to the gun pointed at his chest. The glossy-eyed teen took a moment to register what was going on, gauged the severity of the situation, and simply whispered, "Shit."

"Open up the register!" Jimmy screamed under the neoprene. He pulled the empty backpack off his shoulders and swung it down onto the service stand. "Open it up before I blow your head off."

The stony teen did as he was told and opened the register.

"Put all the money in," Jimmy shouted, still pointing the gun with one hand while swiping candy bars with the other. The kid quickly tugged all the bills out of the till, unzipped the backpack, and shoved the cash inside.

"That's all of it," the pimply kid squeaked. "I swear, I just – " And then he stopped. His bloodshot eyes were suddenly fixed on the tabloid stand beside the register.

Jimmy looked, and there, printed on the front page of *The Mammoth Mirror*, were four familiar faces:

Gal, gaunt and thin, bound and shackled.

Brad, coiffed and contained.

Scarlet, sad and confused.

And there, staring back at him, was Jimmy's own high school senior portrait. God, how the years had screwed him.

The headline read:

**One FINCH in a cage, another on the wind.**
**Have the others flown south for winter?**

Even under the façade of the neoprene face mask, the cashier seemed to have recognized him. "Is that…"

Without thinking, Jimmy pistol-whipped the pubescent prick. The kid fell like the sack of moldy potatoes hidden in Ruby's pantry.

Jimmy stuffed the backpack full of turkey jerky, potato chips, candy, water, and beer. He zipped it up, swung it over his shoulder, and bolted out the door.

*Desperate times…*

*** 

He couldn't believe what he'd just done.

Never in his life could Jimmy have imagined he'd be at the better end of a gun, threatening the life of a nameless cashier for a measly hundred and eleven dollars. He'd counted it all on the way back and couldn't deny that he was more than a little ashamed that he hadn't taken more beer.

The zitty cashier recognized him, and Jimmy panicked. Pure and simple.

Looking back on it, he would've done better to shoot the kid because now, the cops were most certainly searching The Loop for him.

But he wasn't a killer. Not like Gal.

*And not like Brad…*

He was screwed. No doubt about it. He had to get out of town.

Jimmy bolted up the cul-de-sac, past the police tape popping in the wind, turned away from the house that should've been his, and instead crossed Ruby's front yard, jumped over the fence, got down on his knees, and reached up through a small doggy entrance to unlock the kitchen door.

It was only then that he heard the crackle of burning paper and smelled the sharp tang of tobacco in the freezing air.

A Cuban cigar.

"What are you doing here?" Jimmy grumbled.

"Is that any way to greet me?" came that confident, smoky tone he'd grown so fond of. Violent Violet sat on one of the old plastic lounge chairs littering Ruby's back porch. Jimmy allowed his hungry eyes to caress her tatted thighs, memorizing the ink blots he hadn't paid for in months.

"Shorts, in this weather?" he asked. "How did you find me?"

"Don't you remember what I told you our first night together?" she purred, two streams of billowing smoke pouring from her pierced nose. "When I want something, I find it."

"What do you want?" he asked.

"You," she replied with a pouty grin. "Don't you want me?"

Jimmy sighed. He unzipped the backpack, wading his fingers through the pathetic bills he'd stolen, and instead pulled out two beers.

"I don't have any money," he lied, cracking the cans open and offering one to her.

"It's not money I want," Violet answered.

"What *do* you want?"

She smirked. "I want to offer you a job."

*A job?*

"I doubt I'd get a lot of offers," he joked, tipping back his own beer and taking down half in one gulp. God, it tasted good. "I'm hardly a looker."

Violet giggled. "We have enough call girls. No, what we need from you is something a little more covert. Something, I might add, that pays very, very well."

"I'm listening."

"My boss needs something, and he thinks you're the perfect person to get it for him."

"Who's your boss?"

Violet shrugged her strong yet dainty shoulders. "You've heard of him, I'm sure." She took another drag of the cigar and blew out half a dozen impressive smoke rings. "He will introduce himself when the time is right. And he'll reward you for your services. That is, if you help him get what he wants."

"What does he want?"

Violet fixed her eyes on Jimmy's and, for a moment, he felt a nervous tingle on the back of his neck.

"Gallagher," she said.

Jimmy watched her for a moment, guzzled down the rest of his beer, and cracked open another. *Might as well drink while conducting business*, he considered.

"What does he want with Gal?"

Violet stamped out her cigar on the glass table top, leaving an ashy black streak along its surface. "All I'm allowed to say is that he can get your brother out of Folsom, but he needs your help doing it."

"And what if I don't think Gal should ever get out?" he challenged her.

"That's on you," she answered. He watched as she tugged down the v-line of her shirt, exposing her full and ample cleavage. For a moment, he imagined she was going to tempt him with a bosom he'd already feasted on more than a dozen times.

Instead, she pulled a large wad of hundred-dollar bills from her bra. "This is just a very small piece of his offer."

She tossed the bills into his lap and watched as he eagerly flipped through them.

"There's enough there to buy my services ten times over," she whispered, sipping her beer. "And, in time, I won't even make you pay anymore."

"Why me?" he asked.

"Why not?" she answered. "It was my idea, actually. Who better than you? You're his brother, after all." Violet stood up, swinging her hips side to side as she walked around the table, gently tracing her fingertips along his shoulders. "You're strong. A little extra security is something we need."

She leaned down and pressed a soft, seductive kiss to the tips of his lips, lifting one foot up onto the table to expose the Rorschach stretching between her inner thighs, allowing his male gaze to become hypnotized.

"What is it you want most, James? Money? Stability? The house across the street?"

Jimmy looked up and finally, she had his unwavering attention.

"You help us, and I swear your little brother will never again be a hindrance. You'll get the house. You'll get the money." She smirked, tugging his face away from her thighs as she leaned down to kiss him once more.

"And you'll get me, whenever you want me," Violet concluded.

Jimmy gazed into her devilish eyes and smirked.

"Top it off with a freebee tonight, and I'll consider it."

Violet grinned, and then moved away. "You drive a hard bargain, Mr. Finch." She unslung her purse from the back of the chair and pulled out a single sheet of white paper. "Shall we get it in writing?"

"Your boss is pretty official, isn't he?"

"What can I say? He's a businessman." She handed him a pen and smoothed out the contract in front of him.

"Should I be worried for Gal?"

"Have you ever been worried for him?"

"Touché."

"All it takes is a few strokes of ink," she said. "Then, we'll go upstairs and work out the finer details."

Without even bothering to read the contract, Jimmy Finch signed his life away on the dotted line.

*** 

Just after four in the morning, Violet emerged from The Old Lady's home to a soft, dawn snowfall. Her shoes crunched over the frosted crabgrass as she reached into her purse and withdrew the contract Jimmy had signed hours earlier.

She'd done it.

Whether he survived the next couple days was none of her accord. He was a disgusting excuse for a man.

Now tainted in the filthy gorilla's musk, all she wanted was to get back to the cabin and soak in a hot shower. She strolled down the length of the cul-de-sac, hopped in her Volkswagen Beetle, and sped off past the frozen, glassy surface of Gull Lake.

What she failed to notice was the blue Silverado that followed from a distance.

*** 

Only one thing had been confiscated from Gal's pockets the night Sheriff Larson had arrested him all those months ago. On his way out, his cell phone had been returned to him.

What scared him most was that on the night of his arrest, he recalled having the stag horn pocketknife tucked away in his jeans. Amid the shouts, the tackling, and being half-asleep when he'd been chucked into the back of the police unit, he guessed that Larson found the knife and kept it for evidence.

If the pocketknife found its way into the hands of the prosecution, and if it could be proven that Gal had plucked it out of Daphne's neck the morning he'd buried her body, he could very well be facing the death penalty.

Gal was led down a final, claustrophobic corridor, and stepped out into a chilly winter sunlight. He shivered once, his footsteps echoing across an empty parking lot.

Well, almost empty.

"Hey, little brother."

Gal stopped dead in his tracks. It wasn't Scarlet who'd come to pick him up.

It was Jimmy.

# TWENTY ONE

# Pine

Two hours on the road, and not a single word was spoken.

Gal kept his eyes fixed through the passenger window. Red and green hills whipped past as they sped through Nevada. Far off on the horizon, he could just make out the snow-capped peaks of the Sierras.

Further still they drove in silence.

Gal desperately wanted to sleep, but too many questions were buzzing in his head.

*Whose truck is this? Did Jimmy steal it? Where is Scarlet? Where did the bail money come from? Did they sell the house? Why Jimmy?*

Yes. *Why Jimmy?*

Questions interwove with sickening reflections.

*He's the reason I went to prison. He's the reason I've been stuck there. He's the reason I've been starving. He's the reason I've been rotting.*

*Jimmy screwed me over.*

"I'm sorry," Jimmy muttered.

"Fuck you," Gal replied.

"I had to do it, Gal. I heard you on the phone, I heard you confess.

What was I supposed to do? They would've come for all of us."

"I didn't kill her."

"I don't think you did. But, you and Scar – you should've called the police when you found a dead hooker in your bed, you dumb shit."

"You sold me out."

"I'm sorry."

"No, you're not."

"You would've done the same to me, Gal," Jimmy growled. "Don't deny it."

He was right. Had Gal discovered Jimmy confessing to a crime that could get all his siblings in trouble, especially Scarlet, he would most definitely have offered him to the police.

"I gave you a running start," Jimmy had the nerve to remind him. "Don't forget that."

He had indeed. Enough of a running start to find the wind-torn shelter in the channels of Silver Lake. Enough of a running start to learn how to defecate in a hole. Enough of a running start to run straight into a trap laid by Sandy Castro. Enough of a running start to think up a few people who might have actually killed Daphne.

He was done. He wanted answers.

"Did you kill her, Jim?"

Jimmy slammed his foot on the brake, nearly sending Gal straight through the windshield. The back tires fishtailed, sending smoke into a fierce wake behind the truck. The acrid smell of burnt rubber stung Gal's nostrils.

"What did you say?" Jimmy's knuckles whitened as he gripped the steering wheel.

"Did you kill Daphne?" Gal repeated.

Gal heard the grinding of Jimmy's molars, could see that all-too-familiar snakelike vein pulsing in his temple, could feel the burning anger radiating off his massive shoulders.

"Why would I do that?" he asked, a little too calmly.

Gal had the feeling that he was moments away from getting his nose caved in. But for once, he didn't care.

"You've always wanted the house, Jim. You know that. I know that." He glanced at the side view mirror, thankful that nobody had had the misfortune of driving behind them. "Somebody was in the house that night. You knew where the spare key was."

Gal softened his tone, less accusatory and more inquisitive.

"I'm just looking for answers. Framing me would've gotten me out of the house for good." He watched his eldest brother closely, and was astounded when Jimmy turned to face him.

Jimmy's normally angry eyes were defeated. His massive shoulders slumped. His grip on the wheel loosened, and his apelike hands dropped to the torn leather seat.

"Do you really think I would do that to you?" he asked, low and broken.

For the first time ever, in a confrontation with his less loquacious older brother, Gal wasn't quite sure how to respond.

"I'm sorry," Jimmy whispered.

"For what?"

"For being a shitty brother. For not being there for you when you needed me. Ever." His shoulders began to tremble. "I'm not perfect, Gal. Far from it. But I would never, ever go out of my way to hurt you. You're my little brother, before anything and everything."

The vanquished look on his face told Gal everything he needed to know.

"Okay, Jim. Let's go home."

An hour's drive led them south beyond Bridgeport. The elevation was kicking in and, after five months cooped up in a cell, Gal popped his ears and unrolled the window.

A blast of cold mountain air caressed his face and sent his wild, white-patched black hair whipping behind him. The familiar scent of pine flooded his lungs, and finally, he knew that he was home.

On either side of the highway, a five-foot snowbank had compressed into a wall of white slush. Clouds rolled in from the east as the sun set in the west. As much as Gal had wished for the warmth of the sun in winters past, he was excited for his first Christmas snowfall this year.

"Pull over for a sec, Jim," Gal called over the roar of the wind. "I need to write my name in the snow."

Jimmy pulled the truck to the side of the highway, and Gal hopped out. He glanced at either side of the highway and saw nobody else on the road, then relieved himself, drawing a cursive **G** in the slush. He thought of Mrs. Montgomery, his third grade teacher, and how pleased she would be to see that his cursive had survived after all these years.

After all that had happened to him.

He heard footsteps behind him and guessed that Jimmy planned to add a scribbled **J** into the snow.

A sharp prick pierced his neck. A syringe pushed an unseen liquid into his bloodstream. Instantly, his vision faded.

The last thing he remembered were Jimmy's massive arms holding him from behind, and his eldest brother's voice whispering into his ear.

"I'm sorry."

***

He heard his mother's voice.

Her sweet, soft voice calling him from downstairs. It was time for breakfast. He sniffed the air, hoping to catch a whiff of the usual bacon and pancakes she normally cooked on Saturday mornings. He would stuff himself until he couldn't eat anymore, and he never seemed to get any fatter.

His brothers never failed to make fun of how skinny he was, how girls preferred guys with muscles, rugged guys, something that Gal would never, ever be.

*Don't mind them,* his mother would say, *you have a metabolism most people would kill for.* She'd always known the perfect words to make him feel better. Words to make him feel like a king.

He sniffed the air again, but all he could smell was the scent of damp, musty pine. The air was thick with it. He wondered if the roof had sprung a leak under the weight of all the winter snow.

His bed was much too firm beneath his back, bony shoulder blades pressed uncomfortably into the mattress. He tried to roll over, but his shoulder struck something hard above him. He tried to bend his knees, but they knocked against a wooden barrier. He reached down for his blankets and felt only damp denim stuck to his legs.

*I never wear jeans to bed.*

Gal opened his eyes and found himself lost in complete darkness.

*This isn't my room.*

He called out for his mother, but all that emitted was a weak, muffled gurgle.

He tried to open his mouth, but his lips were stuck firmly in place. His mouth was stuffed with a thick, fibrous something, the material pushing back into his throat and causing his stomach to lurch.

He gagged.

"Gal?" he heard his mother call softly again. But she sounded different this time.

Weak.

Sad.

Desperate.

"Gal, is that you?" It was strange, bizarrely muted, as though he were listening to her through a block of wood.

He knew that voice, and it didn't belong to his mother. She was dead, after all.

"Gghhaahh…" he responded through the sock. He tried to raise his arms, but they were blocked by that unseen barrier. He reached out to the sides, but again, he could barely move.

The warm fuzziness in his head was slowly giving way to something much more primal. He wanted to move. He wanted to speak. He wanted to yell. He tried to sit up, but his head slammed into something hard.

Strong, electric fingers began to squeeze his brain from within, the warm fuzziness gone now and replaced with a cold, splitting headache.

He tried to clench his fists, but he could hardly bend his tingling fingers. He struck the planks beneath him, above him, and on both sides of him. The barriers reacted with soft, hollow chords.

He was trapped in a wooden box.

*A coffin.*

"Mmmmppph!" he tried to scream. "Gggahhh!"

"Gal," came that stifled voice again. "Gal, be quiet. They'll hear you."

*Amber.*

He tried to call out to her, but the sock lodged deeper into his throat, lips stuck together under what he assumed was duct tape.

"I'm here," she whispered through a small crack in the wood. "Oh my god, Gal, I'm so sorry. So, so sorry."

He heard her begin to sob, heard chains rattle around hollow pipes. She too, then, was a prisoner in this hell.

"It's all my fault," she wept. "I'm so sorry."

Months of pent up anger toward the girl who had knocked him out with a copper pipe suddenly dissipated. She'd only done what she thought was right at the time. She'd been scared of him, scared that he might be capable of murder.

She must have learned the truth.

"Please forgive me," she cried.

He wanted out. He wanted to wrap his arms around her. Wanted to break the chains that bound her to whatever fate she'd been prisoner to for so many months. Wanted to strangle whoever had taken her from him.

Gal forced his wrist to bend at an unholy angle, forced his forearm to squeeze up between his emaciated stomach and the lid of the pine coffin. Struggled to reach his fingertips over his throat.

He heard a sickening pop as his shoulder dislocated from its socket. Agonizing pain shot down his right side. Vomit burned at the back of his throat. He was about to pass out.

He had to fight it.

Not wanting to suffocate in his own sick, Gal gulped it down, tears flooding his eyes as he wriggled excruciating fingertips higher. Finally, he felt the duct tape on his cheek. He groaned and slowly tore the adhesive out of his stubble, peeling it back past his bone-dry lips until the tape fell limp over the left side of his face. He turned his face to the side, using teeth and tongue to push the damp, musty sock out of his throat before finally spitting it out.

"Amber..." he groaned.

"Gal," she responded. "Gal, talk to me."

"Get me out of here," he whimpered, biting back the agony radiating through his shoulder. "Help – "

He heard her chains rattle, heard her body rustle across wood and gravel, heard the unmistakable effort as she tried to reach him.

"I can't. You're too far," she said.

"Where are we?"

"In a basement. I don't know where, Gal— that girl with the purple hair – Jonathan Tanner. And – and Jimmy – "

*Jimmy.*

*How could I be so stupid?*

"Amber, listen to me," he groaned. "We're going to get out of here. I swear."

"We're never going to get out of here," she whispered. "You're in a box, Gal. They – they're going to put you in the ground."

His heart sank.

He hadn't yet considered why he was trapped in the wooden box. And now, it all made sense. The truck belonged to Jonathan Tanner. He'd hired Jimmy to get Gal out of prison, to coax him into a false sense of security.

"Why?"

"Because of Daphne Castro," she said. "I heard them talking. She's the one that helped him escape from prison. He wants to kill whoever killed her. He doesn't care who it is. You and Scarlet buried her. He thinks Brad might have killed her, and that's why he wanted me."

She choked back another sob.

"He's going to kill you, and then he's going to kill all of us."

"But Brad – "

"Brad killed that Burges girl! He took her baby, and he disappeared. He never even came looking for me – " Amber sobbed, unable to hold back any longer.

"Amber, listen to me. We're going to get out of here," Gal told her. He couldn't trust the fear in his own voice enough to believe it. "I'm going to get you out."

He was met with silence.

"Amber?"

"They're coming," she whispered.

His lack of vision in the darkness amplified his hearing. He listened for a moment, and heard boots thumping on wooden floorboards overhead. Heard the rattling of locks unbolted, the jiggle of a door handle, the squelch of an old door being wrenched open.

"Well, well, the pretty little peach is awake," came a smoky voice. "How'd you sleep, sweetheart?"

"Fuck you," Amber whimpered, more than a little broken.

"I'll be back to dose you again, bitch," the smoky voice barked back. "Come on, let's get this over with."

Two pairs of feet thumped down wooden stairs.

"Don't do this," Amber begged. "Please, he doesn't deserve this. He didn't murder that girl. I swear he didn't. Jimmy, tell her!"

But Jimmy didn't answer.

The racking pain in Gal's shoulder became unbearable. Stars shimmered in the darkness. His world began to spin.

"Jimmy, please!" Amber screamed.

"Shut up!" the smoky voice yelled. A sharp smack echoed in the basement beyond Gal's wooden prison, and Amber fell silent.

Fuzzy warmth clouded Gal's mind once more, and unconsciousness took hold of him.

The last thing he remembered was the overpowering smell of damp, musty pine.

\*\*\*

Jimmy Finch pushed the roughly hewn wooden coffin snugly into the back of the old truck and latched the tailgate. He stared at the box for a moment, and then pulled an old memory off the shelf in the back of his mind:

*He was five years old again, sitting Indian-style on the old bear rug his father had brought home from a hunting trip in Colorado. His arms were cradled under a soft, warm bundle, and he was unsure of what to do next.*

*"You're doing fine, Jimbo," his father said. "Just like that. Careful now. Hold his head."*

*Jimmy did as he was told, propping his elbow upward at a slightly uncomfortable angle. The blanket fell away, and Jimmy looked down.*

*A pair of sleepy little eyes stared up at him, plump infantile lips puckered and suckling on a tiny, sluggish tongue.*

*He held the bubbling baby securely in his left arm. He reached down with his right hand to touch the tuft of silken black hair sprouting from his baby brother's head.*

*The baby gave him a tiny smile, and Jimmy smiled back.*

*"I think he likes you," his father said. Jimmy looked up and grinned at his father proudly. Brad was too little to hold him, and Scarlet was still a baby herself. But Jimmy...*

*Jimmy was a big boy.*

*"You have to watch out for him, Jimbo. Remember that," his father said. Jimmy nodded at his father's words and looked down.*

*Little Gallagher gave a yawn and closed his eyes.*

*"He's your little brother, before anything and everything."*

They drove two miles into the dense woods behind the cabin, so deep now that there was nothing around them except for dense, snow-jacketed Jeffrey pines stretching in every direction.

Pungent, smoky fumes left a haze in the cab of the truck as Violet puffed away on a Cuban.

"So, when am I going to meet this guy?" Jimmy asked, hands on the wheel as he weaved around a large mound of freshly fallen snow.

"He should be back later today," she muttered, chewing the end of the Cuban. "He's picking up a Christmas tree on his way back."

"And the cash?"

"You'll get it," she barked, then softened her tone and touched his arm. "Don't you trust me, baby?"

"Of course."

"Stop here," she told him, peering out at a snowy clearing. "This is it."

Jimmy parked the truck, and the pair of them hopped out. Violet put out her cigar in the snow and approached the large hole already entrenched in the earth.

"You sure you're okay with doing this?" she asked with a playful smirk.

"He buried her," Jimmy replied. "Seems only fitting we bury him."

"Tanner's thoughts exactly."

Jimmy unlatched the tailgate, reached in to grab a large shovel they'd brought along, and tossed it beside the hole. Violet hopped into the bed of the truck and pushed on the coffin while Jimmy held the other end. Together, they hoisted it out of the truck and carried it over to the deep grave.

"On three," he said. "One, two, three."

They released their ends of the coffin simultaneously. It fell six feet and landed with a soft thud on the frosted earth below.

"Perfect," Violet whispered. She walked around the hole to plant a soft, seductive kiss on the tips of his chapped lips. "Fill it in. I'll go warm up the truck."

"You got it," he replied with a smirk, then pinched her on the rear.

As she turned, Jimmy picked up the shovel and swung it as hard as he could. The butt of the shovel cracked the back of Violet's skull.

She dropped to her knees, fell forward, and was silent.

Jimmy stepped over her body, walked casually to the truck, and pulled out the crowbar he'd hidden behind the front seat. He walked back to the hole, jumped in beside the coffin, and wedged the crowbar beneath the lid. He pushed all his weight down against the iron and forced the nail out of the top left corner. He repeated the process three more times, lifted off the lid, and pushed it aside.

Jim looked down at his baby brother, passed out inside the wooden box.

"Gal," Jimmy muttered. "Gal, wake up." He slapped Gal's face a few times, but Gal wouldn't wake.

Jimmy grabbed a handful of snow and held it firmly between his palms. After a few seconds, the heat of his hands melted the snow into ice cold liquid. He let the water drip onto Gal's face and finally, his brother began to stir.

Eyelids fluttered back to reveal emerald green eyes. Jimmy smiled, reached up to touch Gal's stringy and matted black hair, and said, "I'm sorry."

Gal smiled a moment, and then his eyes grew wide.

"Jimmy, get down!"

Before Jimmy could register what had happened, the business end of a shovel pierced his back between his shoulder blades, splitting his spine and severing his spinal cord.

The last thing James Michael Finch remembered in life was his baby brother's emerald eyes, staring in horror as he fell face first into a pine box.

# TWENTY TWO

# Blood

∽

The world had been dipped in oil.

Jimmy fell with a fluid slowness, his bulk careening forward in a perfect arc. The shaft of the shovel momentarily resembled a dorsal fin, stuck firmly in place between scapula and ribs.

Spurts of warm, scarlet blood shot from his lips and seemed to hang, glistening, in midair. And as long as it took for them to hang there, so quick were they to fall and splatter across Gal's face.

Gal was dreaming.

He had to be.

The weight of Jimmy's body came crashing down on top of him, pinning him inside the firm wood of his intended coffin. He moaned, unable to move his left side under his brother's dead weight. His right arm failed to respond at all, courtesy of a dislocated shoulder.

Jimmy's cheek rested against Gal's chest, glassy eyes staring at the dusty wooden panels of the casket's interior. For a moment, he appeared to be scrutinizing the craftsmanship, but Gal knew that his brother's eyes would never move again.

Gal choked back the urge to yell his brother's name one final time, knew that calling out to him would never succeed in waking him.

*I have to get out of this hole…*

"You fucker!" came an unearthly shriek from above.

A purple-haired woman stood at the edge of the hole, eyes ablaze in manic rage, clutching a bloody knot on the back of her violet head.

There would be plenty of time to grieve, Gal supposed.

Instead, the sting of searing hatred and the all-consuming ache for vengeance suddenly hijacked his motor functions. Adrenaline pumped a newfound fury into his veins and, before he could register his own strength, he pushed upward with his left arm and leg, temples pulsing as he shoved Jimmy's weight enough to squeeze out from beneath him.

The woman's frenzied gaze settled upon Gal, her teeth bared like a wolf intent on ripping apart its prey.

"You're next!" she screamed, moving onto her stomach at the edge of the hole to reach in and grip the shaft of the shovel. She pulled and pulled, but her aim had proven too perfect, the sharpened spade wedged and unmoving between Jimmy's vertebrae.

Gal reached up and gripped the bottom of the shaft in his left hand. With an almighty tug, he wrenched the purple-haired murderess over the edge of the hole, watching as she fell with an ear-shattering crack against the bottom edge of the wooden casket at his feet.

She gasped for the breath that had been knocked out of her. Her clawed fingers scratched and tore at Gal's legs.

He kicked downward as hard as he could, crunching the sole of his shoe into her face and snapping her nose.

Blood gushed down her chin and throat. She scrambled and tugged herself up his body, landing a firm punch between his thighs that knocked him senseless. She sank her teeth into his groin, and he screamed in agony. Noticing that his right arm was out of service, she pinned down his left. She retrieved the crowbar Jimmy dropped and swung it hard.

White light exploded behind Gal's eyelids.

His right cheekbone crunched under the force of the iron. Outrageous, searing pain stretched down his neck. His vision went blurry, swimming in and out of focus.

Suddenly, something very peculiar faded into view.

He knew that shape. Watched it emerge from Jimmy's pocket. Saw the pearly handle shimmering against the snow.

Gal pushed his wrist lower under her grip.

He stretched his fingertips.

The severed nub of his left pinky wedged under the trigger guard.

The purple-haired woman pulled the crowbar back for the final death blow. She aimed for his temple. And then, she swung.

Six loud gunshots rang out in rapid succession.

A murder of crows cawed and took wing, feathers flapping in the freezing wind. They flew over the deeply dug hole. Down below, the purple-haired woman dropped the bloody crowbar.

She looked down at the skinny, dark-haired man beneath her. She glanced down between their bodies and saw the small gun with the pearl handle. She noticed the barrel smoking against her stomach.

She touched six new holes in her chest, pulled her fingers away, and let the blood drip from her fingertips.

She collapsed on top of him and was forever still.

***

Under a blanket of bleak winter clouds, a sharp ridge glittered white under freshly fallen snow, passing low along the western incline of Bloody Mountain.

If one were to look oh so carefully, one might have noticed the blue Silverado parked just below the crest, virtually unseen behind a large snowbank. It was from here that former deputy Sandy Castro had discovered the hidden valley below, and the small log cabin veiled within.

She had followed the violet-haired woman here two weeks earlier.

"How long have you been back?" Scarlet asked. She pulled her jacket tighter around her shoulders, leaning in close to the dashboard and allowing the heater to warm her fingers.

"Couple of weeks," Sandy answered. She held a pair of binoculars firmly to her eyeballs, gaze fixed on the shadowy figure below. She watched the man swing a large axe against the trunk of a bushy pine.

"Where have you been staying?"

"I sleep in here." Sandy wiped her sleeve against the windshield, un-fogging the cold glass. "Cheaper than a motel."

"You're more than welcome to stay with me," Scarlet offered. "You've already done so much for us."

"I appreciate that. But after everything that's happened, I'm not sure the Sierras are where I'm meant to be." Sandy pressed the binoculars back to her face. "Reminds me of her."

"Did you bury her?" Scarlet asked.

"No," Sandy replied with a sigh. "I decided on cremation. Sprinkled her into the ocean off the Santa Monica Pier."

Sandy lowered the binoculars just enough to shoot Scarlet a knowing glance.

"She's already been buried once. I saw what it did to her, and that's not how I wanted to remember her face."

Scarlet looked down at her lap.

"I'm so sorry," she whispered. "We both are."

"I know."

"So why come back at all?"

"To expose it. All of it," Sandy muttered. "Daphne was part of something that should never have existed. These girls know nothing else, but maybe I can help change that."

"How?"

"The fastest way to kill a business, is to kill its boss."

Sandy passed the binoculars to Scarlet. She put them to her eyes and watched the strange man chop at the tree.

"When I came back to town, I went back to watch Gal's house. I thought that maybe, if I kept an eye on it, Daphne's killer would return." Sandy unscrewed the thermos and sucked down a mouthful of gas station coffee that was much too black and far too cold.

"Couple of weeks ago, a girl snuck in," she continued. "She had purple hair. At first, I just figured it was some kid out with her friends, looking to get into a little mischief by breakin' into the famous Finch Murder House. But, nobody else showed up."

Scarlet watched the distant silhouette fell the large pine tree, and Sandy continued.

"She came back the next night, but this time, she broke into the for-sale house across the street. I snuck around back and heard her talking with someone."

Sandy took the binoculars from Scarlet.

"She was talking to your brother."

Scarlet's eyes widened behind her hipster spectacles. "Brad?" she asked.

"Jimmy."

"Jimmy? But – "

"They made a deal. This broad and her boss came into a lot of money. Three-hundred thousand, to be exact. Said that her boss needed Jimmy to take the money, and – "

"And what?"

"And bail out Gal."

Sandy choked down another gullet of lukewarm joe, giving Scarlet a moment to digest what she'd discovered.

"Why?" Scarlet asked, eyes twitching as she tried to make sense of it all.

"When I first showed up here, back in March, back before I knew about Daphne's murder, I met one of her friends. She told me all about the Sierra Red Lodges. Told me that Daphne was a call girl. Told me that Daphne wanted better for all the other call girls. That she was involved in some very, very shady business."

"What business?"

"Ever heard of a man named Jonathan Tanner?"

The blood in Scarlet's face drained, her skin a sullen ivory. She nodded.

"She told me that Daphne helped him escape from Folsom State Prison." Sandy sighed. "The girl's name was Whitney Burges."

The pieces seemed to be falling into place. "The girl that Brad – "

"I don't think Brad killed that girl," Sandy said. "I think he was framed, just like Gal."

"Then who?"

"The last time I heard from Whitney Burges was when I was down south. She called me the day of Daphne's memorial. I was sitting on the edge of the pier, and she told me about another call girl named Violet. Said that Violet scared the hell out of her. That Violet was Jonathan Tanner's new main girl. That Violet was the reason she wanted to leave the whole thing behind. Brad and the baby were Whitney's way out. She told me she thinks Violet might have killed Daphne."

"But why?"

"Jealousy, maybe," Sandy replied. "Thought that with Daphne helping Tanner out of prison, he'd make her his main girl. The only way Violet could reach the top – "

"— was to kill the competition," Scarlet finished.

"Bingo."

"But Whitney – "

"Whitney, I assume, started asking questions. Violet knew where Gal lived, so it's possible that she also knew where Brad lived. It's possible that she followed Whitney to the steel mill, and then waited until Whitney was alone."

Sandy pressed the binoculars back to her face. She watched as the silhouette tied a rope around the fallen pine tree and began to drag it away.

"It could be that Tanner doesn't realize Daphne's killer is right under his nose. Daphne was obviously his favorite, and he won't stop until anyone who might have killed her is dead."

Sandy sighed.

"Blood for blood."

"So, Gal — " Scarlet whispered.

"Gal is down there," Sandy said. She reached into the glove compartment, pulled out her trusty Glock, and checked to make sure it was loaded. "And he's in serious trouble."

\*\*\*

He was numb.

Not from the biting cold.

Not from the disbelief that he'd been moments from death.

Not even from the shock of having ended the life of another human being. She'd deserved it, after all.

No. What left Gallagher Finch unable to process anything other than the sound of his feet crunching through the snow was the certainty that he would never again hear Jimmy's childish chuckles. He would never again feel his ribs crack beneath Jimmy's bearlike hugs. He would never again be the butt of one of Jimmy's astonishingly unfunny jokes.

Never.

There would be time to allow himself the full measure of grief. There would be time to try and understand why his brother had offered him up to a harsh fate, only to change his mind at the last moment. He never understood Jimmy. And as much as he wished he could have understood his motives, Gal knew that now, he would never get the chance.

It took an hour, Gal supposed, to pull himself out of the hole.

He used his one good arm to pull Jimmy on top of the purple-haired woman, using their corpses as a foundation and angling the wooden lid of the coffin into a makeshift ramp. He slipped a few times, but finally succeeded in gripping the crowbar onto the edge of the earth and pulling himself out.

He would come back for his brother's body. Was determined to do so. But right now, another life hung in the balance. One he might actually be able to save.

The memory of her voice echoed within his skull…

The desperation in her cries forced his full attention on getting back to her…

To break her chains.

Soaked in warm blood and freezing snow, Gal pulled himself into the large truck. The upholstery reeked of cigar smoke, awakening his senses and giving him some semblance of focus. The keys dangled from the ignition. It took a few revs of the engine to ignite the transmission, and then, he punched the gas.

Snow was falling heavily now, and it was getting dark.

One headlight had burnt out, the other sending a weak stream of light onto tire tracks that were beginning to disappear under the snow.

He weaved the truck to and fro between thick, black trunks of large pine trees, back wheels fishtailing in haste. After a few minutes, the trees began to thin out. He shut off the headlight and drove out into the open.

A log cabin stood in the small valley. The dissipating tire tracks led straight to it.

Gal killed the engine.

He slid out of the truck, sucking a pained gasp through clenched teeth. His dislocated shoulder throbbed with a dull, thumping agony. He tucked the crowbar into the waistband of his jeans and pulled the small handgun out of his pocket.

Bloody Mountain rose to the west, its silhouette outlined against a twilit sky. He'd climbed it once, years ago with Jimmy and Brad. He knew its familiar shark-toothed peak. Knew that he was only an hour's drive south of The Loop.

So close to home, and yet so far.

He approached the cabin, its windows dark from the inside. His eyes followed the contour of the valley, noticing a wide path carved deep in the snow, as though someone had dragged something heavy straight to the front door.

And then, he saw it.

There on the front porch was a pine tree, thick and bushy, wrapped and bound in rope.

*A Christmas tree.*

The path it had carved was fresh, and Gal knew then that Amber wasn't alone.

*If I'm going to die, I'm going to die a rugged man.*

He couldn't help but grin at the notion, deciding then and there that his story had finally reached its climax.

*Whether or not Tom DeLevine survives this ordeal is another matter entirely.*

\*\*\*

As Gal guessed it would be, the front door was unlocked.

An invitation.

*A trap.*

He held the gun firmly in his left hand. He nudged his good shoulder against the wood. Hinges creaked as a gust of stagnant, humid air enveloped him like a snug winter blanket.

If he was going to die, at least he would die warm.

Gal allowed his eyes to adjust to the darkness before stepping over the threshold. The final dregs of twilight filtered in through the doorway, purveying shadows indicative of a living room and kitchen. He recognized the flat wood of a dining table, the faint shine of leather chairs and a matching couch. As he stepped deeper into the darkness, a shadow moved in his periphery.

Gal swung his left arm up, aimed the gun, and fingered the trigger.

His reflection stared back at him through the glass of an old television set.

*Easy, old boy.*

Gal passed into a second room, a small antechamber that led into a long corridor, the end of which was shrouded in pitch black. There were two doorways on either side of the corridor, four possible hiding places for whoever was expecting the return of Jimmy and the purple-haired woman.

*Or expecting me.*

Each room he checked, and each room he found empty, save for a couple of cots, and in one, an empty sack of potato chips.

He pressed deeper into the corridor. The pitch blackness made it impossible to see anything. He was forced to glide his hand along the wall, gun pressed between his palm and the wood, right arm dangling uselessly at his side. He followed the corridor around a bend and stopped.

A single, horizontal sliver of light glowed dimly across the floor.

A door.

And behind the door came a soft, recognizable whimper.

Without a second thought, and without regard for what awaited him behind the door, Gal bolted forward through the darkness, found the handle, and gave it a twist. The door gave a loud squelch on its hinges.

The light within seared his retinas.

Blinded, he stepped forward, caught the edge of a stair, and tumbled. He fell forward, swung his left arm out, and prayed for a miracle. He caught the bannister and righted himself, dilated pupils adjusting to the scene at the bottom of the stairs.

*Amber.*

Her golden hair was lank and greasy, falling like sodden curtains around sullen and emaciated cheekbones. Her once eager and hungry eyes were sunken and hugged by purple bags that swallowed her youth.

But still, she was the most beautiful thing the world had ever seen.

Gal rushed down the flight of stairs and fell to his knees beside her. He dropped the gun and held her face in his good hand.

Her eyes rolled this way and that, as though lost in a dream she hadn't been in two hours earlier. Her wrists were bound in irons cuffs, chains rattling around the large sewage pipe she'd been confined to for five long, arduous months.

"Amber," he said, softly slapping her jaw to pull her out of the drug-induced high. "Amber, come on. Wake up. We're getting out of here."

She stared at the ceiling, eyes red and glazed. Finally, she settled her gaze upon him, realizing he was there with her.

"That's it. Come on."

Her eyes glanced over his forehead. They widened in horror.

A swift kick sent the handgun sliding across the wooden floor, into an unforeseen and shadowy corner. Gal swung his head around and immediately fell backward as an imposing shadow fell across the length of the basement.

"You look just like her."

The deep, gravelly voice rattled his bones. He didn't need to ask who this was. He already knew.

Jonathan Tanner towered over him, beard thick and matted, long white hair pulled back to expose a face tattered in winding scars and pitted pock marks. Pine needles jutted from the top of his head, a large axe pressed against his shoulder.

"Hello, son," he said.

"I'm not your son," Gal growled, scrambling to his feet.

"How did you get out of that box?"

Tanner slowly closed the distance between them. Gal shuffled backward, placing himself between Tanner and Amber.

"Let me guess, that big ape brother of yours had a change of heart."

"Fuck you."

Tanner chuckled a low, earth-quaking rumble. "You're tougher than I thought. Maybe there *is* a little bit of me in you."

"What do you want?"

"The same thing your mother wanted," Tanner answered, running calloused fingertips tenderly along the sharpened edge of the axe's blade. "You in the ground."

"You couldn't do it yourself?" Gal probed. "Had to coax my brother and that purple-haired bitch into doing it for you?"

"You're my blood, boy. What kind of father would I be?"

"You killed *her*. You can't you kill me?"

"I didn't kill Annie," Tanner barked. "She was dead when I got there. Head caved in. Blood and brains everywhere. Looking back, I wonder if she did it to herself. Smashed her own head in, because she couldn't stand seeing me in you."

Gal eased the fingers of his left hand into the waistband of his jeans.

"You escaped that box for a reason, boy," Tanner said. "You're more like me than you think."

Gal's left arm was a blur. He swung the crowbar with everything he had. Iron made contact with flesh, splitting Tanner's jaw with a loud crack and sending blood splashing against the wall.

Tanner roared in agony.

In unrelenting force, he swung the axe in a full arc. Gal dove, and the iron blade missed his ankle by an inch. It smashed against the concrete floor. The handle cracked on impact, splinters of wood exploding in all directions as the axe-head spun across the floor.

Gal landed on his dislocated shoulder. Pain detonated along his entire right side. Tunnel vision began to set in, but he knew he couldn't give in.

He rolled over and crawled desperately towards the shadowy corner...

Reached his left hand toward the shimmering pearl handle of the gun...

Grazed his fingertips on the grip.

Tanner's massive hands gripped Gal's shoulders, lifting him clean off the floor and throwing him across the length of the basement. Gal slammed into the opposite wall. Unable to breathe, he glanced up as Tanner approached him.

His time was up.

Fingers gripped to the pearl handle, Gal raised the handgun, pointed the barrel at his biological father's forehead, and squeezed the trigger.

*Click--*

In the time it took for Gal to realize that he'd wasted all six slugs in the purple-haired woman's chest, Tanner lifted him off the floor and slammed him into the wall. Tanner gripped his colossal left hand over Gal's throat and held him in midair.

Gal couldn't breathe.

He choked on his own collapsing windpipe. His eyes rolled back. His vision began to fade. His feet jolted, hanging a foot from the floor.

Tanner brought his right hand up and stuffed four enormous fingers into Gal's mouth, squeezing and wriggling them down his throat, palm gripping his chin and fingertips curling at an unholy angle into his gullet.

*I'm going to die.*

All was fading. All was fuzzy. All was black. All he could hear was the rush of blood in his ears.

All was silent.

The world was gone.

And then, there were gunshots. There were sirens. There were voices.

"Stay with me, Gal," he heard Scarlet whisper.

And then, there was complete and incomprehensible darkness.

TWENTY THREE

# Smoke

~

"How's your arm?" Scarlet asked.

"It twinges a little," Gal replied, adjusting the sling so that his newly relocated shoulder sat more comfortably in its socket. "Better than my throat."

Twelve days had passed since the dark, snowy night Gal came within seconds of death by the hand of Jonathan Tanner. He couldn't remember much, only the dim light of the basement closing in around him. His mind had gone fuzzy until a faint popping coalesced into deafening gunshots, and then all had gone black.

He'd awoken hours later in the back of a police unit, Scarlet at his side, dabbing his head with a cold compress. Red and blue lights flashed in all corners of his peripheries. Scarlet whispered that everything was going to be all right, that Sandy had found Tanner's cabin and burst into the cellar at just the right moment, that she had shot Tanner in the back and watched him fall. She had had to place four slugs in his shoulder and one in his lower spine, which immediately rendered him paralyzed from the waist down.

"Where's Amber?" was all Gal remembered yelling, to which Scarlet shushed him back into his lucid coma.

Sandy had called in Mono County police. Had apparently screamed at Sheriff Paul Larson for not taking the initial call seriously, that other lives could have been spared.

*Like Jimmy's.*

"Merry Christmas, Jim," Gal whispered.

He lowered his head, letting thick and unruly black curls fall over his eyes, shielding his falling tears from Scarlet's view.

She wrapped her arms around him, careful not to press too hard on his right shoulder. She buried her face into his neck, and Gal could feel the heated wetness of his sister's own tears upon his flesh.

Together, they cried as the mortician pushed the wooden box containing Jimmy's body into a large cremation chamber.

"We do have a minister on site," the mortician said. "I can fetch him if – "

"No," Gal barked.

"Thank you," Scarlet interjected with a small sob. "It won't be necessary."

"As you wish."

He closed the large iron door inlaid with a small window, locked it, and then flipped the necessary switches. The dark interior of the chamber erupted in flickering, golden radiance as a rectangle of flames rose under Jimmy's coffin.

"Take all the time you need," the mortician said, and then left the room.

Together, Gal and Scarlet watched through the small window as the flames rose higher, until the box was completely engulfed in flames.

"I love you," Gal whispered, both to Jimmy and to his sister.

"I love you more," Scarlet sobbed into his neck.

They shook, cried, and held each other tight until the small window showed nothing but thick, swirling white smoke.

\*\*\*

*Bruised and battered, but with a newfound confidence that electrified his soul and sharpened his senses, Tom DeLevine opened the large oak door of his cottage.*

*He breathed in the familiar must and mold of the centuries-old logs holding together the foundation of his home and, suddenly, he was content. It was difficult to imagine that only a year had passed since he'd discovered the dead girl. Surely a lifetime had passed. After all, his once strong figure and proud green eyes had diminished into a yellow-eyed corpse he neither revered nor recognized.*

*He lost so much in such a short time…*

*A father he always hated but who he came to forgive.*

*A brother whose allegiance always seemed cloudy, but who eventually saved him from the worms of the earth.*

*The love and memory of a mother that, surely, never loved him at all.*

*Worst of all, he lost the fair-haired woman with the sharp tongue, the only other human being he had ever truly loved.*

*The reality that was Tom's life terrified her, and she'd flown back to the comforts of her past, eager to escape him and all the turmoil that surrounded him. She was gone forever, and he would have to live with it.*

*But, he was home now. He was safe. He was alive. And that was all that mattered.*

*The wooden floorboards groaned beneath his muddy feet as he stepped inside. He tossed his things onto the bed, sat down on the rickety mattress, closed his eyes, and took a puff from his pipe.*

*'Tell your story,' he heard his father whisper from beyond the smoke. 'Finish it before it finishes you.'*

*Tom DeLevine opened his laptop and began to write.*

Gallagher Finch closed his laptop.

*It's done.*

He sat for a moment in that beautiful realization, lost in the comfortable, musty smell of his home. Sure, the impending hard work of finding a publisher loomed on the horizon. Sure, his hearing concerning

Daphne Castro's burial was only a few weeks away. Sure, he faced up to two years in county jail.

But, he would conquer it all, just as he'd conquered the past year of his life.

Jonathan Tanner was back in Folsom State Prison, where he belonged. Sandy had provided fierce testimony against Gal's biological father and his purple-haired accomplice, convinced she was Daphne's true killer. But, since the woman known as Violet was dead, the charge for Daphne's murder would be placed solely upon Tanner's shoulders.

If jail-time was in Gal's future, and he guessed it most certainly was, he would put off the rest of the renovations until he served his time. Much of the electrical circuitry was faulty and needed re-wiring. Smoke alarms went off at regular intervals. In response, he had dismantled the smoke alarms until he could really roll up his sleeves.

Scarlet offered to move in while he was away, to finish the renovations with her hard-earned money so that he could come home to the house of his dreams, but he wouldn't let her.

He would do his penance. The fighting was over.

*It's done.*

He stood up and walked over to the mantelpiece, running his fingertips along the coarse wooden edge of Jimmy's urn.

It was hard to imagine that his big, bulky, apelike brother could fit into such a small box. Scarlet suggested mixing Jimmy's remains with their father, Charlie's. As had always been Scar's plan, they would drive up to Yosemite, hike to the top of Half Dome, and pour both of their ashes over the edge and into the wind.

A year ago, Gal would've called the plan idiotic. A year ago, his father was a murderer and his brother was a waste of life. A year ago, Gal didn't give a shit about either one. Now, however, the idea of giving them a proper sendoff wasn't nearly enough to compensate for the minimal, wasted time he'd shared with both. He wanted more for each of them, and would spend the rest of his life exonerating their memories.

Remy sat on the mantle beside Jimmy's urn. A single green nugget was wedged in her bowl, the last trace of weed that Gal possessed. He considered buying more, sure, but only a piece of him wanted to indulge. The rest of him no longer needed it.

He decided to indulge that little piece of him one last time. He picked her up, lit the weed, and inhaled that final plume of flowery smoke.

An hour later, the rocky shore of Gull Lake crunched under Gal's shoes.

An icy breeze whipped through his hair. He pulled his flannel jacket tighter around himself, walking down the beach until his shoes cracked along the thin sheet of ice surrounding the rim of the lake. Further out, where the murky depths were too deep to freeze through, Gal watched the sunset ripple its shimmering reflection over the whitecaps.

He pulled Remy out of his pocket and, without a second thought, he pitched her high in the air. The resin-packed pipe whizzed through the breeze, arcing into the fading sunlight before she fell with a *plunk* and a splash into the freezing water. Gal watched the rippling, watery circles expand until, after a minute, they faded under Gull Lake's windy current.

*It's done.*

"I thought I'd find you here."

Gal's heart stopped.

There was no way in hell he heard that voice. For a moment, he imagined it was simply Scarlet's voice, distorted by the whipping breeze and the lap of the shoreline. The mind-fuzzing effects of the weed were wearing off, but perhaps it was just an auditory hallucination. It wouldn't be the first time.

"Gal," she said.

He turned and simply stared at her, standing alone on the road beside the stony beach. She looked as beautiful as ever, as though a mere month away had healed her emaciation, her bruises, her defeat. She looked brand new, a phoenix risen from the ashes, sapphire eyes and golden hair glowing in the fading twilight.

"What are you doing here?" Gal asked, his unshaven jaw agape.

Amber offered a sad smile and tucked a strand of hair behind her ear. She chewed the inside of her cheek and let her feet crunch over the shore. She closed the distance between them until they were only a foot apart. She looked up into his eyes, and he could see her hues rimmed in redness.

"I never thanked you for coming back for me," she said.

"What about Milwaukee? What about your parents?"

Amber glanced down at her feet shuffling on the rocks.

"They hated the idea of me coming back, obviously. Said that I was lucky to be alive. Begged me not to. Asked why I would risk everything to come back here."

"So why come back?" he asked.

She looked up at him.

"Because of you," she answered. She reached up to touch his cheek. "Because you're not in Milwaukee. Because I don't feel safe when you're not around."

Her bottom lip trembled.

"I'm so sorry about Jimmy," she whispered.

Without thinking, Gal pressed his lips to hers.

She wrapped her arms around him, and his arms wrapped around her. The remaining distance closed between them until they were nothing but a single shadow, a silhouette against the brilliant January sunset.

Gallagher Finch truly felt like a rugged man.

***

As they moved, the kitchen table shifted, causing three empty wine bottles to clatter. The merlot tipped, rolled along the oaken surface, and over the side. It shattered on the new tile, mere feet from Gal's bare feet.

"Should we stop?" Amber whispered into his ear. Her palm reached up to tenderly wipe the beads of sweat from his forehead.

"No," he grunted softly, holding her tightly against him. "I'll clean it up tomorrow."

She smiled and kissed him again, then buried her face into his neck.

Had she given him any warning that she was coming back, he would have gone to the June Lake General Store and picked up chicken, possibly some potatoes, perhaps a salad. Amber had waved off his worry, assuring him that cheap wine and frozen fish sticks would do just fine.

And in their haste to give each other what they both needed, they had neglected to draw the curtains over the kitchen window.

Had they taken the time, they might have noticed the pair of bloodshot, gray eyes watching them from the shadows outside.

***

He was shaking, but not from the biting cold.

He wanted to look away, but how could he?

He tried convincing himself that it was somebody else, that his third bottle of stolen whiskey had finally gotten the better of him. Tried to convince himself that he was hallucinating, that he was dreaming, that he was passed out in the snow.

He staggered, feet crunching on the ice beneath his feet. He held onto the nearest tree trunk for support. His head swam dangerously, gray eyes burning with hot fury and cold tears.

*How could she?*

He watched in agony as she threw her blonde head back, could just make out the muffled cry of ecstasy through the fogged glass of the kitchen window.

Bradley Finch collapsed onto his knees, keeled over, and vomited onto the freshly fallen snow. He retched, again and again, until nothing else came up. He collapsed onto his elbows in his own sick, sobbing and shaking, teeth grinding as the world spun and folded in on him.

He looked up to find them standing. Gal's backside taunted him. He watched as the waste of life picked Amber up and carried her up the stairs, both laughing as Gal nearly stumbled into the hole that was once the creaky second-to-last step.

And then, they were gone.

Brad reached into his pocket and pulled out a small silver ring. The large black diamond glittered in the moonlight. He stared at it, pressed the whiskey bottle to his lips and drained it. His stomach threatened to dry heave again, but he gulped it down.

Whitney's bloody corpse flashed behind his burning eyelids. She lay in a pool of her own blood, throat slit, bleeding out all over his living room floor. The baby was nowhere to be found, his blanket still warm.

Brad had panicked. Hadn't even bothered to pack a bag. Simply ran out the front door, into the woods, and never looked back.

Jimmy was dead. His son was missing. The world thought him a murderer.

And now, the love of his life had been defiled by the one person he hated most.

*It's all his fault.*

But *she* had given in. *She* had given herself to him. *She* had come back to that son of a bitch with hunger in her heart. Hunger that Brad had never been able to fully satisfy.

He choked back a final sob, wiped the tears from his eyes and the vomit from his lips, and sat up. The world was a kaleidoscope of black, of stars, of shadowy trees, of an aluminum shed.

*It's all his fault.*

His mind went blank.

His legs carried him across the yard, through the trees, and to the shed. He wrenched open the door, and there they were.

Three large containers, the contents of each having been neglected to be recycled for years, oozing down the sides of the tin barrels.

Black, dripping oil.

And Brad was determined not to waste a drop.

*It's all his fault.*

***

He had never felt so warm. So loved. So protected.

Gal opened his eyes.

Through the rays of sunlight, he could barely make out her face, but knew she was there. Holding him. Protecting him. Could see her long black hair billowing in the breeze. Could smell the familiar scent of honey and vanilla. Could feel the cozy tenderness of her arms supporting his tiny back.

*Mommy*, he wanted to say, but his tongue blathered against toothless gums. He blew bubbles with his spit, wriggled his fingers, bounced his chubby infant legs with each step his mother took.

He listened to the comforting crunch of rocks beneath her feet, the gentle lap of water around her ankles, the chirp and whistle of yellow warblers skimming across the lake.

"Gal," came a familiar voice.

But it wasn't his mother's voice.

"Gal!" It called him at a higher pitch, a childlike cry, somewhere in the distance. He knew that voice. Hadn't heard it in ages. But the way it cried his name was beautifully familiar.

*Scarlet.*

Her face still hidden within the brightness of the sun, Gal felt his mother adjust him in her arms. She pulled him from the comfort of her bosom and held him at arm's length instead.

He kicked, wishing she would pull him close again.

His tiny feet touched freezing cold water, and he began to cry. He looked up, and her face was no longer hidden.

His mother's eyes, so oddly beautiful, stared beyond him, blank and indifferent. Her jaw hung slack, her hair falling in lank, greasy curtains over sunken porcelain cheeks.

She wasn't beautiful. Not here. Not now. Not like this.

"Gal!" he heard little Scarlet screaming louder. "Please, mommy, no! Gal!"

The icy water rose up his legs and his stomach, soaking his clothes. He kicked and screamed, cried and wriggled, but his mother's grip was firm and unhindered. The water engulfed his neck, his ears, and flooded his mouth. He couldn't see. He couldn't breathe. He heard nothing but the pulse of blood in his ears and screams muffled beneath the lake.

"Gal!" he could just make out.

This game was no longer fun. He couldn't hold his breath any longer. He gulped for oxygen, and water flooded his stomach and his lungs. Panic electrified his tiny body. He kicked. He screamed. He choked.

"Gal!"

His vision, warped under water, began to fade. Weak, watery light tunneled inward.

"Gal!"

He was helpless. He was drowning. He was dying.

\*\*\*

"Gal!" Amber screamed.

His eyes snapped open, and instantly, he knew something was very wrong.

His clothes were stuck to his body. His eyes burned. He couldn't breathe. He tasted smoke on his tongue. Everything was much too bright. Much too hot.

"Amber!" he choked, trying desperately to fill his lungs with oxygen. His chest burned as, all around him, flames licked the walls and engulfed the ceiling.

Amber coughed in his face, grasping desperately at her chest.

"We have to go!" he yelled over the deafening roar of the inferno.

Gal quickly helped her to her feet and she collapsed against him. She cried and screamed and choked and coughed. He picked her up over his shoulder, her weight pressing against his smoke-filled lungs.

He grabbed the bedroom doorknob and felt his fingers blister beneath the scalding brass. He yelled out in pain and wrenched his hand back, then launched a firm kick at the door. The burning wood burst open as a searing backdraft sucked the remaining oxygen from the room.

Gal held his breath, shielded his eyes from the intense heat, and carried Amber across the landing and into the spare bedroom. His mother's portrait burned on the wall as he pulled open the door to the widow's watch. The deck roiled in flames, and Gal knew instantly that the front door downstairs was their only chance.

"Stay with me, Amber!" he choked, seeing her eyes begin to glaze over, drool and foam dripping from her lips as she suffocated on the thick, black smoke.

He carried her back over the landing and felt the floorboards cracking under his feet, the wood burning away. He pulled his shirt over his mouth, trying desperately to suck in fresh air, but to no avail. His feet bolted down the stairs, burning eyes set upon the large oak front door.

Gal's foot suddenly plunged through the hole of the second-to-last step.

*Crack!*

He screamed in agony as his leg snapped at an unholy angle, sending him off balance. Amber tumbled over his shoulder and landed on her head with a loud thud on the new tile floor.

"Amber!" he yelled, but she was still.

Clenching his teeth, Gal tried to pull his shattered leg out of the hole, but the pain was far too intense. His foot wouldn't budge. The flames pressed in on him. The smoke was too thick. He couldn't see. He couldn't think. He couldn't breathe.

An ear-splitting crack echoed from above.

Gal looked up, and the ceiling collapsed on top of him.

# TWENTY FOUR

# Black

~

Soft, billowing clouds of ash rose in small plumes as a pair of finely polished black boots pressed on through the debris. They stepped over charred beams of oak that once supported a widow's watch which had leaned a little too far to the east. In places among the wreckage, heat continued to rise from glowing embers that refused to burn out.

Only three hours earlier, as a cold February morning drizzle steamed around the freshly extinguished inferno, a parade of firetrucks whizzed into the tiny cul-de-sac to battle the oily blaze.

Two ambulances had arrived on scene, prepped and ready to resuscitate two sets of lungs, and fully equipped to treat even the harshest burns.

Instead, they had driven away, each with a body bag containing the charred remains of Amber Evans, a Milwaukee native, and Gallagher Finch, whose only wish was to restore his family's Gull Lake home.

The Loop would never be the same.

Newly appointed deputy Sandra Castro reached into the pocket of her Mono County Sheriff's Department uniform, withdrew a handkerchief, and pressed it over her nose and mouth. She took long, slow, steady breaths to filter clean air from the ash, then lifted her sunglasses to rub the gooey, blackened sleep out of the corners of her eyes.

She sighed, saddened that she wouldn't need to re-consult with the lawyer down south. With news of Gal's death sure to spread, there would be no need for a trial anymore.

*Not that a trial was ever necessary after Jonathan Tanner's arrest.*

Sandy knew the truth, pure and simple.

Gallagher Finch, a troubled boy with dark hair and an even darker family history, had taken home the wrong call girl at the wrong time. Had been a casualty of the internal war for supremacy among two power-hungry women. Had panicked and did the only thing that made sense to him at the time. And had been fully committed to atone for his sin.

Looking around at the smoldering ruins of the Finch home, it was clear that Gal had met a fate of the ultimate atonement.

*But this… this was no accident.*

The firefighters had reported a heat index that far surpassed a typical brush or electrical fire. The smoke had been too thick and too black. The fire had fought back and fiercely resisted its watery death. Some sort of fuel had been administered prior to the flames. A type of gas or oil mixture, from what they could ascertain.

*An arsonist*, they'd said.

Sandy's boot scuffed through the ashes, her eagle eyes scanning the blackened ground in search of anything that might lead to an answer.

She couldn't help but feel entirely at fault.

This whole thing had Jonathan Tanner written all over it. But he was locked away in Folsom State Prison's highest security solitary confinement cell. Never again would he be able to escape. Never again would he be able to indoctrinate young girls into the dangerous, unjust, and sickening world of dirty old men's filthiest fantasies. She had made sure of that.

But, like both Daphne and Violet, there were sure to be many young women who were furious about their protector's arrest. There were sure to be many young women who harbored bitter resentment for the green-eyed young man they thought responsible.

Had Gal paid for Sandy's victory?

She made her way into the backyard, thankful that the arsonist had chosen a Sierra Nevada winter to wreak his or her destruction. Had it been summer, the waist-high grass now buried under three feet of snow would easily have ignited, sending nearly ten acres of Gal's property up in flames. With how dry it had been in recent years, it could have easily sent the entire Loop into a panic. Thankfully, the fire had been contained.

Dozens of lives had been spared, and only two had perished.

Her boot connected with something buried beneath the ashes, a hollow clunk followed by a clinking rattle. Intrigued, she bent down and brushed aside the powdery cinders.

Paper label blackened and blistered, a whiskey bottle lay scattered in the rubble. Sandy picked it up by the neck between thumb and forefinger, careful not to smudge the glass in case fingerprints remained. She shook the bottle and listened to the clinking rattle once more.

At the bottom of the bottle sat the source…

A small and beautiful silver ring, set with a large black diamond.

She knew that ring. Had seen in many months ago, sitting in a small wooden box on the coffee table in Bradley Finch's apartment above the steel mill. Had enquired about it. Had watched Amber blush and retreat from the room. Had seen the rage hidden behind the second-eldest Finch boy's steel gray eyes.

Sandy felt as though she'd been punched in the gut.

*Brad.*

***

It took three weeks, two bottles of Fuil na Talhainn, and one final sigh for Sandy to finally break the news to Scarlet that one of her brothers had killed the other.

The black diamond ring that Amber never accepted, that Brad carried around until his rage got the better of him, had proven sufficient evidence.

Not to mention his fingerprints had been found on the scorched whiskey bottle.

Sandy stood stoic beside Gal's sister on the shore of Gull Lake. The freezing water lapped gently around the base of a wooden cross buried into the rocky shoreline. An ear-reddening, icy breeze whipped a black scarf and jacket around her robust shoulders.

Only one other person had come to pay his respects.

Fletch, the Sierra Inn's wizened and white-haired bartender, sat on his knees beside the cross, body hunched as he wailed into his withered old hands. Never had Sandy seen such a display of compassion from someone who wasn't a family member of the deceased. Surely Gal had meant something to the old man that Sandy would never fully understand.

Scarlet's face was buried into Sandy's chest. The young woman's small frame was adorned in a black dress and stockings, prescription hipster sunglasses hiding her puffy eyes as black streaks of mascara streamed down her cheeks.

The tragedy had clearly taken its toll. Had Sandy even slightly loosened her grip, she knew Scarlet would've collapsed.

"I'm so sorry," Sandy said, large fingers stroking Scarlet's lank, unwashed hair.

Scarlet moaned for the umpteenth time that afternoon. She shook violently, less from the cold and more from the shock. She screamed in Sandy's arms until finally, she had no more strength in her lungs.

Scarlet lifted her face and whispered, "Find him."

"We're doing all we can," Sandy replied.

"That's not good enough. You have to – I need you to – Please – "

"Clearly, your brother isn't in the best mental state. When we find him, I swear that you will be able to talk to him."

"I don't want to talk to him!" Scarlet screamed. "I want to kill him!"

Sandy wrapped her arms around Scarlet, rubbed her back to quiet her, and remembered how she had shushed Daphne that way when she was a baby.

"What would that accomplish?" Sandy said.

Scarlet wailed.

***

"I'm sorry," Scarlet whispered, face tucked into the crook of her elbow as she stared at the full glass of beer in front of her, clearly not thirsty. Fletch had offered to close the Sierra Inn for the day, save for Sandy and Scarlet.

"Don't be," Sandy replied, taking a deep gulp of her own beer. "If I were in your shoes, I'd be twice as wrecked." She gave Scarlet's arm a tender squeeze.

"I loved him so much," Scarlet said, choking back another gentle sob. "He was my best friend."

"I know."

"He didn't deserve this."

"No, he didn't."

Scarlet clearly had no more tears to cry. "Why would Brad... he was our brother..."

Sandy sighed. "He was drunk. He was mad. He was jealous." She gulped down the rest of her beer and winked at Fletch for another, the old man looking like a sad old dog who'd recently lost its owner.

"I knew she was trouble," Scarlet groaned. She picked up her beer and slugged down half the glass, dehydration finally getting the better of her. "I mean, she was sweet and everything... but why did she have to go after both of them?"

"Girls her age don't know what they want," Sandy guessed. "Hell, I still don't know what I want."

"I can't stop thinking about how her parents must feel. How they must absolutely hate this place. How they must despise our family."

"Some people belong in Milwaukee."

Sandy was both surprised and relieved to find that she had

successfully brought a tiny chortle from Scarlet's lips.

"There it is. There's a laugh."

"God," Scarlet groaned. She sucked down the rest of her beer and Fletch brought them each another. "What a year. My dad, Jimmy, and now Gal. Brad is a murderer." She rubbed her eyes. "What am I supposed to do now?"

"You can always do what I did. Move somewhere else. Start fresh."

"Yeah? Like where?"

"L.A.'s warm this time of year," Sandy joked.

"Pass."

"You could write a book," Sandy suggested.

"Gal was the writer. I wouldn't even know what to write about." Fresh tears glistened in her eyes. "He worked so hard on it. He was so close. So excited to be done with it. So excited to publish it."

Sandy nodded.

Without a word, she reached into her pocket and withdrew a small, silvery brick and set it on the bar top.

"Maybe this will help."

"What is it?" Scarlet asked, wiping her eyes.

"After I found the ring, I kept searching for evidence. I didn't find much, just some burned clothes, some appliances, and Gal's computer. It was burned all to shit, but after I cleared it from the evidence locker, I took it home and was able to pull this out of it."

Scarlet's eyes widened as realization began to set in. Her cracked and trembling lips curved into a gentle smile.

"I can't believe it. Did you – is it – "

"I'm not a computer whiz," Sandy replied. "Not really sure how hard drives work, but I figured if there's a chance it's still on here, you could take it in and retrieve it." She smiled. "I thought maybe you could get it published for him. Like you said, he worked so hard on it."

Scarlet leapt out of her barstool and wrapped Sandy in the tightest hug she'd ever received.

And for the first time in her life, Sandy Castro felt like she had accomplished something.

***

It was on the fifth day of March that Scarlet Finch finally felt as though moving on with her life was a mountain she was capable enough to ascend. She had finally gone back to work, went out with a few of her friends, and finally received the email she had been waiting on for weeks.

A portable heater glowed comfortably on the desk beside her bed as streaks of glittering rain dripped down the inky black of her bedroom windows. She adjusted the rims of her hipster specs and tucked a stray strand of hair behind her ear. The light from her laptop glowed along her porcelain skin as she glanced beside the screen at her favorite photograph.

Green eyes alight, a twenty-something Gal stared back at her with his cheeky grin, giving her a thumbs-up. He was wearing that familiar Gryffindor tank top, the same one she had stolen from his dresser years ago, the same one she had once worn to bed almost every night, and the same one that she would never wear again, for fear that it would fade and fray like the delicate ties of life that had once bound them together.

In the background was the house they had grown up in, the large eye-shaped knot in the oak front door. The wooden slats of the house needed a good stain, the crumbling stones in need of replacement, the sloping deck of the front porch in need of new timber. At the time, he had been determined to fix it all, and indeed he had, before their older brother had burned it all to the ground.

*I can't think like that*, she remembered.

Scarlet opened the email.

*Dear Ms. Finch,*

*Thank you kindly for considering Black House Publishing to represent your brother's book. We would like to offer our sincerest condolences regarding your inexplicable loss. In trying times such as these, allow us to offer our sympathy to you and your family.*

*As you might have seen on our website, for reasons pertaining to our legal department, we here at Black House normally do not accept unsolicited material.*

*However, after reading your email describing your brother, the unfortunate events leading up to his death, and your beautiful account of his determination to finish his work, the senior editors of our organization were naught without a dry eye. There may be a writer in you yet.*

*We gave "The Loop" a read, and we agree that it has mainstream potential. In short, we would very much like to work with you to bring your brother's story to life. We believe that his style, prose, and narrative poise fit well with the books that we help publish. Though he is no longer here in body, we would like to help preserve his memory with the publication of his novel.*

*Please call our office at your earliest convenience.*

*All the best,*

**Elliott Black,**
**Senior Vice President**
**Black House Publishing**


Below was a phone number, an address, and some obscure quote about following dreams through a labyrinth of letters that Scarlet couldn't finish due to the tears flooding her eyes.

*He did it.*

As their father had instructed, Gal finished his story before it ultimately finished him. His words had won over one of the most prestigious publishing agencies on the west coast. And whether a million people purchased *The Loop* or just one, Gallagher Finch would forever be immortalized in his work.

She wiped her eyes, closed her laptop, stretched her arms over her head, and yawned before sidling out of her chair. Bare feet padded across the cool linoleum of her apartment as Scarlet went to the kitchen and made herself a peanut butter and honey sandwich. Having never tried the decadent combination before, she eyed it a moment and then took a bite.

It was good.

Peanut butter and honey. And to top it off, Gallagher Finch.

*I have to hand it to her… Daphne had good taste.*

Scarlet took another bite and walked to the room that wasn't hers. She opened the door and peeked inside.

By the soft, iridescent glow of a Harry Potter nightlight, his tiny back rising and falling in a steady, healthy rhythm, the baby boy slept soundly in his crib.

The same baby boy she had stolen from the steel mill so many months ago.

"Sleep tight, Gallagher," she whispered, and then closed the door.

# TWENTY FIVE

# Clear

೦

For the first time in a very, very long time, Daphne Castro's mind was clear.

*It doesn't matter anymore. This is the last one*, she thought to herself as she reached over the messy and stained bedsheets to pour herself another shot of vodka. She took it down with a scrunch of her nose and a sharp intake of breath.

The client could keep the Evan Williams to himself, could keep the hangover to himself. Daphne definitely got along better with vodka.

She peered out of the dark-haired male's bedroom window and watched the clouds begin to roll through the otherwise clear night sky.

She listened to the soft and unmistakable scratch of a man's razor shaving coarse stubble in the bathroom just yards away. She could hear the water running. She could hear his deep breathing, smiling to herself as she recalled just how warm and velvety his breath had felt along her neck. Her gaze drifted along the walls of the bedroom. His bedroom.

*Al... or was it Gal?*

She admired the small stag horn pocketknife on the dresser. Grinned at the dirty clothes overflowing out of the hamper in the corner.

He'd said that tomorrow was his birthday, after all. Perhaps she'd give him a discount.

*Perhaps not.*

*It doesn't matter anymore. This is the last one.*

Her stomach grumbled. "Al," she purred.

No answer.

*Or was it Gal? Odd name for a boy.*

"Gal," she corrected herself softly.

"In a sec," he replied from the just down the hall. She heard the telltale guzzle and the smack of his lips on the Evan Williams bottle.

"Make me a sandwich," she groaned.

"In a sec, Dani," he answered.

"It's Daphne. Prick," she admonished with a simple giggle, laying back against the sweat-dampened pillows.

"Whatever," he grunted from beyond the doorway.

She considered what the morning might bring. Fresh white snow. Much needed cash. A silent getaway. She was over this life. Over it all. She had done her part. Had helped Jonathan Tanner in his escape so that others like her might fare a great deal better than they had with The Old Lady. Had scared the hell out of the prick that impregnated Whitney.

Had seduced his younger brother.

It had been a fun year, to be sure, but this wasn't her. Not truly. She was still that little girl with messy pigtails. She wanted to go back to school. She wanted to be a veterinarian, to fix animals that were broken. She wanted to buy her own place. She wanted to raise a dog and eventually a family. She wanted to find a man. A real man.

Her stomach grumbled louder.

"I'm hungry," she whimpered. Daphne heard him sigh and then shut off the tap before his heavy footsteps stumbled away down the hall. "I like peanut butter and honey," she called after him. She heard him grunt as he descended the stairs.

*Plop. Plop. Plop. Stumble. Plop. Creeeak. Plop.*

While she waited for her midnight snack, she figured she'd better update the ledger. Holding the sheet over her chest, Daphne climbed out of Gal's bed and pulled a small red notebook out of her purse. She flipped through the countless pages now flooded with the first initials and last names of her clients. A full year's worth. She couldn't believe how full it had become after only one year. Could only hope to forget the men, the memories, the facets of her lowest year of life.

*It doesn't matter anymore. This is the last one.*

She withdrew a small pen from her purse, licked the tip, wrote a cursive 'G,' and then stopped. What was his last name?

"Gal!" she called, hoping to obtain the information.

"In a sec!" he snapped from downstairs.

*Men*, she considered. *They can't make a sandwich and answer a simple question at the same time.* She would have to ask him later.

Feeling a familiar pressure in her abdomen, Daphne tucked the pen into her notebook, padded out into the hall and then into the bathroom. She let the sheet fall and took a seat on the toilet to tinkle, lazily flipping through the pages of her red notebook.

When she was finished, Daphne closed the ledger and thoughtlessly tucked it into the small magazine rack beside the toilet as she took a few moments to flush and wash her hands.

Downstairs, she heard a loud thump and the rolling clatter of a glass bottle.

*Odd.*

Hands still wet, Daphne opened the bathroom door and peeked her head out.

"Gal!" she called.

She was met with silence.

Daphne wrapped her nude figure in the sheet once again. She crept along the upstairs hallway and into darkness. Her hands drifted along the walls in search of a light switch, but there were none to be found.

"Gal!" she called out a little louder. Again, silence. What the hell was going on? Had the drunken asshole fallen asleep mid-sandwich?

"Gal!"

She reached the top of the stairs and allowed her eyes to adjust to the darkness before holding tight to the bannister and beginning her descent. *Step. Step. Step. Step. Step. Creeeak. Step.* Daphne placed her bare feet on cold tile, eyes wide and pupils dilated as she struggled to peer through the pitch darkness.

There was a soft rush of air past her left ear.

A pair of strong hands touched her hips, squeezing them soft and tender through the sheet draped around her nude body. She could only smile at the squeeze of those hands.

"How's that sandwich coming?" she purred, slowly turning in the darkness to face him.

She was surprised to smell a sweetness in the air. A familiar scent that Daphne recognized as...

"Gal, are you wearing perfume?" she asked with a giggle.

She felt his breath upon her face. Warm. Moist. Yet not stained with the reek of whiskey, as she might have expected. His breath was fresh. Clean even.

The strong hands became softer and soon fell away from her sultry hips. Through the darkness, she picked up the sound of his feet softly padding towards the stairs. The second-to-last stair gave that familiar creak before his feet moved quick and soft up the staircase.

*Midnight snacks in bed then*, she considered with a grin.

Daphne maneuvered her way upstairs, feeling her way through the darkness and following the light seeping from behind Gal's bedroom door. She pushed it open and stepped inside.

He was nowhere to be seen.

"Gal? Come out, you turd." She glanced around the room. At the messy bed. At the posters. At the overflowing hamper. Everything in its place.

*All except—*

Daphne Castro let out a loud and bubbling gurgle. She felt the cold steel of a sharp blade pierce deep into the notch behind her jaw and below her ear, cutting through her neck muscle before slicing clean through her windpipe.

Carotid artery severed, she watched as thick ropes of scarlet squirted from the wound in her neck, painting the walls red. Her hand reached for her neck, fingers clutching the stag horn handle of the pocketknife.

Unable to breathe, Daphne struggled to flood her lungs with oxygen. Her beautiful eyes bulged, lungs growing heavy as she suffocated on her own blood.

With all the strength she could muster, she turned to face him…

Daphne peered into a pair of deep brown eyes, hidden behind a pair of red hipster glasses.

*Those aren't his eyes.*

The beautiful stranger twisted the knife out of her neck and sunk it into her chest.

Daphne Castro was dead before she hit the floor.

\*\*\*

Scarlet Finch never intended to keep the boy.

At least, that was the original plan. But after eleven long years of up-all-nights, Tonka trucks, visits from the tooth fairy, bunch-ball soccer games, childish arguments, and goodnight kisses, she couldn't imagine her life without him. He gave her life meaning now.

Much like Gal had, so very long ago.

*He would've been thirty-seven this year.*

She stopped for a moment, hands gripped tightly to twin steel cables, feet planted against a wooden peg bolted into solid rock as she took a moment to catch her breath.

"Come on, Mom!" her boy called from higher up the nearly vertical slope.

"Hang on," she called back, huffing and puffing. "I'm not as young as I used to be."

The air was thinner up here, the sun was bright, but Scarlet had never seen a day as clear as today.

She and Gally, as he preferred to be called by his school friends, had woken up hours before the sunrise. She packed them each a lunch, an enormous bag of homemade trail mix, and water bottles. The energetic youngster carried the load in his backpack while long, spindly legs pushed him effortlessly upward towards the summit. He definitely had Brad's strength, not to mention those steel gray eyes.

Scarlet watched her adopted son climb, then took a moment to survey the rugged landscape.

Rounded granite peaks dominated the panorama, blanketed in thick carpets of pine-green. The sky shimmered a stark baby blue, speckled with occasional wispy sheets of cirrus.

Below, Yosemite Valley stretched north and south, a swathe of grass and Jeffrey pine meadows. She could just make out the hair's breadth of road, a line of ants glittering as they pressed ever inward toward the visitor center.

Scarlet wiped the sleep from her eyes, careful not to lose another contact lens like she had last week. She'd abandoned her trademark red hipster glasses six years ago, and with them, a lifetime of murderous memories...

Striking Annie Finch in the temple with a steel pipe all those years ago. Pushing her down the stairs after she'd threatened to take Gal away from their father. Away from *her*. Watching with matricidal rage as the woman who wasn't her mother died at the base of the staircase.

Stabbing the call girl, Daphne Castro, after coaxing Gal downstairs and lacing his midnight peanut butter with propofol. Watching with love-laced jealousy as she bled out, tangled in blood-soaked sheets.

Slicing Whitney Burges's throat to keep her quiet about Amber's whereabouts. Cradling the hooker's baby as she choked on her own blood, eager to tie the string of murders on Brad. To free Gal from his conviction.

Playing the concerned sister in front of Sandy Castro. Helping the ape of a woman find final solace in the knowledge that her niece's killer had been brought to justice, when in fact, it had been Scarlet all along.

*And it had all been for love.*

The absolute and undying love she'd possessed for Gal since she was twelve years old, when she had discovered his adoption papers in her father's study.

Back then, it had all seemed so simple.

One day, he would discover that they weren't related by blood. One day, he would realize that he loved her as more than just a sister. One day, he would share her affections, and they would finally be together.

One day had never come, and never would. Gal was dead, and yet her love lingered on.

*One day, I'll find Brad, and I'll make him pay for what he did.*

"Mom, come *on!*" Gally yelled from high above.

She adjusted the straps of her own backpack, careful not to shift the box inside, and then gripped the cables tighter. She ascended, picking each step cautiously, planting her feet firmly into each wooden peg as she pushed higher and higher up the final vertical wall. Finally, after hours of trekking, she set foot on the summit, fell to her knees, and smiled.

It took her eleven years, but finally, Scarlet Finch conquered Half Dome.

"We did it, Mom! We did it!" Gally hollered, setting down the food pack.

"You be careful," Scarlet replied. "I don't need you falling over the edge." Scarlet caught her breath, cursing the fact that she was almost forty years old and that her lungs weren't what they used to be. She smiled as she watched her son, deciding now was the perfect time to give him his present.

"I have something for you," she said.

Intrigued, he glanced over his shoulder.

Scarlet reached into her backpack and pulled out an old, stag horn pocketknife. She tossed it and he caught it in midair.

"It belonged to your father," she lied.

Gally ran his fingertips over the rugged handle, unsheathed the blade that held so many secrets, and smiled before closing it and tucking it into his pocket.

"Can we do it, mom? Can we do it now?"

"Yes, G, we can do it now."

She pulled off her backpack, unzipped it, and removed the large wooden box.

"Can I do it?" her son asked.

"We'll do it together," she replied. Holding her son's hand, Scarlet walked to the edge of the precipice. "Ready?" she asked.

"Ready," he said.

She held one corner of the box, and he took hold of the other. They opened the lid and tipped it over. A dusty mixture of ash and bone spilled over the edge of Half Dome, caught a sudden gusty current, and swirled into a milky gray cloud. For a moment, the air was blessed with the mixed, cremated remains of Charlie, Jimmy, and Gallagher Finch.

Her father. Her brother. And the love of her life.

*I love you*, she thought she heard on the breeze.

"I love you more," she whispered back.

And then, the air was clear.

*** 

It took hours to trek back down to the valley.

To reward her son for finishing the hike without a single complaint, she'd insisted on chicken fingers and fries for the pair of them, to which he jumped enthusiastically with an energy reserved for the prepubescent.

"Go wash your hands," she told him once the host led them to their table.

"Do I have to?" he groaned.

"You won't complain about a twelve-hour hike, but you'll complain about rinsing off a little dirt?" she retorted. "You're filthy. Go on. I'll get you a coke."

"Fine," he grumbled, and then trudged off in search of the bathroom.

Scarlet opened the menu and perused the desserts, concluding that a sweet little reward for her own labor was entirely necessary. It was only when she decided on the pumpkin cheesecake and folded her menu that she noticed a beautiful young woman with bushy brown hair and eyes that resembled large, silvery-blue orbs sitting in the booth opposite. Aside from a couple of pockmarks indented in her clear skin, she was quite possibly the most stunning twenty-something that Scarlet had ever seen. In truth, she looked oddly familiar, and Scarlet knew she had seen her somewhere before, years ago.

But it wasn't her looks that had caught Scarlet's gaze.

The young woman was absorbed in a book sporting a very familiar title.

"That's a good one," Scarlet told the young woman, who set the book down and offered a sweet, yet broken smile.

"I figured I should read it," she said. "Bestseller. Won the *Goodreads Choice Award*."

"And based on a true story," Scarlet added.

The young woman bit her bottom lip and nodded, eyes becoming misty, as though lost in a terrible memory.

"I know it is," she said. "In fact, I know the true story a little too well."

"How so?" Scarlet asked, her interest and her paranoia piqued.

"I, um — well, I don't like to talk about it, but — " the young woman replied. "I was there when they found the girl's body."

And then, the truth became clear. She had seen the girl on the news, eleven long years ago, surrounded by her family and wrapped in muddy blankets while an ambulance carried away the corpse of Daphne Castro.

"I finally got the courage to come back here," she said, and then buried her nose back into *The Loop*.

Scarlet watched Madison Fullerton read for a while, the lovely young brunette completely unaware that the woman who'd just spoken to her was entirely responsible for the book in her hands, as well as the events that had inspired it.

When the waiter came, Scarlet Finch ordered chicken fingers for her son and a slice of pumpkin cheesecake for herself.

# SUBSCRIBE AND FOLLOW